My Partner's Wife

By

Michael Glenn Yates

RJ Publications, LLC

Newark, New Jersey

RJ Publications
MGYnovelist@aol.com
www.rjpublications.com
Copyright © 2010 by Michael G. Yates
All Rights Reserved
ISBN 0-9819998-2-4

Printed in Canada

November 2010

1 2 3 4 5 6 7 8 9 10

Chapter 1

As dusk approached on a warm April evening, the black man in the mirror was very pleased with how things were going in his life. He smiled at his reflection, strongly believing that he was indeed the happiest man on Earth. Tonight he knew was going to be a special evening - an indelible memory, in fact. It would be an evening that would forever change his life…as well as Tamala's. Marcus continued standing in front of the mirror getting dressed in his one-bedroom apartment; he was pondering his relationship with his girlfriend Tamala. Tamala and he had had their ups and downs over the last two years but they had grown closer each day inspite of their problems. His writing her that speeding ticket the day they met was the best thing he had ever done. That action had brought Marcus to this point, experiencing the happiness that was now overflowing within him. Life was too short, as he knew firsthand from the death of his partner. It was time to take the plunge. It was time to get married, buy a house, and have children.

Now smiling and shaking his head in front of the mirror, Marcus was amazed at how Tamala and he ended up being the perfect couple. He thanked God daily for his good fortune. Today was Tamala's 27th birthday, and Marcus led her to believe that he had to report in to work and could not spend time celebrating her special day. Unbeknownst to Tamala, Marcus planned to surprise her by going over to her place and sweeping his princess off her feet, showing Tamala the time of her life. Later would be the biggest surprise, giving her the platinum, two-carat, marquise-cut diamond ring that was currently sitting on the dresser in front of him. Marcus thought that Tamala deserved the best of everything; platinum was fitting to express how much he loved her. He did not have a clue as to how he was going to pay off the ring, however, the crowning achievement of platinum was worth the financial stress. Marcus knew that the proposal of marriage was a big step, but he truly felt that Tamala was the one - the one with whom he wanted to spend the rest of his life.

Marcus marveled at his reflection in the mirror. He was not used to dressing up in a tuxedo. Being a police officer does not present much of an opportunity to wear such attire. The black bowtie and sterling silver cufflinks with black onyx inlays were a challenge to put on, but it was important that he looked his best that evening. Marcus had gone all out that night in his effort to impress the future Mrs. Marcus A. Williams. That was another reason he went with platinum rather than gold when shopping for that perfect diamond ring; Marcus wanted to show his commitment to marriage.

Marcus straightened the black bowtie and then stepped back to admire the happy man in the mirror. He was pleased with what he saw: A brotha clad in black tuxedo trousers, black cummerbund, crisp, white, wing-collared shirt, and of course the treacherous bowtie that had given him hell for the past fifteen minutes; tying it had been next to impossible.

Looking at his oval, mahogany-colored, clean-shaven face, he thought, *not bad for someone closing in on 30 in a few months*. Marcus had a faint horizontal scar just over his left eyebrow, compliments of running into the corner of a tall wooden pedestal table as a small child. Despite that small scar and faint wrinkles developing on his forehead and near his eyes, Marcus's reddish-brown skin was very smooth, almost flawless. His sincere but charming smile captivated many women over the years. His straight white teeth and that enduring twinkle in his dark eyes melted a-many of sistas' wounded hearts. Marcus's hair would have been of a soft wavy texture if he had not begun shaving his head a year ago. He believed that his baldpate was currently in style for his age. Tamala loved his baldness along with Marcus's squinted eyes and little ears, which stuck out from the side of his round head. Marcus made sure his shaved-head had the perfect shine as he continued to admire his 6'0", 185-lb muscular frame in the contoured dress shirt.

Marcus put the ring case - containing his life savings - in his right front pants pocket. He then picked up his bottle of Sean John cologne and slapped a small amount of the sweet-smelling liquid on his chiseled face. He no longer wore a mustache, which was also shaved off to match his baldness. He put on the tuxedo jacket then took one final look at his reflection. Pleased with how well the tux fit, Marcus turned around and glanced at the alarm clock on the nightstand. "Well it's 4:33 p.m., *showtime!*" he said. Before leaving the bedroom, he grabbed his keys then picked up from the king-size bed the extra large present, wrapped in gold and topped with a gold and white bow. As he walked through his apartment toward the front door, Marcus stopped abruptly and turned around in his tiny foyer, facing the interior of his apartment in Chesterfield County.

"Goodbye, bachelor pad. I'll no longer be a single man...but a fiancé." He shook his head with a smile then walked out to rescue his princess from the single life.

Chapter 2

The large floor-to-ceiling windows allowed the evening sunlight into the room. Neci Logan, still wearing a white long-sleeved blouse and blue skirt from the workday, sans her red jacket, white stockings, and black shoes, was basking in the brightness from her tan leather sofa in the sunroom. From her comfortable perspective, she could see down into her large backyard. Neci was not concentrating on the neatly adorned deck, the well maintained lawn, or the unattached garage which housed her husband, Eddie's, old Ford Mustang. Neci Logan was pondering her life of late. She was very happy. The biracial woman had two healthy - though rambunctious - little boys, a handsome husband, reliable transportation, money in the bank, and this wonderful home in Woodland County. She also had the best job in the world - a schoolteacher.

Life had not always been so good for her, more specifically for her young marriage. Eddie and Neci's marriage had been less than perfect over the past few years, but the couple was still together. Suddenly, the dreadful past threatened to invade her serenity. The beauty shook off the negative thoughts as her mind shifted to what to fix her family for dinner. Eddie was working, but the boys currently played upstairs.

Neci sat up from the soft sofa. She glanced at the stack of ungraded test papers on the table before her. The beauty sighed, and then pushed back her long raven hair, wishing she did not have to work on the finished exams that night. Neci stood up to walk into the kitchen. As she made her way, she listened to hear what the boys were doing. She heard them rough-housing upstairs then shook her head with a warm smile.

An idea came to her as she walked toward the refrigerator. Eddie had been on his best behavior since graduating from the police academy recently. He finally received his new assignment at the South Precinct. Her husband was now officially among the ranks of the men and women of the Woodland County Police Department. Earlier they shared a quick kiss as Eddie rushed out the door on his first evening since being released from training. Neci was proud of him; he had worked so hard since losing his last job.

Eddie could have easily gone the other way. Again negativity entered her mind and again she shook off the past. She wanted to do something special for her hubby. Maybe later that night, when Eddie got off duty, she could reward him. Plus, she was extremely horny. The package upstairs underneath their bed contained something that would reward her faithful husband. A Naughty Nurse uniform and various sex toys would be a special surprise for her attractive mate. Thank goodness for online service because it was not in Neci's nature to waltz into a sex shop and purchase such items. She giggled softly at the thought. Eddie Logan would later be thoroughly sexed.

***

East Hopkins Street at North 3rd Avenue was abuzz with activity as commuters, pedestrians, bicyclists, and every other form of conveyance crowded the intersection and surrounding streets. The workday was at its end as the fading April sunlight still brought warmth over the County of Woodland in Virginia. The business district was teeming with office buildings and small enterprises. The sights and sounds of building construction and traffic congestion were the norm all year round.

Rebekah James walked along the crowded concrete sidewalk among some wearing business suits and others donning casual clothing. The black woman in her early thirties stood out in all black: a stretch halter top, short leather skirt, and ankle boots. The outfit accentuated her long, brown, smooth legs, augmented breasts with nipples at attention, and long straight brown hair - her weave was more expensive than the outfit. The waning sunlight highlighted her taut brown skin, simply beautiful. Her light brown eyes, contacts, only added to her beautiful round face. With a body like an Amazon and an ass which amply filled out her tight leather skirt, Eddie Logan did a double take when he drove past her. She reminded him of the actress, Stacey Dash, during her *Playboy* photo shoot.

"*Sweet*," Eddie whispered to himself.

Eddie, with his heartbeat racing in sexual excitement, drove his Volkswagen Jetta hurriedly, as fast as one could in heavy traffic, around the block to return to where he had just seen the ebony beauty. The new cop had just left the firing range and was running late for the roll call briefing. He was going to be on solo patrol that night because his new partner, Officer Marcus Williams, was off on leave. Eddie had not met his partner yet, but he looked forward to his first night alone anyway.

Eddie, with work temporarily forgotten, never bargained on seeing this beautiful goddess; he could not resist her. Eddie nearly raced the wrong way down a one-way street. He cursed in frustration then found an avenue that would take him back around the block. He just prayed she would still be there.

***

Rebekah James, real name Bonita Flowers, knew she had another catch. The experienced prostitute noticed the blond-haired white man staring at her as he drove by. The fool nearly ran over a well-dressed man trying to cross traffic. Rebekah worked during all hours of the day and night. But this was her favorite time of day to pick up customers. Rich business men were abundant, the light of day made it somewhat safer, and the streets were too crowded for the cops to set up surveillance on her. Despite the latter, the vice cops in Woodland were smart. They knew her, and she knew them. She kept in the back of her mind that the white dude probably was a cop. Miraculously, she only had two arrests under her belt.

The woman with striking features - flawless skin, perfectly round ass, large firm breasts, and model-like face - adjusted her halter top over her breasts. The stretchy material rubbed against her large brown nipples. Instead of arousal, the material irritated her. One day she would be able to leave this life, but for now this was the only way for her to make ends meet. As Rebekah James reached the corner, she observed the Jetta parked illegally in front of the Rainbow clothing store. She sashayed toward the passenger side of the car where the window was already rolled down.

She leaned in. "Hey, suga." The woman regarded the man behind the wheel of the running vehicle with a keen eye. He was beautiful - blue-eyed and blond-haired. The man could get any woman he desired, so he had to be a cop or a pervert. The interior of the car was clean, too clean. No cop paraphernalia was apparent but that did nothing to dissolve her suspicion of the possibility that he was an undercover police officer.

She looked back into his stunning blue eyes, but before she could speak again, he spoke, "You're one of the most *beautiful* women I've seen in a while." He then glanced coolly into his rearview and side mirrors before addressing her again, "Quick, get in before we get busted."

Pedestrians seemed oblivious to the common scene of the prostitute-john transaction. The coolheaded prostitute accused the young man, "You got cop written all over you, suga.   Go back to the stationhouse and try again wit' somebody else, okay?" Rebekah had planned to walk away.

Eddie shocked the woman by unbuckling his belt. He pulled his dark blue t-shirt out of his Levi jeans and unzipped his pants. Rebekah gasped when she saw the man struggle to take out the biggest penis she had seen during even her three-year stint as a working girl, or in life!

Eddie held the partially-hard, thick cock in his right hand. "A cop wouldn't do this, would he? Now get the *fuck* in before we get noticed." He left his penis out and covered it with his shirt then reached over and opened the door. She stood back then reluctantly got in; she thought about the money, only the money mattered. As Rebekah shut the door and drove off with the good-looking man, Rebekah had the answer to her silent question: this man was a pervert; this type of john scared her more than the police. She had no pimp, only herself and the weapon in her purse. The box cutter just might come in handy as the sun was a few hours from setting on another day.

***

Prostitution was not a profession to be enjoyed. Promiscuous sex for money was how the vocation worked. The pleasurable expression on Rebekah's ebony face betrayed the latter as the act of sex commenced after the exchange of money. The immense gratification she felt, as the large dick entered her pussy, was almost too much to take. She clenched her teeth and with eyes squinted, Rebekah moaned, "*Oh…fuck*!" She thought the long cock was going to puncture her stomach as she struggled to stay on her hands and knees in the backseat. The white boy stretched her pussy to its limits, which made the fuck tight, but so damn good to her.

The enclosed parking deck was nearly deserted due to the end of the workday. The light of day and the overhead lighting was enough for Eddie to see his condom- covered member penetrate and please the whore calling herself Rebekah. With his pants down to his ankles, Eddie stood outside of his car as he pounded her from behind like there was no tomorrow. The vehicle shook violently with each thrust as he gave the woman all he had. The beautiful woman's thick white cum covered the magnum condom she had provided. Eddie felt his thickness expand, growing harder as he watched the shapely brown ass shake with his every movement. Every bit of his dick filled her as his balls slapped against her clitoris, stimulating her even more. She reared back her shapely ass to meet his powerful thrusts, wanting more of the good dick.

"*Shit*!" Rebekah threw back her head as the white boy pleased her beyond belief. She wondered if she should have paid him instead! The whiteness stretched her pussy so good!

Eddie asked breathlessly as the smell of sex reached his nostrils, "*What's your name*?"

"Re, *bekah*!" He thrust his thickness harder inside the tightness of the whore. The prostitute yelled in both pain and pleasure, "*Shiiiiit*!" The shaft of the man's dick stimulated equally her clitoris and G-spot; when he went deep, he grinded against her hairless pussy.

With each deep pounding, Eddie asked the woman again her name, "What's...your...fucking, *real name*?" He bit his bottom lip as he gave sexual gratification to Rebekah.

The stranger's dick was so fucking incredible. The man had made her cum over and over again, within minutes! Without even thinking about it, she uttered the truth, "*Bonita...Olivia...Flowers*! Oh, *shit*! You, motherfucka! *Your*...dick!" She would have given the handsome white man her date of birth, place of birth, social security number, or credit card number, if she had one, because the big dick was that superior. The nameless man reached unbelievable depths as he continued to pound her from behind. The whore could say no more as she thoroughly enjoyed what this man was doing to her wet, throbbing pussy.

"Would...you...come home with me, and fuck my wife?!" Eddie's eyes were shut tight as he imagined the woman coming to his house.

"Yes! I would *eat* her sweet *pussy*! Do it...for free, *you're a fucking crazy white motherfucka*! I *fuck* I would...make...you...watch, me...make her moan...with my...*oh, shit*...with my tongue and mouth...on...your wife's pussy...*oh, God*!" Eddie was fucking her so hard, but so right. She was cumming again, but this one was going to be a doosy.

"*Goddamn*!!!" Eddie shot his load in the large condom just as the whore's pussy clinched his dick as her own orgasm shook her. Sweat poured into his eyes. He was finished with Bonita. It was time to go to work.

Chapter 3

Marcus merged his 2005 Toyota Camry onto Interstate 95 north toward Richmond, the capital of Virginia, from Woods Edge Road in Chesterfield County. He guided the forest green Camry into the heavy Thursday evening rush-hour traffic, among the tractor-trailers and other vehicles, speeding toward his destination. With the sunlight beaming on the left side of his face, he opened the sunroof to let in the late April warm air; the strong smell of diesel fuel assaulted his nose immediately. Marcus tuned his radio to 106.5 FM *The Beat*, the station known for Hip-Hop and R&B.

Marcus jockeyed for a position in the I-95 fast lane as anxiety filled him. He needed music to preoccupy him and soothe his restless soul. Marcus had to quell his mounting nervousness as he made the thirty-minute trek from his apartment off Route 1 in Chesterfield to Tamala's apartment in Henrico County. The rap music currently blaring from the radio only made him more anxious, so he slid in an old Alicia Keys CD and selected track 6. Marcus allowed his mind to relax as the slow jam assisted him in focusing on a long and happy life with Tamala. As the soothing sound of *If I Ain't Got You* played in the background, he began to focus on his game plan for the night.

Marcus had rehearsed for days on how he would propose to Tamala. He imagined looking into her light brown eyes and her freckled light-skinned face, and telling her how much he needed and loved her. He wanted to make Tamala a permanent part of his life. Immediately upon arriving at Tamala's apartment, he would give her the large wrapped gift, still keeping her in the dark about his plans.

Once she was ready to go, Marcus would walk her out to the limo provided by Richmond Limousine, Inc., as earlier he had given specific instructions to pick them up on time at Tamala's address. The plan was for the young couple to be driven to Ruth's Chris Steakhouse for a lavish and elegant dinner. After dinner, they would be taken to the new premiere dance club, Club Le Amour on West Broad Street in Richmond. Then in the late hours of the morning, the limo driver would navigate them to various points of interest in and around Richmond while Tamala and he sipped champagne under the guise of celebrating her birthday. Making passionate love to Tamala in the back of the limo was definitely on the list, but the drive to Church Hill, one of the highest points in Richmond City, would be the highlight of the evening. Marcus would walk Tamala to the very edge of that hill, located a few miles west of I-95 and bow down to her beauty under the starry sky. While being high above the millions of twinkling bright lights of the tall buildings, lines of I-95 traffic, and lowly streetlights below, he would spring the marriage proposal upon Tamala.

***

Minutes later, when Marcus pulled into the parking lot of the Pine Cliff Apartments located on Shrader Court near West Broad Street and Hungary Spring Road, he saw Tamala's black Nissan SUV parked in its designated space. Butterflies fluttered in his stomach as he parked his own car a few spaces down from hers. Marcus turned off the engine and took in the silence. Tamala was indeed his soul mate, the one he would spend the rest of his life with.

Being the only child, with a mother, Angela, who had died of ovarian cancer and a father, Cedric Myrick who was AWOL, Marcus had no real family - other than an aunt and cousin on his father's side who was from Virginia Beach, Marcus's birthplace - to bring Tamala home to for approval. Despite that, he still knew without a doubt that

Tamala was the one. Marcus wished that his old partner could see this day.

Officer T. C. Slater was shot and killed two weeks ago during a domestic dispute. His killer, Rakeem Javon Harper, better known as Rip, was still at large. Detectives Gary Stoner and Chris Bradshaw, the lead investigators on the capital murder case, had run out of leads on the whereabouts of the 26-year-old killer. The Richmond drug dealer had recently setup shop in Woodland County. Keesha Sykes, his abused girlfriend, was being cooperative with the cops. An abundance of cash was found inside the residence, but no drugs. Marcus was lucky to escape injury or death as T. C. died in his arms. Rip was able to escape as the gentle white giant, Officer T. C. Slater, was no more.

Marcus gave a sad sigh as he stepped out into the warm spring air. Pushing the nightmare of his partner's death away, he put his tux jacket back on and thought about his life with his soon-to-be wife. That brought an immediate smile to his face. A smiling Marcus reached into his car and picked up the large gift box from the backseat then closed the door with his foot.

Tamala's apartment, 216-C, was two flights up and faced the parking lot. He made his way to the staircase leading to Tamala's floor, strolling like Denzel Washington - a cool, confident, straight-backed, broad-shouldered stride. He paused at the bottom of the stairs and looked up at the clear blue sunny sky. Marcus said in his deep but soft-spoken voice, "Man, *what* a beautiful evening."

Marcus took in the smell of spring flowers as a nice breeze delighted across his face. Several children were playing catch in the parking lot a few feet away. A young white couple, pushing their small child in a stroller, was making their way toward a crowded playground area just across the street from the apartment complex. *Spring is definitely in full effect*, Marcus thought. *Maybe that'll be*

Tamala and me with our first child in a few years, he considered. He then began to climb the stairs. He reached Tamala's door and took a deep breath. Balancing the big present on one arm, he used his key to enter Tamala's apartment.

Chapter 4

Something was wrong, out of place. Marcus was surrounded by complete darkness as he shut the door behind him and stood inside his girlfriend's apartment. The shades were drawn, shutting out the late evening sunlight. Tamala usually allowed the sunshine in to 'feed' her plants as she would say, so it was strange for her apartment to be this dark at this time of day. Marcus allowed his eyes to adjust before moving away from the closed door. Just as he was fumbling along the wall for a light switch, he heard several muffled thumps coming from one of the rooms off of the darkened hallway just to the right of him.

It sounded as if someone was in a struggle or fight. Marcus's police instincts took over as he slowly walked in the direction of the barely audible noise. He heard a slap followed quickly by a woman's scream. *Tamala!* His heart nearly lept out of his chest and his muscles tightened in his body as fear and stress filled him. Marcus thought about running toward the scream but decided against it. In Marcus's line of work rushing into a circumstance could get an officer killed, and the person he intended on helping. Trusting in that knowledge now was crucial. He had the element of surprise on his side; catching the burglar or intruder unawares was the best course of action.

Once again another one of Tamala's screams drifted from the darkened confines of the hallway. The gift he was carrying fell silently to the carpet as Marcus instinctively reached for his right side searching for a gun that was not there. A cop wears a gun day-in and day-out so it becomes second nature to grab for it when he feels threatened. Marcus remembered that he was not wearing his gun given he was in a tuxedo. For a brief moment, he experienced indecision. It was too dark to try to find Tamala's telephone, which had probably been ripped out of the wall by the home invaders. Turning on a light would alert the intruders to his presence. He thought about turning around to retrieve his cell phone, which was in his car, but he just could not leave Tamala alone with whoever was assaulting her.

Marcus realized that he had no choice but to confront whoever was hurting Tamala. Fear seeped deep within him as he continued walking toward the noise, which grew louder as he stepped into the short hallway. Saving the love of his life was his only concern.

***

Marcus heard the grunting and moaning before he even got to Tamala's master bedroom. Faint candlelight spilled out from the largest of two bedrooms and into the dimly lit hallway. Feeling his heart in his throat and finding it very hard to breath, Marcus slowly walked toward the doorway hoping against hope that he was not hearing what he thought he was hearing. As he stood to the side of the doorway with sweat dripping down his baldpate, he heard not only grunts and panting, but also desire, passion, and wantonness.

As his heart dropped, Marcus tried to listen to the unmistakable sound of his impending fiancée's breathless voice drifting from the candlelit bedroom, *"It's yours damit...ahh-ahhhhhhhh...it's yoursssss!* Lamarrrrr...oh, fuck, it's soooo good! Oh, GOD...yeessss, like that, don't stop! YESSSS that's it, BABY! My pus...my pussy is yoursssss! *Smack my ass again!"*

(SMACK)

"Oh, GOD, Lamar. I love that shit!" Then Marcus heard a sound that had become commonplace to him over the last two years...the sound of Tamala reaching her sexual peak, her climax.

Mere seconds later, Marcus heard a man's voice, "I'm comin'…*shit*, girl…TAKE-MY-SHIT…oooooh. FUCK, oooooooooooooooh FUCK...DAMN, GIRLLLLLLLL! You got, you got some damn…*damn* good pussy, Tamala!"

Then Marcus heard them shifting on the waterbed, the water sloshing from their spent pleasure. The sound of heavy breathing then kissing reached him. The strong smell of sex wafted from the bedroom out into the hallway where Marcus stood against the wall, in total shock. Now the male voice said softly, "Tamala, ya *pussy* really is da bomb." The couple giggled at the latter comment. After what seemed like the longest pause in history, Marcus heard the lovers whispering sweet things, intimate things…things that only lovers share after a great session of sex.

He could almost see Tamala's sexy light brown eyes, her short brown wavy hair, very soft to the touch, her perky round breasts with supple pink nipples, her plump buttocks, and her 5-foot, 110-pound, petite frame lying there sweaty and entangled with her…with her co-conspirator, her lover.

Marcus just stood there, stood there in the hallway with the back of his baldhead pressed against the wall, eyes closed, listening to their intimate whispering. He seemed almost catatonic, frozen where he stood close to that open bedroom door, and a few feet from the couple. He felt as if he was in a bad dream, actually a nightmare. He sighed quietly then opened his eyes. Candlelight continued to flicker into the hallway. Unconsciously, he began to finger the ring case in his right pants pocket. After a few minutes of staring into space, he simply tiptoed out of Tamala's apartment like a defeated basketball player leaving the hardwood court after missing the winning shot in the championship game.

The dejected off-duty cop, unable to confront the reality that the lady of his life was intimate with another man, left the apartment, shutting the door gently behind him. Marcus knew that he was not a saint. In fact, he had cheated in the past on ex-girlfriends, but never on his loving Tamala. She was his world, his everything! The brightness of the sun blinded him as he slowly made his way back down the stairs.

As Marcus reached the ground level, he saw the black polished limo, gleaming in the fading sunlight, parked in front of the apartment complex blocking a row of cars. The driver was wiping down the already shiny limousine with a clean white rag. Marcus walked over to the older, heavyset black man dressed in a nice tux, probably not rented, and dismissed him. He swallowed back tears of pain and rage. Marcus decided to take solace in going to work. Policing was the only way to keep his confused mind away from his latest plight.

Chapter 5

Tamala hurried out of the shower after dismissing Lamar. She felt that washing away the sex from her body would somehow cleanse her mind of the ongoing guilt that she held for sleeping with him for over three months now. She was pissed with Marcus because he was at work; he forced her to spend her birthday alone. Tamala refused to be alone of all days, on her birthday, so she called Lamar and invited him over. As she slowly dried herself then methodically began rubbing her ebony body down with Cucumber Melon body lotion from Bath & Body Works, she thought about both men in her life, Marcus and Lamar.

Tamala had met Lamar at Gyno-Choice Women's Clinic where she worked as the office manager, well, at least until she earned her nursing degree. Lamar was one of the janitors with the cleaning company that provided services to a number of office buildings in Woodland County, including the clinic. Lamar, who was light-skinned, had the evilest gray eyes Tamala had ever seen. Those eyes, not common in black folks, were Lamar's most intriguing feature. His thin mustache, goatee, braids tied back away from his handsome face, and sagging pants that exposed his boxers, all highlighted Lamar's bad-boy persona. Lamar was not her type, but he made her *hot*. Marcus was a good-boy while Lamar was the quintessential thug. She never intended on sleeping with Lamar or anyone else because she loved Marcus so deeply.

Over the last year, Lamar had constantly been coming on to Tamala as she tried to concentrate on her work. She had also begun to sneak looks at him which in turn built her own sexual curiosity. He wanted to take her out to wine and dine her. She would often laugh to herself thinking, *how's this man gonna afford to take me anywhere on his minimum wage salary? He does seem to always have money on him.* In time, she began to enjoy Lamar's special attention. She looked forward to it each day she came into work, but sleeping with him was the last thing on her mind.

One night well over three months ago, Tamala and Marcus had a huge fight over his not spending enough time with her. She felt as if they were drifting apart, that Marcus was simply taking her for granted, and Tamala was sick of it. They used to make love several times a day. Lately though she was lucky to get sex, or simply even be held, two maybe three times a month. He was always too tired because of working his extra jobs.

That same night of the big argument, Tamala gave Marcus an ultimatum: "You either stop working all that overtime, or I just may find someone who will appreciate me." Without saying a word, Marcus stormed out extremely pissed off. She had never seen him so mad during the time they had been together. The young couple had stopped speaking for almost two weeks, hence opening the door to indiscretion with Lamar.

After finally giving in to Lamar's persistent advances, Tamala met him at the Blue Moon Motel at Harland Boulevard and Decker Street way out on the northeast end of Woodland, hopefully away from people she might know. Though the seedy motel was obviously not to Tamala's standards, the sex between the two of them was both new and exciting. Cheating was something that she had never done. She had to admit that sneaking around added something extra to the sexual experience with the young hoodlum. Tamala had been sleeping with Lamar since that crazy night.

In recent weeks when Marcus was at work, Tamala became more bold by having Lamar come to her apartment on Shrader Court in Henrico County. They would look at rented videos, dine in - she refused to be seen in public with

Lamar given her relationship with Marcus - and have sex like they were a dating couple. This reckless behavior with the bad boy set her body on fire unlike any other sexual experience she had had in her life. Tamala set a boundary with Lamar though. She would never make love to Lamar because she only loved Marcus despite his rarely being around. Sex with Lamar was just that…sex; it was an arrangement just to fulfill a physical need. Tamala only shared her infidelity with her best friend, Staci Foster. Staci had often told Tamala that she was going to get caught, and she would lose the best thing she had ever had - a damn good man. In light of the death of Marcus's coworker, Tamala had become extremely worried about him despite her ongoing affair with Lamar.

Now as Tamala pondered her one indiscretion against Marcus, she continued to spread the fragranced moisturizer onto her showered body. She would never admit it to anyone, not even Staci, but she found that sleeping with both a cop and a thug extremely exciting. The 29-year-old Marcus was muscular, stronger, sexier, and made love to her passionately. The 20-year-old Lamar was shorter and thinner, but rougher; he fucked her hard like a roughneck should.

"Damn, I got issues," Tamala whispered as she rushed out of the bathroom to straighten up her master bedroom while wrapping the damp towel around her shapely figure. She opened the window then lit some incense to cover up the smell of she and Lamar's forbidden passion. Tamala changed the sheets on her king-sized water bed and began to vacuum as she kept thinking about this crazy change in her life.

Chapter 6

Sans tuxedo, Marcus was now dressed in clothing more familiar to him - a ballistics vast, navy blue short sleeve uniform shirt with French blue lapels, navy blue trousers with French blue stripes running down the sides, plain black Nike tennis shoes, a heavy black leather duty belt which contained his handcuffs, extra pistol ammo, pepper-mace, ASP baton, SureFire flashlight, Motorola portable radio, and finally the coup de grace, a loaded compact Glock .45 semiautomatic pistol holstered on his right side. Marcus refused to wear the navy blue Stetson hat as he stood tall in his tailored uniform.

Marcus missed the roll call briefing by a few minutes. As he now sat in his supervisor's office, the vindictive sergeant, Dann Sargent, gave Marcus his usual patrol assignment in the southend of the county. The sergeant then told him to pick up his new partner in the squad room. Marcus was not thrilled to meet his partner so soon, but it was inevitable this time would come. After riding alone for the last week or so, Marcus had grown accustomed to solo patrol. Tonight was probably the time not to be alone; Marcus did not know how to confront this issue with Tamala. The situation was too painful to ponder so a distraction would be welcomed.

As Marcus got up to leave, the spiteful supervisor made a sarcastic remark about not getting this one killed, referring to his new coworker. It took everything within Marcus not to punch the older white man in his face. The sergeant smirked as Marcus left to meet his would-be nemesis, his new patrol partner, Officer Eddie Logan.

***

After cleaning up her bedroom, Tamala turned on the small color TV and plopped down onto the waterbed feeling the water waves rolling underneath her. She surveyed the room to make sure that no signs of Lamar were present because Marcus would be coming over after his shift. "Oh, shit!" Tamala saw that her phone was lying on the floor in the corner. She got up and before replacing the phone on the cradle she listened to make sure it was indeed off the hook, paranoid that someone - Marcus mainly - could have heard what went on between the two of them. She hung up the phone relieved. Tamala then picked up the cordless phone again and found that she had no messages; Marcus had not called her from work. That was strange.

Once placing the phone back on her nightstand, Tamala continued to look around the room as she lay back down on her bed. She noticed that something else was not quite right. She could not put her finger on it though. Then suddenly it hit her like a ton of bricks, the portrait of she and Marcus was missing from her bureau. She always hid the photo during the rare nights that Lamar came over. She did not want Lamar to know her personal business, so she always hid the 5"x7" picture. She jumped up and ran over to the bureau and opened the bottom drawer, retrieved the portrait and returned it to its proper place, on top of the bureau. Tamala then bent down and took out a lavender see-through nightgown from a drawer, dropped the damp towel on the floor and slipped the lingerie over her head. Tamala walked back to her bed then sat down to dial Marcus's cell phone which went to his voicemail. She left a message for him to call her. After hanging up she said angrily, "It's my birthday, nigga! You better call me! I don't care how busy you are! This is *my* day!"

Tamala decided to call her best friend Staci to gossip about her latest sexual escapade.

***

The squad room was filled with tables and chairs which faced a podium in the front of the room. The podium had an enlarged image of the Woodland County PD badge on the front of it. Each shift was briefed during roll call sessions by either a patrol sergeant or lieutenant before the team went out. Officers also completed reports and other pertinent paperwork in this room. Marcus was still thinking about Sergeant Sargent's insulting remark when he walked into the large patrol squad room. He was also sickened by the thought of working with a new partner.

The only person in the room other than himself was seated at one of the tables with his head down. Marcus could see that the person was a young blond male police officer, about his age. As Marcus walked up to him, he could see that the officer was looking at a map of Woodland County.

"What, you lost already?" Marcus said with a smile then extended his hand. "Hi, I'm Marcus Williams, your partner."

The startled officer looked up, "Oh, hey. No, I'm just trying to study our patrol area." He then smiled, with deep set dimples on his face which was accentuated by a cleft chin, then stood to shake Marcus's hand. "I'm Eddie Logan."

Officer Logan was a foot or so taller and twenty pounds or heavier than Marcus, very muscular in fact, with closely cropped hair. The man, with a salon haircut, had movie star looks with gleaming white teeth and tanned skin. Eddie would give Brad Pitt, Keanu Reeves, Matt Damon and Ben Affleck a run for their money in the looks department. This pretty boy exuded an air of self-confidence and conceitedness that was overpowering. The most prominent feature on Officer Logan was his penetrating blue eyes. Those eyes seemed to look right through Marcus; it was almost intimidating.

The 28-year-old former UCLA quarterback released Marcus's hand, still displaying that impressive smile. Then he said, "I'm told by Sergeant Sargent - that's an odd name isn't it? Anyway, he told me that we had the toughest patrol in the county. I guess we'll see plenty of action, huh?"

Marcus slyly rubbed his sore hand, hoping that Eddie did not notice it; it felt as if the guy had crushed his right hand with that powerful handshake. "Yeah, we'll definitely see some action."

"By the way, man, I'm sorry about your partner. I was at the funeral - pretty sad. That guy's still out there somewhere running around free."

Marcus not wanting to talk about T. C. said, "Yep. Look, are you new to the area? I mean you looking at that map and all."

"Well, I graduated from the police academy about four months ago, did all of my field training from police headquarters. The southern part of the county is new territory for me."

"Cool. Where are you from originally?" Marcus asked with curiosity.

"California. I used to be a cop there. We, my wife and two kids, moved here last spring. We wanted a nice place to settle and raise our boys."

"Damn. You came *all* the way from California?"

"Yeah, I saw the job announcement on the Internet. Woodland County looked like a good place to raise my family. My wife, Neci, was able to get a job here as a schoolteacher."

"Great. Which PD you come from in California? Our chief's from LAPD."

"I applied there, with LAPD that is, but things didn't work out for me. I worked at a small department, the Red Rock Canyon Police Department in Cantil, California. About...umm, 100 miles north of Los Angeles."

"*Cantil*, California?"

"Yeah, it's a township, just a speck on the map."

"Oh. Never heard of it, but welcome to Woodland County PD. Let me show you around the precinct." Marcus pointed to the rear of the room, "Grab a radio out of the cabinet first. Then we'll have the grand tour and hit the street."

"Sweet," Eddie said as he went over to the radio cabinet to get an assigned Motorola portable radio.

***

Tamala was talking on the phone with her best friend Staci. "The dick is pretty good, girl, but Marcus's dick is bigger," Tamala said as she laughed with her childhood friend. "Anyway, men have done the same shit to us for years, having coochie on the side. Maybe not Marcus but still…"

Staci was an aspiring model and co-owner of Foster's Hair & Nail Salon on 1st Street between East Clay and East Leigh Streets in Richmond with her mom, Bertha. She stopped laughing on the other end of the phone and suddenly turned serious, "Still though, Tamala, messin' wit' Lamar will only bring you lots of trouble; he probably a drug dealer, you better leave him alone, gurl. Ain't nothin' but trouble."

"Staci, you got some fuckin' nerve acting all high and mighty when I covered fo' ya ass, when *you* took ya hot tail to Cancun last summer with Marcus's police friend, Sneak. What kinda name is that anyway?"

"His name's *Emanuel*. His nickname's Sneak."

"*Whatever*. Hmph… *Sneak*. How appropriate…*sneaking* around with a Sneak. So don't try to make me feel all guilty when you ain't no better than me, okay?!"

"*Tamala*, I'm just sayin' *you* got a good man! The fact is that Derrick, my no-good boyfriend is triflin' as hell, plus I know for a fact that nigga been screwin' around on me too. So when Emanuel offered to take me to Cancun, *gurl*, I was justified in goin', so there!"

"Whatever."

"Whatever back at ya *crazy* ass," Staci said, ending the playful argument which had been commonplace between she and Tamala for years. "You using protection, Tamala? Because the last thing you need is to get pregnant by that hoodlum and have his ghetto-ass baby, not to mention catchin' some shit and givin' it to Marcus."

Momentary silence on the line as Staci's last comment sunk in with Tamala, rocking her soul to the core.

"Girl...I know...and you right. I'm just...caught up in this shit right now. Don't know how to get out, you know?" Then Tamala lied, "And yes, I always make that nigga wear a condom." *At least most of the time*, she thought to herself.

"Good, but all jokes aside though, you need to do some serious soul searchin.' Lamar's trouble, Tamala. I'm for real, girl. If he finds out your boyfriend's a cop, shit, all hell's gonna break loose. The man is trouble, you know he's dealin.' Ain't no way in hell a low-rate janitor can have a brand new BMW and cash money galore, plus the nigga still livin' wit' his *momma*? End it, Tamala, and end it quickly! Then you need to work out your differences wit' Marcus. Suppose Marcus would've got killed? You would be mournin' right now, so you need to wake the fuck up!"

"You right. I...I think about that night; Marcus was crazy about T. C. That poor man was shot down like a dog, but I rather him be dead than my Marcus."

"Yeah...me too." To lighten the mood again, Staci quickly added, "So renew your love, girl. Make it right wit' Marcus. Plus, Marcus ain't got no kids and is *fine* as hell, girl, wit' his Taye Diggs-lookin' self."

Both women laughed again breaking the tension of their conversation.

"You *know*?" Tamala said as she enjoyed talking things over with Staci.

More laughter ensued between the two longtime friends.

"Actually, my man look better than some Taye Diggs," Tamala said through her laughter. Her friend always made her laugh and gave good advice, which she never took.

Staci added, "Well, girl, I gotta work in the mornin'; yo ass is off tomorrow, I'm going to bed. I love ya, girl."

"Love you too, Staci. See you tomorrow night, okay?"

"Yep, but I'll give you a call then. Goodnight!"

"'Night." Tamala hung up the phone and just laid there on the bed thinking about her predicament. She tried Marcus's cell phone again, sighing when she got his voicemail once more. She hung up not leaving a message this time. Tamala then picked up the remote and cycled through the channels of her TV, then decided to call her mother, Mrs. Rose Cooper.

***

It did not take Marcus long to give Eddie the grand tour of the building. After about twenty minutes, Marcus led Eddie to the last stop in the building.

"This is our Communications Center," Marcus pointed to the large glass enclosure in the basement which housed the work area of the dispatchers. Several women sat at workstations that contained high-tech computer equipment along with state-of-the-art radio and telephone systems. Most of the women, clad in navy blue workpants and white collared shirts with an insignia of a radio tower on the left chest, wore headsets with mouthpieces.

"Wow. This is sweet! Looks like something out of *Star Trek*."

Marcus marveled at Eddie's childlike excitement. "Didn't you see a similar setup at the main police building?"

Eddie continued to stare wide-eyed into the large glass enclosure, "Never got to see the dispatch center there, and my small PD, where I used to work never had any up-to-date stuff like this."

"Oh. Well, let's go in." The two cops walked in catching the glances of some of the women there.

Out of nowhere came the communications supervisor, Kimberly Thatcher. "Hello, Marcus. Who's this new officer?" Kimberly asked never looking at Marcus but keeping her green eyes on Eddie as if he was her next meal. Kimberly had been trying to get Marcus into bed for the longest, though Marcus resisted her every come-on, so this snub took him by surprise.

Marcus, who had not seen Kimberly since T. C.'s funeral, felt a surprising pang of jealousy as the white girl waited to be introduced to the man who looked like a prince. "Eddie Logan, Kimberly Thatcher. Kimberly Thatcher, Eddie Logan." Marcus made the introductions in the midst of his bewilderment.

Kimberly, who was obviously smitten by Eddie, graciously shook his hand. "Nice to meet you, Officer Logan."

"The pleasure's all mine, Miss Thatcher. And I *really* mean *all* mine."

The infatuated young woman, with fire engine red hair, tried to conceal a giggle. "Please call me Kim."

"Well, Kim. Then I must *insist* that you call me Eddie. I'm assigned to this precinct. Marcus and I are partners." He ogled the redhead as a hunter would his prey. The woman, who moonlighted as a stripper during her off time, felt the sexual heat of Eddie's stare.

"We're glad to have you, Eddie." Kimberly noticed the wedding band on Eddie's finger but was not fazed by it. She thought wickedly, *it's just a piece of jewelry. No big deal.* She stared from the wedding band back up to the tall stranger.

Marcus, getting impatient said, "I'm sorry to break up this little party, but Kimberly, Eddie and I are going out on patrol." Then Marcus thought, *she never told me to call her Kim!* Marcus quickly grabbed Eddie's arm, leaving behind the numerous wandering eyes of love-struck females.

Somehow Marcus knew that female attention like this was nothing new to Eddie Logan.

***

Tamala hung up the phone after a few minutes of talking with her mother. Now she laid on her waterbed, propped up on several pillows, with the TV remote in her left hand, and her right hand gently massaging her swollen vulva. She whispered to herself, "Lamar, you banged the *shit* outta my pussy...wo' it slam fuckin' *out*, damn. Young buck *sure* can fuck." Though she was sore, she continued to stroke herself as her fingers worked their way through the neatly trimmed curly brown pubic hairs. Tamala's fingers parted her tender moist reddened lips, and then used the tip of her middle finger to gently caress the exposed sensitive clitoris. Tamala closed her eyes as she reminisced about the great sex Lamar and she shared a few hours ago.

"Shit...mmm...mmm." Tamala, licking her lips, began gyrating her hips as she increased the pressure of her finger on her most sensitive area, "Oh, Fucccckkkk, awwwww."

After a few more seconds, Tamala started to get fully aroused again. She forced herself to cease the recreation. She needed to save some of herself for Marcus later. The thought of Marcus prompted her to call him for the umpteenth time on his cell. Once again to no avail, she hung up the phone in frustration. Bored, she got up to walk to the living room to make sure that Lamar had locked her front door when he let himself out earlier.

Turning on the light, she found the door closed but unlocked, "Damn it, Lamar! Stupid-ass can't even lock a fuckin' door. I see why ya uneducated ass can't get a job above being a janitor," Tamala said as she locked the door, leaving the security chain loose so that her baby, Marcus, could let himself in later.

As she stood in the foyer with her back to the door, arms folded over her small chest and tapping her foot, Tamala whispered, "You better have a *damn good* excuse for not callin' me, Marcus. It's bad enough ya ass couldn't get off tonight. Leaving me alone on my *goddamn* birthday. Ya fuckin' ass *knew* this day in advance so had plenty of time to request a day off. Ya lucky I don't kick ya black-ass to the curb." She chuckled, knowing that she would never let go of the best thing that had ever happen to her; Marcus was her ideal man. Before she could turn off the light and head back into the bedroom, she saw the large gift, wrapped in gold (with a large gold and white bow) lying on the carpet beside the couch, and froze, "What...the...fuck?"

***

Several hours into their patrol shift, Marcus found out a great deal about Eddie. One thing was that he loved to talk...especially about himself. He was a graduate of UCLA where he played Bruins football on a full scholarship. During his attendance, he earned a Bachelor of Arts degree from the School of Theater, Film and TV. Eddie was born and raised in Beverly Hills, so he came from an affluent family. His wife, Neci, eldest 5-year-old son, Eddie Junior, nicknamed Juny (pronounced *Joon-nee*), and youngest 3-year-old son, Karl were the joys of his life. Eddie loved to restore vintage cars. Finally, he proclaimed to be a strict vegetarian. Eddie told Marcus everything about him except his astrological sign. Eddie did, however, strangely avoid in-depth questions about his former employer, the Red Rock Canyon Police Department.

Marcus realized other things about his new partner that he noticed on the sly. Eddie had a roving eye for beautiful women and definitely knew that he was God's gift. Eddie also had an annoying habit of saying 'sweet' when his excitement got the best of him. Marcus swore to himself that if Eddie said 'sweet' one more time he was going to strangle him and throw his body in the Chickahominy River.

Marcus did not dislike his new partner, he was just having a difficult time adjusting to not having T. C. around. Sargent's comment about not getting this partner killed did not help Marcus's mood either. Despite the latter, Marcus would never admit to himself that he was also jealous of Eddie's perfect looks, his perfect persona, and his perfect life.

"Man, these new Fords are sweet! Thanks for letting me drive, dude!"

Marcus cut his eyes at the hyper 28-year-old, and then simply said, "Anytime, Eddie, anytime. Look, drive down that next alley and cut off the headlights."

Eddie did as told by turning left into a cluttered alleyway seconds later.

"Just before we get to the end, stop and then edge up slowly until you can see the street corner to your left. It'll be Columbia Boulevard at Stark Street. We'll see what's biting tonight."

The area was one of the busiest open-air drug markets in the county. A number of cars drove into the area looking to score crack, powdered cocaine, and heroin twenty-four seven. Young black teens would stand on the corner flagging down vehicles hoping to make a quick buck from their illicit sales.

As the white, marked police vehicle parked just short of the opening to Stark Street, the two cops could see two black males standing on the corner near Columbia Boulevard under a dimly lit streetlight, less than half a block away. Eddie said, "Damn, Marcus, this is a sweet spot! They'll *never* see us from here!"

"But they'll *hear* us," Marcus said sarcastically.

Eddie, missing the sarcasm, said, "In California, we would chase 'em all night long. They dealt hot and heavy there, I tell you. Look, we may have one - sweet!"

An old yellow van with primer and rust spots pulled up at the corner. The two men ran up to the passenger-side door. Marcus grabbed his binoculars and handed them to Eddie. "See if you can see where they're hiding the dope. Watch the dealers closely, Eddie. They'll lead us to their stash, and then we'll make the bust."

Eddie, using the binoculars, could see the two men who actually looked more like boys. The bigger one had a small Afro, and the smaller boy had short braids. They were talking to someone sitting in the passenger seat. Because of the distance and angle of the van, Eddie could not make out the features of the passenger. The smaller of the two boys went to a small drainage pipe and grabbed an unidentifiable object from a hiding spot. Eddie said, "We got 'em now! The drugs are in that hole on the side of the building. Looks like a drainage pipe or some vent."

"Okay, Eddie. Let's hold it down a little. When the van pulls off, we'll make the bust." Marcus could see the same activity but not as clear without the binoculars.

Eddie saw the exchange of money and drugs. As soon as the van pulled off, Eddie slammed the gear into drive and sped the car with blue lights flashing and siren blaring toward the young boys.

"*What* the...!" Marcus was caught off guard by Eddie's stupid heroics as the Ford seconds later slid to a halt causing the young boys to run in opposite directions. Marcus, recovering from the wild ride, said hurriedly, "I got the white shirt! You get the taller one!" Marcus bolted from the police car as if he was being shot from a cannon; he used his portable radio to call in the foot pursuits. The white - shirted youth ran like lightening back down Stark Street. Marcus was gaining on the boy. "*Stop*…you ain't going to get away from me!" The boy kept running.

As they reached a row of empty metal trashcans, Marcus got close enough to pounce on the fleeing teen. Like a bowling ball, Marcus knocked the young man into the trash cans, causing a loud disturbance that brought out the noisy neighbors. The young boy said, "Get off me, you big motherfucka!"

Marcus turned the teenager over then said, "*Who you calling a motherfucka, Ty*?! *What're you doing out here*?! *Damn it*! How many breaks I gotta give you, man?! I know you ain't sellin'!"

Tyreese Coleman smiled up at Marcus. "Didn't know dat was you, Offisa Williams. You pretty fast!"

Marcus had been dealing with Tyreese over the past several months. The 13-year-old had gotten break after break from Marcus and T. C. "Who you dealing for, Ty?"

"Offisa Williams, dey *kill* me if I tol' you dat!"

One of the gathering neighbors said, "Le' that boy 'lone! Y'all ain't got nutin better to do than mess wit' a lil boy!"

Marcus glared at the old woman standing on a porch, but held his tongue. He grabbed the 13-year-old by the collar then walked away from the small crowd. "Come on, Ty." He led Tyreese back to the police car which still had its lights and siren going. Once back at the police unit, Marcus searched Tyreese, found nothing, then put the boy behind the metal cage in the backseat. He then turned off the lights and siren as he sat back in the front passenger seat.

Eddie walked around the corner with the other teenager and Marcus called headquarters to call off any responding units coming to assist them in the foot pursuits. Marcus recognized Eddie's suspect as Devon Harris who would soon be 17 years old. The handcuffed older teen was bleeding from the side of his head. Marcus seeing the bloodied teen whispered shaking his sweaty baldhead, *damn, what now*? When Eddie reached the patrol car, he said to Marcus, "Little fucker was hiding in the park across the street." Then to Devon, "Get your black-ass in that backseat, *fucking* degenerate." Eddie slammed the rear door after putting Devon in the back with Tyreese.

Marcus thought, *naw he didn't call Devon that in front of me!* Marcus, putting it out of his mind, said, "Eddie, go get the dope please."

As the muscular young cop trotted to the side of the vacant building and out of hearing range, Marcus turned around to face the oldest boy then asked, "Devon, how did you get that?" Marcus pointed to the bleeding wound on the left side of the boy's head.

"Fuck you, Williams! You Uncle Tom bitch! Police brutality! I'm gonna sue you bitch-motherfuckers!"

Eddie walked back to the car, "Nothing's there, Marcus, the drugs're gone!"

Marcus thought, *don't tell me that!* He got up to verify for himself. The drainage pipe, sticking out of the wall, yielded nothing but dampness. Upon returning to the police car, he asked, "You search him yet, Eddie?"

"Yep, I found a thousand bucks in front of his drawers, but no dope."

Marcus said, "Okay, let's talk about this."

He huddled with Eddie away from the police car, the young boys looking on in suspicion. Seconds later the two cops parted and Eddie sat on the hood of the car looking dejected. Marcus walked over to the rear of the marked unit and took Devon out the back, uncuffing him. After getting the first aid kit from the trunk, Marcus cleaned the small wound on Devon's head, the bleeding made it look worse than it actually was. Marcus thought, *thank God he doesn't need stitches.*

Several minutes later Marcus explained, "Devon, you know you're on probation, and if I contact your caseworker-"

"That white motherfucker hit me with his flashlight! I was behind the tree, he just hit me! This ain't the '60s, goddamn it -"

"*Devon*, now you listen to *me*! *You're* on probation for selling drugs! All I need is to call your caseworker, and you'll be placed into state custody just like that!" Marcus snapped his fingers. "I'm about to give you a big break, so get the fuck out of here! Don't let me see you selling drugs on *my* corner again! You understand me, Devon?!

"But that white motherfuck- "

Marcus held up the handcuffs he had just removed from the youth. "Try me, Devon! Just try me!" Marcus then said to partner, "Give me the money, Eddie."

Eddie walked towards them and reluctantly handed the wad of cash to Marcus.

"You get a break this time." Marcus held the money in front of Devon's face. "Though I can't prove it, you and I both know that this is drug money. Take it." Marcus handed the cash to Devon. "Now get out of here!"

Eddie looked on in disbelief but didn't say a word.

The boy, putting the one thousand dollars back in front of his pants, started to make a smart-ass comment to the cops but wisely decided against it. Looking at Eddie, Devon put up his middle finger then ran down Stark Street.

Eddie started to chase him, "You little, black bastard!"

"Let him go, Eddie! We'll get him again! Just chill out, *man*!"

Marcus was not happy with what he had just done with Devon. Despite that, he knew that it was necessary in light of Eddie possibly putting their jobs on the line by hitting the young man, along with the illegal drugs they did not find. Marcus walked around the front of the police car and sat behind the driver's wheel, "Let's go!"

Eddie, still looking in the direction that Devon ran, said, "Somebody must've gotten the drugs while we where chasing them, or they sold it all."

"Yep, come on. Please get in, Eddie."

Eddie slowly complied wondering why Marcus did not let the other one go too. "You found something on him?" Eddie jabbed his thumb back towards Tyreese in the backseat.

"Naw. Taking him home."

"What do you mean you 'taking him home'?"

Marcus shot Eddie a look that could have killed. Eddie, not liking that expression on Marcus's face, decided to keep quiet. Eddie thought, *they treat drug dealers like babies in Virginia.*

***

Tamala was very confused about the present left on the floor of her living room. Now sitting with it on her bed, she wondered if Lamar had left the gift before he left the apartment. "He *did* leave the door unlocked. Maybe he went out to his car then came back in to leave it." She shook her head then whispered, "Naw, that stingy nigga ain't leaving shit." Then she thought, *Marcus must've left it this morning after he went home to sleep. Yeah, that had to be it, but why didn't I see it earlier?*

She turned the large present, with its gold wrapping paper and big gold and white bow, every which way in a feeble attempt to locate a card from the mystery giver.

"Damn, Tamala, just *open* it." She whispered as she slowly began to unwrap the mysterious gift found on her living room floor.

Tamala finally got the big box opened. Inside were two additional boxes, one long rectangular box, the other a medium-sized square box. "What in the world...?" she opened the rectangular box first. "Wow! Who sent these? Better yet how did it get here?" Tamala then turned to the square box and slowly began to open it. "Oh, my GOD!" she took out the item and thought that it was the most beautiful she had ever seen. The latter gift had a small tag attached. Still, Tamala was extremely perplexed about the contents of the boxes and still no card indicating who may have sent the gifts. She picked up her telephone and tried Marcus again, once again the phone went to voicemail, and she hung up without saying a word.

"Who would send me twelve long-stemmed yellow roses, and a size 4, black, silk strapless evening gown, from *Bloomingdales* of all places? Only Marcus was romantic enough to send something like this. He paid a *grip* for the gown alone! He must have something planned for tomorrow night. Friday will be *party* night for sure. I'm convinced that he left it this morning though, but why didn't I notice it before? Marcus, you're so romantic. I love you, boo," she said to the empty bedroom dismissing the question as to how the present had gotten into the apartment. "Lamar, I enjoyed our late evening fucks, but I gotta work things out with my man." Tamala smiled as she looked from the expensive gown to the long-stemmed roses. *I got to put these roses in some water*, she thought as she got up and carried them into the kitchen humming the *Happy Birthday* song.

***

An hour later, before taking him home to his mother, Marcus was able to find out from Tyreese who he was dealing drugs for.

The boy only knew the supplier's name to be Red Bone. The man lived somewhere off North Second Street and drove a white BMW. Tyreese had only seen the crack-cocaine supplier a few times. Red Bone dealt directly with Devon, not Tyreese. The smooth-talking man with scary gray eyes terrified Tyreese. Marcus convinced the boy to stay away from Red Bone and Devon. In the meantime, Marcus would try to find legitimate employment for Tyreese.

***

After dropping off Tyreese, Marcus, trying to keep his voice steady and void of anger, asked Eddie, "What happened to Devon's head?"

"You mean the one I found in the park?"

Keeping his head straight and eyes on the road as he drove the police cruiser, Marcus responded, "Yep, the one you brought back with the busted head."

"Oh…" He appeared to be struggling for an answer as his blue eyes darted about, searching. After a long pause, Eddie shoot back with, "I guess the little shit fell on a rock or something."

"Or '*something*'? You heard us talking, Eddie. Devon said you hit him with your flashlight."

Eddie shot him a look of astonishment as his piercing eyes narrowed. "Marcus, what're you trying to say? I know this is our first day and all, but I'm your partner. You're going to believe that little *degenerate*…over *me*?"

"I just want to get the story straight in case that boy's crazy mom files a complaint because of his injury."

"Oh. Well…that's how it happened. He fell down and hit his head." He nodded his head as to say that was his final answer and he was sticking by it.

"Okay then…it's settled. Now one other thing, Eddie."

The ex-California cop glanced cautiously at his partner then said reluctantly, "*Yeah*?"

"The plan was to drive *slowly* to that corner catching them by surprise, not warning them with our lights and siren."

Eddie smiled. "Oh, sorry about that. But you gotta admit, it was *sweeeeet*!"

***

Tamala finally got fed up with Marcus not answering his cell phone, so she called Marcus on the job. "Hello, I'm Officer Marcus Williams's girlfriend, Tamala Cooper. I need for him to give me a call, right away."
(PAUSE)

"*No*, it's not an emergency."
(PAUSE)

Tamala frustrated made an audible 'tsk' sound then replied, "Yeah, I *guess* I can hold."

She waited for a few seconds then the unknown dispatcher told her that Officer Williams was busy on a call but as soon as he got free, the message would be delivered.

"Thanks so much. Goodbye," Tamala hung up and waited for Marcus to call back. As the TV played in the background, she continued to marvel at how beautiful the gown was and could not wait to try it on. She held up the dress biting her lip in deep thought, then said out loud, "I don't have any shoes to go with this, damn, you could've bought me some shoes too, Marcus!"

Tamala grabbed the telephone on the first ring, thinking that it was Marcus. "Hello, baby!" she said with a big smile on her freckled face.

"Hey, baby, you must really miss me!" Lamar said *using his best sexy voice.*

"Oh...it *you*," Tamala said expressing her disappointment.

"What the fuck that mean? 'Oh...it's *you*'!" Lamar expressed mockingly but actually angered by Tamala's disrespectful attitude.

"Nothing I was just playin'. What's up, Lamar?" Tamala asked hoping to throw him off by now sounding upbeat.

"My dick, that's what's up! Girl, I know you got a boyfriend, and you *thought* that it was him calling, stop sweating it. I'm just giving you the time to clear that shit up, that's all." Lamar stated with self-assurance knowing full well he had a pregnant girlfriend in Petersburg. "Besides, that cop can't hold a candle to me, baby girl."

Tamala was so stunned that she sat up in her bed, "Who told you- ?!" she quickly stopped then tried to calm herself down, running her right hand through her freshly-cut hair, "that I was datin' a...a cop?"

Lamar laughed, "Damn, stop being so sensitive, *Freckles*. It's my business to know everything about you, Tamala. Plus I see that motherfucker patrolling my 'hood almost every night. Anyway, don't worry. Our paths haven't crossed - at least not yet."

Not only was she surprised that Lamar knew about Marcus, but also she was shocked to learn that Marcus's patrol beat was where Lamar lived with his mother, in the south side of Woodland County. "Lamar, I don't like your tone. Stay away from Marcus, and how dare you call me like this? We had an *arrangement*; just because I changed up by *allowing* you to come over here, don't give you the right to call me anytime you feel like it, and *don't* call me 'Freckles'!" Tamala was clearly upset now. Marcus's pet name for her was Freckles.

"Calm down. *Damn*, I'm sorry, girl. Hey, I enjoyed our time tonight. When you gonna let me move in?" Lamar laughed but then quickly ceased because he could sense Tamala getting angrier at him, "Okay...Okay, I'm sorry, Tamala. When we hookin' up again?"

Tamala sighed then replied, "Look, Lamar...I need some time to think about all of this. Remember that our *arrangement* is purely physical, no *love*, no *commitment*."

"A'ight, hit me on my cell or pager when you finish needing *'some time to think about all of this,' "* Lamar stated. He added, "But please don't call the house phone, mama gets pissed when people call after ten o'clock on her precious-ass phone."

Tamala rolled her eyes, then remembering the large gift decided to ask Lamar in a round about way about it. "Oh, I forgot, why didn't you give me a birthday present?"

"I gave you that good lovin'."

"Besides that, *Lamar*."

"I paid your rent for you this month, didn't I? When you come to your senses and be my girl, then I'll hook a sista up," Lamar said seriously.

"Goodnight, Lamar, I gotta go."

"I'll holla. Peace, baby, and remember: I can love you better than that cop." Lamar hung up the phone.

As Tamala replaced the telephone in the cradle, she covered her face with her hands, falling back on the waterbed whispering, "What've I gotten myself into?" She just lay on the bed feeling the water waves underneath her small frame, waiting for Marcus's return telephone call. Tamala continued to lay on her waterbed incensed because Marcus *still* had not returned any of her calls. *Shit like this makes it easy for me to fuck someone else, Marcus,* she thought.
***

Several hours later toward the end of their patrol shift, Eddie and Marcus reported in to the precinct for a debriefing which consisted of finishing up paperwork, showering, and changing into civilian attire.

"Eddie, you mind turning in our reports to Sergeant Sargent? I've gotta make a couple of telephone calls."

"No problem. Hey, Marcus!" Marcus turned back toward Eddie. "Look we got a rough start tonight, man. I apologize for anything that I may have said or done that may have upset you. We did things differently in California. You know, with the gang problems there, we didn't take any chances. It is going to take me time to adjust to Virginia law enforcement."

Marcus was glad that the newly-assigned officer was trying to make amends. "Eddie, I hope you give me time to adjust too. I lost a close friend of mine in the very streets we patrolled tonight. T. C. and I'd been partners for a longtime, so bear with me. In time, you and I will be tearing up the south end of the county because there are plenty of drug arrests to be made!"

"Sweeeet, I hear that!" Eddie stuck out his hand, "Once again, I'm sorry that things got rough between us tonight."

"I'll shake your hand on one condition."

Still standing with his hand extended. "What's that, Marcus?"

"You got a hell of a grip. Don't crush my hand this time, dawg!"

The two cops laughed as they shook hands in hopes that their partnership would yield good fruits. While Eddie went to turn in their reports, Marcus went to the squad room to make some important calls. He felt the cell phone on his belt vibrate once again. He picked the cell phone up, knowing that it was Tamala, and he looked at the display screen confirming the caller. "Tam, you've got to suffer a little bit more. I'll talk to you when I'm good and ready." He replaced his phone then sat down and picked up a telephone at one of the desks. He needed a photo of Red Bone. "Detective Pete Sanchez working tonight?" Marcus asked the dispatcher. "Cool. Connect me please."

Chapter 7

The next day, on the east end of the county, at the Gyno-Choice Women's Clinic, Tamala was sitting at her desk working after hours. The doctors and other medical personnel had left after another busy day. Tamala was working late to get caught up on her filing so that she would have a clean slate on Monday morning. She was also waiting for Lamar Phelps who was due in to clean the office this evening.

Tamala knew something was wrong. Marcus had not returned any of her calls to his home or cell. He failed to show up last night to celebrate her birthday. She knew he was not hurt or anything because he worked last night without incident. She even drove over to his apartment early this morning to find him not there. There was no way Marcus knew about Lamar. What else could it be? Maybe he was fucking around on her! Maybe his partner getting killed finally got to him and he needed his space. Marcus refused to talk to Tamala or anyone else about the death. Tamala's concern continued to grow, along with her paranoia, the longer she did not hear from him. *Where the fuck is he? This is crazy,* the hot-tempered young woman with freckles thought to herself on numerous occasions.

Now as Tamala put away patient files, she tried to get her mind off her absent boyfriend by thinking of other things. She pondered about how she and Lamar could have sex like two dogs in heat. Marcus's latest actions, or lack of, made her feel justified in being unfaithful. She picked up the telephone and started to dial the number to the police department when she heard a vehicle outside. Tamala saw a cleaning van pull up out front. *Lamar.* She replaced the receiver. Marcus would be confronted tonight after Lamar was finished cleaning the building. Her pussy twitched and she crossed her thick legs under the desk feeling her clitoris stimulate as her thighs rubbed. Tamala needed some dick; she needed it now.

Seconds later, Lamar and two other men, one an old black man and the other a pimpled-face white guy, came into the office. While his coworkers wore the tan button-up uniform shirt, Lamar had on a white wifebeater and sagging jeans. They immediately began their work in the one-story clinic. Lamar came over to Tamala's desk and whispered, "Damn, you look *fly* as shit in that short-ass skirt." Tamala, who was wearing a tight black skirt with a slit on one side, displayed her shapely thighs as she intentionally sat back from her desk. That skirt and the white blouse came from the Gap.

"Thank you, Lamar," Tamala responded as the young thug grabbed her trash can and emptied it into the large gray plastic receptacle with four wheels.

"Can I get a quick taste?" Lamar whispered to Tamala as he licked his lips.

Looking at Lamar like he had lost his mind she said, "You *crazy*?" She looked around at his colleagues who were busy cleaning, then back at Lamar, "Uh-uh...not here, not now."

The light-skinned man with gray eyes slowly stuck out his long tongue and flicked it at Tamala who immediately felt the warmth of pleasure between her legs.

"Boy, you need to stop, " Tamala said weakly.
Seeing the want in her light brown eyes and her flushed face, he knew Tamala was burning for him. "Come on just a little taste, Tamala. You know I like to taste you when you *raunchy* and been workin' all day sweatin' and creamin' in your panties. Let me taste you." Lamar slowly licked his lips in anticipation.

"Lamar, you're *so* nasty. What about your coworkers?" Tamala said feeling her nipples growing hard through her white, lace bra.

Lamar glanced at his fellow workers then back at Tamala, "They ain't gonna say a word. *I'm* in charge. Come on. Let's go in your boss's office and lock the door. Nobody will ever know," Lamar said with another flick of his long rough tongue.

Tamala creamed instantly in her white, lace thong. She thought, *damn that fuckin' tongue! Should I let him lick my pussy? Fuck, this nigga goin' make me lose my job if we get caught!*

The aspiring nurse, who was in *love* with one man and in *lust* with another, then stood up from her desk and sashayed down the hallway. Lamar looked back at Slim and the white pimpled-faced boy named Roy. They were oblivious to what was going on as one began to vacuum while the other emptied the other trash cans. *Hell yeah, dinna time,* he thought hungrily at the prospect of performing oral sex on Tamala. The thug followed Tamala who had just disappeared into Dr. Patricia Shay's large office.

***

Marcus deleted all the messages Tamala left on his cell phone. The sound of her voice made him both sick and long for her. He thought, *fuck*. He was trying to finish up an accident report as he sat in the empty squad room. He had drawn and redrawn the accident diagram several times without success. He simply could not concentrate. Detective Sanchez left him a photo of Red Bone, but Eddie and he were too busy to follow up on the matter. Eddie was somewhere in the building, probably flirting with Dispatcher Kim Thatcher, the redheaded sex freak.

Last night, Marcus stayed with his friend, Sneak, a Richmond cop. He refused to deal with Tamala before he was ready. He knew she might come to his apartment so he made plans to stay with him. Marcus needed to escape again tonight hoping that Tamala would not come to his job to talk with him. Sneak invited him to a club later that night and Marcus thought that going out may be the very thing he needed.

***

Doctor Shay's office was decorative and had a magnificent view of the Chickahominy River. One side of the office held an enormous book shelf with an assortment of medical books and journals. She had all of her degrees and a host of photographs on the opposite wall. Still another wall showed photos of babies delivered over the years by this highly-respected doctor in her forties. The furniture and other décor obviously had a woman's touch.

Tamala walked over to her boss's large desk and turned to face her lover who was locking the door for privacy. He went immediately to her.

"Turn around! Pull up that skirt! Let me see that *round brown*!" Lamar demanded knowing that Tamala loved it when he spoke roughly to her.

Tamala slowly turned obediently for her roughneck lover. Just the sound of his commanding voice made her that much wetter between her thick thighs. The woman with the short brown wavy hair could barely contain her excitement as she felt the faint sexual throb. Tamala teasingly pulled up her black mini revealing her shapely asset, split severely, but pleasingly, by her white laced thong.

"Goddamn, girl! Mmm, love that *phat* ass!" Lamar stared lustfully and began rubbing his hardness through his low hanging jeans. He walked closer toward Tamala who still had her back to him.

As Tamala gazed outside the large window at the roaring river, she felt as if she herself had a *roaring river* of lust flowing through her body which became swifter as she felt Lamar's body press up against her. *Fuck! This Nigga is the shit! Fuckin' hard dick feels good against my ass! Damn!* She thought.

Lamar whispered, "Freckles, I'm gonna make you my lady." He slowly began to grind his clothed, hard manhood against Tamala's soft but firm bottom. "I'm gonna eat the shit outta your sweet pussy. I ain't never ate *twat* as good as yours. I'm *serious*."

Tamala, breathing heavily and uncontrollably with closed eyes, began to match Lamar's movements against her, pushing into his hardness. "I *love* the way you suck my pussy, Lamar. You can eat me anytime, baby."

"Turn the fuck around, Freckles!"

Tamala complied with the order. The skirt remained up on its own due to her well-formed hips.

"Take your panties off."

Tamala slowly brought her hands up, allowing them to ride along the sides of her thighs then stopping at her narrow waist. Using her thumbs, she hooked her thongs in its waistband slowly pulling down her sexy underwear over her wide hips. As the garment fell to her ankles, she stepped out of them.

"Pick 'em up, Freckles."

Tamala picked up the soiled panties.

"You know what I want you to do, so *do* it!"

Tamala unrolled the thongs and exposed the inner crotch; she began licking her cum from the sexy undergarment.

"Yeah, that's right. Lick that shit," Lamar said with visible excitement now.

Tamala continued to taste her own wetness as she smelled the wild and pungent feminine scent coming from the silky lace garment. She could not believe the *freaky* things Lamar had her doing as of late. Normally after a long workday, Tamala loved to take a long hot bath to soak away the stress of the day. She also loved the feeling of being clean and fresh after bathing. Lamar met Tamala at her apartment once after work. He wanted to fuck her just the way she was…unbathed. Lamar was definitely a freak and he in turn made her one. Their sexual escapades were scary and exciting at the same time. The man could get her to do just about anything!

Lamar kissed Tamala as the thong underwear rested between their faces. "Time to taste the real shit," Lamar said then lifted Tamala's petite frame placing her seated on her boss's desk. He got on his knees and gently pushed her back onto the desk leaving her in a prone position. With her legs pulled back, Lamar grabbed Tamala underneath her generous bottom, bringing her towards his waiting mouth! He lapped greedily upon her hairy mound, loving her taste and the light musky savor coming from her womanhood.

"Shiiiit, baby! Eat that motherfuckin' pussy! Shiiiiiit!" Tamala sat up on an elbow and pushed Lamar's face deeper into her soft brown bush. Lamar's rough tongue penetrated her hot flesh as he sucked hard on her clit. "Lamarrrrrrr…it's sooooooo *fuckin'* good! Suck it, baby, suck it!"

Lamar worked his long tongue in and out of her like a hard dick, driving Tamala to a quick but powerful orgasm. "Fuck me, Fuck me! Shit! You motherfucker! Mmmmmm…Mmmmmmm…Mmmmmmm! You goin' to make me cummmmm! You goin' to make me cummmmmmmmmmmm! Ohhhh, GODDDDD! YESSSSS, right there! Ahh…Ahhhhhhhhhhhh!"

Tamala, with her eyes shut tight, shook violently as she climaxed into Lamar's mouth. Her hips and pelvis began to slow its tempo. "La…mar. You can eat the *fuck* out some pussy, " Tamala said trying to catch her breath. Lamar continued to lick and suck at her. "Okay, okay, stop! Too sensitive! Oh shit, stop, motherfucker!" Tamala pushed his head away from her sensitiveness. She began to giggle as she looked down into the gray eyes of her lover with his braids tied back. Tamala thought, *You fine, motherfucker. Ya gray eyes drive me fuckin' wild.*

The light-skinned young man smiled then pushed her firm legs back exposing her butt. He began slowly licking her asshole. Tamala, laid back with her eyes closed, and then softly whispered, "Damn, Lamar. You're *so* fuckin' nasty. Licking me like that...awww, *shit*! I love it though. I love it, baby. Put your, damn that feels good...put your tongue in my ass, you dirty motherfucker." Lamar was driving her crazy with his tongue; the rough tongue, licking and flicking her anus gave Tamala a sexual sensation unlike no other, as she stroked her clit. When the tongue entered that taboo spot, Tamala thought that she would lose her mind as she released uncontrollable moans of pleasure.

Lamar finally stood smiling with his thin mustache and goatee covered with Tamala's cum. He stepped in between her legs and dropped his jeans. Lamar thrust his throbbing dick deep inside her wetness causing her to scream out in both pain and pleasure. *"Fuck* me, *Bad-Boy*! Fuck me *harddddddd*!"

Chapter 8

Later that evening in her apartment, Tamala was soaking in a soothing hot bath drinking a goblet of Courvosier as silent tears flowed from her reddened eyes. She just could not understand why Marcus had disappeared on her. She called the police department and left a message; Marcus did not return the call. Tamala understood that T. C.'s death may have had a traumatic affect on Marcus, but she could not comprehend why Marcus was being scarce. She whispered, "I miss you, baby. Where are *you*? Why won't you call me back, Marcus?" Despite her involvement with Lamar, she missed and loved Marcus deeply. It hurt Tamala to think about her longtime boyfriend. Still Lamar provided the perfect distraction.

Lamar wanted to come over tonight, but Tamala told him that she had gotten her monthly cycle and did not feel well. She joked with Lamar about his banging her so hard on her boss's desk that it brought on her period. Tamala topped off the lie by saying that her cramps were just too much to bear, but she would call him in a few days. Lamar still wanted to come over to cuddle with her. That bothered her a little; the thug seemed to want something more than sex - a relationship. Tamala did not care for that one bit. Plus Tamala had plans of her own later.

Tamala got out of the bathtub, dried herself, and then went to her bedroom. Upon checking messages, she found none from Marcus. Tamala was *pissed*. "Okay, Marcus. Ya wanna play it that way? Fine with me, Negro." Tamala went to her closet in search of her sexiest outfit. She was going to have some me-time that night. She and Staci had plans of their own.

***

Marcus's shift was over. Freshly showered, he was dressed in a long sleeved lavender shirt with black slacks. He stood before the full-length mirror in the locker room checking out his attire. Marcus decided to meet Sergeant Emanual Chambliss - called 'Sneak' by his friends - of the Richmond Police Department. Being that Rip was a Richmond native, Marcus was hoping that Sneak my have picked up additional information on the killer.

That evening Sergeant Chambliss was working off-duty at a club in Richmond. The club was being visited by a celebrity; Ashanti, Marcus's favorite female musical artist, had a concert at the Richmond Coliseum. According to Sneak, Ashanti was having her official after-party at the new spot, the Club Le Amour, and Marcus was invited. When Sneak told Marcus about this yesterday evening, it was welcomed news - and a nice diversion - in escaping the pain of infidelity and the death of a close friend.

Marcus walked away from the mirror and out of the locker room. As he entered the hallway, he saw Eddie and Kimberly Thatcher talking privately just at the entrance to the dispatch center. They were making goo-goo eyes at each other. Anyone looking at the two could tell that they wanted to rip each others' clothes off and have sex right in the middle of the deserted hallway. Unseen by the potential lovers, Marcus shook his baldhead then got onto the elevator.

Chapter 9

The Club Le Amour was one of the hottest in Richmond. The four-story facility, which catered mostly to African-Americans ages 25 and older, had three dance floors, along with the top VIP floor. Club Le Amour stayed packed nightly. Each dance floor had its own separate entrance once patrons entered through the front foyer. This made it easier to regulate the Virginia Fire Codes by patron count.

The popular nightspot made its debut this past January and was visted often by celebrities which not bad for a building that used to be an old dilapidated warehouse. There was underground private parking for special guests and with its elaborate security system, off-duty uniformed Richmond police officers working the front door and the club's own security people, Club Le Amour was one of the safest clubs in the city.

Marcus pulled his Camry up in front of 727 West Broad Street his sunroof was open, letting in the seasonable warm air from the April evening. This was Marcus's first visit to the club even though Tamala had talked about the popular spot all the time. Marcus was always working overtime and had never had an opportunity to party at Club Le Amour or anywhere else for that matter. The large neon sign, CLUB LE AMOUR, shone brightly above a double line of late-comers. Men wearing hip-hop gear and women scantily dressed in mini-skirts, tight fitting dresses, and even booty-shorts lined the street outside the club. Marcus thought, *Um-Um-Um, fine women here, boy!* He could hear music thumping from within the club as he sat in his car.

The sidewalk was cordoned off with red velvet rope and red carpet led inside the club. Near the large double doors, a few uniformed Richmond cops and several muscle-bound security officers, with headsets and black shirts with white lettering, regulated the flow of the large crowd. Some simply stood guarding the doors, while the rest utilized handheld metal detectors as patrons filed in.

One of the guys looked over at Marcus parked in front of the club and began to walk toward him. The guy was big, black, muscular, and looked mad as hell. As the man got closer, Marcus could now read the white lettering on his tight shirt, *Security*. Marcus continued to sit in his car, hoping that Sergeant Emanuel Chambliss would make an appearance out front as promised. When the man who lookd like a bulldog reached the driver's side window, he barked, "This is V-I-P parking only! Move it, *now*! If you don't, you'll regret it!"

"Hey, Randy! He's with me!"

The big guy, Randy, and Marcus looked toward the sidewalk, near the front of the Camry, where the baritonal voice came from. Marcus was relieved to see Sergeant Emanuel Chambliss. Marcus never knew why the Richmond sergeant was nicknamed Sneak, but he was so glad to be rescued from this *brotha* with the tight black security shirt, who looked like a broke-down Mike Tyson.

Randy, who towered over Marcus's friend, said meekly to Sneak, "Didn't know he was a friend, Sergeant Chambliss. Sorry 'bout the mistake."

Sneak, who was wearing a black tailored Armani suit with a slick pair of Prada shoes, walked over to Marcus's car door and opened it, "Hey, Marc! Come with me!" Sneak then looked at Randy, "Park my friend's ride in the basement parking and hold the keys for me, Randy."

"Yes, sir." Randy, obedient like a loyal hunting dog, jumped into Marcus's Toyota and drove-off out of sight.

Sneak mumbled something into his Nextel then he and Marcus went into the club through a side employee entrance facing the 300 block of Laurel Street. This employee entrance led to a network of stairs and elevators which allowed private access to each dance floor and other areas within the business. Only VIPs and employees could obtain access through this restricted door.

Marcus met Sneak six years earlier when they both served temporary duty on the Greater Richmond Area Drug Enforcement Administration (DEA) Task Force. Sneak, who worked narcotics then, borrowed then-rookie Woodland County PD cop, Marcus, for a six month undercover stint in and around Richmond. Marcus made numerous drug cases during this deep undercover assignment. The two cops had become good friends over the years. Sneak, who was not married, had dated Tamala's friend Staci Foster for a brief period. The cop, who had a striking resemblance to the entertainer Will Smith, was almost ten years Marcus's senior.

Sneak, a veteran member of the Richmond Bureau of Police, moonlighted at the club as the director of security. He supervised other off-duty police officers and a group of security guards at the establishment. Sneak's group of police officers were specially trained in dignitary protection. Celebrities visiting the hotspot were well protected. Tonight the unit was charged with the protection of one Ashanti Shequoiya Douglas, better known as singer-entertainer Ashanti. Several hours earlier, she had blown away the sellout crowd at the Richmond Coliseum with a topnotch performance. Ashanti was now greeting some of her privileged fans at a very private after-party at Club Le Amour.

"Sneak, he ain't gonna mess up my ride is he? That Randy guy was pissed before you came out! He was all *swole-up* like he was gonna hit me or something!"

As the two made their way into the private elevator and up to the VIP floor, Sneak said, "Marc, if Randy wants to remain employed, your car better not even have a speck of dirt on it. I'm personal friends with the owner here, Mister Sharpe."

Marcus, forgetting about his car now, began to get excited at the prospect of meeting a celebrity. "You really gonna introduce me, man? To *Ashanti*?"

Sneak saw the eagerness on Marcus's face. At that moment, Marcus had the attitude of a little kid getting ready to meet Santa Claus. He knew that Marcus was a big fan of Ashanti. As the elevator door opened on the top floor, Sneak said before walking out the elevator, "Marc, you will not only meet her, I've arranged for you to fuck her too."

Marcus stumbled out of the elevator as Sneak laughed at his expense. "That's not funny, Sneak. You shouldn't play like that; got me all nervous."

"Marc, calm down and stop drooling all over yourself; it's unbecoming, " Sneak said cooly with a smirk on his face.

The cops went through a series of security checks, instituted by Sneak who spoke once again into his Nextel. Apparently he was letting the security people ahead know that Marcus and he were on the VIP floor and headed their way. The two friends approached a mixture of Ashanti's security people and Sneak's crew of officers at the entrance to the VIP room. The music, from all three floors below, was somewhat muted, but Marcus could feel the vibration of the music. *Or was that his heart beating too fast in anticipation on meeting his favorite singer*? Sneak looked back at Marcus, "You ready, kid?"

Marcus just nodded.

"Okay then, let's meet your special lady, Marc." Sneak and Marcus walked into the large and crowded well lit room.

***

Tamala and Staci had to park several blocks from Club Le Amour due to the lack of available parking spaces near the club; Ashanti had the club packed. They parked their waxed-down ride in an area reserved for neighborhood residents. Staci prayed that the Richmond PD would not tow her brother's black Jeep Grand Cherokee. The two women dressed in extremely tight dresses, Tamala's white leather outfit - with matching heels - and Staci's black clingy dress, began the long walk to the new club.

Staci said fervently, "It's *my* ass if anythin' happens to that Jeep! Shit, Tamala! We *way* the fuck out in the middle of nowhere, damn! We gonna be tired and sweaty by the time we get to the front door; I spent all day at the shop gettin' my hair did and shit! On top of that we missed the *damn* show! The shop's not too far from the Coliseum, I knew I shoulda bought my own ticket and left ya black-ass!"

Tamala rolled her eyes. "Staci, just calm down! I apologize for the *fifth time* for causing us to miss the concert. Fuck! I-AM-SORRY! OKAY?! *Ashanti* ain't all that no way. I'll give you ya money back for the ticket, so pleassssssse stop ya annoyin' ass whinin'."

Staci cut her blue eyes (thanks to blue contacts) at Tamala. "I'll knock ya short little ass down on this sidewalk, callin' me annoyin'!"

"Staci, *please*! *You* may be taller than me, but I'll *pimp-slap* you silly before you even get a hand on me, bitch! You betta recognize before I pull that weave outta yo head!"

Staci stopped walking, and began doing the 'black-girl neck roll' with hands on her hips, staring down at Tamala. "*Well*? Start pullin' my weave out, 'ho'! That's if you woman enough, with your *skank-ass*!"

Tamala also stopped her fast walk, doing the same head roll with hands on her shapely hips, but bugging out her eyes at her friend and sucking her teeth making a loud popping noise! "Pleeease, bitch! You ain't worth me messin' up my clothes, provin' I can kick yo skinny ass! So *fuck you*! Tired of yo bitchin'!"

The two beautiful women faced each other with flaring nostrils ready for battle. After several seconds, Tamala broke the silence. "This some silly ass-shit. Us out here fussin' about some stupid concert, looking crazy. Ashanti can't sing no way. Let's just go to the after-party and try to salvage this fucked-up evening, Staci. I told you I had no idea Lamar was coming over. I told him *not* to come over! Took me forever to get him off my door step. Damn, had to sneak out my own apartment just to go out tonight. So, please let's just stop arguing and get our dance and drink on! These heels are killin' me and my thong's cuttin' off the circulation in my ass, so let's try to have some F-U-N, FUN! It's Friday night, girlfriend, let's party!"

Staci agreed but rolled her eyes in annoyance, then said, "Tamala, I told you to break it off with that crazy man. *What*, he stalkin' you now?! That's some serious shit! You ain't nuttin but a *chicken-head* to that crazy fool! He givin' you money all the time! Just not right, gurl! You better make-up with Marcus before this shit get outta hand. And stop callin' me outside my name. I ain't no bitch, *bitch*!"

"And I ain't no skank, *skank*!"

After a moment, Staci said, "Okay…I'm sorry!"

Sighing, Tamala said, "Look, I'm sorry too! Plus, girl, I can handle Lamar and Marcus," She said, grabbing her tall friend's arm. "Come on, let's go. Ashanti better make a appearance at this club, or I'm gonna be a *pissed-off bitch*!"

The two friends continued their long trek toward Club Le Amour through the dimly-lit streets of Richmond.

***

Later, after much reflection, Marcus would be less than thrilled with his face-to-face with Ashanti in the crowded VIP room. Just as Ashanti made her entrance then walked past the nervous Marcus, he tried to catch his breath unsuccessfully then said in an unusually high-voice, "HI, *ASHANTI*!" which sounded more feminine than masculine. Thanks to the loud applause, the entertainer never noticed him as she went to a seating area to receive a few privileged fans and members of her entourage.

A smiling Sneak led his awestruck friend out of the room to give him a tour of the rest of the club.

***

As Sneak was showing Marcus around the club, Tamala and Staci finally entered the hot spot. They were on the first floor of the club, the hip-hop and R&B dance room with multi-colored flashing lights that kept in beat with the music. The studio-like room had catwalks along the ceiling and attached strobe and laser lights shining down on the enormous darkened dance floor. Bold women with short skirts danced on the catwalks, risking exposing their assets to the many eager men and even a few eager women below. The extremely loud music seemed hypnotic for the young crowd that danced up a sweat to a Nelly tune. Women's body parts jiggled and wiggled while their male partners ground against their plump rumps during various sex-like dances.

Tamala and Staci weaved their way through the throng of young partygoers and were lucky to find a small empty table, cluttered with half full glasses of brandy or beer, toward the back of the big darkly lit room.

As they sat down, Tamala leaned in toward Staci to be heard over the music. "Since I caused you so much aggravation tonight, drinks are on me.""Gurl, you a'ight. Paid my cover, and *now* my drinks, we just may become friends again."

"Fuck you, Staci." Tamala looked around the crowded darkroom as the couples continued to groove to the Nelly beat. "These *mens* are hard-lookin' up in here tonight."

"Tamala, you gotta admit - this place is off the chain! You think we can get up to the VIP floor?"

"Girl, *please*. All we have to do is shake our young asses at these horny bouncers and promise them *some pussy* and we'll get in to see Ashanti."

"Ya *know*?" Staci exclaimed as both women laughed then high-fived one another.

"Plus since you can't reach Marcus's friend, Emanuel, we got to use our bodies to get what we want. Shit, what's the point in having a hookup, Staci? He must not have much clout. "

"Don't hate, bitch." Staci rolled her eyes. Emanuel should have answered his phone.

Tamala said, "Let's get some drinks in us first then we'll go up to the VIP room. They don't give a damn about the ABC laws up in here; no last call for alcohol."

- 63 -

"Well then, let's get *crunk*," Staci said then looked past Tamala to peek toward the crowed bar. "See that tall brotha standin' by the bar? The man with salt-and-pepper hair?"

Tamala turned to take a look. "*Damn*, he's ugly *and* old as shit! Ugh!" She quickly turned back in her seat from the fifty-something old man with gold teeth and a dark three-piece suit. "They should not only have a dress code, but a *ugly-ass face* code for people like him, lookin' like somebody's grandpa."

Staci laughed, but tried to hide it from the sugar-daddy who was definitely interested in what he saw. "Don't frown, but he was starin' at us when we walked over to the table. He kept sneakin' peeks at us, well mostly at *me*." Staci said that last statement with an air of playful conceit. "That old brotha gonna buy us our drinks, so save your money! Watch and learn from a pro, Tamala." Staci stood up then sashayed her tall frame over toward the bar. Tamala shook her head at her crazy friend.

***

Sneak and Marcus stood in the Security Room of the Club Le Amour just down the hall from the VIP room. The medium-sized room contained an assortment of color security monitors showing various points-of-interest inside the club as well as the exterior. The latter showed the entrances to the large four-story building. Four security personnel constantly observed the monitors for any signs of trouble in and outside of the club.

Sneak pointed to a set of TV screens and said, "Those monitors on top cover the outside, as you can see. That one there, on the top left, covers the front door. Look, there's Big Randy standing near the door; he's the one that parked your car, Marc. All of those monitors at the bottom cover each of the dance floors, except the VIP room; that's private."

"Pretty sophisticated, Sneak. The owner definitely got the hook-up on security. He pay you well, don't he?" Marcus fingered the lapel of Sneak's expensive suit as he checked out the clothing.

"Naw, don't pay much, but it does supplement what I make at the PD. The real drive for this job is meeting the stars when they come to visit, Marc. Many of the entertainers choose to frequent this club after performing in the city. But like I said before, me and the owner of this *moneymaker,* " Sneak waved his arms about the room referring to the successful club, "are good friends, so he takes care of certain expenses. I'll introduce you to him. His office is downstairs on the ground floor. This place has made him a rich man. The club just sucks up the money, Marc, sucks it up like a vacuum; each floor has its own cash room. This club is like multiple clubs in one actually, even got a small comedy club. The first floor is nothin' but R&B and hip-hop. The second caters to our hardcore gangsta-rap lovers."

"I'll meet the owner some other time. I've got a lot of stuff on my mind."

"Man, I'm sorry. You talk to Tamala yet? I mean unless you don't wanna talk about it..."

"Sneak, I'm cool. Just need some rest. But if you can find out anymore about Rip..."

"When you gonna talk to her, man?" Sneak was really concerned about Marcus. Last night, Marcus gave Sneak the full play-by-play of how he caught Tamala with her lover.

Marcus sighed. "Sneak, I really don't know. I…I don't know what to do. This shit is tearing me up. First T. C., now this shit."

"She called me after you left for the gym this morning, looking for you, man."

Marcus perked up with interest now. "What you say to Tam, Sneak?"

"Told her that we talked but didn't say a word about you staying over. She was worried about you."

"Yeah, right."

"She was, Marc. She really sounded down, man. Staci - "

"I hope you didn't tell her nosy-ass!"

"Come on, Marc. I wouldn't do that. But…I gotta remind you that the girls had tickets to the concert tonight. They might show up," Sneak paused when he noticed Marcus looking extremely uncomfortable. The young cop was glancing toward the security people in front of the monitors.

Marcus, self-conscious about Sneak bringing up his personal business in front of the security guys, said, "Sneak, let's step out in the hallway."

Sneak looked from Marcus then to the security employees. "Oh, right. My bad. Let's go." The pair was about to leave the security room but were stopped when one of the security men yelled something about a fight going on in the hip-hop area.

"Come on, Marc. Let's get some of that excitement!"

The two policemen ran out of the room as one of the security men began to radio the problem to other security specialists in that area. The commotion was about some tall woman beating up on an old man at the bar.

***

"Crazy *witch* threw a drink in my face and then scratched me! Look at my cheek and my damn neck! I'm filin' charges!" The older gentleman said as he nursed his wounds and tried to wipe the alcoholic beverage from his dark wet face with a dingy handkerchief. He then looked down at his clothing. "Ruined my suit too! She gonna pay for my suit!" The old man did not realize that his gray and black toupee was all askew of his baldpate. The toupee looked more like road-kill than a hairpiece!

Several security men were trying to figure out who to put out as one of them desperately held onto Staci, who was kicking and screaming, trying to get at the old man who had disrespected her. "Get ya fuckin' hands off *me*! That motherfucka touched *my* titty! Let *me* go!"

The old man, who wore an out-of-date and out-of-style suit, said, "All I did was buy her a drink. She just went crazy. Young gals these days just don't know how to treat a gentleman!"

The security men formed a protective ring around the 'crime scene' thus disallowing Tamala access to her friend. "Y'all big motherfuckers better let my girl go, let her *go*!" When Tamala tried the crawl under one of the men, he grabbed her. She was now being bear-hugged just like Staci. "Goddamn it, put me down, my boyfriend's a *cop*!" The strongman continued to hold onto Tamala that much harder, enjoying the feel of her ample buttocks against his private parts.

As the music continued to thump and bump from a song by Monica, one of the men who appeared to be a supervisor said, "THAT'S IT! THROW 'EM ALL OUT!"

Another security specialist grabbed the old man by the arm. He began escorting the toupee-wearing man toward the front with the other guards who had Staci and Tamala. "Why you puttin' me out? I ain't done shit to nobody. All I did was buy that girl a drink. That's *all* I did!"

The crowd cleared a path for the big security men who forcefully walked their detainees through. Some of the partygoers were pointing and laughing while others danced as the bright-colored lights continued to flash to the pulsating music. As the captors lead their prisoners toward the entrance of the room and into the lobby, the group's march was suddenly halted.

Both Tamala and Staci looked as if they had seen a ghost, each for separate reasons. Tamala was shocked to see Marcus and Staci was equally surprised to see Emanuel blocking the path.

Sneak, not seeing the three prisoners, addressed the man who appeared to be in charge. "Everything alright?"

The leader said, "Yeah, we got it under control." Now pointing to the three troublemakers behind him, he continued, "These people were causing a disturbance, but we puttin' 'em out."

For the first time, Marcus and Sneak noticed the young women held in the clutches of the large security personnel. Marcus's stomach dropped upon seeing Tamala. Sneak broke the brief silence. "Umm, look we'll take control of those two," Sneak pointed at the girls.

The security leader looked as if he was about to protest but apparently had second thoughts as he told his men to release the women. Staci gave each of the guards her right middle finger upon being freed. Sneak smiled and shook his head as he waved Staci and Tamala over to a door which led into a small private room, actually an empty office. The old man who was earlier smitten with Staci, began yelling something about wanting names for warrants as the security guys threw him out of the club. Marcus followed Sneak, Tamala, and Staci into the room. Once they all reached the cramped space, Sneak shut the door behind them, leaving behind the thumping loud music.

"Hello, Staci, you're looking lovely tonight. *Dessert* for my soul, good enough to eat," Sneak said with a smirk on his face. Then he looked toward Tamala. "And Tamala, nice to see you. I'm sorry that you ladies are having a difficult time tonight."

"Emanuel, look we're so sorry. I am *so* embarrassed. But that man touched my breast!" Staci said peevishly trying to straighten out her attire which was ruffled by the security personnel.

"Staci, you have nothing to apologize for. Can I get you ladies something? Drinks, or something to eat?" Sneak offered with a sexy smile toward Staci.

Tamala, looking over at Marcus, answered Sneak, "Naw, this has just been a horrible evening." Then she said softly to her elusive boyfriend, "Hello, Marcus. Why haven't you called? It seems like you've avoiding me. I know you been having a hard time with your boy's death, but I have been sick and worried. I don't understand why you won't talk to me, I want to be there for you. It was my...birthday."

Marcus, who stood away from the trio leaning against a wall with his arms folded over his chest and his head down, blatantly ignored Tamala. Tamala hated to be ignored. She was trying to hold back her frustration and anger.

Sneak, looked back at Marcus, then again to Tamala, realized the tension slowly building between the two. "Well, we can go to a private area and kickback."

"Sneak, I'm out. Thanks for everything!" Marcus quickly left the room in search of Randy and his car keys.

Tamala yelled after him, "Marcus, what *the fuck*'s the matter with you?!"

Sneak looked at the two disheveled women trying to think of something to say.

Staci put an arm around her frustrated best friend then whispered into her ear, "He knows, Tamala...Marcus *knows*."

***

About two hours or so later back in Chesterfield County, Marcus made it back to his apartment as dawn made its appearance. He sat down on his couch in the living room letting out a long sigh, contemplating the events that had changed his life in recent weeks. He constantly thought about his woman being with another man, and almost on a nightly basis saw T. C. in his nightmares, bleeding to death on that unkempt kitchen floor.

Seeing Tamala tonight reminded him of how much he really missed her as well as how much he still loved her. "Damn!" Marcus said to the empty apartment, angry that he couldn't hate the woman who had betrayed him. He laid his head back and closed his eyes trying to clear his head of all thought, an impossible feat as he saw Tamala's freckles and light brown eyes staring at him in his mind's eye. Releasing another long sigh, Marcus was just about to get up from the couch and attempt to get some sleep when the telephone rang.

Staring at the telephone on the end table for a few seconds, he finally picked it up, "Hello?"

"Hey, Marcus. You still up?" The soft feminine voice belonging to Staci asked.

With exasperation, Marcus requested, "What do you want?"

"Look, Marcus, I know you don't like me, but my girl loves you. You hurt her tonight. Why you treatin' her like that?"

Marcus sat up on the edge of the couch in irritation. "Treating *her*, like what?!"

"You actin' like she did somethin' wrong to you. Tamala wants to be there for you, and you won't let her in...*why*?" Staci, who was currently alone in her home, told Tamala, as they left the club, that she would call Marcus and attempt to find out if he really knew about Tamala's affair with Lamar Phelps.

"I ain't got time for this. You just stay out of our business; it ain't got nothing to do with you, Staci!"

"Marcus, I'm just tryin' to help. You're a damn good man." With the help of loneliness and a stiff drink, Staci began to lose focus as to why she had called Marcus. "Maybe Tamala just doesn't realize it, but I do...*I* do. You're unlike any man I've ever met, Marcus. I really mean that, despite how you feel about me. I know you don't like me because I'm fuckin' Sneak...and I have a boyfriend too. But-but I digrass, I mean digress." The alcohol was taking its toll. "You gave Tamala not only the things she needed or wanted...but you gave her your heart, Marcus. A woman needs that from a man." Staci, working on a serious buzz, sipping on her second or third cup of Hennessy, began to think about how her boyfriend, Derrick, treated her...treated her like shit! She took a large gulp of the alcohol.

Sighing, Marcus said, "Staci, I'm tired. Just tell Tam that I'll contact her when *I'm* ready. I need time alone to think...about some things."

Not hearing Marcus, and feeling warm and horny from the cognac induced high, Staci said seductively, "You know, Marcus…you-you look just like *Taye Diggs*. When I first saw you…I was immediately attacted…*attracted* to you, not only because you look kike, damn…I meant look like a movie star, but because I saw that you were a sincere, carin', roooomantic, and truuuuue gentleman. That was a turn-on for me." Staci had candles lit around her small bedroom as she relaxed on the bed. She took another gulp of the dark liquid and then slipped a hand inside her pajama bottoms, feeling the smoothly shaved pussy.

Marcus was shocked by her revelation of being attracted to him. He grew visibly aroused and then asked, "Staci…this…you shouldn't be, we shouldn't be talking like this…um, you been…drinking?" The thought of sleeping with the pretty woman, to get back at Tam, was very strong, erotic, intriguing, and very, very tempting! It would be poetic justice…sweet, sweet revenge! But Marcus quickly dismissed the thought thinking about Sneak…plus he did not want to lower himself to Tam's sleazy level.

Staci, closing her eyes began to stroke her sensitive spot. She said breathlessly, "*Just a little, Marcus, but I assure you that I'm not drunk.* Just being truthful about things…mmmmmm…tryin' to clear the air…oh, *God*…just in case." She felt the wetness on her fingers. She had to release that river. Her middle finger went deeper into the well.

Marcus cradled the phone between his cheek and shoulder. He rubbed his temples in frustration asking, "What you mean? 'Just in case.' "

"Mm-Mm-Mm…oh, God…well it deprends, depends." She envisioned Marcus's nude body lying against hers. Staci was on the verge of cumming. "Um…well…what I mean is…mmmmmm…just in case you might feel somethin' too, and of course if Tamala and you...you know...break up or somethin'. Ain't like I haven't thought about you, sexually. I love my girl but...sometimes Tamala can be...so fuckin' selfish...want it all"

For some reason, Marcus thought that Staci might have been hinting toward Tamala's unfaithfulness, he suddenly became alert. " 'Selfish, want it all'? Staci, you know something about Tam that I need to know?" Marcus obviously needed no confirmation on Tamala's infidelity, but obtaining information on the man who was *loving* Tamala would be huge!

Staci eyes shot open! She stopped pleasing herself and quickly sat up in bed suddenly realizing that she had not only crossed the line with Marcus, her friend's boyfriend, but she was about to reveal Tamala's darkest secret! "Whoa...whoa look, Marcus," Staci was trying to think through her sexual fog brought out by the potent alcohol. "I'm sorry...forget...forget about what I said." She closed her eyes and ran a hand over her face, "I-I'm not in my right mind. Tamala loves you. Just let her back in and work things out with her." Her head swam in Hennessy. "Goodnight, Marcus."

Marcus, seeing the sunlight shine brightly into his small apartment, said, "Goodnight, Staci...get some sleep." After hanging up the telephone, he said, *"What...the...fuck*?!" He fell back onto the couch shaking his tired head marveling at his crazy life.

Chapter 10

A number of days later, on a cloudy, misty, warm evening, Lamar Phelps was involved in a heated argument over the telephone with his girlfriend, Latisha Wyatt. "Latisha, my boy Royal left a few minutes ago! He gonna give you the money you need!"

"I don't give a damn about the money or funky-ass Royal Brunson! You're the one I haven't seen in weeks. I'm carrying our baby, and you treat me like...like I'm nothing to you! I ain't fuckin' Royal, you the one I need to see! If you love me, then start acting like it, Lamar!" Latisha began crying as she finished the brief diatribe.

"Latisha, calm down and just listen to what-"

"CALM DOWN!, CALM DOWN! Two weeks, Lamar, you haven't been down here in *two weeks*! Yes, I need the money you send me, but I need you more, baby! Why...why can't we get a place together...live...on our own?" Latisha cried harder.

Lamar thought, *because I ain't tryin' to be tied down to your ugly, fat, pregnant, stinky-ass, that's why, bitch! Plus, soon I won't need your house to hide my shit no mo'. I'm savin' my money and gonna leave this hick-ass state! Then go legit.*

"*Well*? Say something, Lamar!"

(CLICK)

That loud audible sound was all Latisha heard as Lamar hung up on her once again. He then took the phone off the hook so she could not call back.

As Lamar was walking back through the dining room of his mother's house in the southern portion of Woodland

County, Josephine, his mother, said from the closed kitchen door out of his view, "That hoochie ain't stayin' here with no cryin' baby. And I ain't go'n baby sit either. I raised fo' of y'all…two dead…one in prison…and you, I just don't know about you, boy, which way you headed in life. I try my best."

Lamar picked up his backpack which was still behind the couch where he left it. "Mama, I ain't tryin' to hear that right now. Gotta go to work."

"Work? You just got off *work*. On most days, your job ends at four. It's almost four-thirty now. I know what you do, Lamar; I *ain't* stupid. You're breakin' my heart. You out there in the street doin' God-knows-what."

Lamar, tuning out his mother who was frying something in the kitchen, held the backpack which contained the instruments of his trade, a Smith&Wesson 10mm automatic pistol, a set of small digital scales, numerous packs of small plastic zip-lock baggies, and a large sealed package of powder cocaine. He was going to Royal Brunson's apartment, about five minutes away, to wait until he got back from Petersburg. In the meantime, Lamar was going to cook the cocaine into its potent rocklike form of crack-cocaine. When Royal returned, they would begin the tedious packaging of the rock substance, preparing the product for sell on the street. Lamar's cell phone vibrated on his right hip; he ignored the call knowing that Latisha was the caller.

Lamar opened the door to leave, but was stopped in his tracks as he observed the Ford police car parked across the street. He knew that the dark silhouettes inside were looking at him, the cops were here to pay him a visit. Lamar looked at the distance from his front porch to his BMW then at the distance from the police car to his ride. "Shit, they'll be on me before I get my car started," Lamar whispered as he calmly and slickly let the backpack slide down his left leg then silently onto the floor of the living room.

As soon as he walked out of the door and onto the front concrete porch, leaving his goodies behind, the two cops quickly got out of the shiny patrol car and began walking his way - a white cop with blond hair and a brotha. Lamar recognized the black cop from Tamala's hidden picture then said to himself, "*Ol' boy* found out I'm fuckin' his woman…this should be good." Lamar began to smile as the cops got closer. He looked forward to this confrontation. "Hello, Marcus!" The light-skinned man said that as if Marcus and he were the best of friends.

Marcus was taken aback by the young thug knowing who he was, but he did not show his surprise or irritation at the use of his first name. Both Marcus and Eddie stopped at the fence as Marcus asked the young man his name, though he knew he had the right guy, "Are you, Mister Lamar Phelps - people call you Red Bone?"

"Yep…that's me, but only my *friends* call me *Red Bone*, you can call me, Mister Phelps. Can I help y'all with somethin', Marcus?" Lamar continued to smile at the cops who remained on the other side of the fence in the misty rain.

"I'm Officer Williams, this is my partner, Officer Logan. I ask that you refer to me as 'Officer Williams'. Anyway, do I know you?"

"Naw, but we share a common interest as you already know." Lamar began to laugh.

Marcus assumed that Lamar was talking about Tyreese. He tried to hold in his rage due to the thug's cavalier attitude. "So, you know why I'm here?"

"Yes, Marcus, I know why you're here."

Anger flashed upon Eddie's face at the continued disrespect that the man showed toward his partner. "Maybe you need your attitude readjusted!"

Lamar's smile disappeared as he slapped his chest with both hands then opened his arms in an invitation to fight. "Bring it, white boy! Show me whatcha got!"

Eddie started toward the front porch but was grabbed by Marcus, "No, it's okay, Eddie!" Then Marcus said to Lamar, "All I ask is that you show us a little respect. I'm giving you that consideration, how 'bout you do the same?"

Lamar thought about it for a second then said with a mock smile, "Look, my bad. Okay, you right. How can I help you, *Officer* Williams?"

Marcus said, "I need to talk to you about that 'common interest' we have, Tyreese Coleman."

Lamar started laughing hysterically thinking, *Ol' Boy don't know I'm fuckin' Tamala! Damn!*

The two cops looked at each other, perplexed by the laughing man.

Lamar trying to stop his laughter said, "That'... oh God...that's *our* common interest?" He tried to get himself together as tears of laughter began to fall down his cheeks.

Marcus held in his temper as best he could. "What's so *funny*?!"

Lamar got in a few more seconds of laughter before stopping. "Okay...I'm sorry but I thought that you - never mind. What about Tyreese?"

"Can we go in and talk, Lamar?" Marcus pointed to the front door of 9302 North Second Street.

Lamar thought about his backpack and its contents then said forcefully, "Hell *naw*! We can talk just where we are. What about Tyreese?"

Eddie was suspicious at Lamar's refusal to let them into the house. "You got something inside you don't want us to see, *Red Bone*?" He gave his winning smile.

"Don't allow no *whities* or *Uncle Toms* up in my home."

"Okay, Lamar, that's the way you want it. I'll cut to the chase! I know Ty's dealing cocaine for you. He's a friend of mine. Leave him alone, and we'll leave *you* alone, got it?!"

Lamar said, "First, I don't deal drugs, and second, Tyreese is just a neighborhood kid I took under my wing. Ain't no law against helpin' the kids. I love the kids, Marcus." The thug finished with a grin.

Without warning, Marcus jumped the small fence then leaped onto the tiny porch. Now standing face-to-face with a non-smiling Lamar, Marcus said in a whisper, "I'm gonna say this once, and only once. Lay off my friend Tyreese. You don't so much as say hello to him on the street. If anything happens to him *or* his mother, I'll make it my project to be on your ass twenty-four-seven, you won't be able to push an *aspirin* on the street…now don't *fuck* with me." Spittle from Marcus's mouth landed on Lamar's upper lip as he finished that last statement.

Eddie stood by waiting to back his partner if things got bad. *This is sweeeet, I love a fight*, the blue-eyed cop thought as he took out his ASP baton.

Lamar continued his eye contact as their noses were virtually touching, the tension mounting. Lamar slowly wiped the spit off of his lip, and then said with a smirk, "Okay…you got it. Tyreese's off the hook. I don't need his ass to sell my drugs. I can make plenty of money without him. Shit, I can probably pay your salary, Officer Williams." He was smart enough to know that simply admitting to being a drug dealer was insufficient evidence for the cops to arrest him. The authorities would need more than his admission to arrest and convict him on any drug crimes.

Marcus lingered a few seconds longer in Lamar's face then slowly backed away. He made his way off the porch and past Eddie, walking back to the patrol unit as the sun began to break through the thick cloud cover. Eddie smiled at Lamar then followed his partner.

As Marcus was about to get into the passenger seat, he heard Lamar yell from the front porch, "Hey, *Marcus*, I see we have more than one interest in common! You have a good day!" Lamar waved then turned and went back into the house.

When the cops were back in the car, Eddie said, "I thought you said you didn't know that degenerate."

Marcus, who was trying to think where he could have met Lamar Phelps before today, said, "I *don't* know him, Eddie. At least up until now. Let's head over toward the mall. I got an informant to meet."

"Sure." Eddie drove the Ford away from North Second Street.

Marcus thought, *what other interests do we share, Phelps? What the hell are you talking about, and how do you know me?*

In less than 24 hours, the answers to those questions would be revealed, hitting Marcus like a sucker punch to his gut.

***

Forgetting about his confrontation with Lamar for the moment, Marcus focused his energy back to finding T. C.'s murderer. Eddie and Marcus went to visit Lynch's Trucking Company, located south of the gigantic Rolling Hills Mega-Mall Complex. The owner of the trucking company, Daron Lynch, also known as Weenie, was a large black rotund man in his late forties. Marcus hoped that Weenie could bring clues on Rip's whereabouts since the homicide investigators seemed to have lost all leads to the fugitive. The shady businessman had legitimate and criminal ties throughout the county and beyond; he was Marcus's last hope in finding Rip. Despite Weenie's past success in secretly helping Marcus solve various crimes in Woodland County, the big man would soon find out that Rakeem Harper was not an easy target to locate.

Chapter 11

As the cloudy day finally yielded fully to the bright May sunshine, the Woodland County police car was parked in front of 4350 Cutler Road; this was home to Eddie and Neci Logan and their two boys, Eddie Junior and Karl. The large four bedroom house was tan with brown trim. The tri-level dwelling, well over twenty years old, had a concrete driveway leading to an attached double-car garage. The previous owners added a large rear deck and a spacious sunroom. The sunroom extended over the sloped backyard which overlooked the unattached garage and the alley. Those new add-ons were unseen by Marcus who was seated in the car. An hour ago, Eddie ripped his pants chasing a shoplighter. He had another pair of pants at his house which was a few blocks away.

"Come on, Marcus. Let me show you the place. I also got this Mustang I'm restoring out back in my garage. She's beautiful."

"Naw, I'll wait here. Take your time. Eddie, thanks for covering my back earlier with Lamar."

"That's what partners are for, dude. I got your back, and you cover mine."

"Cool, now go cover your ass. I'm still hurting from laughing at the *ducky* boxers under your ripped pants."

Eddie said, "It *was* kinda funny, wasn't it? He wouldn't've gotten away if it wasn't for that fence. Anyway, you win some, and you lose some. Such is life, dude. Be right back."

"I'll be here." Marcus let down the window allowing in the warm spring air.

Eddie left the car and walked inside his home.

***

Minutes later, Marcus saw a light gray late model Cadillac Escalade pull into the driveway in front of the closed garage doors. One of the doors opened, and a little boy got out and left the full-size luxury SUV. The SUV had tinted windows and a weathered blue bumper sticker displaying the American flag along with white lettering, *Bush/Cheney* '04.

The child had a crop of blond hair and was the spitting image of his partner. Marcus could not remember Eddie's children's or his wife's names. The kid reminded Marcus of the boy that had squirted Eddie in the face at the mall. Marcus smiled again at the thought. Eddie's *Mini-Me* stopped and looked at the police car then waved at Marcus who waved back. The blond-haired kid, who appeared to be about five or six years old, then turned quickly, ran into the house and yelled, "Daddy, Daddy!"

The rear right passenger side door opened and a dark-haired smaller boy climbed out, leaving the vehicle's door ajar. The boy had a darker complexion and appeared to be a couple of years younger than his brother. He slowly walked toward the house before he raced up the steps to the front porch.

"*Karl*, how many times have I told you to stay in your seat and wait for mommy to get you out?!" A frustrated female voice drifted out from inside of the SUV. Marcus could only see a silhouette, a view through the SUV's open rear door, of what appeared to be a woman sitting in the driver's seat fumbling with something. The boy, ignoring his mother, continued to run then he too disappeared into the home. The resourceful young boy had recently figured out how to escape from his child seat. This drove his mother crazy; Eddie, his father, thought that it was amusing.

The woman finally stepped out of the SUV shutting her door. She walked around the front of the SUV to the door her son had left opened. Marcus saw that she was a brunette, with shiny jet-black straight hair past her shoulders. She was wearing sunglasses, a white blouse, a tight black knee length skirt, and black flat shoes. Marcus thought, *damn that woman got a tight body, hips and ass like a sista!* Because of the distance, he could not make out her face, but surprisingly he was becoming sexually aroused. She was carrying a bag of groceries and what appeared to be takeout food in a white plastic bag. Eddie's wife struggled with the heavy door given her hands were full, almost dropping one of the bags. Marcus quickly exited the patrol car to render assistance to the woman in distress.

When Marcus got within earshot, he said, "Looks like you could use some help."

Mrs. Logan was startled for a second, but quickly relaxed when she saw the familiar uniform. "Oh, yes and *thanks*." She handed the tall muscular officer the bag of takeout then shut the SUV door. Facing Marcus, Mrs. Logan sexily threw back her head, flipping her long hair back from her face, then said, "Whew! These boys of mine. You would think that they have no home training. I spend all day at work with other parents' *wild* children, only to come home to my own." Taking off her dark sunglasses and hooking them on her blouse, she said holding out her hand, "I'm Neci, Gerard's wife. You must be…Marcus, right?"

"Yes…umm…I'm Marcus."

The two strangers shook hands. Marcus felt the softness of her hand and noticed how extremely attractive she was as the sunlight highlighted her shiny hair. Marcus fought off an overwhelming urge to reach out and stroke Neci's soft-looking hair which was neatly parted in the middle. The sweet smelling perfume she wore only enhanced her beauty.

Neci exhibited wholesomeness, morality, and gracefulness; she was both regal and stately in her appearance. In addition, without being overt, her behavior, speech, and saunter radiated pure sexiness.

For a moment Marcus thought that he had assumed wrong, that this woman was not Eddie's wife. He wondered who was this Gerard person was so asked, "Gerard's wife?"

"Oh, you probably call him Eddie, but he's 'Gerard' to me," The precocious young woman said after seeing the confusion on the officer's face. Then she gave Marcus the most dazzling smile he had ever seen. That smile could have literally brightened up any dreary day.

That was when Marcus became aware of other extraordinary things about Neci as he looked down into her friendly wide-set eyes. She spoke in a soft husky but very sensual voice, very articulate with a slight accent; Marcus could not place its ethnicity. Neci's large round eyes were as dark and shiny as two motionless ponds under a full moon. Those penetrating eyes, with long eyelashes, seemed to smile as they searched for sincerity or truthfulness in the audience with which she conversed.

The black natural eyebrows matched the thick bouncy hair which cascaded over her narrow shoulders and flowed down her back. She had dark angular features upon a flawless oval face, a slightly upturned cute nose, and kissable, full, moist, red lips. Her deep tanned skin was just the right shade. Neci's perfectly straight white teeth were one of her many astonishing attributes. She was small-breasted and *small-waisted* with a 5'6" hourglass petite frame which came down nicely to her firm and muscular calves. The woman's body was very curvaceous.

As Marcus continued to take in this woman's exquisiteness, he rethought whether or not she was in fact tanned, maybe she was biracial. Neci's features appeared to reflect mixed race. She was simply stunning, breathtaking even. Her beauty was intimidating to Marcus, making him feel oddly inadequate.   This woman could turn heads anywhere she went. Unbeknownst to Marcus, Neci was a former runner-up for the *Miss Texas* beauty pageant a few years back. Eddie Logan not only had his own perfect looks, but he had a perfect woman to match! The two simply complimented one another. Marcus thought dejectedly, *life is so unfair.*

Marcus noticed all of these things through this brief exchange with Mrs. Logan. He tried unsuccessfully to pull himself together. He was amazed that a woman could have this dramatic affect on him. He was purely rattled, and Neci was purely captivating.

Neci smiled then waved her hands in front of Marcus's eyes. The man simply stood there gaping at her. Neci was both flattered and embarrassed by her affect on him. "Hey! *Hello*? Anybody home? Marcus, you okay?"

Marcus came out of his trace then answered shamefully, "No, I mean yes! Sorry…umm…I was…umm. What was it…I was saying?"

Neci gave a quiet giggle, attempting to hide it with her hand. She did not want to make Marcus self-conscious. "I was saying that you probably know my husband as 'Eddie', that's short for Edward…his first name, I refer to him as 'Gerard' his middle name." She finished with that hypnotic smile.

"Yeah, we call him Eddie at work…um…well, I guess I'll go back to the car and wait for him." Marcus wanted to escape. He felt like a nervous high school boy next to this goddess of a woman.

"Don't be silly. Come on in. Have you two had dinner yet? We've got plenty of eats here."

Everything about Neci was spellbinding: the way she talked, her appearance, and even the way she gestured left Marcus wanting more. He held onto her every word. The young man had never experienced a feeling like this. *What am I feeling? Lust? An attraction? Love? Aww, come on! Now that's ridiculous, she's married!* Marcus wondered then smiled unknowingly at the crazy thought.

Neci looked up into Marcus's handsome face then asked curiously, "What're you smiling about?"

Marcus, caught off guard, tried to think of something to cover the truth behind his smile. "Umm...Umm...we...uh, Gerard and I, I mean, Eddie. We were at the mall and, and some kid got barbecue sauce all over his uniform, I was just remembering that. Eddie and I laughed all the way here."

Amused by Marcus's nervousness, Neci just said with an alluring smile, "Oh."

"Umm...Gerar, Eddie and I came by so that he could change his uniform. We really need to get back on patrol. We'll probably grab a bite to eat somewhere in our patrol area."

"Well, Marcus, make sure you come back on your day off, when you have more time. You're welcome anytime, you know."

"Sure...umm...Missus Logan. I'll do that. I'll come by sometime."

"Do I look like an old lady to you?" Neci asked with that captivating smile.

Marcus thought, *you're the most beautiful woman I've ever laid these tired eyes on. You ain't no old lady, You fine as HELL!* He answered instead with sincere obliviousness, "No, ma'am. Why do you ask?"

Neci laughed with a slight upward tilt of her head then said with that beautiful mesmerizing smile and constant eye contact, "Marcus, I'm twenty-eight years old, we're probably about the same age. Please cut the 'Missus Logan' and 'ma'am.' If you don't mind me calling you Marcus, then please, by all means, call me Neci. "

"Okay, Missus, Neci, I meant to say just *Neci*, minus the 'Missus.' I'll call you that…Neci." This woman really made Marcus nervous. She exuded independence, intelligence, self-assurance, self-control, and class. Despite those things and more, she was still down to earth.

"You sure you don't want to wait inside?"

"Um…yes, ma, yes, Neci. I'll be okay…in the car. Thanks for your kindness though." *Why am I acting like some love sick school boy?* He thought.

"Well, if you change your mind, just walk on in."

"Yeah, yes, thanks, Neci." Marcus turned and began to walk away, his heart pounding in excitement.

"Hey, Marcus?"

The cop with the sweaty baldpate did an abrupt turn around, "Yes?"

Neci looked down at the bag of takeout that Marcus was carrying then said with a sexy chuckle, "Unless you intend on eating all of that *in the car*, I would like a little of it to feed my hungry boys, if you don't mind."

Marcus looked down at the forgotten bag in his hand, "Oh, I'm so sorry, Neci! This is *embarrassing!*" He handed her the bag of food.

"Marcus. You have *nothing* to be embarrassed about. It was sweet of you to help me like you did."

Wow, she called me sweet! Stop that! Just be cool! Marcus thought. He then said to the young woman, "No problem. Nice to me you...Neci."

Giving him that warm, radiant, genuine smile, she said, "Nice to meet you too, Marcus. I'm serious about you coming to visit us, so don't hurt my feelings." She finished the latter with another chuckle that sent pleasant chills throughout Marcus's body, making his stomach do flip-flops.

"I promise. I'll drop by sometime."

"Okay then. Oh, and take care of my Gerard out there...he's all I've got. Goodbye, Marcus."

"I'll watch his back. See ya, Neci."

Just as Marcus made it back to the car, he turned to see Neci on the front porch struggling to open the storm door. He started to go back and help her when he saw Eddie in a fresh uniform open the door for his beautiful wife. They exchanged greetings and then kissed deeply. It pained Marcus to see the young beauty held in the arms of his partner. Neci walked into the house as Marcus obtained a last glance of her posterior. Marcus thought lustfully, *Whoa! That butt would put both J.Lo's and Kim Kardashian's asses to shame!*

As Eddie strolled back toward the cruiser, Marcus felt ashamed for checking out his partner's wife. *What's wrong with me? That's his woman! Get your shit together, Marcus!* The young cop chided himself as he got back into the patrol car.

When Eddie arrived and took over the driver's seat again, he said, "I see you've met the family." The two policemen sat a few minutes before pulling off.

Marcus replied, "Yeah, they're nice, Eddie. What're your boys' names again?"

"My oldest is Eddie Junior, named after me of course. We call him Juny. My youngest is Karl; he's pretty shy, really quiet."

"Your oldest is the spitting image of you; that boy looks *just* like you, Eddie, but Karl looks more like your wife."

"I love both my boys, but Juny's my favorite."

"Neci, your wife, seems to be a very nice person." Marcus tried to convince himself that he was not attracted to the lady.

"Yeah, she is. My wife is a philanthropist. She loves people; human interaction is a strong interest of hers. She's always volunteering at shelters and stuff. I tell her all the time that you can't be nice to everybody; there are lots of degenerates out here."

Marcus said, "Eddie, we can use people like her in the world. Hell, makes it easier for us if she turns someone away from a life of crime."

"But she's *too* trusting, Marcus. One Thanksgiving, when we were in California, she brought this homeless family to our house for dinner! Can you believe that? No joke, Marcus, I wore my gun the entire time under my shirt for fear that those people were going to *jack* us in our own home. When I say things about her trying to help every soul in this world, Neci just laughs and calls me antisocial. The woman sees the good in everyone she talks to."

"Now, Eddie, I do agree with you on that - having strangers in your home can be…well, *dangerous*."

"But despite her love for people, I'm lucky to have her. She's the brains of this operation, this marriage, definitely my better half. So where to, Marcus?" Eddie put the Ford into drive and drove away from his home.

"I'm kinda hungry. Let's get something close to our patrol before Sargent calls us to his office for being out of our area too long."

"Dinner sounds good to me. How about that Mexican restaurant on Shady Tree Road? I can get a veggie dish."

"Yeah, I love Mexican. Let's do it, " Marcus said.

"Sweeeeet!"

Marcus shook his head at Eddie, then he reflected upon the extraordinary woman - Neci. Peace filled his heart, a feeling that had eluded him since his recent troubles.

The police car headed back towards Ghetto Town.

Chapter 12

Marcus was exhausted. He had worked until 7:00 a.m. looking through files on Rip and Lamar Phelps. He could find no apparent link between the cop-killer and drug dealer. *So once again, what other 'common interest' do Phelps and I share?* Marcus thought as he became frustrated.

The past several hours were not a total lost. Marcus was able to get Tyreese a job at the Woodland Lumber and Paper Company. Sergeant Mike Wessel of the Petersburg Police returned Marcus's call and was happy to get Tyreese on the boxing team. Marcus and Eddie's partnership was coming along okay. In fact Eddie had invited Marcus over to his house to see his latest vintage automobile restoration, an early model Mustang. Marcus, who had no desire to see the old Ford, did look forward to seeing Eddie's wife again. He felt guilty about his hidden agenda but Neci did say that he was welcome to visit anytime. Eddie stressed that he would be working an off-duty security job later that night at a nightclub in Ghetto Town, so Marcus had to call him before 10:00 p.m. in order to set up a time to hook-up the next day.

***

Under the May morning sunlight, Marcus pulled into a parking space in front of the Chester Estates. He was glad to be home. The long shift and then drive were tiring. Going to bed was the only thing he looked forward to, despite having the next few days off, because Marcus was both physically and mentally exhausted. He was not bothered by the daytime noise because he had his trusty earplugs in the nightstand to help him sleep.

A large 17-foot orange and white U-Haul truck was being loaded by several young brothas as it sat parked near the front entrance to the stairs leading to Marcus's apartment. Marcus spoke to one guy who was carrying a beat-up end table as he walked down the stairs then to the truck. Marcus went up to his apartment on the third floor, number 9. As he got to his door, he saw Chondra Moore, the VSU cheerleader who lived beside him, standing just outside her door. Chondra, clad in an orange and blue VSU tank top and matching tight, short shorts, was giving instructions to two men who were carrying a large headboard. "Morning, Chondra." Marcus was surprised to see the woman wearing a shorter hair style, which really highlighted her pretty face, over the usual long straight black hair. Her petit frame, a gymnast's build, over firm muscular brown legs, provided a solid beautiful body.

"Hey, Mister Marcus!" She walked away from the men as they carried the item down the stairs. "You gonna miss me?"

Marcus's tired mind finally realized that Chondra was moving. "Why you leaving?"

"Mister Marcus, I told you that I graduate in a few days. Remember the invitation I gave you? It was several weeks ago now."

"Dag, Chondra…I forgot." Marcus had no intention on going to her graduation, but did at least want to get her a present. "You going back home *now*?"

"Well, yeah. Sort of. My parents wanted to get this moving stuff out of the way so that we could make plans for the graduation. Plus after graduation I'm headed to FSU for orientation, I'm going for my master's!"

"Whoa, Chondra. That's great. And yes, I'm going to miss you."

Chondra began to look behind her then past Marcus to make sure the open air hallway was void of any witnesses including the football team members who were grateful enough to help her move that day. Marcus even looked around himself, wondering what she was looking for.

Without warning, Chondra walked up to Marcus and wrapped her arms around his broad shoulders. She interlocked her fingers behind his neck then on tip-toes, pressed her perfect body against him. Marcus instantly got aroused as he felt the intense body heat from the much younger girl.

Chondra looked up into Marcus's eyes then said, "I've always wanted to do this." She tilted her head then closed her eyes and kissed Marcus passionately, slowly prying open his mouth with her moist soft tongue. Marcus responded by putting his arms around her small waist just above her taut bottom and offered his own tongue into the mouth of his neighbor; both tongues became very acquainted with one another. The wet fiery kiss immediately caused a hard bulge in the front of Marcus's slacks. Feeling the swelling from him, Chondra in turn did a slow grind against it and moaned. As the kissing and grinding slowed, Chondra hugged Marcus then stood away from him. The two, breathing heavy, smiled a knowing smile.

"*Damn, that was the shit*! Got me all *wet*. I always knew we had the *hots* for each other, " Chondra said breathlessly then gave Marcus a girlish laugh. "It's too bad I'm leaving."

"Probably a good thing, Chondra. Plus I don't need no drama from your boyfriend."

"Yeah, Jovelle's crazy. *Don't worry*, he's working today. We'll keep this *our* little secret. Maybe our paths will cross again someday."

"Maybe. Look, Chondra, I don't know if I'll make the graduation. I'd like to send you something though."

"Mister Marcus, you've done so much for me since I've moved here. Plus that kiss was present enough." Some of the guys were coming back up the stairs to move more of Chondra's possessions. "Well, I gotta go." The young lady winked then went into her apartment.

Marcus let out a sigh then entered his own apartment.

***

As soon as the door opened, Marcus thought that he was seeing an apparition when he glimpsed the woman sitting on his couch. As his door shut behind him, Tamala, who was obviously pissed, asked furiously, "You fuckin' that *heifer*, Marcus?!"

Marcus tried to remain calm as he placed his keys on the kitchen counter. He put his hands in his pants' pockets in a feeble effort to hide the hard-on caused by Chondra's surprise kiss. Distracted by the U-Haul truck earlier, Marcus had walked right by Tamala's vehicle without noticing it. Tamala being in his apartment while he was out was okay under normal circumstances. Both have long established that the other could come and go unannounced to their respective homes due to their monogamous relationship hence the reason they had keys to each others' apartments. But in light of recent events, Marcus was very uncomfortable as well as offended with Tamala invading his space; she was not welcomed.

"First of all, lower your damn voice, and second, Tam, what're you doing here?" Marcus leaned against the counter, his hard-on abating, with his arms now folded across his chest. He did not want to get in proximity of the woman who was dressed in a pink pajamas short set. It was readily apparent that Tamala had slept overnight at Marcus's apartment.

"I'm your *girlfriend*. Remember? Or did that *'ho'* out there make you forget that."

"Leave Chondra out of this."

"*Oh*, you defendin' her now? Chondra, the *'ho'*?"

"Fuck you, Tam."

"NO, fuck you, MARCUS!

"Chondra's not the 'ho' around here."

"What the *fuck* is that supposed to mean?!"

"What do you *THINK* it means, TAMALA?!"

"Stop being a *PUNK* and tell me what the *fuck* you tryin' to say, Marcus! Damn, be a man for once, you got somethin' on your mind, then say it! Be a MAN about it!"

"Bitch, you wouldn't *know* a real man if he bit you on your fat ass!"

"I *hate* that word! Don't you *EVER* call me a *bitch*!"

Marcus sounding childish, "Tam's a bitch! B-I-T-C-H...*BITCH*!"

Tamala thought about charging after Marcus but thought against it. She was shocked by his cruel words; he had never talked to her that way. Marcus calling her names really stung. She thought of a hurtful comeback then said, "Your dead momma's a *BITCH*!"

The apartment grew so quiet that Marcus could hear his own heart beat. It took a few seconds for Tamala's comment to take effect. Common sense left him when it did. Marcus came after Tamala.

Marcus got within striking distance as he bit down on his bottom lip, ready to lash out at the small woman, who sat defiantly on his couch. Pursing her lips and squinting her eyes up at the raging man, Tamala's demeanor dared Marcus to hit her as he stood hovering over her with his fists balled. Marcus took a deep breath then slowly walked away from Tamala. The rage and hatred in the room were thick.

Marcus walked over to the only window in his living room. He opened the blinds to let in some sunlight because he knew that sleep would now be a long time coming. He could see the Wawa next door. He thought about walking over, leaving Tamala to argue by herself, and getting himself something to eat.

After a few minutes, Tamala said calmly, "I've waited long enough for you to 'think over some things' or whateva the *fuck* you're supposed to be doing. Staci couldn't tell me all you said to her over the phone. You been dissin' me and shit. Then at the club the other night, that *shit* was foul, Marcus. I didn't kill T. C., so why you treatin' me like I'm nothin' to you? Or are you cheating on me, maybe that bitch next door is comfortin' you, huh? Yeah, that's *right*! I *saw* that shit...what y'all were doing out there in the hall, *tonguing down* each other. Once again, I'm your girlfriend, and I deserve-"

Marcus quickly turned away from the window facing Tamala. "Are you *really* my girlfriend, Tam?! A loyal, devoted, and faithful girlfriend?"

"Yes, Marcus!" Tamala frowned in a mixture of anger and confusion, "Why the fuck you ask that? I've always been there for you!"

Marcus walked over to where Tamala was seated then stood before her making direct eye contact. "Are you *my* girlfriend, or someone else's?"

Tamala was caught off guard and looked away from Marcus's intense stare. "Don't be trying to turn this shit around on me. You the one got busted. Kissin' that triflin' bitch out there. "

"Tam, Chondra's my neighbor. She's leaving here for good. Yeah, the *goodbye* kiss got out of hand, it was wrong, my bad. Now, answer my *goddamn* question: Who are you fucking? Believe me, woman, I ain't the one *cheating*!"

Tamala tried unsuccessfully to look Marcus in the eyes as she answered, "I ain't *fuckin'* nobody. How dare you kiss that girl, Marcus?" She felt exposed, naked.

"Let's cut to the chase, I'm tired of this shit…all the fucking lies. I got something for your ass. What you need is a wake-up call. And I know just what you need to bring you back to reality." Marcus said with a menacing chuckle then walked away from Tamala disappearing into the back bedroom.

Tamala thought, *damn, what's he tryin' to get at, askin' me who I'm fuckin'? Does he know? Naw, I was too careful. Marcus don't know shit. Got his head in the sand.*

Marcus came back out of the bedroom with his right fist balled up.

Tamala saw a wild look on his face again, actually in his eyes this time. *This nigga's really gonna hit me now*, was her thought. Slight fear filled her as Marcus slid the coffee table out of the way then knelt in front of her.

Speaking very softly to the woman that betrayed him, "Tam, you meant the world to me…"

Tamala thought, *Meant?* Her fear increased added by *total* confusion.

"…I've remained faithful to you throughout our relationship. Okay, I've been tempted, but who hasn't been tempted by the opposite sex? The fact is, I've never cheated on you, Tam…*NEVER!*"

Still kneeling in front of Tamala, Marcus slowly brought up his large fist and held it in front of her face. Tamala's heartbeat raced in alarm. "Marcus, don't do nothin' stupid. Remember, you're a cop and could lose your-"

Marcus opened up his fist and revealed the black velvety ring case. With his left hand, he opened the small container revealing the engagement ring. He heard a gasp come from Tamala, who was in awe of the ring's beauty - a two-carat, marquise-cut diamond platinum ring. Tamala knew jewelry.

"Tam, I was devastated by T. C.'s death, still am. But something else fucking crushed me into little pieces. You see, Tam, I actually took off the evening of your birthday, I had plans to be with you." Marcus handed her the open case with the ring prominently displayed. As she held it, her mouth stood open in shock, looking from the gleaming jewelry then back to Marcus, he walked back to the window. As he looked out at the busy activity at the Wawa, next door, and at the crowded roadway of Route 1, he continued his diatribe, with his back to Tamala.

"I came over to your place that night, Tam. I was filled with so much joy. I was happy as hell despite T. C.'s death." Marcus smiled and shook his head at the memory. "Damn, I was on a high, unlike anything I've ever felt. Everything was going my way for once. I had my soul mate, and a job that I loved. For weeks, I've planned this…T. C.'s death only sped up my plans, life was too short, I thought. I came into your apartment hoping to begin our new life together."

Tamala knew what was coming; she wanted to become invisible. She began to tremble as she held that ring. Her mind flashed back to sex with Lamar that night. Then she had a sudden revelation, *Oh shit! The present…the roses…the dress…Marcus! Please God…don't let him know. I love Marcus, Jesus! Don't let him know!*

Marcus continued speaking, "I had that ring with me...the one you're holding right now. I wasn't going to give it to you right away. I came over pretending to take you out for a surprise birthday dinner."

Tamala held her head down and closed her eyes. She felt as if she was going to throw-up. She sadly thought, *Marcus was going to ask me to marry him...my dream come true. This is so unfair. I can't believe this shit.*

"I heard noises coming from your hallway. It was dark, Tam, inside your apartment. I thought, I thought that someone was hurting you, thought someone had broken-in and was attacking you. I didn't know what to do. I didn't have my gun. I left my fucking cell phone in the car, so I couldn't call for help. All I could think about was saving my baby, saving you, Tam."

Tears fell from Tamala's closed eyes. She thought, *Please, Marcus, don't say anymore. Make him stop, God. Make him stop talking about this!*

"I walked down the hallway...and my life ended. You really hurt me, Tam. I've never experienced such an *intense*, *emotional* hurt in my life. I'm so *pissed* right now because despite what I found out about you, I'm still so much in love with you, Tam. I *want* to hate you, but don't know *fucking* how! Because of *all* this love I have for you and I can't do *shit* with it now. Hmm...what am I going to do with this *dead* love I have for you, Tam?! It's dead because you killed it."

Tamala started to sob. The words cut her like a knife. She wondered how she could fix this.

"I couldn't believe the shit I was hearing from inside your bedroom. Tam, I *still* can't believe it. I won't let my mind think about it, even *now*...shit's almost funny. Just like I closed out the pain of T. C.'s death, I did the same with what I heard coming from your bedroom. Heard you call his name too. Can't remember the name right now, but that don't matter. Funny thing, Tam, I didn't have the balls to face you or…him. I just…just fucking walked out of there, somehow hoping that it was all a bad dream, somehow hoping it would go away. Ha, ha…joke's on me though. Took my ass to work…acting like nothing fucking happened. Life's fucked up, Tam. Really *fucked up*. Life's a bitch…then you live, *not die*. You live through heartache after heartache…pain after pain! Then? *Then*, and only then, you fucking die!"

Marcus slowly turned around from the window and faced Tamala. "Who was he, Tam? Are you still fucking him? Do you love the motherfucker? Was he the only one, What did I do? What did I do to deserve you cheating on me? Guess I wasn't man enough for you, huh?"

After a pause, Marcus stared at the crying woman on his couch. He felt no sympathy as he raged, "Don't just *sit* there all quiet! Give me *something*, goddamn you! Give me some *fucking* answers, Tam! *Anything* that will *take this fucking hurt away!*" Marcus successfully held back the tears trying to spill out from his eyes. He would not give her the satisfaction of tears.

Tamala cried tears of remorse as she covered her face. The ring that she held was being covered with her guilty tears.

After what seemed like an eternity, Marcus said quietly, but through clenched jaws, as Tamala continued to cry, "I'm waiting, *Tam*."

"I…I'm sooo sorry, baby. Oooooh, Marcus!" Tamala could not stop the tears long enough to speak as she stared forward into space.

"Who is he, Tam? That man who caused all this fucking pain in my life. He took you away from me! Who's the man, the man who's *fucking* you! Come on, Tam. I'm waiting…give me the fucking name of the man I'm going to kill!" Marcus made Tamala cry that much harder, but he waited patiently for the tears to subside.

Tamala slowly began to get her tears under control as she wiped her reddened eyes and damp face with her pajama top. She cleared her throat then whispered hoarsely, "Marcus, lately you haven't been there for me."

Marcus became more enraged by that statement but held his peace.

Tamala, would not make eye contact with Marcus, but continued, "You…you were always working your overtime jobs leaving me alone, night after night. You stopped giving me attention, Marcus." Tamala felt that this was very difficult to talk about; however, she pressed on through tears and sniffing.

"I met someone, Marcus. Someone at work…well…he doesn't work there actually. He's a contractor…a janitor. He was always tellin' me how good I looked, how beautiful and attractive I was. It felt…it felt good, Marcus. It felt good hearin' that. You stopped tellin' me those things. You stopped holdin' my hand in public. You became so…so…"

After a few seconds, Marcus frustrated by Tamala's faltering, demanded, "*Say* it, Tam. The damage has been done, don't worry about hurting my feelings now. Fuck! Say it."

Sighing, Tamala said, "You became so borin', Marcus…*predictable*."

"Humph." Marcus could not believe what he was hearing.

"This man has brought excitement back into my life." Then she looked at Marcus and shook her head as she said sincerely, "And no, I don't love him. I-I cheated, Marcus. I'm sorry about that. He means nothin' to me. I've only been seein' him for a few months. This is the *first time*, Marcus. This is my first and only mistake. *I love you so much*, Marcus. I don't want to lose you, baby. Please-please forgive me, Mar- "

"The *name*, Tam. Who's this man? I want to know now."

Tamala, now looking down at what would have been her engagement ring, did not feel any need to withhold the name any longer. "Lamar. His name's Lamar Phelps, you don't know 'im."

When Tamala finally glanced up, Marcus appeared as if he had seen a ghost. Almost the same look he had given her when he walked in several minutes ago, finding her in his apartment. Marcus's eyes showed shock and revulsion. He held one hand over his stomach. When he shook his head as if in denial she asked reluctantly, "What's wrong, Marcus?" Tamala frowned in confusion then concern.

He looked at her, actually through her. "What did you say his name was?"

"Lamar, Marcus. What's-"

"*No*...the whole name, where does he live, Tam?" Marcus was waiting for the other proverbial shoe to drop.

It hit Tamala then...Marcus was familiar with her lover. She looked away in shame as she mumbled, "Lamar Phelps. He lives in Woodland County with his momma. He drives a white BMW."

It took Marcus a moment to register what Tamala had just said. He felt something inside of him explode, felt lightheaded. He whispered, "*Fuck.*" Marcus glanced around his apartment; he briefly wondered if he was dreaming! His eyes focused back on Tamala then reality hit. "Get out! Get the *fuck* out of my home, you *fucking, whore!*"

Tamala began crying again as the realization began to sink in that her relationship was over. She wanted to die. She gave a pleading look. "*Pleeeeasssee*, Marcus, give me another chance! I love-"

"*Shut up! Don't say those words to me!*" Tamala jumped as Marcus yelled between clenched teeth. He took a breath to compose himself then continued calmly, "Phelps is a lowlife, a drug dealer who coerces children to sell his *crap*. So, Tam, please get away from me. I may not be responsible for what I might do to you if you don't leave." Marcus could not believe what he was saying or feeling. He really wanted to hurt someone, possibly kill someone. This type of passionate hateful feeling had never come from him until now, as his body trembled in stark fury.

Marcus had never physically hurt Tamala, or anyone else. When they argued, she was the confrontational one. Marcus had never raised his hand or ever raised his voice to her, so his angry display was very uncharacteristic. As Tamala looked at the man she loved, she saw that Marcus intended on carrying out the implied threat of harming her; she saw murder in his eyes. Fright struck her at this point. She quickly placed the engagement ring on the couch and went into the bedroom to retrieve her overnight bag and other personal items.

A minute or two later, she emerged from the bedroom still wearing her pajamas. She made a beeline to the door then abruptly stopped. Without looking at Marcus, she put down her bag and purse, and removed a key from her key ring with shaky hands. Tamala, whose eyes were swollen from crying and still streaked with tears, walked over to the kitchen counter and placed the key to Marcus's apartment on the counter. She walked back to the door, picked up her belongings, and then left Marcus's apartment, probably for the last time.

All his life, Marcus reacted to pain, hurt, or suffering the same way. He treated it like cancer; regardless of how much he loved someone, if that person brought emotional pain in his life, he cut them out without haste. Much like a surgeon who encounters cancer or a diseased organ in a patient and then cuts it out; Marcus did the same with those who brought him heartache. Now Tamala had become cancerous to him. She would be proficiently and quickly cut out of his life. No matter how much he still loved her, Tamala would soon cease to exist to him.

Marcus thought, *After my cancer's removed, the pain will be gone, once Tam's out of my life, I'll be left feeling numb, but I look forward to that.* Marcus stared for several seconds at the closed door - the one that Tamala just walked out of. He finally whispered, "Thanks, Tam, maybe now I can begin to heal."

Marcus went over to the Everlast speed-bag in the corner, a leftover from his boxing days but still used daily to keep in shape, and stripped off his shirt. He began hitting the apparatus with all of his might. He tried desperately to shut out the pain that was trying to overwhelm him, but the pain was winning.

Chapter 13

The loud, irritating alarm coming from Marcus's bedside clock woke him up later that evening at around 9:30 p.m. He reached over groggily and felt for the clock, then slammed off the alarm. As he set up in bed, his mind was cloudy because of insufficient sleep. Despite the foggy thoughts, Marcus remembered clearly the overwhelming rage that had possessed him earlier. That anger scared Marcus - *would I have really hurt Tam if she hadn't left my apartment?* That was the question going through his mind. The scary part was that he could not honestly answer it.

But hurting Lamar was another story. *Is he worth me losing my job? Hell naw! Tam, if that's who you want to be with, then have at it. But if Lamar fucks with Ty or his mom, then Lamar's ass is mine.* Marcus still could not believe that Tamala was actually involved with a drug dealer - the type of person Marcus was sworn to arrest. The thought occurred to him that maybe Tamala was on drugs or something, hence her association with Phelps.

Marcus could not sleep after Tamala had left. Their argument had left him livid. Before going to sleep, Marcus thought about calling to apologize for his harsh words, but remembered her brutal words to him. Could he let Tamala just walk out of his life with out fighting for her, fighting for their love? He did not know for sure. Then he thought, *why do I have to be the one to make amends? What she did was unforgivable. She let another man inside of her body, then made that comment about my moms! And I'm* not *boring!* As Marcus pondered those things, he drifted off to sleep around 4:00 p.m.

Now as Marcus sat in bed, rubbing his tired face, he tried to remember what he had to do as depression slowly enveloped him. He had set the clock to wake him at 9:30 p.m. for some reason. Marcus was supposed to call somebody or maybe meet someone when he got up; he could not get his tired mind to focus. Finally he remembered, *call Eddie to set-up a time tomorrow to help him with his stupid car.* Marcus felt the burnout from all the recent stress, worry, and battles of life settling in his body and mind. He also felt out of shape, remembering that the last time he went running was the morning of Tamala's birthday. Working out on the speed-bag was not enough to stay fit. He tried to focus his mind to call Eddie despite the lack of desire to spend off-duty time with his partner.

Marcus flipped the covers off his partially-nude body then sat on the side of the bed. "What's his number?" He said out loud. Marcus picked up the telephone receiver and looked at it as if the piece of equipment would reveal the home telephone number of his partner. "Got it...5-5-5-6-0-7-7, " Marcus suddenly recalled the number. With the telephone's keypad illuminated in the darkness of his bedroom, Marcus slowly dialed the number. Shamefully, his only motivation to this unwanted contact with Eddie was his wife, Neci. Despite the hectic night before and the horrible fight with Tamala, Marcus could not stop thinking about the exquisite woman.

***

Neci Johnson Logan had a long hard day. She needed to escape. Eddie was working an overtime job, and the boys were asleep. She went into the large bathroom which contained a double sink, a huge shower stall, and her beloved jetted tub, her oasis! Neci stripped out of her grubby clothing and put on a black silk robe. She began to run the hot water in the oversized Jacuzzi-like tub.

As the tub started to fill, Neci began to add bath crystals and moisturizers to the steamy water. The bathroom's aroma was exhilarating to Neci, already beginning to take away the pressure of today's events. Once the water level reached her desired point, Neci turn off the water then activated the jets. As the water bubbled, she walked over to the built-in entertainment center (TV, VCR/DVD player, and stereo/CD player) with surround sound.

The lights automatically dimmed as she turned on her favorite jazz CD. The soft music by Walter Beasley led her back to the tub. Neci thought about lighting the aromatherapy candles strategically placed around the vast tub, however, lighting all of those candles was just too exhausting to even think about. She wisely decided to forgo the candles tonight. When Neci undid her robe, preparing to enter the tub, the telephone rang, bringing her back to the reality of a hectic life. She started to ignore it, but thought it might be Eddie calling to apologize or, heaven forbid, her parents in Texas calling because something dreadful had happened.

She worked her way back to the bedroom towards the ringing telephone. "Okay-okay, I'm coming, hold your horses."

Neci picked up the receiver. "Hello?"

Silence on the other end.

Neci becoming irritated said, "*Hello*? Who's there?"

Marcus was not prepared to hear the woman's husky bedroom voice; he was caught off guard then quickly said, "Hi...um...*Neci*? This is Marcus...you know...Eddie's partner. I...um...was supposed to call him...uh, before he left for his OT assignment. We...um...are getting together tomorrow, I'm helping him with his Mustang. He...um...he told me to call to set up a time." After fumbling through that, Marcus felt like an idiot. He sounded like a child, caught doing something bad, trying to explain himself to a parent. He thought, *why does this woman make me so nervous?*

"Hello, Marcus. I'm sorry, Gerard left already. Can I have him call you back tomorrow? He won't be in until well after two o'clock in the morning." Neci said with her mind still on the waiting bath.

"No…I'll just call him back in the morning. May I leave my number though?"

"Sure, go ahead." Neci did not have paper or pencil within reach to write down the number. She relied on her uncanny ability to memorize numbers. That ability in part had led to Neci becoming an excellent math teacher.

"5-5-5…6-5-5-4. He can call me anytime. I'll be here pretty much all day tomorrow. Ain't got a thing to do…I'm just…here, no where to…go." He suddenly realized how pathetic the latter sounded.

"Okay, Marcus. Gerard will probably sleep in late, but I'll make sure that he gets the message."

"Thanks, Neci. Look, may I say something? I mean I don't want to hold you up."

Neci looked towards the entrance to the bathroom and the waiting tub. Getting into that tub was all she wanted to do. When Neci answered Marcus, she tried to sound polite, despite being slightly annoyed, "Sure, Marcus, I've got plenty of time."

"I just want to thank you for being so nice to me yesterday. It was really nice of you to invite me over and all. I guess what I'm trying to say is, I'm a pretty good judge of character. Your niceness is just so uplifting and genuine…feels good to see that in people."

Neci was touched by the heartfelt words from this stranger. "Marcus, I meant everything that I said yesterday…you were such a gentlemen…I really appreciated your help with holding my bag." Then a question suddenly came to her. "May I ask you something?"

Marcus, sitting on the side of his bed, said, "Sure."

Neci smiled when she asked, "Are you nervous by nature…*shy*? Given you're a police officer, I can't see you being like this on your job."

Marcus thought for a moment then decided to be forthcoming as he answered, "Well, Neci, I seem to always make a fool out of myself when I meet a, look don't take this as a…umm…*line* or come on, but pretty women make me nervous and…a little shy." Marcus then told Neci about the Ashanti incident a few nights ago.

After Marcus's account, Neci sat down, on her bed, as she chuckled at the cute story. "Wow! I'm sure you still made a great impression on Ashanti. And thanks for the compliment…an old married woman like me likes to hear that she's pretty once and a while."

"Well…I'm sure you hear it all the time. You really are a *beautiful* woman…inside and out." Marcus felt that his comment was a bit forward as well as corny. He regretted the words as soon as they came out of his mouth.

"Marcus, you're making me blush…you're *so* sweet. And no, I don't hear it all the time, but thanks again. Just when I thought that you were Mister *Shy-Guy*."

"Well, I…um…just tell it like it is, Neci…this world is full of people lying to one another, nobody wants to be truthful about anything. I go to work day-in and day-out with people lying to me. Then have to come home and deal with the same… Anyway, Neci, it's just so nice to meet good people like yourself. I-I just get so discouraged with life sometimes. I don't know...here lately...I see nothing but negativity, and that makes me negative."

"You sound...so sad, Marcus, so defeated. Why are you so discouraged?"

(SILENCE)

"Marcus, I'm sorry if I'm prying, I didn't mean to."

Marcus thinking about the separate events of Tamala and T. C. replied, "Things have just been terrible...life hasn't been a joy recently. I'm beginning to think that God's pissed-off with me." Marcus chuckled for Neci's benefit to lighten the mood some then added, "I mean with all the things that are going wrong in my life right now. But I won't bring you down with my problems."

"Gerard told me about your other partner...I also read about it in the papers, and of course on the TV news. *You* could've been killed also, I hate Gerard working this job. I'm sorry that you had to go through something like that."

"Yeah...me too."

(SILENCE)

"You mentioned dealing with lies at home. So...what did she lie about, Marcus? I didn't see a ring on your finger so I'm assuming that you're not married...leaving the only logical answer that your girlfriend did something to hurt you."

Marcus, who was slumped down on the bed, sat up wide-eyed. "How did you know that?"

Neci being comical said in a mock serious voice, "I have *ESP*, Marcus. I know *all* and see *all*."

The two strangers laughed. Marcus felt his gloominess melting away.

"Are you comfortable talking about this with me? Please feel free if you are…I promise not to share it with anyone else, including my husband." Neci said the last with a light chuckle.

"It's strange, Neci…but…somehow I do feel comfortable…telling you. I think…this is weird, but I feel like I can trust you. I'm not much of a talker."

"Well, I'm your personal psychologist tonight but I warn you my fee's pretty steep."

"Doctor Neci, if you can solve *my problems*, your fee will be well worth paying."

"I'm listening, Marcus…seriously."

With that, Marcus shared his recent story of betrayal, lost love, and pain, with

Neci. This would be the beginning of a special bond with an unlikely confidant - his partner's wife.

***

"I told ya, Tamala! I knew this shit was gonna happen! Damn, girl! Ya shit was raggedy from the get go! Lettin' that nigga stay over, *knowin'* full well Marcus had a key to ya crib! That was just plain stupid, Tamala, not one of ya brightest moves. When ya called me at work this mornin', I knew the shit had hit the fan. How do ya know Marcus ain't goin' after Lamar?" Staci was at Tamala's apartment in Henrico County sitting across from her on the loveseat. After she left the salon this evening, she rushed right over to hear the details.

Tamala had called Staci over for some much-wanted advice on how to right the wrong she had done, however, she did not need a lecture from her best friend - at least not now.

"Staci, at this point I-I just don't know what Marcus is capable of doing. You should've seen the look in his eyes - scared the shit outta me. Durin' all the time I've known him, I've *never* seen him act like he did. That temper came outta nowhere." Tamala, shaking her head, shuddered at the memory of Marcus's demeanor.

"Outta nowhere? Ya fucked another *man*, Marcus found out 'bout it, then ya call his momma a *bitch*? Damn, Tamala, you my girl and all, but I would've had a tempa too. Ya ass lucky ya made it outta there before he beat ya senseless; shit, I would have." Looking towards the kitchen, Staci changed the subject. "What you got to eat, Tamala? I'm hungry like a bitch."

Tamala looked at Staci as if her friend had lost her mind.

Staci, seeing the look on Tamala face, said naively, "What?"

"My life's in shambles, Staci, and all you can think about is feedin' your face?"

Getting up and walking into the small kitchen in search of food, Staci replied, "Girl, just let Marcus cool down. You know that man loves you. Give it time, Tamala...you two will be back together soon enough." She began raiding the refrigerator.

"Staci, but the *look* in his eyes-"

"Didn't you hear me? Marcus loves you, girl. Let him cool down and swallow his pride, then ya need to go back beggin' for a second chance. Men love that shit, girl. First, ya gotta dump that nigga. Cut Lamar the *fuck* loose!" Staci found a chunk of baked salmon, and some wild rice. Heating the items in the microwave, she added as an after thought, "Get what ya can from the nigga first, then cut him the *fuck* loose."

The tall woman put the heated food on a plate and then made her way back to the living room. Sitting back on the loveseat, she continued her advice, "Then wear some Victoria's Secret and go over to Marcus's place and do ya thing, girl. Suck that *dick* like ya never sucked it before. Make that motherfucka forget all 'bout ya fuckin' somebody else. Power is in the *pussy*; use it, girl, *pussy power*! You'll see!" She pointed the fork at Tamala then used it to take a bite of salmon.

"Staci, you're raunchy as hell, girl. But-but...you ain't heard the worst of it." Tamala looked down nervously at her hands.

Staci stopped eating feeling that Tamala was about to drop a bombshell, "*What*?"

"That night when Marcus came over and caught...caught me with Lamar..." Tamala was staring into empty space, tears welling up in her eyes again.

"Tell *me*, girl. What? Marcus hit ya, Tamala?"

Tamala shook her head then focused on Staci. "He was planning on proposing to me."

"Uhn-*uhn*? Get the fuck outta here! Proposing as in marriage? Ya lyin', Tamala, ya lyin', girl!"

Tamala slowly shook her head then looked down in shame as the tears commenced to fall again.

Staci, putting down her food, whispered, "*Goddamn*, Tamala."

***

Under dim lighting, Eddie Logan enjoyed seeing his thick cock buried deep inside of Dispatcher Kimberly Thatcher. As he took the fiery redhead from behind, her thick cream covered his bare dick with every thrust of her shaven pussy; he loved to *raw-fuck*. Kimberly's curvy and dimply ass bounced with the hard pounding Eddie delivered. The smacking of sweaty flesh, animalistic grunts, and wild ravings could be heard throughout Kimberly's elderly mother's home but her nearly-deaf mother was oblivious to the noise. The aroma of late night sex permeated the small sparsely decorated bedroom, Kimberly's room since childhood. The canopy twin bed, now without the canopy, shook and appeared unstable as it creaked loudly in concert with the naked lovers.

"*Oooooh-ooooooh-ooooooh-ooooooooooooooh-ooooooooooooooooooooooooh*, my pussy, my pussy! Hurt…" she was forced to catch her breath. "*…my pussy! Hurt* it, baaaaaaby! *Yes*! Hurt my fucking, *pussy*!" With eyes closed and long hair hiding her face, Kimberly boldly reared back then bit her bottom lip as Eddie pumped her faster and harder.

The blond-haired handsome man blocked out Neci, the boys, his ailing back, and even the threat of sexually transmitted diseases as he tried to *hurt* Kimberly's womanhood. The saying, *a stiff dick has no conscious*, was true in this case; a stiff dick also made one stupid. Eddie had no guilt or regret as he cheated on his wife. Neci was the furthest thing from his mind at this moment.

Now his eyes locked on a fellow pole dancer sitting in the corner. The mousy looking brunette, with a *banging* body, watched the couple intensely while working her small dildo on an overly large clitoris. Eddie's blue eyes glanced down to her dick-like clit; he could not wait to taste the nude woman with no name. His only concern was whether or not the tiny bed would hold three horny people.

***

After Staci left Tamala's apartment, still in shock over Marcus's ruined marriage proposal to her best friend, Tamala had another visitor - Lamar Phelps.

"Why not?! You said that y'all broke up! Plus now he knows about us. We ain't got to hide this thing no more. Let's do this!" Lamar was frustrated by Tamala's stubbornness over the two of them getting together. Now that her cop boyfriend was out of the picture it was possible to have a relationship.

Tamala, equally frustrated, hopped off her water bed wearing only a pair of tan lace panties. She began looking for the remote to her TV. "I never said Marcus and I *broke up*!"

"Anytime a brotha take back his key and tell you to *get the fuck out*, if that ain't a break up, then *damn*, tell me what is?!"

Tamala searched frantically for the TV remote. Finding it, she turned on the TV in hopes of tuning out Lamar.

"I know why you avoidin' us getting together. You still don't believe me do you? You still believe that motherfuckin' cop, what do I have to say or do, Tamala, to prove to you that I don't sell drugs? He told you a straight-up lie!"

Tamala still wondered how Lamar had so much money all the time. He was just a worker, though a manager, at a local cleaning company; no way he could afford to constantly give her money and have all those expensive amenities. As of late, Lamar was even talking about buying her a new car, a *Mercedes-Benz*!

Tamala stood at the foot of the bed holding the TV remote facing Lamar. She looked into Lamar's cold gray eyes then said with an attitude, "Marcus also told me that you make kids peddle your drugs on the street corners. Is *that* a lie too?" Her left eyebrow arched for emphasis.

Lamar gave Tamala a hearty laugh as he lay in her bed. "How I look makin' somebody sell some drugs?" After additional laughter he added, "Plus if I was a drug dealer I'd never trust some child to sell my stuff. Now can we talk about us, Freckles? Come on back to bed; let's at least make love again."

Tamala gave a sigh and sat hard on the bed causing it to wave. As she flipped through the various channels, she spoke to Lamar with her back to him, "I'm the one that gave him his key back. He just needs some time to cool off. Marcus is still *my man*."

After several seconds, Lamar chuckled, "In the meantime you got me up in your apartment fuckin' me like there's no tomorrow. When I stick my *shit* in you, you hollerin' *my* fuckin' name, not his! What's up with *that*?" Lamar smirked in triumph.

Tamala became incensed then immediately stood up and faced Lamar. "Get out, Lamar!"

Trying to look innocent, Lamar said, "Come on. Look I'm sorry, Freck- "

"I *said* leave, Lamar!"

The two stared at each other for what seemed like an eternity. Lamar slowly got dressed.

As he started to walk out the bedroom, a smile slowly spread across his face. "Call me when you ready to talk about us. By the way, let Marcus know that if he tries to come at me again, it will be his last mistake. I ain't nobody to fuck with. He needs to stay out of my bidness. My bidness now includes you. You belong to me now, not Marcus. Later, Freckles."

Tamala's breast heaved up and down with every angry breath she took. She tried her best to calm down. She did not relax until she heard the front door shut behind Lamar. She thought briefly about calling Marcus to warn him but quickly thought against it. Staci was right. Lamar was trouble. Tamala must think of a way to rid the thug from her life.

***

Well over one hour and counting, Marcus and Neci lost all track of time as their conversation flowed like two old friends catching up. Marcus not only talked about Tamala and T. C. but also shared tales of his colorful childhood, and past failed relationships with the easy-to-talk-to Neci. He was amazed at how effortless it was to open up to her. Marcus was not quick to trust, so revealing personal details of his life was not typical. Neci was touched by Marcus's loving persona and his recent plights, particularly the account of his ruined romantic evening and proposal to Tamala.

Neci gave him a few words of encouragement, and she even shared some of her own personal issues over the years. Marcus was comfortable to talk with. Neci, like Marcus, was also not quick to trust others, but Marcus exuded integrity. It was uncanny how at ease Marcus made her feel. She shared a good portion of her past with the man she had met just twenty-four hours ago.

Being from San Angelo, Texas, Neci was an only child born to a doting father (African American), Dr. Benjamin T. Johnson, a loving mother (Puerto Rican), Sara Cortez Johnson. Her father was a prominent cardiothoracic and vascular surgeon at Saint Anne's Regional Medical Center. Dr. Johnson also had a private practice where her mother worked as a registered nurse. They were affluent and well respected in the community. Both well-educated parents were now in their fifties.

Due more to embarrassment than trust, Neci did not share with Marcus the mess her husband had caused in Cantil, California, when he worked at the Red Rock Canyon Police Department - a mess that had forced them to flee to Virginia in the first place. The dirty little secret, which they left behind, almost tore their fragile marriage apart, not to mention that if the secret had been exposed, it could have rocked the little town of Cantil with much scandalous embarrassment.

Neci concluded by saying, "Now, I'm trying to earn my Master of Education degree at VCU, but Marcus, it seems almost *impossible* to attend my classes plus raise two boys along with trying to please my husband. If I ever finish, I'll work on getting a doctoral degree…one day."

"Neci, there is no doubt in my mind that you will become Dr. Neci Logan one day."

"Wow! I like the sound of that. Thanks for the encouragement, you're too sweet."

Neci was taken aback when she saw that it was well after midnight. *Time really does fly when you're having fun,* Neci pondered.

As if he had read her thoughts, Marcus said, "Boy, look at the time, I'm so sorry to have kept you on the phone so long."

"Oh, no apology necessary, Marcus. I really enjoyed talking you…this was…*really* nice. I'll have Gerard call you in the morning."

"Thanks…" Marcus had the strong urge not to let Neci go. The feeling came out of nowhere.

"Good night, Marcus."

"You too, Neci."

When Neci hung up the phone, she walked back into her bathroom. Sitting down next to the tub overrun with soapsuds, she looked thoughtfully at the whirling soapy water. She reached down and turned off the jets, calming the now lukewarm water. Neci continued to look into the water of the wasted luxurious bath as the Walter Beasley CD repeated softly in the background. Somehow the long phone conversation with Marcus did more than any hot bath could ever do to melt away her stressful day.

Neci was both intrigued and frightened by that latter revelation. She was fascinated because Marcus someway *fed* her; the stranger satisfied something within her restless soul. Neci was afraid because she did not want what happened in Cantil, California to repeat itself here in Woodland County.

The confused beauty opened the tub's stopper, releasing the water down the drain. As the swirling soapy water slowly abated, Neci prayed that the budding yearning within her would also soon disappear.

***

Months later, Marcus continued to reflect upon the exotic beauty, Neci. By helping Eddie with the restoration of the Ford Mustang, Marcus was able to see Neci on a regular basis. Innocent telephone conversations and those frequent visits to the Logan home brought about a close relationship between Marcus and Neci; the sharing of furtive glances soon became a private game between them. The fleeting looks soon turned into outright stares; the two began looking into each other's eyes as if trying to read the other person's thoughts. Eddie was oblivious to the slowly developing bond between his wife and his partner.

Marcus and Neci rationalized, independently, that there was nothing wrong with a man and woman in today's society being close friends. The simple fact was that Neci was married to Eddie, and Eddie was Marcus's partner; an affair was inconceivable. As they continued the innocent telephone interactions behind Eddie's back, it never occurred to them how close a bond they were developing.

Chapter 14

Woodland County was blessed with a bright sunny, but hot, Saturday afternoon in July on the day of the police department's annual picnic, which featured the much anticipated *Spouses versus Cops* softball game at Arrowhead Historical Park. The scorching sunlight promised to bring its sweltering heat before the day was over. The heat shimmered across the ground and along the tops of the outbuildings throughout the public park. The local meteorologists predicted another weekend of stormy weather which had not come to fruition. The dusty sun-parched ball field could use the impending rain.

The game commenced that morning at 10:00 a.m. Organizers hoped to finish the competition before the humidity and temperatures in the low 90s gained a foothold on the day. Participants in the game wore softball jerseys provided by the county, the wives, husbands, girlfriends, and boyfriends of the police officers wore white jerseys with *Spouses* screen-printed in black lettering on their backs, and the officers donned light blue jerseys that said *Cops*. The spouses, once again, beat the police officers during a hard-fought contest by an embarrassing 10-point margin. The men and women of the Woodland Police Department blamed the loss on the effects of the oppressive heat.

Now the large crowd of police officers, city officials, spouses, children, and friends gathered for lunch under the two gigantic pavilions near Softball Field #3, where the battle was just lost. The sun set high casting its punishing heat down upon the almost barren earth. The pavilions provided some comfort from the hot weather, with the help of a mild westerly breeze. The aroma of hotdogs, burgers, BBQ ribs, and steaks mingled in the muggy air. The opposite side of the pavilions yielded a panoramic view of the Chickahominy River in which Marcus Williams found extremely peaceful. The river was calm today; a slow lazy journey later emptying into the James River. Marcus sat across from Eddie and his family as chatter surrounded them. He watched as Neci catered to her children's needs. She was stern but gentle. She demanded order from her boys, and they gave it. Neci, in some ways, reminded Marcus of his own mother.

"Now eat your food like good boys," Neci said, sitting down before her own plate. She had a slight Hispanic accent which Marcus found, even in this public setting, very sultry. Marcus tried not to stare at Neci each time she got up to get food or condiments for her hungry family. Her untucked white jersey almost looked like a nightshirt over her tight black shorts. Neci's firm muscular legs and well-defined arms glistened with sweat. Marcus now knew that the yellowish-brown skin was due less to tanning and more to her Latino ancestry. Throughout the morning and into the softball game, Neci and Marcus played that staring game which had become commonplace between them. At one point Neci smiled then winked at him. Marcus was caught off guard by her explicit action because he was used to her nervously turning away and twisting her hair as they secretly glanced at one another, always without words or gestures.

Now as Marcus looked across at Eddie, he noticed that his partner was grimacing. Eddie had played horribly. The final insult was his dropping that fly ball in left field; the error was a big embarrassment to Eddie. He had been quiet ever since, despite his earlier trash-talking with the spouses. Marcus thought that Eddie took the game too seriously thus missing out on the fun of it.

"You okay, Eddie? You look like you're in pain." Marcus asked.

"I'm alright…must've pulled something, that's all." He slyly rubbed his back, ignoring the grilled vegetables that Neci placed before him.

He studied Eddie and his family who sat to his right. Neci sat closest to Eddie with Karl then Juny beside her. *The perfect family*, Marcus thought. He envied what Eddie had: someone to love, and someone to give it back. He prayed that Eddie appreciated what he had.

As loneliness, self pity and depression invaded him, Marcus excused himself from the Logan family and walked out into the late July heat. It was almost difficult to breathe in the stifling thick air as he searched for solitude. Neci secretly watched Marcus walk away. She noticed that he seemed aloft since they had sat down for lunch. She saw the sudden sadness on his face as he stood up and walked toward the river. Neci squinted at the bright sunlight reflecting off the water, but continued to gaze at Marcus until he disappeared behind the tree line, walking parallel along the sluggish rippling river.

***

"It's not the end of the world you know."

Marcus thought that he was dreaming as the familiar voice startled him out of his light nap along the Chickahominy. He had lost all sense of time; he slowly looked around as he lay in the shade of the trees on the riverbank, trying to locate the owner of that voice. When he looked behind him, he saw her and smiled.

Neci stood behind him, and she enjoyed seeing Marcus's face light up at seeing her, a total turnaround from his behavior earlier. It really felt good to be greeted in such a way, to be appreciated by someone who was obviously glad to see her. An hour ago when she watched Marcus walk away from the pavilion, he really did look as if the end of the world was near.

"Oh, hi, Neci." Marcus quickly sat up on his right elbow. "I, I must've dozed off. Felt good, so cool in the shade." Marcus pointed up toward the cover of the large water oak tree. Looking sheepish, he said, "I must've been tired. *Has* to be almost five or ten degrees cooler under here, I bet."

"I don't know about that." Neci laughed as she fanned herself with her petite, delicate, manicured hands and then said, "Feels about the same to me. Hard to escape this *hell-hot* heat, Marcus. Seems to me, they should've held this picnic during the spring, rather than in the middle of summer."

She walked closer then sat to his right, crossing her legs out before her. Marcus's heartbeat increased at the beauty's close proximity to him; she was actually close enough to kiss. Despite the light sheen of sweat that covered her body, he could smell her clean scent, maybe shampoo, shower gel, or perfume…flowery. With her raven hair tied back in a long ponytail, he noticed Neci's smooth light brown skin and her perfectly shaped nose, admiring just how perfect the woman truly was.

The sunlight and closeness allowed Marcus to fully take her in. He was amazed at how the woman simultaneously exhibited both her African American and Puerto Rican features - the full lips, the nice rear, those curvy hips, and the muscular legs attributable to the former, then the strong angular facial features, dark hair, slight Latina dialect, and skin tone of the latter. He could watch Neci all day, enjoying every eyeful.

Without warning, Marcus's thoughts became verbal, "You're so beautiful, Neci, simply gorgeous." The slip of-the-tongue shocked him. Marcus was quickly embarrassed for having revealed himself to her this way, so openly...*too* openly. He was starting to shed his shy persona around her. He slowly sat upright with his legs sprawled out in front of him, Neci and he now sat shoulder-to-shoulder facing the river with the reflection of the bright afternoon sun.

Upon hearing those wonderful words, in Marcus's deep but soft-spoken voice, Neci immediately felt her body flush, her skin tingle. She began to feel lightheaded; her nipples were suddenly extremely hard and sensitive against her sports bra underneath her jersey. Neci flushed more as she felt herself moisten and that familiar, pleasurable throb between her legs. She asked herself, *what is this man doing to me, doing to my body?*

Neci quickly tried to regain her composure, saying, "Thank you." She changed the subject, hoping to focus attention back on Marcus. She said, looking intently into his eyes, "So...what're you doing out here all by your lonesome?"

Marcus thought, *that husky voice...mmm, mmm, mmm.* He then answered as he looked into her sparkling doe-like eyes, "This heat was getting to me, needed some shade." Marcus's right shoulder slightly touched Neci's. The brief intimate contact did not go unnoticed by the pair. Both quickly averted their eyes, glancing back toward the flowing river. The eyes are indeed the window to one's soul; neither wanted to reveal their innermost private and intimate thoughts.

Neci knew that he was not telling the truth about why he left the picnic. She returned her sincere gaze to the attractive man. "You looked so sad when you left us, didn't even eat your lunch. What's wrong, Marcus? Or maybe you'd rather not talk about it with me."

Marcus searched her face and saw her genuineness. "I feel as if I can talk to you about *anything*, Neci," Marcus said in a tone a bit too affectionately as he stared at her passionately. Feeling embarrassed again, he said in a normal voice, "But I'm cool, I'm cool." He turned back to the river, not comfortable sharing his pity-party with Neci. Marcus did not want her to feel sorry for him, like in some of their past telephone conversations.

Neci suddenly had an idea. "Hey, Marcus. I have this coworker, at J. L. Nelson Elementary School. Her name's Gayle Batts. Gail teaches Spanish, pretty ironic huh? You know, with me being fluent in the language, thanks to my momma's persistence. Anyway, we're both teaching summer school and-"

"I didn't know you were teaching this summer, Neci."

"Yes, just for extra money."

"Oh."

"She's single and umm, you know…you're not seeing anyone. So I was thinking that maybe you and Gail could-"

"I'm sorry, Neci…I…I'm just not ready…not ready to start seeing anyone. I appreciate your thoughtfulness, but…" Marcus trailed off, not knowing what to say or how to feel about Neci trying to set him up on a blind date.

"You're right. I apologize, I have no business trying to-"

"Neci, there's no need to apologize. Thanks for caring, okay?"

As if she had read Marcus's mind earlier at the pavilion, Neci said, "Okay, Marcus. I just hope you find her…I mean a woman that can make you happy."

Marcus looked deeply into her dark eyes and wanted to say that he had already found that woman…*Neci*, but instead he said, "You're a good woman, Neci, I really appreciate your friendship."

Neci peeked back toward her right and Marcus followed her gaze. The boys were sitting down under a big tree, well away from the riverbank, playing with a toy truck and what appeared to be action figures. The four of them - Marcus, Neci, and the boys - were all alone near this stretch of the Chickahominy River.

"Marcus asked, "Where's Eddie?"

Neci focused back on Marcus as she answered, "He said he was going to ride with someone to the store, a stupid beer-run I believe."

Marcus had a sneaking suspicious as to who that someone was…Kimberly.

"Neci…are you…" Marcus was on the verge of asking her if she were happy with Eddie, but thought wisely against that, then asked instead, "…umm, doing okay?"

Neci thought that that was an odd question, but smiled and answered, "I'm okay, why?"

Marcus lamely responded, "I was just curious." He thought, *just curious? Shut up, Marcus! You're making a fool outta yourself.*

Neci glanced in the direction of her children again, making sure they obeyed her earlier command to stay away from the river. "Well, I better get the boys back, when Gerard returns we'll be leaving shortly after." She turned back to face Marcus, "I'm feeling sticky, I *hate* hot weather, Marcus. Not as bad as Cantil, but close!"

"Yeah, I guess I'll head on home myself."

Neci asked earnestly, "You want to join us for dinner later tonight?"

Marcus wanted badly to say yes, but did not want to seem pathetic or without plans on a Saturday night, so he told a little white lie. "I...um...I have this friend...Sneak, Emanuel Chambliss. He's a cop in Richmond. I'll probably hang out at one of the clubs with him tonight. Nothing special...just something to do." Marcus knew very well that he would simply go home and turn in early.

"Well I hope you have a good time. But if you change your mind or if your plans change, please come over."

Marcus stood and then helped Neci to her feet. Still holding her hand as they stood face-to-face, he said, "If I decide not to go, I'll call you guys." Marcus felt electricity as he held Neci's soft hand in his. The contact gave him life. He believed with certainty that releasing her now would bring him sudden death. *Neci, Neci, Neci, why couldn't I've had met you before* he *did. You are so right for me!* Marcus thought in wonderment.

He looked intimately into Neci's glistening eyes, getting lost in them. His body tingled and his stomach fluttered. She stared directly back into Marcus's eyes. Neci's eyes held him captive, slowly making him come unglued. Neither of them said anything, both in their own private thoughts, simply enjoying the moment.

Without warning, Neci reached out with her free hand and gently brushed away some dirt and a few blades of grass from off his shaved head. Neci's hand lingered upon him for a split second then went back down to her side. "You're a very handsome and *sweet* man, Marcus. Your eyes...your *enthralling* smile...*my God*...it...*your* smile warms me. Any woman would be lucky to have you for a mate." She found Marcus's shyness and emerging boldness with her a major turn-on. The many glances and bold looks at her both scared and excited her, pushing her to reciprocate. Neci thought, *Marcus, when you look at me, just like you're looking at me right now, I feel free to be me...bold...passionate...totally open to you...in every way. I feel as if we're all alone in our own little world. Just you and me, free to...STOP IT! God, please help me with this! Marcus is making me feel...so...so sexual!*

Marcus continued to look down into Neci's jet-black eyes and then at her full moist lips. He had the strong urge to kiss this woman, his partner's wife.

Neci wanted to touch him again, caress his face. She then felt guilty for having such a strong desire for intimacy with this man. *I'm married, with children. I'm not in high school anymore. But...he makes me feel like I'm a teenage girl again. Makes me feel vulnerable, desirable, I want to be submissive to him...he makes me feel out of control. Hello, God, I need help here! I've got to get this under control. I'm just lonely, that's all...think...this is not right. Marriage counseling for sure now! Plus this is Gerard's partner and friend!* She thought with deep frustration. She gave Marcus a heavy sigh then whispered, "I've...better go, Marcus." She slowly released his hand then quickly turned away, walking towards the boys. "*Juny, Karl,* let's go find your daddy!" She gathered them up and the trio left the riverbank by way of one of the many trails in Arrowhead Historical Park.

Marcus felt as if he was in a trance. He just stood there as Neci and the boys disappeared along a path which led back toward the pavilion. With the soothing sound of the river in his ears, and those *flutters* deep within his stomach, he suddenly had a mind-blowing and life-altering epiphany. He found himself both amazed and shocked by the unexpected revelation...he was falling in love with Neci Logan.

Chapter 15

The Logans' light gray Cadillac Escalade sped down Deer Chase Road at a dangerous pace, much too fast for the narrow two-lane road. There was nothing along this stretch of roadway but tall thick growing trees. The hot sun barely shone through because of the overhang of those trees over the blacktop road.

As Eddie Logan drove seventy-five miles per hour in a fifty-five mile per hour zone, he was livid. He was mad that he made an error in the softball game. He was angry that the cops lost to the spouses. What really set him off was that Neci caught him in the parking lot with Kimberly Thatcher.

Earlier, Eddie and Kimberly had gone to Bubba's Marketplace to purchase a twelve-pack of Icehouse. Instead of going back out to the heat of the day when they returned to the park, the pair decided to stay in the air conditioned Escalade. When Neci and the kids walked up on them, Eddie was sitting a little too close to Kimberly and being in the backseat did not help his case any. After Kimberly sheepishly walked away without a word, Eddie gave the lame excuse that he was helping his coworker look for her missing contact lens. He stressed to his wife that one of his coworker's contacts had fallen out of her eye, as they sat up front, and was blown back to the rear of the SUV, by the powerful air-conditioner.

Now as the Escalade raced down the road, Eddie unsuccessfully tried to explain for the fifth time that nothing was going on between Kimberly and him.

"Goddamn it! What else do I need to say to convince you?! Nothing *fucking* happened, we were just having a few beers, Neci!"

Junny, who sat in the back with his younger brother Karl, said, "Mommy, daddy say a *baaaaaaad wooorrrddd*." Both boys seemed more interested in the argument between their parents than the Disney DVD, *Finding Nemo*, which was playing for them on the video display.

Neci was so upset that she did not hear her eldest son. "All the way in the *backseat*, Gerard?! *What*?! You think I'm *stupid*? I'm *not* stupid!" Neci started that trademark nervous habit of twisting her hair, after she took it out of the long ponytail.

"Kim is just one of guys, a dispatcher. Like I said, her fucking contact fell out and-"

"I don't care if her eyeball blew out of her head - you and that woman had no business sitting together all *chummy* in the backseat of *our* car! That slut!" Neci stopped abruptly then looked back at the boys and began to feel ashamed of arguing and using the word *slut* in front of them. She turned back to her philandering husband trying to be much calmer. "That woman's *definitely* not one of the guys, the way *she* dresses. Gerard, her blouse was so tight. She wasn't wearing a bra. And those short-shorts showed the cheeks of her... " Neci caught herself for the boys' sake again then whispered, "You know...her *a-s-s* was sticking out from the bottom of her shorts. *Disgusting*, Gerard."

Afraid of the speed that Eddie was driving, Neci said, "And slow down before you kill us all!" Neci was incensed. She was mad for breaking her own rule of not arguing in the front of Juny and Karl. But she could not control the hurt and anger of seeing her mate in the backseat laughing and giggling with some strange redhead.

"I'm trying to get home so that I don't have to listen to your *never-ending* nagging!" Eddie shot back.

Neci crossed her arms as her eyebrows shot-up in anger, but said in an eerie calmness, "*Oh*? You think I'm nagging you now?"

"Yeah, *nagging*. Nagging for nothing! You're blowing everything out of proportion, Neci, as always!"

"Humph! As if I didn't have a reason to make a big deal out of this." Neci sighed then turned back in her seat facing the road which sped dangerously before her. "I said *slow down*, Gerard, *now*!"

Eddie gave his own sigh but obeyed his wife.

The kids set directly behind their parents facing the flipdown video screen which played the Disney movie. Karl, the splitting image of his mother, turned his sippy-cup upside down and watched the punch slowly pour out of the cup and onto his lap. Juny, with his daddy's blond hair, simply looked out of the window then occasionally at his fighting parents. He put his fingers in his ears, and squeezed his eyes shut. It was no longer fun to hear his father say bad words.

Neci silently wondered if infidelity was slowly creeping back into her marriage. She quickly closed off thoughts of Cantil, California and what occurred there. She suddenly felt nauseated. Neci was also beginning to wonder if Eddie could control his unusual sexual cravings and not repeat Cantil here in Woodland. She knew that she could control her inner wants and desires as suddenly an image of Marcus's handsome sweaty face popped into her mind. His soft touch was electrifying. It also felt good to touch him. She saw herself stroking Marcus's ebony chiseled face, the face of an Adonis. Neci had never been with a black man sexually. Despite her father being African American, she felt more inclined to date Caucasian men during her single years; eligible black men were rarely in her circle.

The thought of being with a black man, Marcus, was somewhat intriguing. With her eyes closed, she smiled as she looked at Marcus's thick kissable lips, and those bedroom eyes. In her mind she gazed at his muscular arms. She wondered how they would feel wrapped around her. Whenever Marcus stood facing her, he towered over her, making her feel so vulnerable; she *wanted* to be dominated by him. And those intense eyes of his. She thought, *the way he looks at me, the wanting, the desire in those eyes. Oh Marcus, today you got my panties so…*

Eddie glanced over at his wife, "What the *hell* are you smiling about?"

Neci was startled and looked over at her husband then became embarrassed because of her intimate thoughts of another man. "What? Nothing, Gerard, just drive, *please*. I'm, I'm getting a…umm…a headache."

Neci looked forward again at the long lonely highway in front of her. She suddenly realized that she was now no longer sure if she could control herself if a compromising situation arose between her and Marcus. She thought fervently, *I must guard against that! It's also my duty to ensure that Gerard doesn't stray again. My marriage is sacred to me. Unlike some women, I take my vows seriously.* Neci was far from being a devout Catholic, but her faith and heartfelt wedding vows convicted her. Those latter thoughts and beliefs did nothing to alleviate the growing desire that she had for Marcus.

***

Later that evening, around 11:30 p.m., at her lover's home, Staci lay beside the sleeping figure. Her cellular telephone had been ringing all day, she thought that it was her boyfriend, Derrick, trying to locate her. Had she checked the caller-ID, she would have seen that it wasTamala calling.

She had to put the phone on vibrate so that she could enjoy her evening with Sneak, whom she recently started seeing again. Staci had the day off, so she knew that it was not the hair salon calling for her to work.

This time when Staci heard the phone vibrate as it was clipped to her purse strap on the nightstand, she grabbed it to peek at the number on the display. Sneak had just pulled out of her and was now fast asleep. Staci was relieved because Sneak and she had been going at it all day, and she was both tired and sore. They had planned to go to the club tonight, but got wrapped up with each other, two horny lovers aching for a sexual release.

Staci saw that the displayed number was Tamala's. She pressed the green talk button to take the call. "Hey, Tamala, how you- "

"Girl, where you *been*?! I been callin' ya house, the shop, and this cell number most of the day and ya ass was nowhere to be found!"

"I love you too, girl! Now, chill-out, what's wrong?" Staci felt her lover stir next to her in the bed. She whispered, "Hold on, Tamala."

Staci got up and put on the tight red skirt that Sneak had pulled off of her hours ago. She walked out of the bedroom and into the living room, sitting topless on the couch.

"I'm back, Tamala, what's wrong?"

Tamala whined, "Where you been, *Staci*? I had a shitty day and no one to share it with."

Staci told her how she spent her day on this hot and lazy July Saturday.

"You fuckin' him again, Marcus's friend, *Sneak,* from the club?"

"Tamala don't trip. I ain't married, he ain't married, so it's cool. Now get up outta my business and tell me what's up, girl."

Tamala calmed down enough to relay to her friend that she followed Lamar to an area in Petersburg. She saw him meet a plump pregnant female and give her money outside a rundown house. The young girl obviously had feelings for Lamar given the way she was trying to cling to him as they talked on the front porch. Seeing enough, Tamala got out of her SUV and walked down the block to confront the two. Lamar struggled to keep the two women from fighting as he dragged the pregnant girl into the house. He then walked Tamala to her Jeep and tried to calm her down by giving her money.

Lamar told Tamala that the woman was a girlfriend of one of his boys. Lamar said that he was helping them out financially until they could make ends meet. Tamala saw the lie in his gray eyes. Anger overtook her as she slapped Lamar so hard that his cheek quickly became red from the assault. He simply stared coldly at her in silence. She saw something in Lamar's eyes after that slap, something scary, something that she could not describe but that caused fear to creep into her soul. Whatever that "something" was, it prompted her to get into the SUV and drive away before Lamar could react.

Staci sat riveted on the edge of her seat until Tamala finished. "Damn, I woulda cut that nigga! And you shoulda kicked that big bitch's ass! She can't get away with that shit!" Staci, getting pumped up, looked over at the clock on Sneak's table across the room. "Oh hell *naw*! We gotta handle this now! You wanna go back down there? It's late but I'm down with whippin' her ass!"

"Naw, Staci. Like I said she's pregnant. She 'bout ready to give birth and shit."

"Yeah, the bitch probably pregnant with Lamar's baby! Now I know you ain't dumb, Tamala. You know she probably called his ass, and he went runnin' down there to gi' her some money or somethin'. Don't be no fool, girl!"

After several seconds of silence, Tamala said in a near whisper, "I know, Staci. I know. Had the nerve to give me some money...like he gave that pregnant bitch."

Staci loved to gossip. She was almost salivating, "How much that nigga try to gi' you?"

"He pulled out a wad of money, gave me two thousand dollars!"

"No *shit*! You lyin', girl! Whatcha do, Tamala? Did you take it?"

"*Hell* yeah. I mean he pissed me off and shit, but hell yeah, I took that nigga's money! He was gonna take me shopping before this shit happened, so the money was mine anyway, fuck *him*!"

Staci was in awe, "Damn, *two-grand*?"

"Yep...he been trying to call, but I'm gonna make him suffer for a while."

"Don't play wit' that thug, girl. You know he dealin', Tamala, you playin' wit' fire. In fact, I thought you were tryin' to break it off wit' him."

"I'm so lonely. And I-I'm not sure what he doing, how he makes all that money, Staci."

Staci asked, "Well, I tell you what you need to do, girl. You *need* to get back with Mar- "

"*Staci*, I don't need that right now! Marcus and I, we through. It's over."

"I ain't never seen you give up wit'out a fight, girl. Marcus is one hell of a man, you better get him back before someone else catches his eye."

"Look, Staci, I just wanted to get this thing that happened today off of my chest…I'm going to bed now."

"*Oh*, I bring up Marcus's name and now you gotta go! You know you still in love with him, right?"

"It ain't that easy, Staci, and you *know* that."

"The only thing I know is that if I had a man like Marcus, my ass would be at home wit' him right now, wearin' his fuckin' weddin' ring, gettin' that *good* dick. Wake up, girl, before it's too late. Marcus is worth-"

"*Goodnight*, Staci!" Tamala hung up before Staci could respond.

Staci looked at her cell phone then sighed. She whispered to herself, "Tamala, you're makin' the worst mistake of your life if you stay wit' Lamar. Nigga's nothin' but trouble." Staci got up and rejoined a slumbering Sneak in the bedroom.

Chapter 16

Neci climbed out of her jetted tub, dried herself, and then sat nude on her bed. Wearing a towel over her thick wet hair, she moisturized her taut light brown skin as the larger wet towel lay on the floor. The boys were fast asleep, and she was more than relaxed as *he* popped into her thoughts again. Her body tingled with pleasure. Neci had not seen or heard from Marcus since Saturday, after she had left him standing alone by the river. She knew that her other half was with Marcus at this very moment. The two men were gallantly protecting the citizens of Woodland County.

As Neci rubbed down her soft skin, she wondered if Marcus thought about her as often as she about him. *I feel so childish, thinking about you this way*, she believed. Thoughts of Marcus and the soothing bath made her body hot, in fact her body was on fire. She said softly, "Now I need a cold shower, *this* is crazy."

The central air-conditioner did nothing to relieve her sexual heat. Neci got up and walked back into the large bathroom, retrieving a clean dry towel from the small linen closet. She returned to the bed, and then sat on the dry towel which was spread beneath her. She picked up the small bottle of scented oil and poured a portion of the contents in her hand. She looked over at the clock…10:45 p.m.

Neci whispered, "I can't believe I'm going to do this, got to get my mind off of Marcus and on my marriage."

Neci had some slight hang-ups about self-pleasure. Grading papers or attending to her own college studies often kept her occupied on those rare occasions she needed that self-attention. Tonight such attention was necessary to quell her inner fire.

Lying back onto the fluffy pillows, she rubbed her hands together and began to slowly massage her body with the sweet smelling oil. With her eyes closed, she imaged that Marcus was massaging her now. His eyes were on hers, so intense, burning her with his passionate stare. In her mind's eye Marcus was wearing a pair of silk crimson red pajama pants, showing his bare muscular torso. His strong large hands gently stroked her naked body, getting her hotter. When his hands softly touched her stiffened nipples, her hot spots, she felt like screaming with pleasure. In the fantasy, Marcus lightly squeezed her right nipple with his thick fingers causing Neci to moan with intense pleasure.

Neci whispered, "*Oh* my. *Damn, papi*. You…you're sooooo good…Feels sooooo good. Oh, *papi chulo*…Mmmmmmm, "

The ringing telephone on the nightstand rudely interrupted Neci's vivid fantasy.

"Nooooooo! Ugggggh, who's *calling* at this hour?!" Neci quickly sat up wiping her hands on the towel, feeling like a child caught in a deviant act.

In frustration, Neci snapped up the phone, "*Yes*?!"

It was Neci's mother.

"O nada, Mamá…estaba…mirando la televisión." Neci said, and then thought in frustration, *Yeah, right, just watching television*.

***

Marcus sat alone in the small locker room; his shift ended over almost an hour ago. Still clad in his uniform, Marcus was sitting with his back to one of the lockers. He was still trying to get over the death of his partner. Rip, his killer, was out free as a bird while T. C. lay rotting in the ground. Tamala was still on his mind, but not like before.

To make matters worse, today had been Marcus's thirtieth birthday and no one called to acknowledge the special day. No one cared. Marcus was tired of being unhappy, tired of being alone. The only thing that brought him happiness was Neci and Marcus felt guilty for his illicit thoughts of the beauty because of Eddie. He and Eddie were really getting along. Eddie had his back out there on patrol. But still...Neci: the beautiful woman captivated Marcus. Marcus had an epiphany. He smiled to himself as he thought, *maybe telling Neci how I feel would purge me of my feelings for her. Then what? I don't know, but telling her feels right. Gotta put this behind me.*

***

Weeks passed. Marcus pulled up into the visitors' parking lot. Her car was still parked in the teacher's parking area. He could not get the woman out of his mind, no matter how hard he had tried. He and Eddie continued to work on the car at the Logans' garage out back, not the parking garage attached to the house. Marcus and Neci continued to play the silent staring game. It was now time to confront the woman about the way he truly felt for her.

As he sat in his Camry, Marcus thought, *where do I expect this to lead? I tell her that I'm attracted to her, then what, dumb-ass? This isn't a good idea. I mean, Neci is just a nice person...she's just being friendly with me...she has no interest in me...at least not romantically, purely as a friend. I mean come on, Marcus, Eddie has the movie star looks and gift of gab, hell, what would she want with me? But damn, the way she looks at me. I can't be imagining that...can I? That day in the park after the softball game, I saw it in her eyes...the attraction for me. Naw, I can't do this. I won't do this to my partner. Eddie has his issues...I know he's screwing Kimberly. But still, is that reason*

enough for me to try and get with his wife? No. Marcus, go
back home, leave this place.

Instead Marcus, wearing a cool Ralph Lauren Caribbean
blue polo shirt and tan cargo shorts of the same brand,
slowly got out of his car and walked toward the long three-
story building on the north side of Woodland County. He
could not believe that he was finally going to do this.
Marcus had been driving to this place over the past couple
of days, only to quickly leave in fear of making a fool out of
himself. But today was the day to put his cards down on the
table for Neci to see.

The office was just ahead, just inside the front entrance
according to the sign Marcus just read. Someone there
would be able to direct him to Neci. The marquee out front
read that summer school hours ended at 3:00 p.m. which
was an hour ago. With fear and apprehension, Marcus
walked into J. L. Nelson Elementary School with a nervous
heart, hoping to finally reveal his feelings to the 4th grade
math teacher.

***

"I give you the best that life has to offer. The least you
can do is suck it every now and then. I eat you out...why
can't you give it back?" Lamar was tired of her excuses for
not performing oral sex on him.

Tamala had the day off; she was seated before her
computer trying to complete an assignment for a psychology
class that she was taking at John Tyler this summer as
another class toward her nursing degree. Lamar came over
promising to leave her alone, saying he just wanted to be
around her. She was too busy for company but reluctantly
agreed to his coming over.

"Look, Lamar. I told you when we first started this that I
don't do that."

"I bet you sucked that cop's dick. Didn't you?"

"That was different, *Lamar*."

"Oh, so you admit that shit. You sucked his dick but won't suck mine. 'Sup with that? And what the fuck you mean '*that was different*'?"

Tamala turned away from the computer and gave Lamar a look of annoyance. Her homework assignment was due by midnight for this difficult online course. "Marcus and I had been dating one another for a longtime. During that time, I got to know him and his habits. I wonder about you and *your* habits. Meaning I ain't gonna suck *your* dick!" she turned back to her computer frantically attempting to finish her work.

Lamar was upset by that comment but turned on because he saw it as a challenge. He stood up and took out his hardening penis, putting it on Tamala's right shoulder. "*He* likes you, Freckles…kiss 'im. *Please*?"

"*Boy*, get ya dick off me. Why can't you let me do my work? *You* promised."

Looking sad, the light-skinned thug sat back on the bed. Tamala looked back at him. Lamar still had his manhood hanging out.

Tamala had to admit that she was tired and needed a break from homework. She also admitted to herself that she needed something else too. With Lamar staring at her with those freaky gray-eyes, she stood and then slowly slid out of her tight jean shorts revealing her wet pink cotton panties. She meant what she said about not reciprocating oral sex with Lamar, but she was not about to give up the exciting sex; she needed to be penetrated…and now.

Tamala made Lamar layback onto the bed. She pulled her panties aside, gripped his dick, and slowly sat down on him. Inch-by-inch, enjoying the unhurried breach of her increasing wetness. "Shit, Lamar…you…mmmmmm…you got some good dick, baby, *fuck*." She closed her eyes and enjoyed the ride.

***

Marcus recited it repeatedly in his head, *room 311, room 311, room 311*. He was amazed by the familiar smell of the school. All schools smelled the same. The scent of old books, waxed floors, and cleaning products, just like from his childhood. He walked up another flight of stairs to the third floor and rounded a small corner into the hallway. The long hallway, brightly lit by the sunlight and fluorescent lighting, was deserted. Marcus read each room number, just to the left side of the door, in his head, *hmmm, the odd numbered classrooms are to my right…301…303…305…307…309. Ah, here it is, room 311.*

Marcus stood frozen at the entrance of the open doorway, standing just to the right of the door thus out of view of anyone inside. Underneath the room number, 311, was a yellow rectangular paper sign with the name *Mrs. N. J. Logan* over the word *Mathematics* printed in black magic-marker. Marcus tried to will himself to walk into the classroom but his mind refused to listen to his body. He suddenly lost his nerve then did the prudent thing…turned to leave the building, flee before he was seen. He walked quickly back down the hallway. Marcus looked back occasionally to make sure Neci did not see him make his escape. Looking back one final time, he felt relief as he made it to freedom. Marcus breathed easier as he rounded the corner leading to the stairs, literally running smack into someone.

"Umphhh!" The sound released out of Marcus rather loudly.

"*Hey!*" Neci said in surprise.

Marcus nearly knocked Neci down as she was stepping onto the top landing after leaving the downstairs teacher's lounge, with bottled water in one hand and papers in the other. As she was about to tumble back down the steps, the quick-thinking Marcus grabbed her before that could happen. The papers scattered about and the bottled water flew back and bounced down the stairs. Neither immediately recognized the other due to the sudden collision.

Holding the woman in his arms, Marcus said, "God, I'm so sorry, *Neci*?"

"Marcus, *hi*! What're you doing here?" Neci then thought the worse, and asked with alarm in her voice, "Something happened to Gerard or the boys?" Her wide dark eyes, framed with long black lashes, searched his eyes for an answer.

Still holding Neci tightly in his arms, not with enjoyment, but with great embarrassment, Marcus answered, "Eddie and the boys are okay. Everything's fine...ummm.   I-I...ummm...I-I   was...ummm...in the...ummm...the neighborhood. I just came by to say hello."

Neci smiled in relief then in joy at seeing Marcus. She loved it when he got flustered in her presence.

Neci asked playfully, "You sure were in a hurry."

"Yeah...I...ummm...ummm, look let me help you with this mess I made." He released Neci from his gentle grasp.

Marcus ran down the stairs and retrieved the bottled water then joined Neci in picking up the scattered papers. After the documents were collected, Neci faced him with that bright winning smile.

"Come on, let me show you to my classroom, Mister Williams."

Marcus, feeling like a buffoon, obediently followed the beautiful woman back to room 311, wearing a tight but conservative fuchsia skirt and crème-colored blouse.

***

Neci gave Marcus a brief tour of her medium-sized classroom. They were standing at Neci's desk, which was extremely neat and clutter free. The six large windows on one side of the room allowed in the bright sunlight. Marcus could see his car parked downstairs out front shimmering in the heat of the day.

"That's pretty much it, Marcus. I spend my entire day here teaching and molding young minds. We at J. L. Nelson strongly believe that the children are indeed our future." Neci giggled at her statement which sounded more like a public service announcement, then nervously pushed back her lustrous hair behind one ear, exposing a diamond earring.

Marcus, enjoying her presence, retorted, "Either y'all teach 'em here or Eddie and I'll teach 'em out in the streets at the school of hard knocks."

"We definitely don't want that, do we? The school system hopes to make your job easier, at least in theory."

Marcus said, "Yeah."

An awkward silence followed; neither knew what to say.

"Well..."

Marcus said, "Well...umm."

Neci looked outside, "It's hot out there...isn't it?"

"Yeah, I wore these shorts hoping to cool down a little."

Neci looked back towards him. "Hmmm. Nice outfit, Marcus. You *definitely* look cooler." Without meaning to, she sounded a bit too seductive as she gazed upon his body.

"Yeah, your outfit looks nice too," Marcus said. Then he thought, *'your outfit looks nice too'? Good comeback, Romeo!*

Neci said, "Thanks."

"Ummm, well…" Marcus glanced out of the window, "it's hot out there today."

Another uncomfortable silence loomed between Marcus and Neci as the conversation finally petered out. Marcus could hear the ticking of the clock as nervous sweat sprouted upon his baldpate. He tried to think of a clever opening to bring up the reason he came to visit her. As he stood there speechless, feeling like a fool, nothing came to him. It was so easy talking to Neci over the telephone but face-to-face was another thing, especially when he had planned to tell the woman that he had strong feelings for her. Neci looked at her watch a couple of times and now looked out of the window again, and then back at her watch, as if she had somewhere to go.

Marcus, unable to stand the silence any longer, gathered his courage and said, "Look, Neci…I need to talk to you about something, something that has been on my mind for a while."

Neci peeped at her watch again then stated, "Okay…you appear as if you have something on your mind." She pointed to a chair in the corner. "Pull up a chair, bring it over next to the desk." Neci took a seat behind her desk.

Marcus retrieved the chair, and he brought it back to where Neci was now sitting. She looked like Marcus felt - nervous. Neci resisted the urge to twist her hair which usually comforted her. Her stomach started to churn with emotion.

Marcus did not waste anytime; he started speaking as soon as he sat down,

"I...ummm...I-I...ummm." He could think of nothing else to say at that moment. He immediately thought, *come on, Marcus, get it together...just...just say it. Tell Neci how you feel about her!*

Marcus tried again. "Look...I've only known you for...ummm...a few months. But since that short time I've really grown to like you a lot. You've been so nice to me, Neci. So caring...so *nice...*"

Neci looked away from Marcus as she sat with her hands clasped on her desk, seeming to be searching for something on her large desk calendar. Her left hand started to go toward her hair, that nervous little girl trying to come out. She made a conscious effort to return her hand back to the desk. She knew what Marcus wanted to express.

"I don't know of any other way to say this...I mean with Eddie, Gerard, being my partner...this is hard to say."

Neci was now biting her lower lip, as if waiting for the guillotine to drop. She had a knowing expression on her face; Marcus was smitten with her and that was not a good thing.

"I have enjoyed our many talks, Neci. We've talked just about everything under the sun. I don't trust a lot of people, but I feel as if I can tell you anything. You've really helped me to get through my breakup with..." Marcus temporarily forgot his ex-lover's name, "...Tam. I just wanted to say...look the fact is that I'm very attracted to you, Neci. Never felt such a strong feeling for anyone, any woman, in my life."

Neci now had her palms flat against the calendar, still staring intently at that calendar to avoid Marcus's intense but sincere stare. She looked as if she was upset in hearing those words coming out of Marcus's mouth. Actually she thought, *what did I do to bring this on? He has indeed gotten over his shyness with me.* Neci found the latter thought scary but exhilarating because she wondered if she could resist Marcus if he persisted along this course. She was not upset with Marcus, but with herself for allowing this *thing* to somehow develop. Neci also wondered whether or not she could continue to hide her own feelings about her husband's partner. Staying committed to her marriage was something that was important to her. She could not allow anyone to interfere with her union to Eddie. *There is no excuse for infidelity, no excuse at all,* Neci thought.

Marcus, becoming alarmed and concerned with Neci's expression, continued talking despite her negative body language. "I wanted to get this off my chest because I can't stop thinking about you. When-when I lay down at night, my thoughts are of you. When I get up in the morning, there you are again…on my mind. You're *constantly* on my mind, Neci. I guess…I know this can't go anywhere, you know with you being involved and all…married to Eddie, but…I just wanted you to know. Maybe telling you somehow would give me peace…maybe help me to stop thinking these deep thoughts about you…about…us. I guess I've said all I needed to say." Marcus immediately felt foolish.

Neci continued to look down at her desk. It seemed like an eternity before she finally turned her head slowly and looked seriously, with her dark sparkling and intelligent eyes, at the crestfallen man sitting to her left.

"*Wow.*" Neci looked back down at her desk as if addressing the furniture. "Marcus…I…don't know how to respond." She chuckled nervously and then said, "This is…wow. I don't know what to say." Neci paused for a few seconds and focused upon Marcus once again. Suddenly, a serious expression appeared upon her face, thoughts of Juny, Karl, and her husband crashed into her mind. She continued with a furrowed brow, "I don't think we should-"

The light tapping at the open door interrupted Neci's response to Marcus's diatribe.

For a brief second, Marcus was petrified to look toward the door because he had a very bad feeling that Eddie would be standing there. How would he explain visiting his partner's wife? He braved himself and turned toward the soft knocking. A Caucasian woman in her fifties wearing an ugly multicolored sundress stood in the doorway. A man and woman, also white, in their twenties stood behind the older woman in the hallway. All three seemed hesitant to enter the classroom.

"I'm sorry to interrupt, Missus Logan, but Mister and Missus Parker are here for their conference about Billy."

Neci stood, and Marcus followed her lead.

Marcus turned to Neci and whispered, "I'd better go. Thanks for your time, Neci."

Before Neci could respond, Marcus quickly walked toward the door nodding at the trio as he left the classroom.

Neci thanked the other teacher for escorting the parents to the classroom before dismissing her. She asked the couple to have a seat. Neci excused herself, for a moment, not sure what to do. When she stood just outside the door, she watched Marcus walk hurriedly down the empty hallway. Neci thought about calling after him but decided against it. Marcus vanished as he walked towards the stairs.

Neci walked back into her classroom to prepare for the parent-teacher conference, which was the reason she'd stayed late that day. Marcus dominated her thoughts throughout her meeting with the young parents.

Chapter 17

The antiquated homes on Cutler Road sat on small lots; most of the houses were only a few feet apart. In contrast, Eddie's and Neci's home had some seclusion due to ample space and hedges on both sides of the structure which provided welcome privacy from the close-knit community. The rear of the Logans' tri-level home had two distinct characteristics: one, a large three-sided sunroom - walled by floor-to-ceiling rectangular shaped windows with decorative blinds - on the back left side of the house that jutted-out from the second floor, and two, a roomy deck just off the kitchen area that was separated by patio doors on the right rear of the home. The deck was furnished with a large patio table set and an expensive high-tech gas grill. Leading out from the deck were several wide steps which led down to a spacious, sloped backyard.

Numerous feet from the home and to the left sat an unattached garage which housed Eddie's workman tools, and the partially-renovated, 1965 convertible four-speed Ford Mustang. The gutted, primer, two-door vehicle sat on aluminum wheel-ramps as it stood waiting and ready for additional work. Eddie planned to paint the vehicle candy-apple red. Installation of the engine, dashboard, seats, carpeting, convertible roof, and other accessories were still uncompleted. Realistically, Eddie and Marcus had a great deal of work left on the vast project.

A few days after visiting Neci at her school, Marcus drove into the Logans' rear yard from the paved alley then parked behind the work garage. Eddie was at the Advance Auto Parts store picking up additional supplies thus running late. Marcus would simply wait in the garage until his arrival. He was just too embarrassed to face Neci again. Marcus tried to tell Eddie that he had a cold and could not come over to help with the Mustang, but Eddie persuaded his partner to stop by anyway.

Now as Marcus sat on a barstool in front of a large metal fan, waiting for his partner, he noticed that his stomach was doing flip-flops from nervousness. He wondered if Neci knew that he was coming over. He felt silly hiding out in the garage but in light of the fiasco at the school with Neci, Marcus surely had reason to hide. A few minutes after his arrival, Marcus heard foot steps coming toward the garage. His nervousness subsided as he was relieved that Eddie had finally arrived. The sooner they got started on the work, the sooner he could get back home. When the small side door opened, Neci walked in instead of Eddie.

"Hi, Marcus, Gerard just called. He had to run to another parts store and would be much later than anticipated. He tried calling you on your cellular." Neci was wearing a white tank top, a pair of blue jean shorts, and brown sandals. She was holding a bottle of Budweiser that she handed to Marcus.

"Thanks." Marcus was not much of a drinker but the August heat made him thirsty.

As Marcus gulped down half of the foamy cold fluid, Neci, with her thick hair wrapped up due to the heat, watched him. She obviously wanted to talk to him further. Marcus lowered the brown bottle and stared back at her.

"I'm sorry you're not feeling well. Gerard told me that you were sick...something about a summer cold?"

"Yeah, I didn't want the boys to catch it so I thought it was a good idea to wait out here."

"I see." Neci glanced down briefly then back at Marcus. "That's kind of you."

Neci gave that winning smile which lit up her youthful face and said, "Look about the other day, Marcus…"

Damn, she's going there! Marcus was mortified. The last thing he wanted to talk about was the embarrassment from the 'other day.' "Umm, Neci, you, we don't have to bring that up. It was all a *big* misunderstanding…I read something in you that wasn't there…I'm sorry if I've offended you."

"No offense taken. I was just caught off guard. But I would like the opportunity to address it, that is, if you don't mind." Neci looked at him earnestly.

Marcus did mind, but said, "Sure, go 'head."

Neci continued to stand as she gathered her thoughts. "I was flattered by your words but maybe what you're feeling is loneliness, you know, from breaking up with your girlfriend, Tamala. This…*bonding* that we've experienced over the past few months may have been the result of that, of your breakup with her which lead to your attraction…to me."

"Actually it isn't, Neci. What I feel toward you is genuine, it's no rebound. I'm over with what I had with Tam. She killed what we had. I admit that it still hurts, and I still care for her. I maybe even miss her from time to time. But once again, what I said to you at the school was really from the heart. As crazy as it sounds, I've *connected* with you, Neci. On a level I've never experienced with a woman. That *connection* made me want to be closer to you…*intimate* with you."

Neci started tingling all over as Marcus exuded confidence from his candor with her. *Being 'intimate' with him,* Neci pushed the erotic image from her head. *This man knows what he wants, and he wants me…whoa! Focus, focus.*

Marcus continued, "So you don't have to treat me like some hurt little boy with a crush," he finished with a smile.

"Okay." Neci decided to be honest, at least partially. She looked down at her hands folded in front of her then up at Marcus as she said, "I've spent years trying to keep my marriage together, Marcus. Gerard and I almost separated due to infidelity, which nearly destroyed our marriage. I still believe in my vows and will do everything in my power *not* to allow unfaithfulness to creep its way back into my marriage. I *love* Gerard and our children. I just can't betray them, Marcus. It's my *duty* to keep this marriage together."

Marcus thought about Eddie and Kimberly, and then about Eddie's lack of commitment or duty to his marriage. "I respect that Neci; the last thing I want to do is cause a riff between you and Eddie. I care for you too much to bring problems into your life…into your marriage. I…I just wanted to express my feelings to you." Then Marcus suddenly thought of a burning question that he needed answered. "May I ask you something?"

Neci said slowly, "Sure…ask away."

"Am I reading you wrong? I mean…are you attracted to me too, Neci?"

For what seemed like an eternity, Neci finally said, "No…what I do feel toward you is a close friendship." She finished the lie by saying, "That's the *only* thing I feel for you."

Marcus felt like he was drowning in a deep pool of water and could not catch his breath. "Okay…I understand."

Neci looked down then said, "I hope I didn't hurt your feelings. Don't think you have to make yourself scarce around here, Marcus." She then looked into his eyes. "Like before, you're always welcomed here, even if you want to call and just need to talk. It's okay."

Marcus, still allowing the other stinging words to sink in, simply said, "Thanks."

Neci smiled brightly then said, "So, now that you're over your 'summer cold,' when you and Gerard are done for the day, I expect you to join us for dinner…okay?"

They both laughed at the lame summer cold excuse.

"Dinner would be nice, Neci."

"Well then, it's settled. Can I get you another beer?"

"Naw. Thanks though. I'll just hang out here until Eddie shows up."

"Alright, if you need anything, just-"

"Walk on in. I remember. Thanks, Neci."

Neci smiled again then left Marcus with his wounded thoughts. Knowing that Neci had no feelings beyond friendship toward him was both devastating and heartbreaking. He upturned the beer bottle and drained the rest of the cold alcohol.

***

Later that evening in the kitchen as dusk began to settle upon Woodland County, Eddie sat at one end of the table drawing a caricature for the laughing boys who sat on each side of their father. All three were engrossed in the drawing as Marcus sat with them facing the small window over the kitchen sink. Earlier, Neci had prepared a deliciously seasoned stir-fry dish with shrimp, chicken, an assortment of vegetables, brown rice, and of course Eddie ate his portion without the meat. A light wine was served with the meal while the kids drank milk or fruit juice.

Now Neci stood with her back to the group washing the last of the dishes. Marcus offered to help, but Neci waved him off. Marcus tried desperately not to gaze at the beauty, but he was losing the battle. Marcus glanced over at Eddie, who continued to instruct the young boys in the art of drawing. He talked softly to them as they asked questions and waited patiently for their turn to draw. Marcus then took a chance and glanced up at Neci. The tight jean shorts highlighted Neci's nice firm buttocks. The middle seam ever so gently separated the plumpness of the woman's behind, making it even fuller.

Marcus felt his manhood growing in the midst of his voyeurism. He swallowed slowly enjoying the rearview of Neci. He noticed her nicely shaped hips that led to a petite waist. The golden color of her arms and shoulders appeared soft to the touch. Oh, how Marcus wished he could feel the texture of her skin, the warmth of her flesh. His gaze went up to the petite neck which was exposed given her hair was pinned up. Kissing Neci's neck gently, the nape, the deep hollow, tasting her skin with his tongue, and making her moan in pleasure were only to be done in his futile fantasies.

Marcus ached and yearned for such a chance, a hopeless opportunity to make love to the woman who now stood just a few feet in front of him. He could almost reach out and touch Neci if it was not for the dinner table that separated them. Despite the coolness of the central air-conditioner, Marcus was developing beads of sweat upon his baldhead. His heartbeat was racing as he took in the full view of the sexy and desirable young woman. Then as he continued to stare at Neci, he noticed that he too was being watched. His stomach immediately tied in knots as he became frozen in terror with his hand caught in the proverbial cookie jar.

Through the mirror-like reflection of the small window in front of Neci, he clearly saw that she was staring at him intensely. It almost made him gasp in embarrassment as a result of being caught checking her out. But what kept him cool as he looked in awe at the woman's reflection in the window was the expression on Neci's face. She had a hint of a smile as she glanced back into Marcus's eyes. Neci's expression said two things according to Marcus's interpretation: one, I see you checking me out, but it's ok, and two, I want you just as much as you want me.

Neci then slowly looked away from him and continued to wash the remaining dishes.

Marcus thought, *when is this cat and mouse game gonna end...damn!*

Chapter 18

Neci and Eddie lay nude in bed after a brief session of sex, or as Neci secretly called it - 'a quick bang.' Eddie had not made *love* to her in years. Instead of slow and methodical lovemaking, like what was performed in the early years of their marriage, Eddie nowadays delivered a hard and sweaty *fuck*, often leaving Neci sore and unsatisfied and talking to him over the years about their sex-life had been futile. Sex between them had become both mediocre and boring, no thrill and no spice.

Eddie now lay sound asleep beside his beautiful young wife who herself was wide awake in the dimly lit room. Something was bothering her as she lay amongst within the sweaty and rumpled sheets. She could not pinpoint what had just struck a nerve with her. She was just on the cusp of consciousness when it came to her. The revelation jolted Neci out of her near slumber: her loving husband, the man that promised to love and cherish her for the rest of his life, whispered the name of another woman just before he had climaxed. She struggled to recall the name, but it escaped her. As she lay back down, a tear rolled out of her left eye into her ear. She had a perfect view of the nighttime sky through the window near her. Though she could not see the moon from her vantage point, she could see that it shone brightly.

Over the past few months, she tried constantly to ignore the warning signs: her husband was having whispered telephone conversations over either the house phone or cell phone. He would claim to go to the store for a few items only to return hours later empty handed. He signed on for overtime jobs but neither his payroll checks nor the bank accounts reflect the extra money. Finally, his staying out late until the wee-hours of the morning, with little to no explanation as to his whereabouts, did little to alleviate Neci's suspicions.

Neci thought back to when she saw her spouse alone with that woman in the parking lot, in *their* car, after the softball game last month. The way he was all *chummy* with her as they sat closely together. The name came back to Neci in a flash, and she whispered in defeat toward the window and the moonlit sky, "*Kim's* her name...she's a dispatcher. That's the name you called out instead of mine, you *bastard*. It'll be a long time before I open my legs to you again, Gerard." The words went unheard by her husband who remained in a deep sleep. *Catching a STD from your husband should never be the concern of a faithful wife*, Neci thought as she now faced this hard-cold fact, unfortunately she had been down that road before with Eddie. The cesarean scar on her lower belly served as a constant reminder. That C-section was due to Neci actively being treated for a curable sexually transmitted disease thanks to her prodigal husband, who passed on the disease during the latter stages of her pregnancy with Juny. Neci had tried everything to break Eddie of his past cheating, brief separations and threats of divorce were only temporary fixes; old habits would yet again takeover her husband.

Now with sadness, Neci realized that infidelity had again struck her fragile marriage. Strangely enough though, she did not feel totally heartbroken by this revelation. In fact she had a mixture of relief in the midst of her discontent. That former feeling confused her greatly. She thought, *my husband's screwing another woman. Why do I feel relief, and not pain?* Neci truly did not have an answer to that question as emptiness suddenly filled her soul. Then her thoughts went to another man...Marcus; elation gradually replaced her emptiness. Neci unexpectedly realized that Marcus was the panacea for her emotional pain. *Marcus*, she thought unsurprised.

Before sleep could take Neci, she began to have endless thoughts of Marcus and wondered what he was doing at that very moment. Her mind then proceeded to wander into forbidden territory, without guilt. Neci fantasized about how Marcus would take her, how he would make love to her. Neci shuddered as goosebumps covered her body with the intriguing thought. She pondered, *how would it feel to have Marcus inside of me?* Somehow, Neci knew that it would be more than 'a quick bang' as she placed a shaky hand between her legs.

Chapter 19

A week had passed and Marcus lie sleeping in his tiny bedroom. The tired cop was having a vivid nightmare.

In the real world, the ringing telephone on his bedroom nightstand, pierced through the dream just as Rip fired-off several bullets at T. C. and at him. The sleeping Marcus began to groan and stir despite the deep slumber that had overcome him, thanks to almost twenty-four hours of working overtime during the past few nights. The ringing phone thankfully stalled the nightmare but not before he watched T. C.'s head explode. He awoke with a violent gasp.

Now as Marcus lie awake in bed, deep under the covers with the air-conditioner blasting, he was disoriented and afraid. Amazingly the fatigued man began to drift off again; thirteen hours of sleep was apparently not enough for the overworked and exhausted officer. The persistent phone started up again, stopping only when the Verizon answering service picked up the call. Finally the telephone got through to the sleeping man...*RING, RING, RING*.

Marcus bolted upright as the blankets slid off his lean nude frame. He was covered in sweat, but did not notice the sudden chill from the air-conditioner biting into his skin. As his heartbeat raced from the fading nightmare, Marcus struggled to realize where he was. The semi-darkness of the cool bedroom and his grogginess confused him as he desparately he took in his surroundings. The green glowing display of his clock showed just after 10:00 p.m.

Marcus had no idea what day it was having slept most of the quiet Sunday away. He also did not know what drove him out of his much-needed rest. The nightmare disturbed him, but it had now faded completely. Gradually he realized that he was home and quickly covered his cold body. He had to urinate but did not get up. Instead he slowly lay back down and again sleep tried to take him...*RING, RING, RING*.

"Shit," Marcus croaked as he groped for the loud electronic apparatus. "*Yeah*?" He answered quite perturbed.

"*Marcus*? Did I wake you?"

The familiar female voice did wonders in waking him fully. She had his full attention as his senses sharpened. He struggled to sit up.

Marcus cleared his throat then said, "Hey, Neci...naw, I'm good...just...just chilling." Marcus rubbed the sleep from his eyes and tried to sound wide awake.

"Liar," Neci said playfully then laugh warmly.

Marcus said through a yawn and a smile, "You got me. Been working my ass, I mean my butt off...sorry. I don't know if I'm coming or going right now. Boy, this is a pleasant surprise."

"You must have really been knocked out. I feel guilty for disturbing you."

"Don't sweat it. What's up?"

"I need to see you, Marcus."

Marcus's heartbeat increased again; this time not from his nightmare. He thought he had misunderstood her. "*Really*? Ok, I can meet you somewhere...umm, let's say tomorrow first thing?"

"If it's not too much trouble, I need to see you tonight, right now, if you can."

Marcus was pleasantly shocked that Neci would want to see him but that pleasantry quickly turned into concern. Plus this is the first time Neci had initiated a telephone call to him. Something seemed out of place; something was wrong. "You okay, Neci?" He sat up further with his back to the cold headboard.

Neci was silent for a few seconds before she answered, "Just…I…need to talk. Please, I, I wouldn't ask if it wasn't important. Let's meet somewhere private, somewhere neutral. You know…people may get the wrong impression if we…are seen together."

"Right. I understand completely." Marcus was thinking about his apartment as a meeting place until she made that statement. Plus he did not want to offend Neci by suggesting such a bold spot, his bachelor pad, to meet. His thoughts then flashed to his partner. "Where's Eddie?"

"Gerard…went *out*. He'll probably be gone for a while, I'm sure of that. Back to his routine. The boys are at the babysitter. So, I'm free to see you." Neci refused to mention that she and Eddie had had a big argument just before he stormed out the door. She refused to have sex with Eddie ever since the night he called out another woman's name making it known he was cheating again. When he tried to have sex with her tonight, Neci was not having it. Eddie was angry with his wife but some of that fury seemed contrived, almost as if he conjured it up as an excuse to leave the house for the night.

Marcus noted resentment and disgust in Neci's voice when she talked of Eddie. Suddenly a safe place to meet came to mind.

"Okay. I've got the perfect spot, Neci."

***

Marcus arrived at the designated meeting location just shy of midnight. The last Sunday in August yielded a cool but comfortable night. The full moon, high above, lit Arrowhead Historical Park almost as if it were daylight. The pavilions, concession stands, various storage buildings, and empty ball-fields stood out clearly under the eerie moonlit night. On the other side of the fields, hidden by a stand of trees, was a man-made lake, Lake Sequoyah. Under the bright moonlight, the lake which was popular for fishing and boating gave the illusion of solid ice.

Marcus sat in the Camry with the windows down taking in the cool fresh air. His car was parked on the side of the paved entranceway, just before the locked barricade which stretched across the asphalt roadway leading into the park. The parks in Woodland County were closed up at night to prevent vandalisms and parkers from entering after dusk.

Marcus reflected on that hot day last month in which the softball game was played. That humid day was in stark contrast to tonight's record breaking low temperature of 49 degrees. Marcus looked at his watch and saw that it was now 12:05 a.m. Neci told him that she would be there by 11:45 p.m. He wondered if Eddie had come home and surprised her. He surmised that she probably would not show up if that were the case. Before hanging up the phone earlier, Marcus gave Neci his cellular number in the event she needed to call him. He checked his cell phone to make sure it was on and confirmed that it was; no missed calls or messages.

Marcus settled back into his seat waiting nervously. He hoped that the police would not find him sitting here. It would be hard to explain to a fellow officer why he was out here in the middle of nowhere at this late hour. His other worry was getting caught with Neci. Marcus did not want to think about those implications. Originally he thought that the park was a great place to meet, hindsight thought differently!

Marcus wondered what Neci wanted to see him about. *Was she reconsidering the possibility of something more than friendship with me?* That thought was too exciting to even hope for.

One of the workers at Parks and Recreation gave Marcus various keys to several of the parks' gates and buildings. If an emergency occurred after hours when Marcus was on duty, he did not have to call out a park official to gain entry. Tonight the key to Arrowhead Park would be for his personal use.

Marcus saw a set of headlights coming from the main entrance of the park behind him. He gripped the steering wheel subconsciously as he held his breath. He relaxed when he saw the big Cadillac Escalade pull up behind him; Neci had arrived.

Marcus quickly exited his car unlocking and then opening the gate; he motioned for Neci to drive through into the shadowy park. He reentered his car and drove just inside the gate. After re-securing the barrier, he told Neci to follow him. Marcus wanted to drive deeper into the park and be hidden from view.

***

Thirty minutes later, Neci talked about everything under the sun as they walked along the Chickahominy River. As they enjoyed the moonlit river traveling towards its ordained destination, Marcus and Neci walked a portion of a dirt path that was pitch-dark due to the moon being blotted out by the overhanging trees. The tall trees themselves were silhouetted against the bright full moon casting menacing shadows throughout the darkened park. The park's late-night atmosphere gave Neci a haunting and desolate feeling while at the same time she was exhilarated by the company of her friend. The comforting manly presence of Marcus walking beside her made Neci feel protected. *Marcus wouldn't let any ghosts or goblins harm me*, she thought in jest.

When the conversation fizzled out they walked in silence as the sound of the river could be heard softly in the background. Neci seemed to be having trouble bringing up whatever she brought Marcus out there to talk about. Marcus waited patiently and did not want to push her. It was not until they made the full circle back to their cars, an hour or so later, when Neci finally got to the point of this clandestine meeting.

Neci sat on the hood of the Toyota looking beautiful in the moonlit. Her lush dark hair radiated under that natural lighting as it flowed down her back. She wore a baby blue fleece designer sweat suit. The word *Lacrosse* was stitched in white across the plump bottom of her pants. Marcus did not know if the word referred to the sport or a brand name, in fact he did not care. It simply looked great where it was. Neci noticed that Marcus's outfit showed off his muscular body; his physique had distracted her from the moment Marcus got out of his car to open the gate to the park. Marcus's black, tight- fitting Under Armour workout clothing and sleek pair of Nike running shoes definitely held her attention. His athletic build was a turn on that Neci tried in vain to ignore. Marcus's long sleeve turtleneck and leggings staved off the coolness of the late night.

Neci looked up at the bright moon. "It's beautiful out here at night - *so* serene, *peaceful*." She looked at Marcus. "Thanks, Marcus, for choosing this place."

"No problem. I wanted to put you at ease." Marcus saw that Neci hugged herself against the night chill. "You sure you don't want a jacket or something? I have one in the car."

Neci gave Marcus a sad smile then answered, "No, I'm fine, thanks."

Neci looked down at the ground seeming to be deep in thought. Suddenly she glanced at Marcus as she started to twist her hair, "My marriage is not going well, Marcus. Gerard and I are in trouble…can't hold it together anymore. I, I don't have any friends here, I mean…other than you. I needed to talk to you about it, in person. I *trust* you. We've shared some painful secrets as well as some happy moments during our brief friendship, right?"

Marcus nodded in agreement but kept quiet. He did not want to quell Neci's thoughts.

Neci continued, "You know how I feel about you, and you've expressed how you feel about me." She shook her head in frustration. "This is hard for me to talk about, and I hate to involve you in my marriage. With you and Gerard being partners and all, plus you and I having…this *secret* friendship, I struggled with…with meeting you tonight, Marcus. Gerard is cheating on me with another woman. He's throwing away our marriage which has forced me to come to you."

Marcus tried to contain his excitement. He thought, *Neci must have caught Eddie with his pants down…literally. His cheating ways have finally caught up to him. Now Neci's reconsidering the possibility of us having something more than friendship.* Marcus could not contain his joy.

Marcus interrupted, "I'm glad you've come to me. Neci, I don't know where this may lead, I mean with us seeing each other, but I promise you that I won't cheat on you. You're the dream woman for me, Neci. I have never met anyone like you. We'll take it slow and see where it'll lead because I know with children involved it'll be tough with us being together. As for Eddie and me being partners, *he* messed things up, not us, so why should we be punished if we want to be together."

Neci frowned then said, "*Marcus*...I think you're misunderstaning my intentions with you tonight. For that I apologize. I've come to you for help. Hoping to *save* my marriage, not *sabotage* it."

"Huh?" Marcus felt the sinking feelings of dread, confusion, embarrassment, and disappointment deep within his gut. "I thought...I don't understand...why did you meet-?"

"Marcus, I wanted to see you face-to-face because I want to know the truth...I know that you won't lie to my face."

"Neci, I'm sorry, but what are you talking about? What do you want from me then?"

Neci answered with irritation, "I *need* to know who my husband is fucking."

***

Eddie's Volkswagen Jetta pulled in through the alley then turned into the backyard of the Logan home on Cutler Road just after 2:00 a.m. He parked near the garage that housed the vintage Ford Mustang. Eddie had not been out back to check on the car lately. He loved to look at the partially-restored vehicle as often as he could because it was his passion, his drug. Upon assessing how much more work needed to be done to finish the project, Eddie was disappointed as he remembered that Marcus would not be helping him to complete the restoration.

Eddie locked the garage and walked up the grassy slope toward the rear deck of the house. He hoped that Neci would be asleep because he was tired and pissed off so did not want to hear her nagging about him staying out late. He was upset because he had searched high and low for Kimberly and could not find her. Eddie called her home phone as well as her cellular - no answer at either. He even drove by the Pure Pleasure club where she stripped, then finally the police precinct - still no Kimberly. He wondered where the hell she could be at this time of night.

Eddie let himself in through the sliding patio doors and worked his way upstairs to the master bedroom. He stopped suddenly just after entering the open door to the lit bedroom. The bed that he shared with his wife was made up.

"*Neci?*" Eddie became afraid and wondered if Neci had left him. He frantically looked around for signs of her abandonment. He checked the closets and drawers for missing clothing, but nothing appeared to have been taken. After searching the entire house, Eddie was in a panic when he discovered that she was nowhere to be found. His panic went into overdrive when he found that her SUV was gone. It was parked neither in the driveway nor inside the attached garage. *Where the fuck is my wife? Where would she go?* Eddie tried to calm himself enough to think things through. He went back upstairs to the bedroom where he left her earlier that evening.

Eddie scanned the room for any signs that would explain Neci's absence. His eyes stopped at the telephone and caller ID device next to the bed. Eddie walked over and searched the unit to see if she had received any emergency calls that would prompt her to leave the house. The only calls to the house were 'UNAVAILABLE' or 'OUT OF AREA', all possibly telemarketer calls from the week they were gone, despite they had registered with the national Do Not Call list. No real recent calls because family and friends knew that they were away.

Eddie was baffled, but quickly got an idea. He picked up the cordless telephone and pressed the redial button to display the last number dialed. The small display screen revealed the phone number 555-6554. Eddie stared at the number because it was very familiar but he could not place it. He pressed the talk button which automatically dialed the displayed number. After three rings the answering service activated, the familiar voice gave instructions to leave a message. Eddie slowly hung up the phone without leaving a message. He stood in the bedroom even more confused and said as he scratched his thick blond mane, "Why the hell would she call Marcus?" A crazy thought entered his mind, *could she and Marcus...? Hell no!* No *way!* Eddie quickly dismissed the idea and concluded that Neci probably dialed Marcus's number believing that Eddie had gone to visit Marcus after arguing with her. Eddie chuckled, "Everyone's fucking missing - Kimberly, my wife, and my partner, *fuck*!"

Eddie dialed his wife's cellular and immediately got her voicemail. He hung up the phone and stripped down then got into bed still not believing that his loyal wife left the house at such a late hour. *She could've at least left me a note. She probably went out looking for me. She'll be back.* Sleep eventually overcame Eddie as his wife stood in a moonlit park with the man Eddie entrusted with his life nightly while they patrolled the dangerous Ghetto Town.

***

"It's a *simple* question, Marcus!" Neci was furious as she stood before him. Marcus had been evading the question ever since she asked it thirty minutes ago. Neci knew that there was no way two men could work together and not discuss sexual conquests. She knew how men were; Eddie and Marcus were no different. She did not share her own suspicions that Kim the dispatcher was her husband's mistress.

Marcus was exasperated. "Like I keep telling you: Eddie don't talk to me about stuff like that. Yeah, we're close in some respects, but we don't talk about *sex*, Neci!"

Neci was tired. She did not want to take out on Marcus her personal problems and frustrations. He had been sweet and kind to her but the need to confirm her husband's unfaithfulness consumed her.

As the moonlight shined upon them, Neci stared for truthfulness in Marcus's eyes. After several seconds, she gave a great sigh and said in a near whisper, "Look, Marcus, I'm...sorry. I've been here with Gerard before. The harder I work to keep this marriage together, the harder he works to tear it apart. I'm just at the end of my rope." Silent tears streamed down her face as she thought about that horrible secret in Cantil and how they were forced to flee from there like fugitives.

Marcus *did* tell her truth. He really did not know for sure if Eddie was screwing Kimberly Thatcher or any other woman. He did feel guilty for not at least telling her about his suspicions; he felt as if he had betrayed her. As Marcus looked at the pain and exhaustion on Neci's face, he felt rage toward Eddie. *Why would he put her through this? I would die to have someone like her. In fact, I would die to have her!* The feeling became so strong that Marcus automatically reached out to console the crying woman.

"*Don't*. Please don't, Marcus."

Marcus remained frozen with his arms outstretched toward Neci.

Neci wiped away her tears as she said tenderly, "I can't trust my feelings. The last thing I need is for you to hold me right now."

Marcus slowly dropped his arms. "I'm sorry. I didn't mean nothing by it. I just wanted-"

"I know, Marcus. You're so sweet. I wish..." Neci stopped. It did not matter what she wished. She was married to a man who did not appreciate her, and before her stood another man who would give his all to make her happy. *God, he looks so sexy in that outfit.* Neci closed her eyes hoping that the sudden sexual urges would pass. Her body tingled with pleasure.

"You okay, Neci?"

Neci opened her eyes and whispered, "*No.* I have thought about you everyday without fail, Marcus. I had thoughts about us, thoughts that a married woman shouldn't have for another man. So being in your arms, even for comfort, would only make things...you know."

"Yeah, I know - complicated."

Neci slowly nodded and wiped away her remaining tears then said, "We better go."

"Yeah, okay. You going to be okay to drive or do you need more time here?"

"I'll be okay. I'm sorry for getting you involved in this; I was desperate and needed answers. I didn't mean to put you on the spot."

"Why don't you just confront Eddie, Neci?"

Neci shook her head. "Gerard's a good liar. He's always denied these things in the past. He should've pursued that acting career; he probably would've earned an Oscar by now. Anyway, thanks for your time, Marcus." Neci then walked over and got into her SUV.

Marcus looked in her direction then got into his own car to lead the enigmatic woman out of the park.

***

The two would meet at least twice more during the following week. They would just walk and talk about nothing. Enjoying the park at night was exhilarating. But mostly Neci and Marcus enjoyed each other's company. No touching, no kissing, just talking and enjoying the friendship. Despite the innocence of it all, both felt the heat of their mutual attraction. If they continued to see one another, things would get out of hand. Neci, without warning, thought that it was best to cease all telephone calls and face-to-face interaction to work on her marriage without distraction. Marcus was devastated.

Chapter 20

Early November arrived with much cooler weather. The time for the Annual Fall Police Officers' Ball had arrived on a crisp Saturday evening. This event gave the officers, their spouses, and some select dignitaries an opportunity to dress up - men in tuxes and women in sleek evening gowns. The extravagant affair spared no expense when it came to providing an assortment of exotic foods, entertainment, and *lots* of alcohol.

This year's hosted location was the Omni Richmond Hotel at 100 South 12th Street. Within walking distance of the grand hotel was Brown's Island, surrounded by the James River, the Canal Walk, and the historical Carytown district with its narrow cobblestone streets lined by archaic buildings. The Omni's spacious and ornate Magnolia Room with its vaulted ceiling, brass chandeliers, cherrywood wall paneling, adorned with brass wall-lamps, and original artistry depicting paintings from early periods of Richmond, served as the grand ballroom for the annual dance. The fireplace was the centerpiece of the gigantic room, adding intimacy and a cozy ambience. That large, elaborate, stone fireplace sat burning in the rear of the room unobstructed by tables or other furniture. A service kitchen, with banquet servers, was to the left of the room. The private bar, on the opposite side, was operated by two male bartenders. Numerous round tables with white tablecloths were placed methodically about the room.

The tables were adorned with expensive china, polished flatware, crystal, flowers, candles, and other elaborate place settings. A shellacked wooden dance floor was in the center of the room with a small raised stage near the front, against the wall but in between the two entrances. As Johnny Slick and the Midnight Players performed a plethora of contemporary music and hits from yesteryear, well over two hundred guests listened or danced throughout the night.

Marcus arrived late, walking into the left entrance clad in a tuxedo well after 12:30 a.m. although the event had begun at 9:00 p.m. He had had trouble tying the bowtie to his rented tux - nothing new there. A combination of ineptness, nervousness, and anticipation of seeing Neci had just made knotting a bowtie too difficult. He strolled further into the dimly lit room and stopped to scan for familiar faces. Hoping to spot Neci, Marcus struggled to find anyone that he knew. With an organization employing over 600 people, it was easy to be in the midst of unfamiliar faces. Marcus also quickly noted that very few guests were African American but he was used to this because of the limited number of blacks at all that worked for the Woodland County PD.

Marcus looked to his right at the band on stage. The band was playing some oldies song that Marcus could not recall. Only a few couples were dancing while the rest either mingled or sat drunkenly at their tables. All the men, with exception of the police brass, wore black tuxes while the women were clad in a variety of colored evening gowns. The room smelled of food, alcoholic beverages, and an odd mix of colognes and perfume. Either the heat from the units or just all of the bodies made the room very humid. Finally Marcus saw a familiar face and he quickly made a beeline to the black man who was a former NBA player.

"Hey, Captain Holmes!"

The lieutenant-turned- Captain Jeffrey Holmes stopped dancing with his wife and pivoted toward the voice. "Marcus! Man, nice to see you." The tall soft-spoken man turned back toward his wife. "Katrina, you remember Officer Marcus Williams; you met him at one of our charity basketball games." His wife, who wore a light colored evening gown, did not have a clue who 'Officer Marcus Williams' was.

The slim black woman with short curly hair, who was about the height of her very tall husband, looked down, and greeted Marcus with a subtle nod. "Nice to see you again."

"Same here," Marcus then addressed Jeffrey as he continued to search the crowd for Neci, "You seen my partner around, Eddie Logan?"

"You mean the new guy with the blond hair?

"Yeah."

"Umm, I saw him with, I assume, his wife. They left about thirty minutes ago. He was kinda tore-up - too much to drink."

Marcus was crestfallen but desperately tried to hide it.

Captain Holmes noticed the sudden look of despair on Marcus's face. "Damn, you okay, man?"

His wife discreetly elbowed him then whispered, "Watch your mouth, honey."

Marcus felt his stomach drop as the realization hit him that he was too late; he had missed the opportunity to see Neci. "I'm cool, Captain Holmes. Hey sorry to interrupt y'all's dance. I'll see you later. Nice seeing you again, Missus Holmes."

"Marcus, when you gonna call, so we can get together?"

"I'll be in touch. Oh, congratulations on getting captain…represent, *brotha*." Marcus walked toward the bar.

***

Meanwhile not too far away, Neci stood outside in the hallway near the restrooms. Eddie was currently in the men's room trying to get himself together. He had been

- 176 -

throwing up for close to forty minutes now. Neci was ready
to go home. She had to help Eddie to the restroom because
he was so drunk. He had come out a few minutes ago but
quickly ran back in to empty whatever was left in his
stomach.

Neci could not see the entrance to the ballroom, but she
wondered if Marcus had showed up. Eddie told her that
Marcus said he might drop by. She thought, *apparently he'd
changed his mind.* Despite her decision a few months back
to tell Marcus that they should cease contact, she missed
him more than she could have ever imagined. The telephone
conversations and the late night walks in the park this past
summer were a pleasant escape from her humdrum life. She
also missed confiding in Marcus. Above all, she secretly
missed being pursued by him. Neci and Eddie still had not
had sex since the night he called out that woman's name
when they were making love. She refused to sleep with a
man she believed was cheating on her. Neci confronted
Eddie about her suspicions a month ago but of course he
denied sleeping with another woman. He remained adamant
that *'Kim was just one of the guys.'*

Neci stood between the restroom doors as people went
in and out. She was about to knock on the door to the men's
room when Eddie came staggering out. His tux looked as if
he had slept in it. She thought, *it really is time to go.*

"I, I'm okay, Neci. Let's go back in."

Neci frowned and looked at him incredulously. "Are you
crazy, Gerard? You look a mess, and I'm ready to go!"

"Ne, ci, I, I freel...*feel* better, one more hour. I nam, *am*
having frun...*fun*. Let's go back *in*!" Eddie quickly
staggered toward the ballroom.

"Hmmph!" Neci was frustrated then thought, *I can't
believe this. He's embarrassing me and himself. I should*

leave him, but I'll never forgive myself if something happened to him. She mumbled as she followed her drunken husband, "*Damn* you, Gerard."

***

Marcus had an expensive glass of diet coke in his right hand as he pondered leaving the party. He resigned himself to being alone for the rest of his life. He thought, *maybe a little Bacardi rum in this coke will do me some good before I go home. Then maybe I can sleep instead of tossing and turning, thinking about my messed up life.* Just as Marcus was about to turn back and walk to the bar for the rum, he saw Eddie stumble into the right side entrance to the room. For a second, Marcus thought he was seeing things. It was not until he saw *her* walk in also that he believed that there was a truly a God in heaven, and that he was not seeing things.

Neci was struggling to catch-up to her staggering husband. She looked humiliated and pissed at the same time. It was no wonder why: Eddie looked like Otis, the town drunk, from Mayberry. His bowtie was undone and his tux was completely disheveled. They made their way to their table near the right side of the ballroom, conveniently near the bar. Neci was wearing a strapless black evening gown with a high slit near her shapely left thigh. The form-fitting silk gown, which showed off every curve of Neci's voluptuous figure, had vertical rows of silver beading that wrapped around the shirred bodice to the hem. Her stunning V-shaped diamond necklace matched perfectly with the dangling diamond earrings. Neci's black high-heels also had silver beading. She wore her long hair up with a few curly strands hanging down the sides of her radiant face. Marcus thought 'beautiful' was not enough to describe Neci that night. She had the sexiest sashay that Marcus had ever seen

in a woman. 'Elegant' was the word that came to mind
when he watched her.

Marcus stood in a trance, gaping like a madman as the
couple sat down and was quickly greeted by a waiter. Once
he remembered to breathe, Marcus finally began to contain
his excitement. He sat his coke down on a cluttered and
abandoned table then made his way across the crowded
room toward the Logans.

***

Eddie had just ordered another vodka mixed drink - this
time a Purple Passion. He asked his wife, "You want
somethin' to drink, dear?"

Neci sat fuming. "*No*, Gerard! Are you trying to drink
yourself to death or what?"

"*Braby*, we paid to *havre* a good time, let's enjoy this,
okay?" The waiter sat the drink down in front of him.
"Thanks, *kiddo*." He immediately partook of the fruity
drink. "*Awww*, that's sweeeeet." Eddie then gave a loud
involuntary burp.

"Do you have to be a *pig* too? *That's it*. You've got five
minutes to finish that drink then I'm leaving *with* or *without*
you, Gerard!" Neci glared at her husband.

Eddie started drinking the moment he got to the ball.
Seeing Kimberly Thatcher with her date, some balding
white man in his thirties, made Eddie jealous. Kimberly had
her red hair flowing freely down her back just the way
Eddie liked it. The balding man was hanging onto Kimberly
as if she were his lifeline. Kimberly would occasionally give
Eddie a playful look then she would kiss her date. Eddie
knew that Kimberly was doing that to upset him, but Eddie
could not control the effect it had on him. He did not love
Kimberly, but she was the only sex he was getting these

days. The last thing he needed was some other man moving in on his girl.

Now Eddie tried to find reprieve in the alcohol; drinking helped him to escape.

"Hey, partner." Marcus stood before them.

Both Eddie and Neci looked up at the voice.

Eddie was happy to see his patrol buddy, "*Marcus*! I knew you wouldn't - "

(BURP)

"Ex...excuse me...knew you wouldn't let me down, come on have a drunk, a drink!"

Marcus laughed then said, "Naw, man, but it's time to cut you off for the night." Marcus then smiled down at Neci. "Hi, Neci. You look lovely tonight. It's been a while."

"It has been. How've you been?" Neci was ecstatic to see Marcus. She suddenly became self-conscious about her hair and makeup.

"Been a little busy. Did I miss much tonight?" Marcus said looking around the ballroom.

Neci looked over at her husband who was drinking himself into a stupor. "Not much. Gerard has been my entertainment for the evening."

"Honey, you know you love it when I'm pickled. Damn, just saying that word makes my mouth tickle. *Pickled! Pickled! Pickled! Pickled!*, Hey, *pickle* rhymes with *tickle*!"

"Cut it out, *Gerard*." Neci said under her breath then looked back at Marcus. "Sorry, have a seat." She glanced at her watch. "You're *really* late."

Marcus sat across from the pair. "I...umm, had some trouble with my tie."

Neci looked him over with a smile. "Well, you look debonair, Marcus." *My God! You look handsome!* Neci thought to herself.

"I think…I'm gonna-" Before Eddie could finish his words, he promptly vomitted on the floor then passed out with his head on the table.

Neci gazed wide-eyed over at the embarrassing sight and gave a heavy sigh. She looked at Marcus and asked shamefully, "Could I trouble you to help me get him in the car? I hate to ask." Some of the guests were already laughing and pointing at the scene.

Marcus looked deeply into her dark eyes, "It would be my pleasure, Neci."

Neci flushed but loved the way he admired her with his eyes. "I need to grab my wrap from the coatroom."

"I'll meet you in the lobby." When Neci left, Marcus then began the task of getting Eddie up on his feet as hotel workers attended to the mess left behind.

Chapter 21

Marcus pulled into the familiar alleyway as he followed the Cadillac Escalade to the Logan home. Before leaving the Omni Hotel, Marcus insisted that he help Neci bring her husband home instead of simply into the SUV. He parked just past the garage where the unfinished, vintage Ford sat. He stepped out into the cold November air not wanting to leave the comforting heat of his car. The frosty air immediately penetrated the tux he wore. Neci got out of the SUV and walked up to the deck to open the patio doors while Marcus proceeded to get his drunken partner out of the passenger side of that SUV.

"I lovvvve yoooou, Marcus. You'rrrrreeeee the greatest, dude!"

(BURP)

"I'm drunk, ain't I?"

Marcus had his arm around Eddie as he assisted him in walking towards the house. "Yep, you drunk, Eddie. Please stop breathing on me. And for *God's* sake warn me if you get sick again, okay?"

"Okee-dokee, bluddy!" Eddie said with a salute making buddy sound like *bloody*.

Marcus eased the man through the patio doors.

As Neci pointed, she said, "Take him all the way to the living room. I'll be there in a second." She stayed behind to lock the patio doors.

Neci then walked around them and led the two men up the stairs to the top floor. Marcus followed her to the left and down the hall. "Put him on the bed in there." She pointed into the guest bedroom. Neci had no intention on sleeping in bed with her drunken husband that night. The guest bedroom would be perfect for him. Marcus supported Eddie as he guided the man down onto the queen-sized bed. Eddie quickly drifted into a drunken fog. Marcus, sitting on the bed winded, looked up at Neci and then said comically, "Please *don't* ask me to undress 'im."

Neci laughed, "He'll be fine." She took off Eddie's shoes and motioned for Marcus to follow her.

***

Minutes later in the kitchen, Neci and Marcus sat across from one another at the table. They were both drinking hot cocoa. Neci had removed her jewelry and was now relaxed in her soft pink bedroom slippers wearing her hair down over the black evening gown. She was telling Marcus about her work in the classes she was taking at VCU. Neci was currently working on a thirty-page research paper differentiating home- from traditional-schooling.

"It's due by Christmas but I'm going to need an extension. Once I graduate from VCU, I'll take a long break before tackling those doctorial courses. I don't even like thinking about it, to tell you the truth."

Marcus said after listening patiently, "I wish I had the drive to go back and finish my degree. I have so much debt right now. Shoot, the last thing I need is to pay on a college loan, that's if I could even qualify for one. But you'll become that college professor in no time, Neci."

"Thanks, Marcus. And thanks for helping me with Gerard. I'm so embarrassed about the way he…" She shook her head as she thought back on Eddie's drunken adventure.

"It was no problem. Cops get drunk at these events all the time. No one really even noticed."

Neci smiled, "You're just too sweet, but *stop* lying, everybody from the Chief to the young woman cleaning up Gerard's puke will remember this for a longtime. It's going to be a while before I can show my face around another police function. Can't take him anywhere." They laughed together.

"In all seriousness, Marcus, let me reimburse you the money for the ball. You weren't there long before Iasked you to help me with Gerard."

"Neci, I don't want your money. The only reason I came there in the first place was to see..." Marcus tried to stop a slip-of-the-tongue.

Neci asked innocently, "To see...*what*?"

Marcus said in a whisper, "I've missed you *so* much. No matter how wrong it may be, I do. You looked exquisite tonight. You're the most beautiful creature I've ever laid eyes on, Neci."

Neci looked down then hesitantly said in her own whispered voice, "I've missed you too, Marcus." She stared back at the attractive bald man and then said, "I hated not seeing you these past few months. I thought it would be best not to see you, but-"

"I totally understood your reasons, Neci. You're committed to your marriage and your children. I really do respect that. I admit that it hurt in the beginning, shoot, it still hurts, but I understand."

"I didn't mean to hurt you, Marcus."

"I know."

The conversation suddenly halted for neither knew what else to say on that subject. The only sound in the room was the ticking of a wall clock somewhere in the house.

Marcus broke the silence, "Well, I'd better go. It's pretty late."

Neci glanced at her diamond-encrusted Movado watch. "Yes it is. We've got mass in the morning." She focused her attention back at Marcus. "The boys are at my coworker's home for the night, a last minute babysitter. I'll be getting up early to pick them up before church. I'll walk you out."

Marcus put on his tux jacket and they both proceeded to the patio doors. Once outside on the deck, Neci thanked Marcus once again for his helping her with Eddie, who was still sleeping off the alcohol.

"Woman, you gonna catch your death out here in this cold."

Neci smiled and said lightheartedly, "Look at *you*, sounding like somebody's momma, acting like you care 'bout little ol' me."

Marcus took off his tux jacket. "Let me show you how much I care for you." In an act of gallantry, he draped the jacket around Neci's bare shoulders then gently kissed her on the forehead, still holding onto the jacket as if he were embracing her instead.

They stood close to one another. Marcus wrapped his arms around Neci in the darkness of the late night as they stood breathing in each other's warm air. Neci stared up into Marcus's handsome face as her eyes adjusted to the darkness of the cloudy night. He stared back into her eyes, and Neci felt a fire burning within her. She shivered but not because of the coldness. The tender kiss to her forehead caused her body to tingle in warmth. She was surprised at the effect that the intimate gesture had on her.

"Your turn," Marcus challenged in his deep voice, feeling high from the experience.

Neci continued to stare at Marcus, heart thumping fast with nervousness. She looked at Marcus's sexy bald dome. He was broad shouldered in his crisp, white, wing-tip collared shirt, bowtie undone. She was suddenly overcome with desire for him. Neci's sexual inhibitions were completely abated.

Without thinking, Neci slowly closed in the distance between them, their bodies now touching. She could feel the heat from his hard muscular body, the pleasant smell of his cologne now in her nostrils. She wondered if he was as nervous as she was, for at that very moment, Neci did not know what she was going to do. Suddenly, she tiptoed and kissed him lightly on the lips, then she returned flatfooted back to the wooden deck. The brief kiss felt good to her; it felt right.

Marcus could not believe this was happening as his heart began to race with excitement; Neci's moist, tender lips had just touched his. He wrapped his arms tightly but gently around her small frame and slowly eased his lips towards hers. Marcus kissed Neci. Their nervous lips tried to find a comfortable niche as the two tongues met. Marcus tasted the remnants of cocoa as Neci began to moan with pleasure.

Neci's nervousness all but disappeared as she allowed her body to submit to the will of this tall, dark Adonis who held her tightly. She in turned wrapped her arms around Marcus's thick neck, subconsciously stroking his head and feeling the tautness. Neci felt Marcus's hardness grow against her flat stomach as her wetness increased. She sucked on Marcus's long tongue as if it was his growing hardness. Their lips finally jelled into the perfect kiss that became intense, harder, and deeper. The couple's sexy muffled moans could be heard as they breathed noisily through their noses, their hot breaths releasing into the cold air like raging bulls. Marcus's large hands slid down the arch of Neci's slim back and rested just above her shapely butt.

Marcus grew bolder as he cupped her ample behind and pulled her closer to his erection. Once again, Neci tiptoed but this time to feel Marcus's erection against her own increased throbbing. She moaned uncontrollably as she felt his manhood rub hard against her swollen clit. Her nipples ached for attention. She wanted Marcus to plunge deep inside her wetness. Both Neci and Marcus disappeared into their own world, becoming lost in their own world; they were alone together in body, mind, and spirit. Neci became his water, Marcus became her food. At that very moment, neither one of them could survive without the other as they kissed hungrily.

They kissed this way for almost ten minutes before it slowly...very slowly...began to wind down. The powerful kiss became softer as their tongues darted back and forth into each other's mouths, probing, teasing, and pleasing. Marcus then kissed Neci's cheeks, chin, nose, and finally her neck; the latter spot drove her wild. She mumbled in Spanish; Marcus had no clue what was said but it sounded extremely sexy. Marcus ended by slowly kissing her again on the forehead. They were both left breathless by the passion just experienced.

Marcus looked deeply into Neci's eyes. "Now do you know how much I care for you?"

Neci, on fire, answered excitedly with a slight tremble in her voice, "This...is not good, Marcus. Nothing...but trouble."

"Yeah, I know."

The experience left her shaken, but pleased. "What...what should we do?"

Marcus continued to embrace Neci, looking down at her, stroking her coarse hair. "If you felt what I just felt...then how can we...contain this?"

Neci feeling secure and comfortable in Marcus's strong arms said jokingly, "You shouldn't answer a question *with* a question, Marcus. But...but, what *did* you feel?"

"I felt, feel that I could fall madly in love with you, Neci. That's how I feel."

Neci's mind whirled because she felt the same way but was afraid to voice it. Instead she said, "All of that from *one* kiss?"

Marcus nodded, "Yep."

"I repeat, Marcus, 'trouble.' "

"Like I said, 'Yeah, I know.' "

Neci said softly, "I-I'm scared."

"Me too, but we can be scared together as we make love."

She smiled then cocked her head as she looked at him curiously. "*Okay*...what does that mean?"

Marcus rethought his response then smiled self-consciously. "Hell, I 'on't know. But it sounded kinda romantic." Both of them laughed.

Neci gently pulled away from Marcus and handed him his jacket. "It's been an *interesting* evening, to say the least."

"Yes, indeed it has been *very* interesting."

"Good night, Marcus."

"Night, Neci." Marcus gave her a quick peck on the lips. He looked at her longingly then left the deck to get to his car.

Neci stood in the bitter cold as Marcus drove away. She stood alone on the deck holding herself to keep warm long after Marcus left. Neci was thinking about the insatiable kiss, and how it took her away. *If a single kiss could yield so much passion and emotion, then the act of making love would...*

Neci shook her head. She was afraid to ponder it any further. She turned and went back into the warmth of her home. Her thoughts turned to Cantil. She did not want what had happened there to repeat itself in Woodland County, but she felt powerless to stop what was happening with Marcus. If that was the case, horrible things could be in store for all involved. Neci tried to block out Cantil - that dark period in her and Eddie's life.

***

Later as she lay alone in her bed, Neci felt that sleep would not come; dawn was approaching as uneasiness filled her soul. The source of her unease lay in the bedroom down the hall, deep in a drunken sleep. Before finally drifting off to sleep, Neci had a strong premonition that the nasty little secret, left back in Cantil, would indeed repeat itself.

Chapter 22

Three days later, Marcus was finally able to call Neci. She had been on his mind constantly since the night of the ball. Eddie was busy writing an offense report in the squad room. Marcus took the chance and called her on his cell phone as he sat in an empty interrogation room. As he dialed her number, his heart was racing, looking forward to hearing Neci's voice.

***

Neci was seated in front of her desktop computer in the multipurpose room in her home, wearing a pair of white Victoria's Secret pajamas covered with little red hearts. She had the fireplace going which gave the room a serene atmosphere which was able to stay that way with the boys finally put to bed. The large room was decked out in contemporaty home décor which brightened the space even without the burning fireplace. A few weeks ago, Neci moved her computer desk to this room, so that she could see out of the sunroom's large floor-to-ceiling, rectangular-shaped windows. Not that the view of her backyard was spectacular, but the panoramic sight gave her a sense of not being closed in. Neci suffered with a mild case of claustrophobia. The sunroom eased the affliction.

Now as Neci sat before the Dell computer screen, wearing a pair of reading glasses to help reduce the strain to her eyes, she realized that she had writer's block as she attempted to complete her college paper. All she saw on the screen were meaningless words. Neci pressed the delete button getting rid of a paragraph she had typed twenty minutes ago. In frustration, she tried to refocus on what she needed to convey to readers but before Neci could develop a workable concept, the telephone rang. With a sigh of resignation, she went to answer it.

"Hello."

On the other end of the telephone, Marcus felt warmth cover his body upon hearing the husky sensuous voice. "How ya doing, Neci?"

The butterflies in Neci's stomach were immediate. "I'm doing great, Marcus. Glad to hear from you. What've you been up to?" Neci sat down on the plush couch with her legs under her. She was trying not to sound too excited about hearing from him.

Marcus answered in a serious voice, "Thinking about you."

Neci frowned in confusion, "You're working right, with Gerard?"

"Yep...we are at the station completing paperwork. Umm...Eddie is writing a robbery report."

"Oh. Was anyone hurt?"

"Naw, just routine stuff. Happens all the time where we patrol." Marcus quickly changed the subject. "Look I don't have long. I've got one question. You having regrets...about the other night?"

After a pause Neci said, "No, I keep replaying it in my head. I think about that...*our kiss* more than I ought to." She gave a nervous giggle.

"I want to see you."

"*How*, Marcus? I, I mean with me having Juny and Karl...it's, it's just so hard to get away. And...despite us crossing the line with our kiss...I, I don't know if I can do it again...or do something more than...you know, more than a kiss. I'm still confused about my feelings for you." Neci suddenly felt awkward.

"Neci, I know you're busy with the children, work, and your college courses. I was just wondering if you could just slip out like you did when we met a few times in the park…maybe one night get a babysitter when Eddie's out late…umm, I just want to see you, we don't have to kiss or anything else. I promise." Marcus wanted to put her mind at ease.

Neci loved the idea of seeing Marcus again, but it was just impossible. "He'll suspect something. We'd be taking a big chance…it's just too risky, Marcus. Plus meeting you in that park…late at night…we might get caught."

"I know a place where we can go…and feel comfortable."

Neci asked softly, "Where?"

"It's this club I go to on occasion. It has several dances floors, I know the owner…well actually I know a Richmond cop who works there sometimes. It's mostly a black club. With you being pretty much new in the area-"

"I'd stick out like a sore thumb, Marcus. I may be *half* African American, but you forget that I don't *look* the part."

"It's not like that, Neci. I was just trying to say that no one will recognize you. I really, really, *really* want to see you. *Please*?"

Neci yearned to see him again also. "Marcus…I can't make you any promises." She bit her lower lip then asked, "Where's this place…the club?"

Marcus was hopeful. "It's at West Broad and Laurel in Richmond. It's the Club Le Amour. We could meet there or I could pick you up somewhere. *Shoot*, I can even arrange for you to simply drive up front and one of the security men will park your car and bring you in to me."

"*Oh*? You have it like that, Marcus?"

"Yeah, I *got* it like that." Marcus joked smiling to himself.

"Make me feel like a movie star, huh?"

"Whatever it takes, Neci."

Neci then wondered about Marcus's intentions. "Meaning 'whatever it takes' to get me into bed?"

"Neci?"

"*Yes?*"

"You mean more to me than just sex. Having a good time and just hanging out with you is all I want, *honest.*"

Neci was touched and relieved by Marcus candor. "When and at what time?"

"How 'bout this Saturday? Umm…does eleven or midnight sound good?"

"Okay…I, I may meet you there…but if Gerard's here at the house…"

"I understand."

Neci said, "Marcus?"

"Yeah?"

"I can't promise you that I'll be there, please remember that. I may lose my nerve."

"Neci, I totally understand your situation, I just miss you like crazy."

Neci felt her stomach drop in both fear and excitement. "*God*, I…miss you too, Marcus. This is all just so…unbelievable, so sudden. You made me feel so good the other night…" Neci almost added that Marcus probably could have had his way with her…if he had pushed the issue…she thought against telling him that little secret. *It's been a long time since I've been that wet. Come to think of it, I don't know if I've ever been so excited, whoa!* Neci pushed the thought from her mind. She subconsciously took her hair out of its ponytail then started twirling some of the strands, feeling a sexual warmth spreading as she was powerless against pondering the haunting and powerful kiss.

Neci had not had sex since August; she was increasingly horny and almost yielded to her husband's advances the night before. Here she was a married woman who could not trust her own husband enough to have sex with him. *Married life's not supposed to be like this!* Neci thought in anger and frustration. Marcus was really making it difficult for her to stay faithful.

"...so keep that in mind for next week too. Okay, Neci?"

Neci was in such deep thought that she had tuned Marcus out completely. "I'm sorry, Marcus. What did you say?"

"Dag, you falling asleep on a brotha? Must be losing my skills. What were you thinking about just now?" Marcus teased.

Neci played with her hair trying to think of something to say other than the truth. "Oh, nothing, I was...trying to write that paper I told you about. I'm having trouble focusing."

"Okay, it's like that? Gonna keep secrets from me now? A paper got you that distracted?" Marcus continued to toy with her.

"You're *too* scary...you see right through me. But some secrets will stay just that - *secrets*." Neci laughed softly, loving that Marcus was so in tuned with her.

"Gawd, you have the sexiest laugh, not to mention that beautiful voice."

This man is making me sooooo wet. I've got to get off this phone! Neci said, "You're just trying to get into my panties. It takes more than flattery to undress me, Marcus." Neci could not believe what she just said. She sat with her mouth open in shock.

Marcus was caught off guard by the comment and took a few seconds to recover. "Okay? What *does it take* for me to get into your panties?" Marcus toyed with her a bit more.

Neci stroked her thick hair back from her forehead. "Trust. It takes *trust* to win me over." *Good answer, Neci.* She secretly congratulated herself. Neci was enjoying this sexual game of cat and mouse.

"Do you trust me, Neci?"

Without even having to think about it, which scared her somewhat, Neci responded softly, "Yes, Marcus. *Totally*." Neci felt liberated upon the unexpected revelation of having absolute trust in him.

Marcus almost did not hear the response because Neci spoke it so low. He had to swallow hard to keep from getting excited. Without warning, the door to the interrogation room opened, Eddie stood in the doorway holding paperwork.

"There you are! Jarvis told me he saw you duck in here - oh sorry, dude, didn't know you were on the phone." Eddie saw the cell to Marcus's ear. He then whispered, "Just had a question about the property sheet but catch me when you're done." Eddie shut the door leaving Marcus with his heart in his throat.

Marcus said quickly to Neci, "Hey look, sorry, I gotta go!" He snapped his phone shut thinking that that was a close call.

***

Neci stared at the handset perplexed. "*Huh*!" She slowly replaced the telephone on its receiver. Neci went back and sat before her computer. She would never be able to do any work on the paper tonight. The sexually stimulating conversation left her *hot*! Their banter and the long sexy kiss would dominate her thoughts for the rest of the evening. Neither sleep nor homework will be achieved. Meeting Marcus in some dimly lit club may not be a good idea. Plus the stress of getting caught was just too much. Despite those negative points, the prospect of his company was exhilarating. Neci headed upstairs to take matters in her own hands; then maybe sleep would come.

Chapter 23

Saturday night, early Sunday morning, the Club Le Amour was crowded as usual. Marcus looked at his watch for what felt like the one-hundredth time…1:05 a.m. He had been pacing the main lobby, which led to all of the multi-themed dance floors, since arriving at the popular entertainment spot well over three hours ago. The thumping music, though muted by the closed doors, gave him a headache.

Marcus had two major financial choices - one, purchase some much-needed groceries, or two, pay on the high remaining balance of his monthly Verizon telephone bill. He decided to do neither. Instead, Marcus chose to get a new wool suit for tonight's occasion. He was wearing a 3-piece burgundy suit, a matching open collared shirt, and black crocodile/alligator print shoes, all ordered from the *Steve Harvey Collection*. Sneak turned him on to the bargain purchase at Freeman's. He really wanted to impress Neci tonight, so living outside his means, just for tonight, was okay. Marcus took one last look around the vast lobby. He observed some of the patrons leaving as more began to crowd in.

Now resigned to the fact that Neci was a no-show, Marcus decided to head home and quickly remove the clothing. He did not want to sweat too much more in the suit because he hoped to return the items to the clothing store. The suit was not only too expensive but also too baggy for his taste.

Marcus started walking back through the crowded lobby. Before retrieving his car, he would double check with security to see if his date had somehow shown up without his noticing. He nearly made it out of the lobby before he ran into her, Tamala Cooper.

Tamala, carrying her coat, was accompanied by her tall friend Staci. Staci, wearing a black top and black leather pants with matching boots, was the first to speak.

"*Hello*, handsome." She stood back to admire his clothing. "Boy, you lookin' goooood in that *suit*...hot!" She exclaimed.

Marcus felt ill at the sight of the two, his stomach started to churn as he said, "Thanks, how y'all doing?"

Staci spoke up when she realized that Tamala was not going to talk to her ex-beau, "We doin' fine, Marcus."

Tamala looked just as uncomfortable as Marcus felt. She wore extremely tight black jeans, a red sweater, and black heels. She continued to stand silently, pretending to be checking out the crowd around them, as Staci continued to engage her ex-boyfriend in conversation.

"How you and Sneak doing?"

"His black-ass had to work tonight. 'Posed to meet us here later, but cancelled, so I'm gonna cancel the pussy allotment for this week too."

Marcus wanted to get out of this place but tried to remain composed. "Dag. You got my boy on an allotment, huh? That's *cold*, Staci."

"Not as cold as his bed's gonna be."

Finally Tamala, who looked everywhere but at Marcus, said, "Staci, let's go. Momma making me go to church with her in the morning." Tamala looked back toward the front entrance in hopes of escaping from this scene. She did not know how to handle seeing Marcus all dressed up and looking *extremely fine*.

"Okay, girl, *chill*, damn." Then Staci mouthed to Marcus, "She still loves you, Marcus."

Marcus was beginning to sweat. "Look…umm, I gotta go too. Nice seeing…umm, y'all. Tell Sneak long time no see, I've been too busy to get up with him."

"Okay, Marcus. We'll see ya."

Marcus, breathing a sigh of relief, quickly walked away toward the front entrance making his own escape. He was relieved to be free of the two young women who began putting their coats on to prepare to leave. That relief turned to shock when he saw Neci walk in through his escape route. She had yet to see Marcus as she stopped to remove her overcoat. Neci was the image of perfection, achingly and devastatingly beautiful. Men, and even some women, ogled the striking woman.

Neci wore a skintight black mini-dress and carried a black and silver clutch. The garment showed off her shapely muscular thighs and that hourglass figure. The dress was covered with silver glittery swirls, and the small garment's thin straps tied over each firm, tanned shoulder. The top was cut not only to push up her firm round breasts, but it was also made to highlight that anatomy. Her black and silver heels firmed up her taut calf muscles, making her smooth legs appear longer than they actually were. Her jet-black wavy hair flowed down her back. She had the thick hair combed over to the right leaving a part on the left topside. Upon seeing Marcus staring greedily at her, Neci's model-like oval face lit up as those red full moist lips smiled in a greeting.

Marcus stood frozen in the middle of the lobby with people walking in and out the club, in both fear and excitement. In front of him, with her radiant smile, was the most attractive woman he had ever seen. Behind him was his ex-girlfriend and her crazy hot-tempered friend.   He realized that he had two choices: he could walk over and welcome his date thus unleashing the ghetto twins, or simply walk out of the building ignoring Neci and lose her forever. Marcus thought, *maybe a third option could be to grab Neci and run like hell!* Knowing that the latter would not work, he made his decision.

Marcus slowly walked toward the beauty.

When he stood before her just to the side of one of the front doors, Neci said shyly, "Sorry I'm late, Marcus. Things got…complicated at home."

Marcus was still mesmerized as he grabbed Neci's right hand and kissed it. "First of all, you look, *delicious*! There are no other words to describe you." That made Neci melt inside; she almost cried before this handsome gentleman. "And now for less pleasant matters, what happened at home?"

"Oh for the first time in weeks, Gerard suddenly decided to stay home on a Saturday night. I almost didn't come but told him to watch the boys while I went out for a change! Marcus, we got into a *huge* argument; I came close to calling the police. Wouldn't that have been great, the cops at our home. Anyway, he finally calmed down and here I am." She spread her arms wide reinforcing her latter comment.

Marcus took her coat and said in a sincere sexy voice, "Yes, indeed; here you are."

Neci discreetly covered her mouth as she giggled, "Marcus, stop leering at me. You're making me self-con-"

"Wanna introduce your *friend*?"

Marcus almost forgot about Tamala and Staci behind them. He was very surprised that Tamala's voice was the one behind him. He turned trying to think of how he was going to handle this. He then stepped back to allow a proper introduction between the three women.

He looked over at Neci to his right and noticed her angst, but proceeded with the introductions anyway, "Neci, this is Tam, *Tamala* and her *pal*, Staci." He then looked over at the two women on his left, "Tamala and Staci, this is a very good friend of mine, Neci."

Neci recognized Marcus's former girlfriend's name. She suddenly became guarded but spoke cheerfully to the women who in turn ignored her. Both Tamala and Staci looked back and forth between Marcus and Neci as if expecting further clarification from Marcus as to his relationship with this woman. Then *something* caught Tamala's fault-finding eyes.

"Who this white *bitch* steppin' out on?" Tamala accused as she pointed toward Neci's left ring finger adorned with a gold wedding ring set. Tamala continued, "Ya ass gotta be steppin' out on somebody!"

Neci's dark eyes first grew wide then narrowed in caution as she stared down the short, freckle-faced woman. Neci never said a word but stood her ground.

Marcus was furious. "Oh, *now* you can talk, Tam? A few minutes ago you couldn't even say a simple hello to me, now you up in my business."

Tamala stared at Marcus, "Hell *yeah*, motherfucka! Bringin' this white 'ho' up in here disrespectin' black women! *What*...you couldn't find no black woman, Marcus?! Least I can deal with *that* shit." Tamala then looked Neci up and down. "But you got some nerve bringin' this *white* bitch up in here! Fuck! You know this is one of my clubbin' spots!"

Marcus thought, *black women love using that worn out racial argument when they see a brotha with someone other than a sista.*

Staci with her hands on her hips said to Tamala, "Tell 'im, girl." Then to Marcus, "Got *some* fuckin' nerve, Marcus." Now Staci tried to stare Neci down as she asked with a serious neck-roll, "That a weave in yo' hair, white girl?! 'Cause I know hair - looks like a weave to *me*!"

Neci said calmly to Marcus but kept her eyes on the two agitated women, "Marcus give me my coat. I'm leaving."

"But-but…Neci, don't pay them no-"

"*Give* me my *damn* coat, Marcus!"

Staci said, "Oh naw she didn't!"

Marcus complied with Neci's request and handed over the coat.

Neci knew better than to put on her coat in the midst of these crazy women. Past experience had taught her that these women were the type that would jump you while being defenseless when putting one's coat on. When she was growing up, Neci was constantly fending off jealous females who hated her because they claimed Neci thought she looked better than them, or acted if she was better than them. Throughout high school, she was always having to prove herself as "normal." As a result, she had never felt part of any one race, group, or clique; no one welcomed her. Loneliness was a way of life for her. Neci's exotic beauty, mature manner, and superior intelligence set her apart in school; her female peers hated her for the most part. She was forced into fighting them; this was the only way to prove herself worthy or to gain respect. Trying to gain normality in her young life was a constant.

Now even in adulthood, she had to protect herself just because of being what she was - her true self. Neci knew all the tricks of dirty fighting so she walked out slowly carrying her coat, still watching the angry women.

Staci continued to stand behind Tamala as she said, "Yeah, ya better leave, *bitch*! Go'n back to the white part of town!"

Marcus stared in sadness as Neci disappeared through the front doors. He immediately turned toward the women, infuriated. "Y'all are two of the most *ignorant, ghetto bitches*, I've ever met! Y'all need to fucking *grow up*! Goddamn you, Tam! You fucked up *my* life! *You* started this shit." He then pointed his finger in her face. "I was nothing but good to you, and you *fuck* some drug dealing *faggot* behind my back. I fuckin' hate you for that! Fuckin' *hate* you, Tam!" Tamala was taken aback.

Marcus glared at Staci who was equally afraid of the man's outburst, only because Tamala shared with Staci her fears about Marcus possibly hurting Tamala someday. "And *you*…fucking my friend, Sneak! Knowing full well your ass has a boyfriend, cheating your *damn* self! So I got a right to see or *fuck* anyone I want, married or not!" He pointed at Staci. "*Fuck you*!" Marcus then pointed his finger back at Tamala. "*and fuck you, Tam!*" Marcus turned and stormed out of the club, just as security was running in, leaving both Tamala and Staci stunned.

***

Marcus searched the sidewalks around the massive club, knowing that security could not have retrieved Neci's SUV that quickly. Then it occurred to him that maybe she had parked on a side street and had not taken advantage of the valet parking offered by him. If that was the case, Neci could be anywhere at that moment.

On a hunch, Marcus ran toward the corners of Broad and Laurel Streets. Once at the corner, he sprinted south down Laurel Street in hopes of finding Neci.

Marcus was frantically searching for the offended woman. Finally at North Laurel Street and West Grace Street, he looked up and down Grace Street, but saw no one fitting Neci's description. He rubbed his face in frustration then whispered, "I've got to find her."

Marcus jogged further down Laurel Street as his rapid breath was visible in the cold of the mid-November night. When he reached West Franklin Street on the outskirts of the open campus of Virginia Commonwealth University where Neci was working on her master's degree, he searched up and down that roadway - no Neci. Empty cars belonging to students and patrons of the surrounding clubs lined both sides of the narrow two-lane street.

As the chilly air stung his face and lungs, he continued his futile search, glancing across the one-way street toward Monroe Park which was partially cloaked in darkness. The bare trees gave the park a Gothic or haunted look and feel. A feeling of impending dread filled Marcus. He shrugged off the strong emotion to focus. Neci had to be close.

A few cars drove by as Marcus slowly scanned right in the direction of the Cathedral of the Sacred Heart, Grace and Holy Trinity Church, Richmond's Landmark Theatre, and other buildings which sat deserted this time of night. No foot or vehicle traffic in that direction either. He reached for his cell phone then remembered he did not have it on him. It would not have been of much use anyway because he never got Neci's cellular number. With a heavy frustrated sigh, Marcus turned around to walk back to the club, but something caught his eye.

A dome light was turned on inside of one of the vehicles parked in the front of a row of tall buildings, VCU coed dormitories, along the left side of West Franklin Street. Marcus could not make out the type of vehicle because several other parked cars partially blocked it from his view. He was hopeful as he began walking east on Franklin Street, a half block away from Laurel. The streetlights reflected dimly on the familiar vehicle.

"*Thank you*, God." Marcus could barely believe his luck when he saw the rear end of the light gray late model Cadillac Escalade SUV, Neci's vehicle. As he slowly walked toward the driver's side window, Marcus could now see her behind the steering wheel, under the dome light, wiping tears from her mascara-covered face. Neci was apparently trying to catch her breath due to running all the way to her vehicle. Marcus thought, *Damn, Neci, you faster than Gail Devers!* Though only a couple of blocks from the club, the trek was a *long* couple of blocks.

Marcus knocked on the window, as lightly as possible, hoping not to startle her. "Neci?"

Upon seeing the bald man in the nice burgundy suit, Neci yelled through the closed window, "*Go* away, Marcus! Stay away from me!" She started the SUV.

"*Wait*!" Marcus opened up the driver's door. "*Please*, Neci, let's talk this out."

Neci blew her nose into a tissue then said, "Leave *me* alone, Marcus! GO AWAY!"

Marcus said softly, "That was a bad scene back there."

"NO SHIT! Marcus, please go! Just leave me alone!" Neci tried to pull the door shut. "*Move!*" She was becoming hysterical.

Marcus blocked the door with his body. "You're too upset to drive. Let's just talk, okay?"

"Talk about what, Marcus?! Maybe discuss how you let those women talk to me like that?! You just *stood* there, didn't say a damn word!"

"It, it just happened so fast. I had no idea they were there…I, I should've known better than to meet you at the club. I'm sorry I put you in that position, Neci."

"Yeah?! Well, I'm sorry too, Marcus!"

"Neci, look please just calm down…you're upset."

"You damn right I'm upset! I'm upset with those girls back there, trying to judge me! I'm upset because Gerard put me in this predicament! I'm upset with you for making me *want* you! And, and…!" Neci was trying to hold back additional tears then said softly, "Most of all…I'm upset with myself…because… because I know better. I should've never come here tonight. Please get away from my car. I'm going home to my family, where I belong."

Marcus felt that he was losing Neci even before he ever had her. "Look, Neci, I'm sorry, please tell me what you want."

Once again, Neci blew her nose then looked at him. After a thoughtful pause and a sarcastic laugh, she said pensively, "Marcus, I obviously don't know what the hell I want." Shaking her head, frowning, she continued, "This would've never worked, you and me. Can't you see that *now*?"

Neci gave a long sigh, "You're a handsome, intelligent, and sexy man. Marcus, you're a perfect gentleman, everything I need and want in a man. But…but the fact is that…I'm *married*, happy or not, to Gerard…and I have two precious boys. I, I don't know what I was thinking…I just don't know." She then said with stark finality, "Goodbye, Marcus."

With slumped shoulders, Marcus pleaded, on the verge of tears himself, "Don't you *deserve* happiness, Neci?! You deserve *love* and happiness! I have all that and more to offer! You can't leave me! *Please* don't go! God, you just don't know how much I *need* you, don't *go*!" He stood there looking haggard with his arms stretched out wide almost if he expected her to run to the safety of his embrace. Marcus whispered shaking his head, "It can't…can't end like this, *not* like this, Neci. Give me a chance to make you happy, even if just for a little while." Marcus swallowed back tears.

Marcus's words had a profound effect as Neci's frown quickly faded. She was deeply touched by his fervor. Her shiny dark eyes searched him closely. Upon seeing the desperate and defeated expression on Marcus's face, as if his survival depended upon her very existence, she was finally overcome with compassion for this man. She could not help but to soften for a man to whom she should have never opened her heart. At that very moment, Neci wanted Marcus more than ever.

Neci sighed then turned up the heater in the SUV, and said sympathetically, "Get in, Marcus. It's freezing out there."

***

"So that's what you've been dealing with the last two years, from her?"

Marcus thought for a moment. "It wasn't all bad; Tam and I've had our good and bad moments, just like any other couple."

Neci and Marcus were walking along the Canal Walk near Brown's Island, which was a buzz of activity during the hot summer weather but now a cold and desolate concrete canal front this time of year. The canal was made up of a series of steps, iron railings, barred gates, and walls. The top portion of the walls, containing the narrow strip of water in between, acted as walkways. The stretch of the Canal Walk, well over a mile, had become a poplar attraction for tourists and natives alike. Now, the well-lit concrete walkways contained the almost motionless dark and chilly waters which eventually led into the vast James River.

A few minutes earlier, after Marcus got into Neci's SUV, she drove them around aimlessly, neither one of them saying a word, each in their own private thoughts. When the SUV turned onto East Byrd Street, passing the River Front Plaza, Marcus asked Neci to make a right leading to Haxall Point. He then directed her to park the large SUV in a small parking area just off Haxall Point, across from the canal.

Now under the pale moon as Marcus and Neci continued their walk side by side, they finshed their discussion about the night's episode with Tamala and Staci.

Neci interlaced her arm into Marcus's. "What attracted you to her?"

Marcus enjoyed feeling the warmth of Neci body close to him. "In the beginning, we seemed to have similar interests." Marcus then smiled as he continued, "Would you believe that I met her on a traffic stop? Humph, even wrote her a summons."

Neci looked over at him earnestly and then asked, "Do you still love her?"

Marcus paused for a second. "I guess on some level I still care about Tam, but in love? I can honestly say that she has killed those feelings."

Neci stopped walking grabbed Marcus's arm tighter. "Good."

Marcus looked down at her as he questioned, " '*Good*'?"

Neci smiled intimately up at Marcus then said, "I could never consider allowing you inside of me if you still had *loving* feelings for another woman." She then thought, *Okay Neci, where did that come from? Slow down!*

It took a few moments for Marcus to process what was just said. He finally replied in shock, "Okay."

Neci tactfully and quickly changed the subject, "It's really cold out here." She began rubbing her arms due to unwisely leaving her coat behind.

"*See*, told you to grab your coat." Marcus, doing what any real man would do, took off his suit jacket and draped it over the woman's shoulders similar to the night of the police officers' dance.

Marcus now facing her, asked, "How's that?"

"Well, it would be even better if maybe you could kiss me, Marcus." Neci continued shyly, "That'll probably warm me up a little."

Without hesitation, Marcus pulled the petite woman into his arms, kissing her as if it would be the last time. Their lips melted together instantly much like the kiss of old lovers rather than a couple just learning each other. Marcus's suit coat fell onto the cold concrete. He felt the stretchy material of Neci's dress in the palm of his hands as his excitement grew. He could feel the curves of her hips, her taut buttocks, and then the arch of her back. Marcus moved his hands up and began to caress her long, thick, heavy hair; it was fragrant and soft to the touch. For both, this kiss was more intense and passionate than the one shared on the night of the dance.

***

Minutes later Neci said as she caught her breath, "See? I'm…not so…cold anymore."

"Good."

As Neci continued to be held by Marcus, feeling his manhood growing against her, she said, "We better get back. Gerard's already furious over me leaving tonight. Staying out *all* night will just make matters worse."

Marcus looked into her eyes as the water in the canal reflected in her dark orbs. "Want me to follow you home…make sure he don't do nothing stupid?"

Neci searched his face for sincerity. "You'd do that for me, wouldn't you?"

Marcus whispered, "I'd do *anything* for you, Neci."

Neci was suddenly dizzy with excitement and enchantment. It was a good thing Marcus was still holding her or she would have fallen. "You sure know how to sweep a woman off her feet."

"When can I see you again, Beautiful?"

"Marcus, you've got me in a trance right now. But…uhh…I, we're going away next week for Thanksgiving, to California. We leave early Monday morning, even got someone to cover my classes for the short week. I'm sure Gerard told you we're visiting his parents. Then for Christmas, if he can get off, we're going to visit my parents in Texas. Doesn't seem to be enough time to…" *Time for what?* Neci thought.

Marcus felt a sudden sadness then responded, "Yeah he did tell me that y'all were going away for turkey day weeks ago, but I forgot."

Neci saw the sadness in his eyes then said reassuringly, "I'd love to see you when I get back, maybe meet somewhere for lunch. We're returning next Sunday. How about that Monday after?"

Thinking about Neci being gone for a whole week *and* Christmas depressed Marcus, so he rebounded, "Instead of lunch, how 'bout breakfast and lunch at my place. Skip school that whole day; let me pamper you."

Neci became a little nervous. She loved the sexual thrill that she felt when she was with Marcus but the concept of actually being intimate with him, Neci could not grasp. Maybe it was too soon, if ever. "Whoa, we'll be taking a big chance meeting at your place, wouldn't we? With Gerard knowing where you live, maybe that wouldn't be such a good idea."

Marcus reluctantly agreed. The apprehension in Neci's body language and her voice did not go unnoticed. She was developing cold feet. Making her comfortable was the key. "We'll take it slow, go at your pace. No pressure. You call me when you can get free, okay?"

"Okay…" She wanted to say more but nothing came to mind.

Neci gently released herself from Marcus's warm arms. "I'd better get home. Need to get back home before Gerard gets suspicious. I'll drive you back to the club to get your car."

"Yeah, sure. I'm going to miss you, girl. Wish I could see you before you leave for Cali." Marcus also wished that he could freeze this moment in time, basking in her presence.

"Would be nice." Neci tiptoed slightly, despite having on heels, and kissed him lightly on the lips. "Going to miss you, too."

"Take this with you, Neci." Marcus stooped slightly, placed his hands on both sides of her face, and then gently kissed her forehead.

Neci feeling warm tingles throughout her body said, "Wow. I love that, when you kiss me there. Seems *so*…special…*so* intimate."

"Just a kiss for your soul. Enjoy your trip, but come back safely to me."

"I will, Marcus."

Marcus picked up his coat and then gently draped it back around her shoulders. He took her hand as they walked back to the SUV with hopes of seeing one another immediately after the upcoming holidays. Thanksgiving and Christmas came and went. Neci and Marcus were both miserable having not found the time to see each other. As the New Year approached, they wondered if being together would ever happen.

Chapter 24

Marcus was sitting on his couch in front of the TV sulking as usual, this time at the prospect of facing the New Year alone. Last year this same time he was contemplating the proposal of marriage to Tamala; now, he had finally accepted losing her to another man. As he channel-surfed, he thought how pathetic his life had become. Marcus went from the possibility of being happily married to chasing another man's wife. He also continued to struggle with T. C.'s death and his murderer's escape. Sneak called earlier wanting to know the scoop on the married white girl that Marcus brought to the club. Marcus refused to talk about it. Marcus was sick with not being able to see Neci.

Marcus sighed in annoyance as the phone rang next to him.

"Hello,"

"El está loco, ¡Marcus! ¡Tirando cosas-destruyendo la casa! Los niños están

llorando-él está borracho, ¡Marcus! ¡Estamos encerrados en el cuarto! ¡El va a tumbar la puerta! ¡Ven a ayudarnos!"

The female voice boomed into Marcus's ear as he heard muffled yelling, banging noises, and crying in the background, he asked, "Who is *this*?! I can't understand you." After a split second, Marcus recognized the frantic voice. "*Neci*? What's wrong? *Slow down*! Speak English!"

Neci was huddled in Juny's and Karl's room with them beside her in the closet. The closet door was open but the door to the room was closed and locked, as Eddie continued to yell for her to 'open the fucking door.'

Neci had no idea that she had just spoken Spanish. She tried collecting herself as best she could but continued to shake in fear. "Gerard's lost it!" Neci's emotions overtook her again, *"He's been drinking all day, Marcus! We're locked in the boys' room, so he can't get to us, but he keeps saying he's going to kick the door open! Please!"*

"Neci, you've *got* to calm down!"

"Help us! He'll listen to you! I don't want to call the police! He'll lose his job! Please come now!"

"Alright, alright, Neci! But look, if he gets in there, call 9-1-1 anyway, *okay*?"

"Yes, just hurry!"

Marcus slammed the phone down then ran into his bedroom to get dressed.

***

Thirty minutes after traveling at breakneck speed, Marcus finally slid the Camry to a stop in the backyard of 4350 Cutler Road at 10:20 p.m. He ran to the patio doors and of course found that they were locked. Marcus went to the front door and began ringing the doorbell. After a few seconds he got no response, so he banged on the door. Earlier, Marcus tried to contact Neci from his cell phone several times, but he only got a busy signal which was a bad sign.

The front door swung open. Eddie stood there, shirt unbuttoned, wearing a pair of tan dockers, with a vacant drunk look. "Who the fuck's at my door?!" the hairy-chested drunk yelled.

Marcus remained calm though he wanted to pounce on his partner as he said, "Hey, Eddie. What's going on? I was in the neighborhood and thought I'd drop by. Can I come in, man?"

Marcus stood there in the darkness as Eddie frowned trying to identify his caller. Eddie began to look calmer, but was extremely intoxicated, as recognition showed upon his face. "Yooooo, Marcus! Dude, *clome* in!" Eddie staggered back to allow Marcus access into the house.

Marcus shut the door behind him and stood in the foyer as he asked, "Is everything alright, Eddie?"

Eddie, with his blond hair in disarray, stood swaying from side to side. "I'm *dwunk*, again!"

Marcus glanced around. He saw that holes were in the plaster of the walls going up along the stairs, a sign of Eddie's rage. "What happened to the walls, Eddie? Where're the children and your wife?"

"I'm dwunk, Marcus."

Marcus, trying to be patient, asked again, "Where's Neci and the kids?"

"I'm dwunk as hell, partner." Eddie wobbled in place, appearing ready to pass out.

Marcus was losing his cool. "*Eddie*, don't make me ask you again. Where's your family?!"

Eddie stood tall then barked, "Don't come in my house, *my house*! Don't push me around! I'm in charge! This is *my* house, partner!"

Marcus walked up to Eddie and stood nose-to-nose with him, repulsed by the strong stench of stale alcohol on Eddie's breath. Marcus said, threatening, "Eddie, just give me a reason to clock your ass! Answer *me, goddamn it*! Where's Neci?!"

"Marcus?" Neci hesitantly walked down the stairs toward the men. She had most of her hair pinned up with a few loose strands along the sides of her head. Neci had on a long white silk robe. "I think it's okay now." She then turned her attention to her husband, "Gerard, everything's okay, right?"

Eddie looked from Marcus then toward his wife. "I'm sorry...too much to dwink." He focused his attention back to Marcus. "I'm sorry, dude. So much is going on." Eddie suddenly thought about Kimberly Thatcher and his ailing back. "The pain just won't go...won't go away, Marcus." With that, Eddie lowered his head and started to sob.

"Marcus?"

Marcus answered Neci but kept his eyes cautiously on Eddie, "Yeah?"

"Can you help him upstairs?"

Marcus just stood there staring at his partner with caution and pity.

Neci pleaded, "Marcus, *please*?"

Marcus glanced up at Neci then back at her crying husband, and sighed, "*Come* on, Eddie. Time to sleep it off." He grabbed Eddie by his arm and escorted the sobbing man upstairs to the master bedroom at Neci's instruction.

Eddie allowed Marcus to guide him. "I'm sorry, Marcus. I'm so sorry."

 "I know, dawg. Come on, watch your step. Time to go night-night."

***

Several minutes later, Neci and Marcus sat side by side on the flight of stairs; they were on the landing closest to the living room. Neci explained wearily as she looked down at her hands resting on her lap. "He came in ranting and raving about *something*, I couldn't understand him. Gerard just went *crazy*, scared the boys to death. He went into their room and woke them up. Marcus, he was yelling at them about not picking up their toys in the great room." She then glanced over at Marcus sitting to her left, "He was literally drunk out of his mind." Marcus listened with grave concern.

"During Christmas, we didn't have such a good visit with my parents, much like Thanksgiving with *his* parents; most of his drinking stems from that visit. Anyway, my father gave Gerard a hard time. I *hate* my father sometimes. He knows how Gerard's family treats us. Despite that, he turns around and treats Gerard the same way. Daddy acts like Gerard's not good enough for me. Sometimes he's no better than Gerard's parents. Since we got back two nights ago, Gerard's drinking has gotten worse. Tonight after I tried to stop him from bothering the boys, he started in on me in the hallway near their room. He got so out of control. Anyway, Juny and Karl eventually went back to bed. I didn't come out of their bedroom until I heard you downstairs. I'm tired of living like this, Marcus. Just *sick* and tired. *Look* at the holes in my walls!" Neci gave a great sigh.

Marcus waited a moment to make sure she had finished before he said, "I tried calling you and got no answer."

"The phone's probably off the hook."

It was then that Marcus noticed a small red mark on the left side of Neci's cheek. "Did he *hit* you?!" Marcus touched the spot and Neci flinched.

"I'm okay. I know it sounded a lot worse over the phone but really this was an aberration on Gerard's part. He's not really the violent type; he's usually very sweet and calm-natured."

Marcus stood up with the intent to confront the now-sleeping Eddie; he wanted to give him a lesson on how to properly treat a lady.

Neci gently pulled Marcus by his hand, causing him to sit back down.

"It's *okay*, Marcus. *I'm fine*."

"Eddie hit you!" Marcus stated the fact.

"Marcus, it was *inadvertent*, I'm sure. Now please just calm down. I'm *okay*, and the boys are *fine*, they're asleep now. All is well with the Logans."

Marcus brushed her hair back gently, revealing the entire left side of her beautiful face. Neci turned her head to gaze at him as she said with a tender smile, "By the way, Happy New Year, Marcus." She desperately wanted to change the subject.

Marcus leaned in toward her and lightly kissed her forehead then kissed the small bruise on her left cheek. He was surprised at what he now saw on her face; the confused, scared, and slightly bewildered look vanished from her eyes. It was replaced by sultriness. Neci slid closer to Marcus and began kissing him fully as if trying to satisfy a hunger. Suddenly, she stopped. Neci stared intensely at Marcus for several seconds as if trying to come to some sort of decision.

Neci said, "I'll be back in a minute or two. Please don't leave."

Before Marcus could respond, Neci went up the remaining flight of stairs to the top floor. He saw her turn right disappearing from his view. Shortly after, he heard water running. It sounded to Marcus to be coming from the shower in the hallway bathroom.

***

Much later after he heard the shower stop, a perplexed Marcus heard Neci walking back down the hall then saw her walk into the master bedroom where Eddie was sleeping.

Neci was still wearing the white silk robe, but now freshly showered, emerged walking back down the stairs and grabbed Marcus by his hand. "I had to check in on the boys. Come with me; I've got a surprise for you," she said breathlessly.

Neci led Marcus downstairs to the familiar hallway passing the laundry room, and game room. Neci turned on the light after they entered the spare bedroom across the hall from the half bathroom. She then shut the door and walked a shocked Marcus to the full size bed which contained four small pillows, tan sheets, and a brown comforter.

Marcus remembered the room from his last visit, the day Eddie almost caught him slobbering down Neci. The same old wooden desk covered with a typewriter and a slew of papers, a chest of drawers, and the small closet without a door were highlights of the small cluttered room with beige carpeting. A few lackluster paintings covered the beige colored walls. An old wooden cuckoo clock, which still worked but lost its *cuckoo*, hung on the wall facing the bed. Neci released Marcus's hand then went to the closet and retrieved a medium-sized cardboard box. She opened the box and began taking out the contents - various-sized colored candles. Neci started placing the candles in different locations around the room. After setting one down, she lit each with a yellow bic lighter.

When Neci finished the task, she told Marcus as she pointed to the wall at the right of the door, "Turn off the lights please."

Marcus complied and the tiny bedroom was filled with an abundance of glowing and flickering lights making the room very cozy and intimate. The room began to fill with a variety of pleasant scents that Marcus did not recognize.

"Nice, huh?" Before Marcus could reply, Neci said with elation, "Now for my surprise." Neci went back to the closet and picked up something from the back of the cluttered top shelf. She came back and faced Marcus then handed him a small box wrapped in shiny green paper and topped with a red bow. "Merry Christmas, Marcus."

Marcus looked at the wrapped gift not knowing what to do with it. "Neci..." He then glanced up at her. Neci was smiling as the candle light reflected in her dark eyes. "I can't accept this. I didn't even give you a birthday gift let alone something for Christmas."

Neci giggled then said, "Stop being silly and just open it."

Marcus sighed in embarrassment because he felt inept in not reciprocating the kind gesture. The top of the wrapped box could be lifted without tearing off the wrapping. Marcus opened it to reveal white tissue paper which concealed the contents. Upon lifting the paper, he discovered a polished thick gold chain - a man's bracelet. He took the gift from the box and saw a small charm dangling from the bracelet - a tiny gold puffed heart charm. Marcus stood there watching the candlelight reflect from the gold heart as it swung from side to side.

Neci, smiling widely, enjoyed the mesmerizing look in Marcus's eyes. "You like?"

"Wow..." Marcus finished as he looked at Neci, "...it's beautiful."

Neci said very softly, as she gave him a heartfelt expression, "I've just given you *my* heart, Marcus. Please take care of it."

As Marcus looked at the beautiful woman, he said, "I will."

"Promise?"

Marcus nodded his head, "Yes, Neci. I promise."

Neci, satisfied with Marcus's answer, said, "Great!"

Marcus placed the bracelet and attached pendant on his left wrist. "I'll keep it close to me, always." He laid the empty gift box on the small nightstand next to the bed then walked closer to Neci kissing her on the forehead.

Neci sighed and said softly, "I love it when you do that, Marcus. It makes me feel so special."

"Because you *are* special, Neci."

Neci gave Marcus a long lingering look then slowly stepped away. She dropped the lighter into the empty cardboard box which had contained the assortment of candles, then lifted the box off the bed placing it back in the bottom of the closet. She walked back and stood a few feet from him with a serious look on her face.

"I've been a devoted wife, been both faithful and loving to Gerard during our years of marriage. However, I've got nothing to show for my devotion to my husband other than misery and heartache. I can't begin to share with you the hell Gerard has put me through."

Neci sighed as she continued, "For once in my life I, I *do* want to be happy. I want to feel loved, even if it *is* only for one night." She crossed her arms over her body, holding herself.

Marcus slowly stepped closer to Neci. He could smell the flowery scent of shower gel upon her body. He took hold of both her hands and looked deeply into her eyes then asked softly, "You sure about this?"

Neci smiled nervously shook her head. "No…I'm not."

Both Neci and Marcus shared a small chuckle at the straightforward reply.

Marcus unpinned Neci's hair and allowed it to fall freely upon her shoulders. He then said tenderly and confidently, "You're right. It's about time that you experience some happiness, Neci. Tonight it's *my* job to ensure that you do." Keeping his eyes on hers, Marcus undid the silk belt on Neci's robe then gently opened the garment and slid it off, allowing it to fall silently to the carpet.

When Marcus stepped back to admire Neci, who wore a matching set of white silk bra and panties, she subconsciously crossed her arms in front of her lower torso. The experience of having two children left Neci with a few stretch marks and a slight belly bulge. The subtle pooch, along her otherwise flat abdomen, persisted no matter how much she dieted or exercised. A faint transverse scar, from the cesarean section performed in order to deliver her son, Juny, could be seen just above the low cut front of Neci's panties. But Marcus noticed none of those flaws due to the dangling jewelry, a piercing which extended out from the skin fold at the top of Neci's navel and past that bellybutton.

The gold jewelry sparkled as Marcus knelt down to examine it in the dim candlelight. "This is sexy, Neci. I would've never guessed you had one of these." He gently moved her arms for a closer look. Six gold beads hung vertically, all had a precious stone attached which faced out. The top bead of the jewelry, which was attached to the top of the navel, was adorned with a diamond. The piercing extended along a gold curved bar revealing the remaining connected five gold beads, which pointed down toward Neci's panties. Four of the beads were also decorated with various-sized diamonds with the last bead containing a pink sapphire. Neci recently purchased the jewelry from BellyBella of Beverly Hills, a Christmas and birthday gift to herself. Belly-rings were something that Neci wore to detract from her flaws, especially during beach season.

Neci looked down to watch Marcus inspect the jewelry. She could feel his hot breath on the crotch of her panties and his large hands on her hips. Her eyelids fluttered when she felt a tingle between her legs; dampness began to spread there. Marcus, seeming to sense Neci's excitement, gently kissed her stomach.

Neci sighed as her heart rate tripled as she began to feel weak in the knees.

Marcus kissed her much lower, at the crotch of her panties. He felt the soft smooth fabric with his lips and tongue.

Neci closed her eyes as her entire body tingled with pleasure, the exhilarating feeling of Marcus rubbing against her sensitivity was almost enough to make her climax. If he kept it up, Neci may very well release her mounting pleasure. His large hands stroked her slowly from her hips down to her shapely legs. She wanted to grab his head and gyrate into him, but she desperately resisted the growing urge, trying to maintain control.

Marcus could smell the familiar sexual scent radiating from Neci's panties as he also felt the warmth and softness of her smooth skin with his hands. He began kissing her up toward the belly jewelry, where he took the two-thousand-dollar body art gently into his mouth. He slowly sucked the entire piece of jewelry into his mouth as his lips then pressed against her stomach. Marcus surprised her when he inserted his tongue into the hollow of her navel.

Neci felt the tongue and Marcus's hot breath along with the gentle but sensitive tug upon her navel, giving her a sexually intense feeling never experienced from this part of her body. Her nipples rose to attention as she placed her hands behind Marcus's baldpate, guiding him deeper into this sexually unexplored area.

"Ooooh, Marcus…mmm…oooh, baby," Neci hissed.

The more Marcus sucked upon the piercing the more Neci moaned with pleasure. The very act left her lightheaded, woozy, but extremely turned on, uninhibited even. The only sounds in the house were the heavy breathing of ecstasy from the forbidden lovers and the ticking of the cuckoo clock.

Marcus slowly stood up, displaying his own sexual excitement through his baggy jeans, then said seductively, "Tonight's all about *you*. In line with my official police duties, which are to protect and to serve, I've already protected you tonight. Now it's time for me to *service* you, Neci."

With that said, Marcus tongued Neci down hungrily, and she kissed him back with equal intensity. He then scooped her up into his strong and powerful arms placing her on the bed as they gazed intensely into each other's eyes. Marcus indeed had plans to please Neci unto satiability, *Kama Sutra* was about to be unleashed upon the wife of another.

Chapter 25

Tamala laid comfortably in a set of pink pajamas on her new living room couch. Tonight, the newly-purchased, large Sony plasma TV was on. Tamala appeared to be looking through the TV rather than at it. She was deep in thought as she slowly looked around the apartment, a complete transformation of its former self. Brand new leather furniture, a few new appliances, lamps, a surround sound system, electronics, game consoles, African art and artifacts, and new bedroom furniture in both bedrooms, adorned the apartment. She also had enough clothing to wear once for each day of the New Year.

Lamar had completely accessorized Tamala's home over the past few months. He had all but moved in; most of his time was now spent in Henrico with her. Tamala was not a woman without common sense. She had known for some time that her mysterious boyfriend could not afford such luxuries on a mere janitor's salary. Even the materialistic Tamala drew the line at obtaining things by illegal means. Off and on, Tamala had been pondering Marcus's accusations against Lamar, that he was a drug dealer.

Lamar's temper was also of concern; he showed fits of rage not toward her really, but at the equally-mysterious thuggish people he dealt with. The whispered telephone calls, extended errands for days and even weeks at a time, secretive meeting spots, and lots and lots of money, all those things solidified Marcus's allegations. On top of all of that, Tamala heard that Lamar had a baby by some woman in Petersburg. Tamala suspected that the young woman who confronted her on Harding Street last summer was the mother of Lamar's child. The red warning flags had been up and flying for a while, but largely ignored by Tamala, at least until now.

Tamala was on a mission tonight. She waited patiently for weeks to take advantage of one of Lamar's absences. When the moment came a few minutes ago, Lamar claimed that he needed to make a quick 'run'. Tamala received a kiss from him then began to ponder where to look for his stash as he made his way out of the door.

Now as Tamala proceeded to get up from the tan leather couch with its rich new smell, she believed that Lamar was hiding his wares in the back bedroom which was unused. *That's the most logical place for that nigga to hide his shit*, Tamala thought. She turned on the light in the smaller of the two bedrooms. Tamala stood in the doorway, searching, scanning, looking, and thinking. She went to the closet. She opened the double sliding doors to reveal many boxes of men's athletic shoes, sweat suits, and clothing for the club scene. On hands and knees, Tamala began rummaging through the numerous sneaker boxes. Years ago, Tamala saw a movie about a drug dealer who made so much money that he hid his cash and drugs in his shoe boxes. After minutes of sweat, her search was futile even after searching the tennis shoes themselves. *Maybe he respects me enough to keep his shit at his momma's house*, Tamala thought as she stood up before the closet with its doors wide open.

Tamala looked around trying to think of where someone would hide something of value, something that they did not want found. She eyed the closet again then wondered if Lamar would hide drugs in the abundance of clothing items hanging in there. She did not think so as the distant sounds from the TV drifted in from the front of the apartment. Her eyes then went to the bed. *Maybe under the fuckin' mattress or underneath the bed?* she pondered. Tamala walked over to the bed and knelt down to peek underneath. She saw nothing out of the ordinary. Just as she was about to stand, Tamala saw the silver serrated metal box with a metal handle on the top.

"Now that was not here before we got all this new shit. Fuckin' nigga better not be hidin' drugs in my house! I'm not catchin' a charge behind *no* motherfucka, you better believe that shit!" Tamala was angry as she reached for the metal box and pulled it out into the light. The medium-sized toolbox-like container had a small master lock in the hasp. "Fuck! How am I gonna get into this bitch?" She scratched her head and looked about the room.

Tamala got up leaving the box on the carpeted floor in search for something, anything, that would get her into the vault-like container in hopes of revealing Lamar's secrets.

***

Several minutes later, Tamala returned to the bedroom with an old craftsman screwdriver that she found in a kitchen drawer. She knelt to pickup the heavy box then placed it on the queen-sized bed. Tamala positioned the screwdriver between the hasp and the lock and then commenced to pry frantically as droplets of sweat covered her forehead. After several more minutes, she heard a loud metallic breaking sound as the screwdriver gave way against the resistance of the lock and hasp. The broken hasp flew apart and the screwdriver sailed across the room, hitting the wall.

"*Shit!*" One of Tamala's fingernails broke off, down to the tip, and bled. "*FUCK!*" Tamala put the finger in her mouth hoping to ease the pain as her eyes watered. She then blew on her finger trying to stop the burning pain to no avail. "Just got these fuckin' nails done too, *damn!*"

Slowly curiosity overruled the pain in her finger; she sat on the bed and opened the latch to the lid. Then she lifted the lid, with its hinges at the rear, with ease. What Tamala saw made her forget all about the throbbing pain in her slightly-bleeding finger.

Inside the metal box were several sandwich-size, clear, zip-baggies which contained a white powdery substance. The baggies were packed in tightly and protected by the cushioned inner walls of the box. The walls, top and bottom of the metal box, were padded with a gray spongy material. Tamala had no idea what to do as she stared in utter disbelief at the cocaine being stored in her apartment.

"The *fuck* you doin', Tamala?!" The voice boomed behind her.

Tamala's heart virtually stopped in fear as she looked up toward the sound of her boyfriend's angry voice. With fright in her eyes, she saw Lamar peering down at her from the open doorway. She could not find her voice to reply as Lamar's cold gray eyes seemed to burn red in anger. The usually-outspoken young lady was stunned to silence as the man's eyes continued to glare dangerously at her. She sat frozen on the bed with her hand caught in the proverbial cookie jar.

Lamar was wearing a black cap, jeans, tennis shoes, and a leather *Philadelphia Eagles* jacket. "You snoopin' behind my back? I buy you shit left and right, and you betray me by goin' behind my back? *Bitch*, you don't know who the FUCK you messin' with?!"

Lamar walked toward Tamala and grabbed her up by the collar from off the bed. As he held the terrified woman against wall, he slapped her hard with the back of his right hand knocking her down to the floor.

"Aaaah!" Tamala cried out as she hit the floor. She braced her body waiting for Lamar to inflict additional punishment on her. Tears of pain and fear spilled out of her closed eyes. Tamala wept loudly and hoped that Lamar was not going to kill her.

Lamar calmly reached down to retrieve the metal box closing the lid. He then walked to the closet, which was still open, to acquire what he had returned to the apartment for. He bent down and retrieved his pistol out of an old gym bag hidden behind several pairs of his shoes and empty boxes; Tamala's hunt missed the gym bag. Still holding the metal box, he put the handgun in his waistband then walked back toward Tamala.

"Shut that cryin' up! Ain't no need for cryin'! You knew what the fuck was up! I got's to do this to survive, baby!" Now referring to the metal box, he continued, "This is my key out of poverty! Tired of being po', workin' for fuckin' peanuts! Now don't you *ever* go behind my back again! There's one thing I *can't* stand. And that's a nosy bitch! As long as you're my woman, I need your trust and respect! I gotta know that you got my back, Tamala!" Lamar then examined the box under his left arm. "Stay out my shit! Now I gotta get a new container…damn, woman!"

Tamala continued to lie on the floor crying silently and holding the right side of her reddened face, still feeling the sting of Lamar's smack. Fear clouded her thinking as she turned away from his accusatory gaze.

Lamar knelt down in front of Tamala. "Look, Freckles, I'm sorry. I lost my temper, but you shouldn't have gone through my stuff." He reached out to stroke her hair and she flinched. "It's okay, baby. Look, I'm goin' to get you that brand new Mercedes-Benz, baby. You know I love you, Freckles." After a couple minutes of uncomfortable silence, Lamar said, "Well, I see that you're upset. I got some shit to take care of. I'll be back later and we'll do somethin' fun tomorrow, okay?"

Lamar leaned over to kiss Tamala who slid away from him. "Woman, you shouldn't be like that. Stop cryin', I didn't hit you that hard." He sighed, "Tamala, look I gotta go. We'll make-up tomorrow."

Lamar stood up and slowly walked out of the room with his cocaine.

Tamala did not relax until she heard the front door shut behind her boyfriend. She put her right thumb in her mouth and cried harder, pulling her knees up into her chest. She thought, *I'm in some shit I can't get out of now.* Tamala had no where to turn, not even to her close-friend Staci. She was trapped. Tamala was afraid that Lamar would never let her go, especially now that she knew his true occupation - an armed street drug dealer with an out–of-control temper.

Chapter 26

As Eddie Logan slept his drunkenness off and the Logan boys dreamed the night away, two floors below them, in the tiny spare bedroom, Neci Logan lay breathless on the bed void of bra and panties...waiting for Marcus to finally take her.

Minutes earlier, after placing her gently upon the bed, he kissed, nibbled, and sucked every inch of Neci's body, deliberately ignoring all of her obvious sexual spots. Teasing her into a frenzy was his only goal at the time. Her body burned in the places where he kissed her...her neck, shoulders, arms, even her armpits, her torso, inner thighs, behind her knees, her calves, and her diminutive red polished toes, but Neci learned tonight that the arch of her back was another of her sexually sensitive areas. Afterwards, he slowly removed her bra and wet panties, tossing the garments to the floor. The tender and attentive lover then stepped back and gazed at Neci so lovingly that she nearly cried tears of joy!

Now as Marcus stood at the foot of the bed. He admired Neci's nudeness as the candlelight threw shadows upon her well-toned body; the flames lit up her dark eyes which squinted seductively at Marcus. Her mouth parted as she laid waiting with bated breath in anticipation of the forbidden sex. The woman's long black hair was sprawled about the pillow, ever so sexy. Neci had two thickened blackberry-like nipples that were surrounded by caramel-colored smooth areolas. Those nipples were set prominently upon her petite, but supple breasts. The dark nipples stood out in stark contrast against her perfect tawny-colored skin. Marcus could not wait to taste them.

Marcus's eyes roamed down her slim torso, past the ornate jewelry at her navel, and continued all the way down to her toes. Neci had a hint of black hair surrounding her sex. The triangular thatch was shaved very closely, almost bald. The short fine hairs appeared soft to the touch. The thick dark folds of Neci's inner lips resembled that of calla lily in full bloom. Her delicate petal-like lips were slightly parted, revealing the pinkness of her inner sanctum. Marcus noticed her nectar glistening there, Neci was extremely wet, excited, and ready for him.

Neci watched Marcus staring intently at her. He made love to her with his eyes. She thought, *oh my God, it's so amazing what this man does to me.* Marcus began to undress…taking off his shoes sans socks, his teal sweater and shirt, the baggy jeans, and finally the dark blue boxers. As Neci stared at the naked muscular man standing at the foot of the bed, it took everything within her to keep from jumping on him and taking him sexually.

Neci saw that Marcus had a well defined physique; his fitness was the result of his years in the boxing ring. His broad shoulders, muscular arms and chest, led down to a narrow waist, and large thighs. His six-pack abdominals were one of his best features. The candlelight flickered upon his dark body as his pectoral muscles flexed upon his hairless chest, Neci was attracted to hairy men but Marcus's overall sexiness made up for what he lacked in hair. Looking at his tall, dark, lean, but muscular-cut frame, intensified Neci's excitement…the feeling was intoxicating.

Neci's eyes immediately went to Marcus's long thick hardness. It pointed straight up *almost* to his stomach. The throbbing anatomy excited Neci so much that she gasped in pleasure. Neci wondered if Marcus would be a gentle lover as she watched, mesmerized at his bobbing member. The dampness between her legs increased even more. Her breath deepened in expectancy, and her nipples tingled in anticipation. She reached up and gently squeezed her right breast, teasing the hard large nipple with a soft pinch. Marcus went to Neci upon seeing the sexy image of her touching herself.

***

Though almost an hour had elapsed, time seemed to have slowed down for the lovers as Marcus worked magic with his tongue.

"¡Eres un amante tan atento, Marcus! ¡No puedo esperar sentirte dentro de mi ser! ¡Ay- Dios, su lengua...ay-*papi*...eres tan increíble!" Neci indeed felt as if she was intoxicated with her eyes shut tightly.

Hearing Neci speak in her native dialect, made Marcus work even harder to please this beautiful woman, the Spanish language sounded so erotic under sexual duress. Marcus continued to suckle her erect nipples, tasting their sweetness in his mouth and elongating each one with a fiery intensity. He masterfully massaged her large swollen clit as Neci gyrated her hips to meet his large hand. Marcus put one of Neci's breasts completely into his mouth as he now worked his tongue very slowly around her smooth areola. He bit down lightly on each nipple, making her moan even more as he expertly bit and suckled upon those hot spots of hers.

Neci whispered breathlessly as she began to reach an orgasm, "*Suck...it harder...baby. I, oh-God, like it like that.*" She grinded harder against his stroking finger, feeling the building orgasm! "Marcus...you're going to make me...cu, cum! Don't make me cum yet, baby! I need you inside me, *now*! Oh-God!" Neci tried to grab Marcus's thick rigidness, but she was so disoriented, by the wonderful feeling her lover was providing, that she failed in her quest.

Marcus ignored Neci's plea to not make her *cum* as he inserted the tip of his middle finger inside of her, now using his thumb to continue massaging Neci's sensitive spot. He continued going from breast to breast trying to give equal attention to both, driving Neci wild!

"I, I, Oh, Marcus! *Cumming*!" Neci's head shot back sharply in pure elation. She could not catch her breath as she was about to reach her sexual peak! She gyrated even wilder against Marcus's hand, clinging to the comforter as if her very life depended upon it! Tears of pleasure spilled from her half opened glistening eyes, as she erupted fiercely against her lover's hand!

"Oh, Marcuuuusssss! *Aaaah*, *mmmmmmm*! Sooooo, goooooood, Marcuuusssss!"

Marcus, feeling her trembling body and firm thighs closed against his hand, gradually reduced the pressure against Neci's now oversensitive clit. She was sweating and lay with her eyes closed, appearing as if in a trance. She was in seventh heaven!

***

Upstairs, Eddie awoke suddenly. He had one of the most intense headaches ever. He had no sense of time or of his whereabouts. He stroked his achy throbbing head, and then realized that he was home. Still in a drunken fog, he tried to sit up in bed but slipped on the wet satin sheets.

"*Shit*."

He could not believe how much sweat was on the sheets. Then the smell hit him! The wetness was not sweat, but vomit!

"Yuck."

Eddie groggily sat up then painstakingly got up out of bed, now swaying in the darkness of the large bedroom. It was not long before his sour stomach produced yet another spew of smelly vomit.

"Oh, help me, God! Gotta…stop drinking. Take me out my *fucking* misery."

Eddie coughed and gagged as his vomit covered the carpet and his already ruined shirt. He stripped off his shirt and stumbled slowly into the bathroom throwing the shirt into the darkness. The sudden memory of slapping his wife earlier came clearly through the drunken haze.

"God! What's wrong with me?"

Guilt gripped his tired body. He turned on the bathroom light only to quickly turn it off as the brightness produced a blinding wave of pain to his eyes and head. After relieving his bladder, Eddie setout to apologize to Neci, who he believed was now sleeping down the hall in the guest bedroom.

***

Neci was still on cloud 9. Her head was spinning with the after effects of one of the hardest orgasms she had ever experienced. Marcus began slowly nibbling down toward her stomach, and Neci soon felt her legs part widely as his hot breath matched the heat between her legs. Though she was still on another planet, Neci could feel the gentle probing and tasting of his long tongue, taking in her essence but being careful to avoid the still too-sensitive clit. At a snail's pace, the tongue explored her deepness, then suddenly began to lap hungrily. He enjoyed the softness of her black pubic hair. The neatly trimmed triangular patch of hair gave off a clean flowery scent under his nose.

Neci's eyes were still closed, trying to recover her energy. "What…are you, you doing to me, Marcus? My God! Your *marvelous* tongue!"

Marcus enjoyed the sweet tangy taste of Neci's love. He kissed the thick inner lips then licked from the bottom of her sex to just short of her clit. He eventually made his way back up to her face and began kissing and tonguing her passionately.

Neci could smell and taste her own familiar juices as she returned Marcus's exciting kiss. She felt him position himself between her legs. The lean, dark, tall, muscular body of Marcus Williams was now on top of her. The kiss intensified as both Neci and Marcus anticipated the act of lovemaking. The large head of Marcus's manhood gently grazed against the clit.

Neci thought in excitement, *He's about to stick me, God, yes.*

She then felt him pressed against her opening. The wonderful heat and feel of Marcus's throbbing cock made Neci break the ferocious tongue kiss.

Neci whispered passionately in his ear, "*Oh, Marcus.*"

She held Marcus tightly, waiting to feel him fully. When Marcus's thickness finally penetrated her, she sighed with pleasure biting down on her lower lip, feeling him inch by inch slowly making his way deeper inside her. Neci's body was on fire!

***

The guest bedroom was empty! Eddie was perplexed for a moment.

"Where's my wife?" he whispered.

Eddie then searched the boy's room along with the rest of the entire top floor for Neci. She was nowhere to be found. Then a thought occurred to him, *Neci's probably working late on her college studies; as always.* Eddie wanted desperately to right the wrong he caused upon his wife, both past and present marital transgressions. He loved Neci and had to make amends if he had any chance of saving their fragile marriage. Eddie staggered down the stairs.

***

Neci broke the kiss while burying her head into his shoulder. She whispered, *"Marcus…your…cock…feels sooooo good inside of me."* She opened her legs wider and pushed with her bottom and thighs in order to meet his strong and methodical thrust!

Marcus continued to drill gently and slowly inside of Neci, the long stroke seemed to go on forever! Finally when Marcus's length reached its hilt, Neci felt and heard his testicles smack wetly against her firm buttocks.

"My, *my* pussy! Your big *cock*! Feeeeels *too* good!"

When Marcus began to grind against her, Neci could not believe the pleasure that this man was giving her. Her closed eyes rolled back into her head as Marcus's powerful movements stimulated her clit.

"Oh, Marcus!" She held on to him even tighter, yielding herself to her lover.

Marcus then short-stroked the beauty underneath him then demanded softly, *"Look* at me, Neci." He gently pushed her wavy hair away from her face.

Neci struggled to open her eyes to meet Marcus's intense gaze as she continued to match his manly strokes. She was soon able to focus on his handsome face. Neci wished that this moment would last forever in the candle lit bedroom.

Marcus looked into the dark eyes of the biracial beauty as he pleased her slowly with his long hardness. "You're my goddess, my queen, Neci. I worship you as we are now joined as one, making you *my* lady, *my* woman, for I am now *your* man. I appreciate you and respect you." He increased his pace inside of her then continued.

Neci said excitedly, "Oooooh, *Marcus*!" Her eyes remained anchored to his.

Marcus was in love with his willing prey. "Neci, I'd die for you. I need you like I've never needed any other woman in my life. I mean that, baby. I mean that from the depths of my heart, my soul. Thanks, Neci, for rescuing me. I feel soooo fucking complete, I am now *whole*." Marcus then grinded Neci deeply.

Neci's eyes shut uncontrollably as she gasped, "*Ahhhhhhh, Goddddd*!" Tears escaped from her closed eyes as she wrapped her arms tighter around Marcus's wide muscular back. She was deeply touched by his heartfelt words as the man continued to please her thoroughly.

With wet eyes, Neci searched his again, then demanded, "Make love…damn, sooooo good, *Marcus*. Make *love* to me!" Marcus seemed to throb stronger and grew larger inside of her. He slow-grinded Neci again, staying deep within her.

***

Eddie, through his alcohol-induced haze, was now worried. Neci was not in front of her computer as he had expected and she was not in any of the rooms. Then relief came to him when he realized where she was.

"She's downstairs in the spare bedroom, *idiot*." He grabbed his head as another wave of dizziness and intense pain hit him. "Damn, my *head*. Got to get something for this pain…"

Eddie shuffled back to the living room and then proceeded downstairs to where his partner was making love to his wife. Once on the bottom level of the large house, he made his way down the semi-darkened hall, lit by a small nightlight. As he walked toward the spare bedroom, he could see that the door was shut.

Eddie smiled through his pain, showing the dimples that attracted so many women over the years, as he anticipated the makeup sex he would have with Neci. "I've found you."

Eddie stopped suddenly as he passed the game room to his right. He backtracked and stood in the open doorway, looking toward the mini-bar in that room.

Eddie said softly, "Maybe a quick drink will knock out this headache. I'll just have one drink, and *only* one."

Eddie, ignoring the spare bedroom, stumbled his way toward his friend, the booze.

***

Marcus felt the tightness and the wetness of his lover, especially against his thick shaft. He concentrated on pleasing her with every inch of himself. He slowly raised himself up and almost completely out of her then gave her just the tip of his thickness, making circles and teasing the opening of Neci's wetness. Without warning, he drove himself deeply back inside of her, stroking her faster than before. Marcus's piston-like thrusts brought Neci to the pinnacle of sexual bliss.

Neci's head thrashed from side to side as her thick long hair flew wildly about with some strands plastered against her sweaty face. "GOD! Marcuuuuusss, yesssssss! Like that, *baby*! Just like that! Oh, *papi*! Give me that big cock, *papi*!" Neci grabbed Marcus's tight buttocks and held him firmly. She suddenly stopped her thrashing to look deeply into his eyes. Neci wanted to connect further with her lover, seeing the love in his eyes. The lovers then kissed again as their sweaty bodies flowed in perfect sync to their own music, to the magical and mystical song called love.

***

The bottle was turned up, all the way, as the dark liquid flowed out and down Eddie Logan's throat. The beverage burned but had the desired effect on him: the headache was replaced by sweet bliss. Eddie was now in his own familiar world, a world with no pain or worries, an instant escape from reality which seemed to be spiraling out of control these days.

It was at that moment that Eddie heard a familiar sound. The sound was muffled but unmistakably well-known. It drifted through the walls of the adjoining room, the spare bedroom. Before he could grasp the source of the noise, Eddie slowly passed out as he sat on the floor against the bar. In the darkness, the empty bottle fell to the carpet as Neci had yet another orgasm, continuing to moan in that familiar intonation that Eddie knew intimately.

***

Marcus made love to Neci throughout the night. Feeling her inner walls gripping his manhood, along with the heat of her sex, was almost more than he could take. As they both set out to please the other, the lovers explored every position imaginable. She tasted him while he tasted her, once again. At one point Neci took control and sat atop of Marcus, riding him ever so slowly. But soon Marcus regained control, putting her legs up against his powerful shoulders, giving Neci deeper thrusts. He also took her from behind, and when he reached the depths of her, she cried out uncontrollably in Spanish. Neci lost track of the number of orgasms she had. The couple lost all track of time during the torrid act as they whispered adoring words, increasing their unspoken love for each other. Finally, as Marcus climaxed hard deep within her, Neci buried her fingernails into his back leaving scratches as she came with him. Marcus loved her with an intensity Neci had never experienced, an intensity that was felt deep within her soul.

***

Later the spent lovers were covered in sweat and exhausted as Marcus lay on top of Neci. As the scent of their passion filled the small room and their connection now complete, Marcus held her tightly, still somewhat rigid inside of her, while Neci cried silent tears of joy and pleasure. She thought, *I've finally found him - my knight in shining armor.* Princess Neci had finally been rescued by her handsome prince. For once in her life, Neci felt free, unrestrained, happy and truly loved. She clung to Marcus, never wanting to let go.

***

As dawn approached, Neci and Marcus laid within the tangled sheets. The candles had long since burnt out. Marcus was not sure as to whether or not he had drifted off to sleep; this enchanting time with Neci had been surreal. He simply could not believe that they made love through the night. Marcus felt as if he was in a trance the entire time he loved the beautiful woman. They were both insatiable, they could not get enough of the other's love. Marcus was currently on a sexual high. He was confident in his ability to please a woman, but the explosive way Neci responded to his touch, his kisses, and finally with him being inside of her, was unlike anything he had ever experienced.

Now, Marcus spooned a sleeping Neci, replaying every moment of the wonderful evening. The beginning rays of sunlight penetrated the closed curtains near the left of the bed. He tried to make out the time on the clock which hung on the wall, but the room was still too dark. He raised his left arm to glance at his watch and saw instead the gold bracelet with Neci's dangling heart; his watch currently lay on an end table at his apartment. Marcus smiled at the dangling jewelry then focused his attention on Neci. He moved the sleeping woman's thick hair away from her neck and then kissed her there. She stirred slowly.

Neci began to purr with her back still to Marcus, "*Mmmmmm*, hey, baby. You keep kissing me like that you may get something *else* started." Marcus kissed Neci on her neck again, making her giggle. She turned to face him, covering her mouth afraid of morning breath, then said, "You're *bad*, Marcus."

The lovers laughed quietly. When the laugher gradually died down, Neci and Marcus stared intensely at one another. They dangerously ignored the urgency of the starting day. He stroked her hair, and she his smooth face. After a couple of minutes, it dawned on both them what the familiar look was in the other's eyes. But neither was brave enough to verbally express what they saw due to the uncertainty and nature of their illicit relationship. The look in both of their eyes was crystal clear. The lovers could no longer deny it for the look of love was too strong to ignore.

***

Several minutes later, the loud knocking at the door shattered Neci and Marcus private thoughts. Marcus was about to leave before the interruption. His heart raced as he waited and hoped that Neci locked the door behind them last night. As both of them sat up in bed, they heard the angry voice.

"Open the *goddamn* door; I know you're in there!" Eddie pounded on the door again.

Marcus looked for a place to hide. The door-less closet was too small to get into and the bed too low to crawl under. Nowhere to hide.

"Let me handle this, okay?"

Marcus whispered, "I'm open for any suggestions at this point, Neci." The last thing Marcus needed was to be trapped in here with Neci and nowhere to go. He would be forced to hurt Eddie and have to deal with the consequences afterwards. But one thing for sure, Marcus would protect Neci and her kids at all cost.

Eddie tried turning the door knob again. "Unlock this door, and let me in *now*, damn it!"

Marcus looked at the window. He pondered, *maybe, I can-*

Neci interrupted his thoughts and said in a near whisper, "Get behind the door, Marcus. He thinks I'm in here alone. I sleep down here on occasion to get away from him when he's drunk. *Trust* me."

Marcus stared at her then sighed as he got up and quickly dressed assuming the position behind the door. Neci put on her bra and panties then quickly donned her robe. She scanned the room for any signs of last night's escape from reality. Neci saw nothing but the burnt candles which were not out of the ordinary, she burned candles from time to time to help her to relax.

Neci went to the door as Marcus stood in place then said through the door, "Gerard, I'm going to open this door, but you'd better behave. You understand?"

"Neci, I'm sorry about last night, just open up. I want to make sure you're okay."

Neci took one last look at Marcus then braced herself for the confrontation with Eddie. A split second before Neci opened the door Marcus got a glimpse of the empty gift box, which held his bracelet and puff gold heart, sitting on the nightstand. Before Marcus could warn Neci, the door opened, blocking his view.

Eddie was dressed in the same tan Dockers from last night, sans shirt of course. "Hey, sweetheart. I apologize for being an ass last night. My head's aching from all the drinking I've done. I'm going through some hard times right now, you know about it. Just have patience with me. I didn't mean to hit-"

"*Gerard*, apology accepted. Give me a few more minutes of sleep. I'll fix breakfast for you and the boys." Neci glanced back at the cuckoo clock on the wall then added, "It's still early yet." She looked back at her husband, "Go back to bed, Gerard."

"Only if you come with me."

"No!" Neci's stomach churned as the sour odor of alcohol assaulted her nose.

"How 'bout I sleep down here with you then? We can cuddle." Eddie gave his best smile. Neci used to fall for those dimples and blue eyes, now red, all the time. Those attributes no longer had the desired effect on his wife that Eddie hoped for.

Neci was getting impatient; her lover stood just a few feet away from being discovered by her alcoholic husband. "*Look*, Gerard. I'm tired. I didn't get much sleep last night because of *your* tirade. Let me sleep, then we'll sit down and discuss things."

"Things? What things?"

"I'm just talking, Gerard. Go back to bed, please."

"Okay. But you accept my apology?"

"I told you that I accepted it."

"Sweeeeet!" Eddie started to leave but something caught his eye. "What's that?" He pointed at the nightstand.

Neci looked where he had pointed and her stomach sunk. "Oh, *that*? That's umm, that's…nothing. Just an old box I had. "

Eddie staggered further in the room, bumping Neci back a few steps. "Let me see." Eddie's back was now to Marcus who instinctively balled up his fists. If Eddie turned around, he would be face to face with his partner.

Neci remembered Marcus putting on the bracelet, so nothing should be in the box. She pushed Eddie back out the door then grabbed the box off the nightstand slamming it down into his hands. "*There* you want it, it's yours! Now, *let me sleep, Gerard*!"

"Okay, okay. You don't have to raise your voice. I love you."

Neci felt torn and awkward all of a sudden but had no choice but to respond, "Love you too. Now go back to bed." She shut then locked the door leaving Eddie in the hallway.

Neci motioned for Marcus to step away from the door, who felt sick at hearing her express love for Eddie. She did not want her husband to hear her talking to Marcus. She whispered, "Where did you park last night?"

"In the back, where I always park."

"If Gerard sees your car, we're in trouble, Marcus."

"Look, don't panic. Just go out there and make sure he goes back to bed. Distract him and I'll sneak out. Simple as that. It'll be fine, I promise." He held her hand reassuringly.

Neci sighed as some of her fear dissipated then said, "Okay."

Marcus smiled. "Being with you last night is worth being in this little…dilemma."

"Marcus, don't let this go to your head, but you're an *excellent* lover. I've never *in my life* felt anything close to…well, you know…to our wonderful… lovemaking. It was…"

"*..Powerful.*" Marcus finished her statement.

Neci smiled in amazement. "*Yeah*, but…how did you know I was going to say that?"

Marcus looked at her seriously then answered, "Because we're connected now. We're one, Neci." He then held up his left arm dangling the gold bracelet and continued, "Plus now I have your heart, *remember*?"

Neci smiled. "Yes, darling. I remember."

With that, the two kissed deeply sealing their unspoken love for each other then formulized a plan to get Marcus out of the house unscathed.

***

Eddie had remained on the other side of the door, although he could not hear the whispered conversation between Neci and Marcus. He never suspected that his wife was in the room with someone else, however, he had sensed that something was not right. He looked at the empty gift box in his heads and thought that the answer lay within. Curiosity made him peek into the box - nothing. He crushed it in his fists.

Eddie, frustrated, slowly walked back down the hall then back up the stairs into the kitchen with a nagging feeling about his wife. Neci was no longer her usual self. Not to worry, Eddie had already put into place *certain measures* that could shed some light onto the matter. He decided that from here on out he must be even more vigilant. Neci must be watched closely. He must set out to find the answers behind his wife's recent strangeness. Eddie vowed to get to the bottom of it even if it killed him.

Chapter 27

Thirty-six hours after their indiscretions, Marcus was going nuts as he had not yet heard from Neci. Eddie had been unusually quiet that night as they answered a few calls during a heavy snowstorm which gripped the area; Marcus's partner said next to nothing. His silent partner and his guilt were getting the best of him. Marcus had no choice but to call Neci to make sure she was okay. That chance came when he and Eddie stopped briefly at the precinct to turn in reports to Sergeant Sargent. While Eddie took the paperwork to Sargent, Marcus bolted to an empty office to make the hurried call.

The sleepy husky voice of Neci answered on the third ring, "Hello?"

Marcus, sitting in the dark at the records clerk desk, closed his eyes taking in the voice of the woman that he had made love to the night before last. "Sorry to wake you, Neci. Needed to hear your voice, check on you."

Neci, wearing a long burgundy sleep shirt, feel asleep on the couch in the great room with the gas-burning fireplace glowing behind her, lighting up the dim but toasty room. Now sitting up and suddenly alert, Neci said, "Marcus, I've missed you like crazy! I just couldn't find a way to call with Gerard here."

"I understand. I feel so much better now. Been worried that maybe Eddie...well never mind, I'm glad you're okay. Would've tried my cell earlier but didn't charge the battery."

Suddenly growing concerned, Neci asked with a frown on her face, "What about Gerard? Why are you worrying, Marcus?"

"Well…he's been…so quiet tonight. The man has barely said a word to me all night. It's like pulling teeth to get him to talk to me."

Neci relaxed then said, "Oh. Gerard's just upset with me." She intentionally left out that they argued about going back to California, and Eddie's threat to rape her. Neci continued, "He's been trying hard to get back into my good graces. I refuse to have…well, you know how it is."

"No I don't, tell me how it is."

Neci sighed, "Gerard wants…you know, sex. I refuse to sleep with him for various reasons but especially now."

" 'Especially now'?"

"Marcus, how can I put this?" Neci paused to get her words right, "You have my heart, remember? I can only give my heart to one man. I've never been the type to sleep with more than one man at once. It, it may sound silly to you but I value that so much. Making love is so precious to me…so… giving. I don't take it lightly; having someone inside me is more *spiritual* than physical. Sounds crazy…I know. Plus my body belongs to you now, *not* Gerard."

Marcus said, "Doesn't sound silly or crazy at all. I admire that. Wish I could make love to you right now, just for sharing with me."

"I'm now going to sleep apart from him, which is not going to go over well - sleeping in separate bedrooms. Well, enough of that worry." Neci then said slowly, "Marcus, it was so…so wonderful, the way we…*you know*…made love." Neci shook her head at the sensual memory. "I've never been loved that way…" Neci forced back tears, tears resulting from the lingering memory and tears of longing…longing to be in Marcus's arms again.

Marcus said, "Making love to you felt so right, Neci. You know, I can still taste you on my tongue."

Neci put a hand between her thighs as her clit ached for attention. "*Marcus*, you're getting me hot, so behave."

"Your pussy tasted so good, Neci. I've never tasted anything so delicious in my life."

Neci whispered breathlessly, as her hand made its way further between her legs, "*It's mean of you to get me this way.*"

"What 'way'? Say it, we're both adults here. Speak freely."

"*Wet.*"

"Tell me, Neci. What's wet?"

Neci was surprised at her sudden adolescent shyness, "My…you know…"

Marcus's own excitement was building as he pushed, "Naw, I don't know. Come on, Neci. Say it. Wanna hear you talk dirty."

Neci knew she had talked seductively when they made love the other night, but did not remind Marcus of that fact. She said softly, "My *pussy*."

"Damn, Neci. You sound so sexy with that accent, the way you say 'puuuseee.' Say something else…something raunchy."

Neci said gently, "Marcus, stop encouraging me. And stop making fun of my enunciation." She touched her wetness.

"You playing with that sweet pussy?"

Neci reluctantly answered, "Yessss. How did you know?"

"Do you have on panties?"

Neci gave a whispered reply, "No...I don't."

"Taste it for me, Neci. Your cum."

Neci said seductively, "Marcus, you're *so* bad."

"Taste your cum for me, baby."

Neci placed a finger inside of herself then brought it up to her mouth. She sucked her moistness off her finger. "Mmmmm. Tastes *very* sweet. I can't *believe* I did that for you."

Marcus growing hard asked shakily, "You ever tasted your own cum before?"

Neci was very hesitant in answering such a revealing question but after the other night what could she *not* share with Marcus? "Yes, lots of times." She heard Marcus's excited breathing over the phone. Neci grew bold at her sexual power over him. "That excites you, doesn't it, Marcus? Me *tasting* my pussy." The husky voice teased.

Marcus tried to contain his growing excitement as he said hungrily, "Yes, it does actually." An intriguing question popped into Marcus's mind and then he asked, "You ever tasted another woman's cum before, or at least fantasized about being with another woman...*sexually*?"

It took a few moments for Neci to answer the blunt question, it caught her totally off guard, even though it was commonly asked by men. Neci finally answered with mock displeasure in her voice, "I *can't* believe that you asked me *such* an offensive question, Marcus!"

Marcus seeing through the charade pressed on for an answer, "Well?"

Neci was very quiet for a few more moments, thinking, then said, "No comment. I'll just let you wonder about that."

She laughed playfully enjoying teasing the wonderful man on the other end of the telephone.

Let down, Marcus swallowed back his excitement then simply said, "Damn…"

Neci suddenly became serious then expressed sadly, "I wish that you were inside of me right now, baby. I miss you so much, *it hurts*."

"Yeah…miss you too, Neci. I've never felt like this for anyone."

"How do you feel, Marcus? About…about me?" Neci regretted asking such bold questions, but she desperately wanted to gauge Marcus's feelings.

"I'd make you my wife right now if I could," Marcus answered with conviction.

The response took Neci's breath away. It was not the answer she was looking for but more than addressed her question.

Marcus asked, "You okay?"

"Yes…you're just too sweet. You made love to me as if I *were* your wife."

"In my heart you are, Neci. You're *constantly* on my mind. It makes me crazy not talking to you, or not seeing you. In fact, I'm not whole until I'm with you."

"Oh, Marcus. Stop before you make me…cry."

"I need to see you again, like right now."

"Me too, but it may be a while, this is so...complicated, Marcus."

"I know, baby. But I don't care how long it takes to see you. As long as I have something to look forward to, give me a date or time when I can see you. That's all I need, Neci. *When* can I see you again?"

"I'm sure that I'll be out for the rest of the week due to the weather, no school with all that snow out there. Ummm...how about we plan something next week? Maybe the weather will break. I can get away any afternoon, maybe take a couple of hours of personal time, but I've got to get back before my last class."

"First chance you get, Neci, call me at home or on the cell. We can meet at the park, you know Arrowhead park where we-"

"*Beat* you guys in softball, and where you and I had our late night walks, I know the place," Neci said good-naturedly.

Marcus smiled as he said, "Neci, you didn't have to take it there. We'll beat y'all this coming summer."

Neci retorted jovially, "Sure you will. Keep thinking that."

"I look forward to your call and seeing you next week."

Neci asked enduringly, "You wearing my heart, Marcus?"

"Afraid to wear it at work. I might lose it. But I got it tucked away safely in the front pocket of my bullet-proof vest...close to my *own* heart."

"Good. You'll always have a piece of me with you."

"Until I see you, please call me from time to time when you get free."

"I'll try, darling. Just hearing your voice takes away some of my loneliness for you, Marcus."

"Same here, Neci. Well...I better get back."

"Be careful, Marcus."

"I will."

The "*L*" word was on both of their minds but was left unspoken once again, neither one of them had the courage to be the first to say it.

"Well…goodnight, Marcus."

"Goodnight, Neci."

The two hung up simultaneously, both feeling the warmth that the conversation brought to them on this cold, cold January night.

Chapter 28

The following week, the afternoon sun shone brightly in the sky but did little to warm the hard cold earth. Most of the snow and ice from the previous week had dissipated. During the winter months, there were only certain portions of Arrowhead Historical Park opened during the day. Avid runners, joggers, mountain bikers, and the like frequented the trails in their quest to stay in shape during the cold months.

There was a scattering of parked vehicles throughout the park as Marcus made his way into the vast area. As he drove past each parked car, he observed that some were occupied while others sat empty. Marcus thought, *hmmm, lunch-goers or maybe lovers*. The gray barren and leafless trees appeared to be stretching toward the brightness of the sun, in hopes of obtaining some manner of warmth on this brutally cold day. Marcus parked in a secluded spot then left his car running to keep the heater going. As usual, Neci was late but called Marcus thirty minutes ago and assured him that she was going to make it. She got held up due to a 'minor crisis' at the school, something involving a fight between a student and teacher during one of the lunch sessions.

Marcus was not hopeful until he saw the gray Cadillac Escalade drive through the park pulling up beside him. Marcus, wearing a heavy black jacket and blue jeans, turned off his car. He got out and met Neci as she rounded the front of her SUV. Neci was wearing black leather high heeled ankle boots, a black tweed skirt with white specks and a matching jacket over a long sleeved white blouse. Her hair was combed back and braided with a single long ponytail, *Lara Croft* style. Once again with her shiny raven hair slicked back, Neci's youthful Latina facial features were really highlighted, especially in the sunlight. The thick but trimmed eyebrows, the wide dark eyes with long lashes, and the cheeky smile, were prominent against Neci's smooth tawny skin tone. She was simply radiant. The lovers embraced tightly.

"Oh, God, this feels so good, Marcus." Neci said into Marcus's shoulder with her eyes closed.

"I never want to let you go, girl." Marcus enjoyed the sweet scent of Neci's perfume and the warmth of her body.

The couple then kissed...and kissed...then kissed some more.

Neci said breathlessly when the kiss ended, "*Okay*? That was *great* as usual. Come on, hop in with me, Marcus." She led Marcus back to the SUV. He opened her driver's door then trotted back around to the passenger side and got in.

Marcus looked around the SUV. "Nice...very nice. Tan leather seats...*nice*. Didn't notice this the last time." He held out his cold hands toward the heater vents. The gold bracelet and heart charm dangled along his right wrist.

"I see you've brought *my* heart!" Neci said with glee.

Marcus, with his hands still held out, responded, "Like I said before, your heart's always with me, Neci. Man, this heat feels good. Cold out there, ain't it?"

"Yes, but the kiss heated things up quite nicely. Wouldn't you say?"

"Come here for another one then."

Neci reached over the center console and tongue-kissed the bald man.

Neci pulled back with sultry eyes then whispered, "You're going to send me back to school with wet panties, Marcus."

Marcus glanced toward the rear of the spacious SUV interior. He looked past the middle seats and all the way back to the bench seat. He then stared back at the sexy lady beside him. "You don't have to go back with panties at all. Come on...follow me."

Marcus got out and reentered the SUV through the rear side door and Neci did the same from her side. The two giggling lovebirds squeezed between the middle seats and plopped down on the rear bench seat. With Neci to his left, Marcus pulled her to him and kissed her deeply.

"I can't express how much I've missed you, Neci." Marcus then kissed her again.

As the bright sunlight shined its rays through the tinted windows of the SUV, Marcus took off her jacket and started to unbutton her blouse.

Neci nervously scanned the surroundings outside then asked through her sexual excitement, "You don't think we'll get caught out here do you?"

"We'll be okay; kinda kinky being out in the open like this though. The possibility of getting caught is a sexual thrill." Marcus undid the snap on the front of Neci's beige silk laced bra and greedily took her left breast into his mouth. As he gently sucked the dark nipple, it began to elongate, becoming fully erect.

"*Oooh*, baby..." Neci felt the gentle tugging of her thick nipple. Marcus's tongue worked expertly on the small breast. Neci stroked and kissed the top of his baldhead. As Marcus licked, bit, and sucked her, Neci enjoyed the pleasurable throbbing commencing between her legs. She needed his attention badly down there.

As if Marcus read her thoughts, he kissed her breast goodbye and got down on his knees in the cramped space.

Taking off his coat, he then pulled up Neci's skirt over her firm bare thighs. She lifted up her bottom to allow him to slip off her beige silk laced panties. Neci smiled when she saw Marcus place her wet panties in his jacket pocket behind him. He then pushed her skirt up along her waist and pulled her gently to the edge of the seat, spreading her legs and exposing her sweetness. She laid her head slightly against the top of the seat, keeping her intense eyes on her lover. Neci interlaced her right hand into his left.

Marcus could smell the sweet sex as he inched closer to her nectar. Neci anticipated Marcus devouring her; she bit down on her lip in ecstasy. She nearly cried out in elation upon feeling Marcus's slick tongue graze the sensitive, tight, forbidden opening between her ample buttocks. The tongue then trailed slowly up to her wet thick pussy lips with a final stop at her swollen clit. He began to flicker his tongue quickly across that area of her sex. Marcus pulled up Neci's hood to give special attention to the clitoris.

"*Uhhhhhhhhhh*, yes, baby. It feeeeels soooo good, Marcus." Neci moaned with her eyes closed and allowed herself to be loved by Marcus's wild tongue. She grabbed his baldpate and started gyrating against his face.

Marcus paused in his action then asked, "Like the way I eat your pussy, Neci?"

Neci opened her eyes and look seductively at Marcus. "*Yes*…God yes!"

Marcus toyed with her as he asked, "Want me to stop?"

Neci said in her sexy husky voice, "Please keep going, Marcus. Don't…you *dare* stop!"

Marcus asked playfully, "What you want me to do, Neci?"

"*Eat that sweet pussy, baby.*" Neci opened her legs wider and pushed Marcus's face hard between her legs.

Marcus stuck his hard long tongue inside of her making her moan loudly. He made love to her that way, for a few minutes, as her black peach fuzz tickled his nose. He tried to suck her dry causing her to cry out even louder in ecstasy. Marcus felt his hardness straining against the tightness of his jeans, begging to be freed. Several minutes later he pulled away from her and stretched up to kiss her, both of them tasting her sweet juices, both of them breathless.

Marcus got up and sat to the right of her again. He undid his jeans and pushed them down to his ankles along with his black briefs. The long length of his cock pointed skyward as it throbbed for attention. "Come take a ride with me, Neci."

Neci whispered seductively taking hold of his meat, "Let me take *you* in my mouth first." She smiled then got up allowing her skirt to fall back into place. She knelt before him, taking Marcus's thickness deep into her mouth and throat. Neci sucked Marcus as she massaged his anatomy with her right hand. They locked eyes, looking deeply at each other.

"*Fuck!*" Marcus nearly fainted at the sensation and sight of the beautiful woman performing oral love on him. Her tongue did slow twirls around his thick cock.

Neci then licked his large balls still keeping her eyes on Marcus. She found his sensitive spot underneath his cock, at the swollen head. Marcus had to stop her before he came. Neci chuckled at his excitement, loving her control over him.

"Come ride this thing, girl."

Neci got up and raised her skirt to prepare for the joining with her lover. Just as she stood, her head bumped the headliner of the SUV. "*Owww*." Both then cried out in laughter.

Marcus asked with a smile, "You alright?"

Neci, embarrassed, answered, "I'll live." She began to reposition herself. "Let's give it another try."

Marcus still smiling, said, "Don't knock yourself silly now."

"You are so crazy, Marcus." Neci successfully straddled Marcus taking hold of him and guided the massiveness towards tender moist lips. She felt him slide slowly inside of her as she lowered herself. "Ooooh-*God*, Marcus. You feel so *damn* good, you fill me up just…just right, baby." She put her arms around his neck.

Marcus, holding her around her slim waist, felt her wetness and tightness envelop him. Neci's walls began to squeeze his cock after she settled upon him. "*Damn*, Neci, you keep doing that, and we're gonna end this before it gets started."

Neci laughed seductively then kissed him. The sexy woman, with sultriness in her dark eyes, stared deeply into Marcus's. Neci slowly reared her hips back and forward, grinding her lover. She gazed at Marcus wantonly through half-opened eyes as she felt his pulsating thickness deep within her.

Neci slowly raised herself up and down on Marcus, feeling him glide in and out of her. Suddenly a white sedan drove by slowly. She stopped her stride, hoping that the occupants of that car could not see through the tinted windows. She felt like a fish in a fishbowl for the world to see. Once the car passed, Neci relaxed again as she began to gyrate, squeeze, and then make both long and short strokes along Marcus's stiff cock.

As her lover moaned, Neci once again stared deeply into her lover's eyes and said softly, "Feel that *wet* pussy, Marcus? It's all yours, baby. It's yours and no one else's. Te quiero, Marcus. Quiero todo lo que tenga que ver contigo. Ahora soy tuyo, papi chulo."

Neci had to verbalize the precious but forbidden words, professing her love directly to Marcus was just too deep and complicated right now. Spanish kept her deeper feelings hidden from him but still allowed her to express them safely. She threw her head back and closed her eyes; she loved him so much.

Neci reached back and grabbed his knees for leverage. The intensity of their lovemaking was taking them both away again. A place where only the two lovers could go, only Neci and Marcus could escape to this place...total bliss, *heaven*! Neci increased her sensuous gyrations as her sex swallowed Marcus's throbbing manhood.

"*Damn*, Neci. You gonna make me cum up in you." Marcus kept his eyes on the passionate woman.

Marcus heard her say breathlessly as her seductive movements became frantic, "*Oh, Marcus*! *I'm about to make a mess all over your* big cock! *Cum with me,* baby! *Oh, God, it's so gooooood*! Please cum, *now, uhhhhhhhhhh, Marcus*!"

The two came quickly and held each other tightly as their hearts raced with passion and exhaustion. Their love gyrations continued but at a much slower pace as the lovers began to wind down. After several more minutes, Neci reached down to where they were still joined and touched their wetness. She shyly brought up her hand then said seductively, "Let's taste *our* love...*taste* what we've made."

The sexiness of the act compelled Marcus to comply with the demand of the woman who now held his heart. She placed her slim moist fingers into his mouth then lean in towards him. They tasted their love hungrily then kissed passionately.

After the feast and the electrifying kiss, Marcus said, "I love it when you speak Spanish while I'm inside you. What did you say?"

Neci smiled then replied, "Ummm...I may tell you someday." She kissed him then suddenly looked at her watch. With wide eyes, not believing how fast the time had passed, she said, "My God, I'm late! I've got to get back to school, Marcus!"

Neci slowly raised herself up, and Marcus slid out of her. "Mmmm, feels just as good coming out," she said with fervor.

Marcus watched her straighten up her clothing. "Don't worry. You look great, Neci."

"Sorry to rush off. God, I'm dripping wet." She raised her skirt slightly as the wetness trickled down between her thighs. Neci then glanced at Marcus with a sheepish and apologetic expression as she said, "I'm going to need my panties back, Marcus. I'm a *human* Niagara Falls."

Marcus laughed then said, "I understand. But you owe me a pair next time."

"Okay. It's a date, now hurry."

Marcus retrieved the garment then handed it back to her. He watched the woman frantically make her way to the front of the SUV. The love he had for Neci ached within his heart. He sighed then quickly dressed and followed the hurried young lady.

Chapter 29

At 8:37 p.m. Panera Bread at 11 Mall Avenue, just east of the Rolling Hills Mega-Mall Complex, was not crowded with the usual college students, preppies, and business cliental from lunch time to early evening with their laptops and iPods amidst food and drinks. It was definitely not the kind of eatery visited by the run-of-the-mill street cop, but Eddie loved the place. The upscale sandwich shop specialized in hot gourmet soups, made-to-order sandwiches, bagels, salads, pastries, and other desserts. The brightly-lit bakery-café had a cozy atmosphere with the help of a warm fireplace, modern décor, and intricate but intimate layout. It was an excellent haven from the night's cold.

Marcus and Eddie, on their meal break, sat in a booth closest to the restrooms. An older gentleman in his fifties, a young woman with an infant, and a family of four, were the only other customers dining this evening. Eddie feasted on a veggie sandwich along with a tomato and pepper bisque. He slurped the latter very loudly and washed it all down with a diet soft drink. Marcus had a smoked ham and Swiss sandwich with lemonade. He was a little upset because he forgot to ask for a side of mayo.

Marcus put down the dry sandwich and addressed his partner, "So, Eddie, what's been eating at you lately, man? For weeks, you've been like...in a daze. Trying to talk to you," Marcus pointed toward a wall, "is like trying to engage that wall over there in a conversation, what's up?"

Eddie was in the midst of taking in another spoonful of his bisque. He put down his spoon and gave considerate effort in thought before answering, "Well, got a lot of things...a lot of stuff on my mind."

Marcus waited patiently.

After several more seconds, Eddie continued, "Things are not going well at home."

Marcus cleared his throat and put on his game face to ask, "You mean with Neci?"

"Yeah…she…she's just different. It's hard to describe."

" '*Different*'? How?"

Eddie gave Marcus a hard and serious look as he responded, "My wife's fucking around. Another man is *dicking* Neci. Can't believe she's cheating on me, Marcus. I don't want to fucking believe it." A single tear streamed down Eddie's face.

Marcus was caught off guard despite his guilt from being intimate with Eddie's wife, and the fact that Eddie suspected infidelity. Hearing his partner say it aloud was still a bit unnerving. Marcus was rattled but attempted to recover as he asked, "What proof do you have, Eddie? I mean, just because y'all aren't having sex or sleeping in the same room ain't proof that Neci's cheating."

A shadow passed across Eddie's face. He stared intensely into his partner's eyes, frowned, then leaned forward toward Marcus who was seated on the opposite side of the table, then blurted, "How the *fuck* do you know we are sleeping in separate rooms, let alone not having sex, Marcus?!"

Marcus frantically tried to think of a rebound as he answered, "Ed-Eddie. First you need to calm down. I'm only trying to help you, man. Second, it's common for couples to stop having sex and sleep in separate rooms when they have problems. I just made an assumption, sorry, *damn*!" Marcus thought, *Good comeback! A little weak, but not bad!* He waited uneasily to see if Eddie believed him.

Eddie stared hard at Marcus for a long time. Marcus felt the beads of sweat popping out off his baldpate. He wanted to swallow but was afraid that Eddie would see that as a sign of guilt or nervousness.

A full minute past before Eddie sat back and relaxed. "Sorry, dude. This thing got me stressed…just don't know what to do. Neci means the world to me, Marcus. I'm not going to let some other guy take her away from me."

Marcus wanted to breathe a sigh of relief but fought that strong urge as his heart beat subsided some. "Eddie, you know Neci wouldn't screw around on you - get real!"

"Marcus, you just don't know the *history*, dude."

Marcus's stomach dropped. He did not like the way that sounded and he thought, *is Eddie implying that Neci cheated on him in the past? Impossible!* Marcus had to know though, so he pressed Eddie for elaboration on his statement.

"What're you trying to say, Eddie? *What*…that Neci's been unfaithful before?"

Eddie did not answer. He combed his hand through the thickness of his blond mane and then finished the rest of his dinner.

Marcus did not like the silence. *What the fuck is he trying to say about Neci?*

"I'm full. Let's roll, dude." Eddie piled his empty containers on of the tray and stood up to leave. He looked down at Marcus and said, "Long story…not gonna get into it. Let's find somebody to arrest." With that, Eddie walked toward the trash receptacles, emptied his tray, then left through the side door.

Marcus's stomach began to ache and not from the partially-eaten dinner left on his plate. He slowly got up to empty his trash then followed Eddie out to the patrol car. Marcus had a very uncomfortable feeling about his relationship with his partner…and the woman, Eddie's *innocent* wife, with whom he was now madly in love.

Chapter 30

Several nights later, Marcus received a telephone call from Neci just after 9:00 p.m. She gave him an unexpected and surprising proposition. Neci invited Marcus over to the house; as Eddie was working an off-duty job, he would not be home until late. With the boys in bed asleep, the timing was perfect and she *needed* him. Marcus was very apprehensive about going to his partner's home. On his last visit he became trapped inside and Eddie nearly caught them in the small bedroom. Plus Eddie's suspicions about Neci's infidelity made it even more likely that they could get caught this time. Eddie may very well NOT be working that niight, rather, possibly setting up a trap for Neci and her secret lover instead.

The more Neci pleaded about how much she needed Marcus inside of her, however, the easier it was for him to give in to seeing the beauty that night. Marcus made a quick telephone call to the police department and verified that Eddie was in fact working security at a dance held at one of the military retirees club. Marcus called Neci back and told her that he was on his way.

***

During the long drive to Woodland County, Marcus thought for the one millionth time about Eddie's statement about his and Neci's 'history' and that *it* was a '*long story.*' It made Marcus question Neci's involvement with him; he painfully questioned whether or not this was Neci's first affair. The thought of Neci being with another man, outside of her marriage to Eddie, was just too much to stomach. It would cheapen what they had - diminish the magic of it all.

Since learning of this, Marcus seriously pondered coming right out and asking her about her possible past indiscretions but lost his nerve. He even wondered if he should warn Neci about Eddie's suspicions. Selfishness overruled that latter thought; Marcus wanted nothing to interfere with his being able to see Neci from time to time. As Marcus got closer to the Logan home, his qualms of getting caught by a jealous husband and his doubts about Neci's past disappeared. He was going to make love to Neci that night and that was all that mattered - nothing else.

***

Neci purred in a sexy voice as she looked up at Marcus, "God, you have an *incredible* body. I love the way you take control over me, over *my* body. You're so powerful, but a gentle lover. The way you take me…you're very intense…I, I just love the effect." She sucked one of her fingers then reached up and began making little circles around and upon Marcus's nipples as she continued, "If I remember correctly, it's your left nipple, right?"

Marcus sat nude on the sofa in the dimly-lit great room of the Logan home, "Yeah, you got a mind like a steel-trap; you don't forget a thing, Neci."

As the fireplace was ablaze behind them, the only light in the darkened room, Neci knelt between Marcus's large thighs on the plush tan carpet wearing only a hot-pink nightshirt. They had just finished a brief session of intense lovemaking. Neci, seconds ago, took him into her mouth. She tasted her tanginess on him. Neci had been in a playful but sexual mood that night; she refused to allow Marcus to climax, torturing her lover with her irresistible sexuality.

As Neci continued to hold onto Marcus's thickness with her other hand, she looked at him seductively then said, "You told me over the telephone the other night, remember during our phone sex? That your *left* nipple was *extremely* sensitive and *me sucking* and *licking* it would have you climbing the walls, right? "

"Something like that."

Neci put Marcus's hardness back into her mouth then slowly massaged it with her soft tongue, sucking the pulsating member.

"Aaah-shiiiittttttt, Neci. Forget my nipple, keep doing that." Marcus enjoyed watching Neci take him inside her mouth. The way she slowly sucked and twirled her tongue made him want to climax immediately.

Neci continued the oral sex but once again refused him an orgasm. She slowly stopped but kept her hand moving slightly along his smooth length then asked, "Remember, what I told you about one of my turn-ons, something I've never done?"

Neci's squeezed his rigid cock as Marcus answered, "Anal sex, you've always wanted to try it."

Neci's dark eyes glistened as she smiled. "That's right. As you know, I'm a virgin back there. I find the thought of you and I doing *that*...rather...exciting, a major turn-on for me. Mmmm...being taken from behind like that, no pun intended, would be pure ecstasy, Marcus." She looked thoughtfully then licked her lips. "Hmmm...maybe tonight's the night for my deflowering, you think?" Neci, released Marcus, and then got up walking pass the silent Samsung 50" widescreen plasma TV and into the sunroom a few feet away.

The large TV, now facing the couch that Marcus sat upon, was in between the great room and sunroom. The high-definition TV could be turned around along its swiveled base making it viewable from either room during any given time. Neci sauntered into the sunroom, walking in between the two-piece sectional sofa and loveseat there, toward the large windows. She faced the set of floor-to-ceiling rectangular windows that gave a view of the backyard. The decorative blinds were up and revealed the lighted yard which was covered with a powdery snow from earlier that evening. The outside coldness looked exotic, like a winter wonderland. Neci took off her long nightshirt then assumed the position, fully naked.

With Neci's yellowish-brown, glistening skin reflecting the light from the fireplace, Marcus could see that she leaned against the window placing her hands on the glass with her back to him, exposing her tight plump buttocks.

Neci licked her red lips and spread her legs wide apart. She then turned her head back toward her seated lover as she said challenging, "Come frisk me, Officer Williams, I've been bad." She turned back facing the window with her shiny long hair cascading down her back. Neci pushed out her plump rear, it jiggled slightly, then she said softly, "*Please* use your *big* nightstick, officer."

Marcus leaped up from the couch unable to contain his excitement then went to the waiting woman. As his stomach fluttered in excitement, Marcus knelt down behind Neci and touched her buttocks, the Jennifer Lopez-like anatomy rippled from the touch. He spread the flesh open and pleasured Neci there as she stroked her clit.

"Aaaah-aaaah…mmm-hmm, that's good, Marcus. *Uhhhhhhhh*" Neci, balancing against the glass with one hand, moaned again, and then whispered something unintelligible, closing her eyes tightly. The woman's breathing became rapid. Her knees were weak due to the pleasure. She felt the warmth of Marcus's long tongue beginning to penetrate her *virgin opening*, gradually preparing her for the later anticipated pleasure of him sliding deep inside her.

Marcus then vacated her anus momentarily and slid his tongue inside her wetness to use as lubrication anally. "Oooh, Baby! My puuussssy! Mmmmmmmm! Haaaaaa-aaaaaaaah, aaaaaawwww, don't you...you *dare* make me cum! Not yet!" Neci's eyes rolled back inside her head in pure exhilaration.

Suddenly, Marcus sensed a presence behind him. He would never be able to describe how he knew, whether a slight sound or just something intuitive, but he knew without a doubt that someone had just walked into the room...that someone was now silently watching the lovers. Neci, still stroking herself to an intense orgasm, was totally oblivious to the newcomer and that Marcus had stopped feasting on her.

Marcus still holding onto Neci's bottom, turned toward the visitor with the shiny essence of Neci covering his face. His misgivings of being caught literally with his pants down had now finally come to fruition. Upon seeing the man's angry face, Marcus's erection immediately withered. As Marcus stared into his partner's steely gaze, he knew that the brief torrid affair with Neci was finally over; both sadness then fear quickly set in.

Chapter 31

"I'm just *tired* of the excuses, Tamala! We been dating long enough! I do *you*, but you don't do *me*?! Ain't going for that shit no more."

Tamala was tired of this same old argument as she lay on the bed covered up by the bed sheets with Lamar glaring down on her. "I told you, Lamar. I don't *suck* dick. And *you* know that."

"You sucked that cop's dick!"

"Like I *said* before - I dated Marcus much longer than I've dated you."

Lamar was standing at the foot of the bed in a pair of red and blue cotton briefs as he asked, "What the fuck that's supposed to mean to me?!"

Tamala was getting nervous. Lamar had not been violent with her since the night she found his secret drug stash. She did not want to upset him to that point ever again.

"*Answer me*, *Tamala*! Stop starin' into fuckin' space!"

Tamala looked at him then said, "I ain't staring in no space. Just thinkin', that's all."

"You *gonna* suck my dick tonight! I've done nothing but take care of you, Tamala! You got everythin' you need up in here! I've turned your *shitty* little crib from nothin' to luxury! That cop could never give you all this shit! The *poor-ass* motherfucker couldn't even pay your car note!"

Tamala was now getting angry. "Marcus was good to me, Lamar! You don't know him so don't speak on shit you don't know about! Maybe he didn't have much money, but he *loved* me; he took care of me with the little bit he did have!" Tamala paused and then glanced down reflectively, "Marcus…he made me happy."

Lamar stared at Tamala in disbelief. "You takin' up for that *punk-ass* motherfucker now? His *broke-ass* couldn't take care of you, I come on the scene and give you everything, *every-fucking-thing*! Now you defending his no-money-having ass? *Oh*, and now you trying to say I don't make you happy, *bitch*?"

Tamala fixed her eyes on him accusingly. "Marcus *would never* hurt me like you did! But most of all he treated me with *respect*! I was just too blind to see it!"

Lamar laughed mockingly at her. "Ha-ha. *Respect*? I buy you all this shit," he looked around then waved his arms about the bedroom and apartment, "and all you can say is that *I* don't fuckin' *respect* you?" He then stared back into her eyes, "Bitch, *please*!

Tamala threw back the bed sheets and yelled, "STOP CALLING ME THAT!" Tears started to well up in her eyes.

"The *fuck* you raisin' your voice at, *bitch*?!

Lamar removed his underwear then walked closer to the bed grabbing Tamala's hair. "I want a fuckin' blowjob *now*. You owe me - fuckin' debt's past due." With his other hand, he held his limp dick in front of her tightly closed mouth. He noticed the look of hatred upon Tamala's face. "Damn, you look like you wanna kill me or something, Tamala. Looking all defiant and shit, *suck it*." His penis now touched her closed mouth.

Tamala released the tears. As they rolled down her face, she made up her mind not to give in to her fear. She continued to look back at him with boldness.

"Suck it…I *ain't* playin'!" Lamar's gray eyes began to burn with anger. He twisted Tamala's hair hard in his tight grip.

"Owwwww! Pleeeeease, Lamar! That hurts, *stop*!"

"Suck-this-dick!"

Tamala looked at him timidly then croaked, "*No*."

Without warning, the back of Lamar's hand came down on her with lightening speed. He slapped Tamala so hard that it knocked her on the opposite side of the bed. He watched her fall to the floor and laughed. Lamar walked over to her and looked down at the fallen young woman with a mocking smile. "Don't make me hurt you, I *do* love you. You gonna do what I say, Tamala?"

Tamala replied softly, "No, Lamar." The woman held her ground.

Lamar smiled wildly then pounced in anger upon the helpless and defenseless young woman. Tamala rolled into a ball in hopes of protecting herself from her crazed boyfriend's blows. As Lamar kicked and punched Tamala severely, she had only one thought before being beaten unconscious: *Marcus, help me.*

***

An optical illusion, a trick of the dim lighting, the stress of getting caught and Eddie's suspicion of his wife's adultery, made Marcus see something, rather someone who was actually not there. Marcus frowned then blinked twice. He thought, *a child?* Then the revelation came; he realized that, Juny, his partner's and Neci's eldest son was staring defiantly at him. Marcus stood face to face with Eddie's miniature.

The butt-naked Marcus said cheerfully, "*Hey*, Juny. What's up?"

The frightened but angry boy replied, "*Stop* hurtin' my *mommy*!"

Neci hearing the voice came out of her sexual stupor and turned toward her son's familiar voice. "Oh, god!" The fully nude woman covered her mouth in shock.

The frightened young eyes of Neci's son pleaded with her, "*Mommy*, Mister Marcus *hurt* you!" Juny then placed his stare back upon Marcus, who continued to kneel before the child. "I'm tellin' my daddy on you, Mister Marcus, you are *baaaad*!"

Marcus glanced back and up at Neci. He saw pure mortification and terror on her face. Marcus reached for her fallen nightshirt and handed it to her as he said to the boy, "Me and mommy were playing a...umm, game, that's all, Juny...we were playing a game that adults play." Marcus still addressing the boy looked back at Neci, who was quickly getting dressed, and continued, "See, Juny, your mom's fine."

The blue-eyed and blond-haired boy ran to his mother and clung to her. Neci looked at Marcus as if for guidance. She held her son with one hand and twisted her long hair with the other.

Marcus told her softly, "It's going to be alright, Neci."

The horror-struck woman whispered, "What if he *tells*...?"

Marcus repeated, "It'll be alright. Maybe I should..."

Neci simply nodded then glanced down as she now held the boy with both arms, "Juny, I'm going to get you back to bed so Mister Marcus can go home now."

Marcus feebly tried to find his belongings in the dim light of the fireplace, dreading what he was about to leave behind. Knowing in his heart but trying to deny the feeling that this episode would put an end to them - Neci and him.

Finally after getting dressed, he took one last look at Neci and Juny standing near the large windows of the sunroom. Neci knelt down before the confused and upset child, trying to calm him, reassure him and persuade him that what he saw was nothing and his father knew all about this *silly game* that *Mister Marcus* and she played. She told Juny that it was not necessary for him to tell his father. Neci prayed that her explanation would work on her impressionable son. Marcus quietly left the room and then let himself out.

***

Later as Marcus made his way through the extreme cold to an alley two streets over where he hid his Toyota, his only thought was on a love that was probably lost now - and fear that Eddie was now apt to do something stupid if little Juny ran his mouth.

Marcus pondered these disturbing and depressing quandaries while making his getaway to his car. As his hot breath produced a small steam cloud into the air, he never noticed the coldness of the night that had numbed his worried face. The sound of the crunching snow, under his hurried footfalls, also went unheard as his anxiety began to increase.

Chapter 32

The very next afternoon, Saturday, the boys ate their lunch and Eddie went out to the garage to work on the Mustang. Neci picked up the cordless telephone from it's wall mount in the kitchen then quietly stepped into the sunroom to call Marcus. She was careful to keep an eye out of the large windows to watch for Eddie's return to the house. Neci, dressed in dark gray slacks and light blue sweater, heard the phone ringing through the receiver, as she took a seat in the sitting area of the room. Just as she was about to hang up, Neci heard Marcus's sleepy voice on the other end. She tried to sound cheerful and non-panicked, just the opposite from what she now felt on the inside.

"It's a bright sunny Saturday afternoon, and you're *still* in bed, wait 'til you have kids then *sleeping in* will not be an option. How ya doing, lazy?"

Marcus wearing only a pair of black underwear, Calvin Klein boxer briefs, rolled over groggily and glanced at the clock. "Dag. It's almost one o'clock." He yawned uncontrollably saying, "Excuse me, Neci, I'd gladly lose sleep if those kids were *ours*."

Neci smiled at the wonderful thought but quickly focused back upon the dreadful and incredibly difficult task of breaking the news to Marcus. She responded, "You're too sweet. We need to- "

"You and Juny okay?" Marcus sat up in bed as the sheets slid off his bare chest.

Neci exhaled sharply then peeked through the kitchen doorway connected to the sunroom and great room. She could hear the boys talking and still eating their meal. "I don't know, Marcus. I've kept Juny as close to me as possible. For the most part he's…pretty much his usual self. I don't know if he'll bring up our situation in front of Gerard." Neci looked back out towards the garage then continued, "But…I just don't know how long I can keep him away from his father, Marcus. I'm, I'm *really* worried about this." Neci was frustrated as she placed her head in her hand, staring at the floor.

"Maybe…Juny will think that it was all some bad dream, you think? He may not have even understood what was going on." Marcus said reassuringly.

Neci answered, "I don't know. I, I really just don't know what to do. If…if Gerard finds out… I'm just a nervous wreck. I didn't get much sleep." She began twisting her hair as she stared once again toward the rear yard.

Marcus gave a great sigh. It was time to be forthcoming about Eddie's mindset. "Neci, I've got to tell you something. I meant to tell you last night…but…but just got caught up…in our moment."

Neci sat up in concern then asked, "What's wrong, Marcus? Did something happen?"

Marcus sighed once more trying to gather his thoughts. "It's…let me explain, it's not too bad."

"*Please*, Marcus. Just say what's on your mind, I can tell it in you voice…something's wrong, isn't it?"

"Neci, Eddie suspects you of seeing someone."

Neci's heart leaped in fear. "What?! Who?! Why didn't you say something, Marcus?!"

"Neci, *please* just settle down. He didn't go into details. Look, he would've told me if he suspected me."

"Great, *Marcus*! That gets *you* off the hook, *unbelievable*!"

"Neci, I didn't mean it that away. Come on, there's no need to get upset."

"Marcus, you shouldn't have *kept* that from me!"

Neci saw Juny peeking through the open doorway at her. The loudness of her voice drew concern from the boy. Neci tried to calm herself as she blew a kiss at her oldest son then smiled. He smiled back shyly and walked back out of sight toward the table.

"I know, Neci...I, guess...I was just selfish."

Neci spoke harshly but in a low voice, "You *damn* right it was selfish!"

(SILENCE)

"Neci, we can get through this-"

"How, Marcus?! My son is very bright, *not stupid*! At any moment now, Juny could tell his daddy that his mommy was having sex with '*Mister Marcus*'! How do you suppose we could 'get through' *that*, Marcus?! Tell me?! *How*?! *Do tell*!"

(SILENCE)

Neci had tears streaming down her eyes. She loved Marcus so much, but the revelation of them sleeping together would no doubt breakup the family. She thought gravely, *Gerard would take my boys from me. I can't let that happen - ever!*

Neci still crying silently broke the silence by expressing sadly, "I can't do this anymore, Marcus. I just...*can't*. Fate is...so damn unfair. I can no longer take the stress of this. Sneaking around...being in constant fear of getting caught. It's...it's just too much. My boys mean the world to me...can't let Gerard find out about us, I'll lose my children, Marcus. We can't do this anymore, *I* can't. It has to…end"

Marcus tried valiantly to keep himself together as he felt the love of his life, slipping *out* of his life. He whispered with urgency, "Neci, *please* don't do this. We can work it out *somehow*. We've got a good thing between us."

Neci saw Eddie slowly walking back to the house with grease or oil on his grimy hands. She tried to swallow down her sadness then whispered sincerely, "Marcus, I'm so…so sorry. Our timing was…it's just so damn unfair. Goodbye, sweetheart." She pressed the 'off' button as she watched her suspecting husband walk up to the deck. *I must somehow make amends…convince him otherwise, s*he thought with resolve. Neci slowly stood up and walked back to the kitchen with her family; she must now somehow begin to live the lie of being the happy wife for the sake of her boys.

***

Marcus stared unbelievably at the phone in his hands. *Neci was gone - gone forever*. He slowly replaced the phone on the nightstand. He did not have time to fully process the devastation of his loss as the telephone began ringing again.

Marcus regained his hope that Neci was calling back as he exclaimed, "*Hey!*"

"Marc?"

Marcus frowned then looked dejected as his hopes were dashed by Sneak's voice. He answered his friend, "Hey, man. What's up?" Marcus rubbed his sad and tired eyes.

"Bad news, brother. Need you to haul-ass over to Henrico Doctors' Hospital. Tamala was involved in some sort of accident. I think she's lying, but-"

"What happened, Sneak?" With his heart racing, Marcus threw back the sheets and covers then swung his legs on the side of the bed. His stomach felt sick with dread.

"It's not life threatening, but Staci found Tamala unconscious inside her apartment. They were supposed to do some shopping this morning. Staci called her but got no answer so she went over, used her key, Tamala was in…in bad shape, Marc. Need you to come, if you can. The good news is that they just took her out of intensive care. You coming, Marc?"

With eyes closed, Marcus lowered his head then rubbed his baldpate saying, "Yeah, yeah, of course I'll be right there." He looked up and stared into space. "Where's the hospital, Sneak?"

"On Skipwith Road in Henrico off Forest Road. You take-"

"Never mind. I'll just Mapquest it. Let me get dressed."

Sneak said, "I'll wait for you in the front lobby and take you up to her."

"Okay, thanks, Sneak. I'm on my way." Marcus ended the call then whispered, "Damn…what the *fuck*?" He then moved quickly to dress and lookup the directions to the hospital on his archaic computer.

Chapter 33

The entrance to the front foyer of Henrico Doctors' Hospital, the Forest Campus, was an architectural wonder. The tall stylish assemblage, just outside of the foyer, was definitely a work of art with large white concrete pillars, topped with several rectangular and crisscross-shaped designs that were crowned with angled roofless peaks. The "framing" design was often a conversational piece.

After finding a parking space, Marcus rushed into the foyer nearly knocking Sneak down.

"*Whoa*, Marc, slow down, man!"

Marcus, wearing a ratty blue sweat suit with Woodland County Police Academy across the front of the sweat top, stopped when he recognized Sneak. "*How's Tam doing*?!" Marcus asked breathlessly.

Sneak grabbed Marcus firmly on his broad shoulders then looked deeply into Marcus's eyes to gain the frantic man's attention. He said in his deep voice, "Brother, relax. The doctor said that Tamala's gonna be okay. She was knocked unconscious but is awake now and doesn't have a concussion. Now, the girl does have some serious injuries - blunt trauma to her face, a broken left arm, and a few broken ribs, but she'll survive."

"Damn, Sneak! What the fuck *happened* to her?!"

"Ummm…she claims that she fell down the front stairs out in front of her apartment building. Supposedly slipped on some ice."

" '*Supposedly*'?"

Sneak, who had on a black skullcap, turtleneck, and slacks, nodded then continued, "She said that she crawled back up to her apartment where she passed out, then Staci found her."

The two cops shared a knowing look.

"She's lying, right?"

Sneak released Marcus then nodded.

Marcus asked, "Lamar?"

Sneak said, "That's what I think but didn't wanna say it, man."

"Have the police been called?"

"Yep, standard procedure for the doctors to contact the cops and Henrico PD just left. They were satisfied that it was just an accident."

"Sneak, we gotta do something. Does Tam's momma know she's here?"

"She's upstairs with her now, along with Staci. Tamala's sisters were contacted too. The good thing, Marcus, is that she is gonna be fine; they got her in a regular room now."

"Take me to her, Sneak."

"Alright, but listen. Be cool up there, okay? No need to upset everyone. Visiting hours ended and won't start back until four p.m. but they letting us stay, I flashed the old badge; security knows we are the police. Also Marcus, I wouldn't mention that we know she's lying about what happened; we'll get to the bottom of it in time." Sneak frowned as he continued, "And one other thing, ummm…Tamala's a little groggy still. Her face is… severely swollen, her left eye is swollen shut. I…I just wanted to prepare you, my friend. She looks a lot worse than she actually is."

Marcus gave a heavy sigh and shook his head at the mental picture. He looked wearily at his friend, "Okay, *please* take me to her."

"Follow me."

Sneak led Marcus upstairs to see the woman that he once wanted to become his wife. Marcus slowly began to seethe with anger, a burning anger that would be impossible to stop if the wrath continued to build within him. With Neci possibly forever being out of his life and Tamala's vicious assault, Marcus could soon become a loose cannon. The two men silently entered one of the empty elevators.

***

Tamala lay in her hospital bed; her window had a view of a parking lot below. The sunlight shone but did not cheerfully brighten up the room given the solemn mood held by all. Through the one eye that was not swollen closed, Tamala watched her mother and Staci standing near the window talking quietly. The other bed beside Tamala's was neatly made up but empty. She was woozy from the medication and extremely sore from Lamar's beating. It even hurt for her to breath because of the broken ribs.

Tamala felt ashamed for putting herself in this position - broken in a hospital bed and lying to the police as to how she got that way in the first place. *Why did I lie to them, all of them, Momma, Staci, and the police? Fear, shame? What?* Tamala thought as she scanned around the semi-private hospital room. She came to the realization that selfishness and greed brought her to this point in her life. *I deserve to be here, I fuckin' deserve this shit!* An angry tear escaped from her uninjured right eye. She was angry with herself and only herself! Her pity-party was interrupted when she heard the door open.

Sneak and Marcus walked in with serious expressions on their faces. Marcus's eyes caught both Rose Cooper and Staci standing near the window. He waved with a brief smile as he greeted Tamala's mother, "Hello, Miss Rose." Then he glanced at Tamala's friend. Marcus's smile disappeared, but he said with a nod, "Staci." Staci nodded back without a word.

"Thank, Gawd, Marcus. So glad ta have ya here." Mrs. Cooper clasped her hands in front of her chest as if in prayer, beaming at Marcus.

When Marcus's eyes settled upon the small form in the bed closest to the door, he gaped uncontrollably. He observed Tamala's injuries just as Sneak had described them but actually seeing his ex-girlfriend in her fragile condition, shocked Marcus to his core. Tamala had an IV drip connected to her right arm. She was also hooked up to various other tubes, electrodes, and monitors, all displaying or controlling her vitals. The shocking part was that Marcus did not recognize the light-skinned freckled-face beauty that he once worshipped; her swollen face was severely distorted. Marcus felt sadness, pity, and then rage upon seeing the beaten woman with her broken left arm held above the bedcovers.

Tamala began crying then turned her head toward the window, away from Marcus. Shame was all she felt at that moment; shame at how she had wronged the man that wanted to spend the rest of his life with her. Now, that man was here to support her at her bedside.

Marcus apprehensively walked toward her. Sneak motioned silently for Tamala's mother and Staci to give them some privacy so the three quietly left Tamala and Marcus alone. Marcus stood at Tamala's side. He did not know what to do or say. Then instincts took over and he slowly reached for her right hand. He held it gently then whispered, "It'll be alright, Tam. It'll be alright..." She turned toward his voice.

Marcus's kindness only made her cry harder. *How can he be so forgiving, so loving after I treated him like shit, threw him away like garbage*, Tamala thought. She felt more ashamed than ever at that very moment.

***

"Then Staci said she found me. I musta fell *pretty* hard, Marcus."

Tamala recounted her *story* to Marcus, who continued to hold her hand while listening intensely. She had calmed down considerably, finally able to talk. Tamala stared up at the ceiling as she relayed her account to Marcus, as if talking to herself. She felt dirty for lying to Marcus but just could not bring herself to tell him the truth. Tamala felt like a failure - a loser in life. Only when she finished her dramatic soliloquy did she make eye contact with him.

Marcus searched her one good misty eye now, as he prepared to question her weak story of falling down the front stairs. He was trying to determine the mental fragility of the woman. He did not want to traumatize her anymore than she already was, but he needed answers. Marcus decided that he must confront Tamala. He thought, *should I beat around the bush, or just be blunt, just come out with it?* Marcus needed a few moments before proceeding. He gently released her hand then slowly walked over to the window which continued to allow in the bright afternoon sunlight. He leaned against it trying to gather his thoughts.

Marcus's eyes caught an elderly white gentleman walking gingerly with a cane from the parking lot. He would walk a few steps…stop…then walk a few more, only to repeat the tiresome sequence. The older gentleman was bundled up, wearing a tan hat and a long black overcoat, due to the cold weather. Marcus could see the man's puffs of warm breath against the coldness of the air. He carried a quad aluminum cane, the type with the four rubberized tips, as he shuffled slowly toward the building. Marcus had an odd thought as he became mesmerized at the man's plight of simply trying to make his way to the hospital's front entrance. He wondered if the gentleman was coming into the hospital due to health reasons, or maybe to visit his ailing wife whom he was totally dedicated to visiting, despite his own failing health and the bone-chilling weather. The man finally walked out of sight as he made it to the building. Marcus had an urge to cheer for the man's accomplishment especially in the midst of not slipping on an ice patch.

Marcus often visualized himself growing old with the woman of his dreams. He wondered if he would just grow old and wither away without ever finding the love of his life. He thought, *Tam left me for another and Neci belonged to another!* Marcus exhaled sharply then walked back toward Tamala. She was staring at him with a look of wonder.

Marcus plopped down on the bed beside Tamala. He stared back at her for a moment. Finally he broke the long silence, "Remember that trip when we drove down to Myrtle Beach, the summer before last? We were standing on the balcony taking in the aroma of the ocean, gazing up at that cloudless blue sky? We both said at the exact same time…'This is heaven', remember that?" Tamala slowly nodded as Marcus continued, "Time and time again we seemed to have the uncanny ability to finish each other's sentences; we often knew what the other was thinking way before words were ever spoken. I could just look at you, and you at me; we could almost read each other's minds. We had a special connection, Tam, a connection that…that somehow became broken over the last year or so." Tamala looked sadly at Marcus but listened respectfully. "Anyway…I don't need a special connection with you now to know that your story's *pure* bullshit. I see right through it. You and I both know what really happened, and you falling down some stairs never *happened*."

Tamala averted her eye. She turned and stared at the ceiling again saying with defeat, "Just let it be, Marcus. What's done is done. Please just let it go."

Marcus stood up and walked to the door then stopped to look back at Tamala. "As hard as this is for me to say,

Tam. I still care for you." Tamala looked toward him with tears once again streaming down her face. "You didn't deserve this. I hate what Lamar did to you. You can't hide what I see…I see that he's put the fear of God in you." Marcus looked down at the floor trying to compose himself. Moments later, after gathering his thoughts, he once again glanced up at the beaten and defeated woman. "You hurt me, Tam, very badly, but you didn't deserve this. Get better." Marcus quickly exited the room leaving the crying woman behind. Once outside the room, Sneak tried to call after Marcus who took the stairway, running. Sneak, Tamala's mother, and Staci looked where Marcus had disappeared then at the door to Tamala's room. They quickly went into the room to check on her.

***

A few minutes later as Marcus drove out of the hospital parking lot, he dialed a familiar telephone number. After hanging up with the arrangements complete, Marcus knew that he could rely on Weenie, T. C.'s and his old informant, to get the job done. After tonight, Lamar will wish that he had never met Tamala Cooper. Rage, hatred, and murder filled Marcus's heart which both disturbed and excited him and he willingly embraced his darker side. Taking out all of life's frustration on Lamar would bring him sweet release. Though Marcus was enraged, he knew that he had just crossed the line with that phone call. It made him a little nervous because several laws would be broken that night; Marcus would not only be in jeopardy of losing his job but in danger of going to prison.

As Marcus merged onto the interstate heading back to his apartment to prepare, he really did not care about the possibility of being arrested. He had lost so much in the last several months. He thought, *it just doesn't matter anymore, my life's over!*

Chapter 34

Later that night, Lamar Phelps pulled up in his BMW and parked near the front of his home in Woodland County - Ghetto Town. Unbeknownst to Lamar, he was being watched. A man dressed in all black waited patiently for the young thug to arrive. He was now crouched in the darkness near the right corner of Lamar's mother's home. The man had been laying in wait for most of the evening. As he watched Lamar get out of his car, the man could feel how stiff his joints were. The coldness could greatly affect his performance, but he was hopeful that it wouldn't too much. As the dark shadows of the night concealed him, the man stood allowing his blood to circulate through his tired and cold joints; he was not as young as he used to be. The man knew that he would only get one opportunity at the younger man they called Red Bone. He also knew that Red Bone was possibly armed, but the man was not worried as his adrenaline began to kick in. He also had the element of surprise on his side so he only had to remain calm and place sole trust in his skills and instincts. The beating needed to be swift enough to keep Lamar from yelling out for help or from pulling out any weapons. The first strike would therefore be the most important; if he failed the mission could turn deadly. A failed mission was not an option; the man must pounce on Lamar quickly, but silently.

Lamar walked slowly toward the house looking down at his keys in the dim lighting of the streetlamp. He walked through the opening of the fence as he discovered the correct key. It had been a while since he stayed with his mother. He would go back to Tamala's place when the 'heat' cooled down. He was certain that Tamala would keep her trap shut and not tell the police who assaulted her. Lamar had been through this before with prior girlfriends:

they knew when to keep quiet after a whipping. He thought, *I had no choice but to teach Tamala a lesson. She'll understand in time, God intended for men to run the house! Keep our women in line. Gotta admit I miss that girl.*

Before he could step onto the porch, the first blow to Lamar's solar plexus was extremely effective as the unsuspecting victim doubled over in shock then pain holding his midsection. The man in black dragged a groaning Lamar to the corner of the house where he had been waiting all night. Once in the darkness, the man quickly got down on his knees and commenced to punching Lamar with lightening speed; the punches and jabs were quick and efficient. The man wore leather sap-gloves, with steel inserts, which intensified his powerful punches that landed on Lamar's torso, back, sides, and midsection. He was careful to avoid hitting Lamar in his face as those punches could kill him instantly. The goal was to beat him to within an inch of his life.

The sickening thuds from the blows were relentless. Lamar had never experienced pain like this before; death would have been welcomed. The whimpering Lamar was finally able to get a reprieve after a few minutes as he passed out from the excruciating pain. The man continued to beat the now-unconscious Lamar who was being thrown around like a rag-doll. The weight from the heavy gloves and the hard punches began to take their toll on the man in black. His arms felt like jelly as his punches slowed. He could hear his own ragged breathing along with his rapid heartbeat.

When he finally stopped the devastating assault it was as if he had come out of a trance or foggy dream. The man in black looked down at the motionless figure and for a moment wondered who the unconscious person was. The man questioned whether or not he had killed Lamar, as that was not in the plan. Fear began to overtake him. The man looked around for witnesses but discovered that he had not been seen due to the lateness of the hour. There was no pedestrian or vehicle traffic and the man was relieved as he focused his attention back on his victim.

The man began to search the inert form below him and found the gun in Lamar's waist band, quickly placing it in his jacket pocket. A further searched revealed wads of money and - crack-cocaine. Those items were also kept as the tired man in black weakly stood up, still out of breath. He took one last look around then down at the motionless man. The man in black proceeded to make his escape, running through backyards then finally to his rented vehicle hidden in an alley. The rented burgundy 2007 Ford Taurus displayed untraceable license plates thanks to a local business man named Weenie. The man fired up the cold Ford and sped away from the area relieved that his assignment was over. He just hoped that his prey was not dead; facing the legal ramifications from a death would be more serious for all involved.

***

The burgundy 2007 Ford Taurus sped through the radar beam going twenty-six miles per hour over the posted speed limit. Recruit Officer Ray Maitland and Field Training Officer Paul Ketcham were traveling south on Elm Street when the speeding vehicle registered 51 miles per hour in a 25 mile per hour zone.

Field Training Officer Ketcham looked over at the wide-eyed rookie then said condescendingly, "*Well*? You gonna go after him or what? Maybe you got more important shit to do, huh, Maitland?"

The pimple-faced rookie had only a week on patrol. He seemed almost shellshocked as he tried to work out in his head the next move.

"*Maitland, turn around* and *chase* the bastard!"

"Yes, sir!" The young man maneuvered the Woodland County Police Department patrol car slightly to the right side of the road then whipped the marked unit left to make a wide U-turn.

***

The man in black was so focused on getting back to Richmond to place the original license plates back on the car and return the rented Ford back to the rental depot off Broad Street that he did not see the police car coming from the opposite direction until it was too late. His mind went immediately to his victim's contraband which was currently still in his pockets - the pistol, money, and drugs. He would be through if caught by the police. The man hit the accelerator increasing his speed even more. In his rearview mirror, he saw the flashing blue lights of the patrol car attempting to catch-up to him. The man in black was now the prey.

***

Field Training Officer Ketcham said calmly, "Okay, son, just take it easy; let the patrol car do the work. *See*? We're gaining on him."

Officer Maitland was pumped, "Yes, sir!"

The senior cop, nursing a painful stomach ulcer, shook his head and informed dispatch that they were in pursuit of a speeding, dark-colored vehicle. Between giving their directions to the dispatcher, he tried to keep the young rookie calm. "You're doing fine, son. Don't over accelerate;

even though there's very little traffic out here you still gotta clear your intersections."

The young cop said, "Yes, sir!"

The senior cop just prayed that Officer Maitland did not get into a wreck and that they got through the pursuit safely.

***

The man in black made several evasive turns and still the police car was keeping pace with him. *I've got to get out of this before more police cars join in, then it'll be over for sure*, the man thought as fear gripped his soul. Then an idea occurred to him. He knew Ghetto Town like the back of his hand.

***

"Sir? He, he turned out his lights!"

"Keep your cool, son. We need to get closer so we can get a tag number off the car. Just keep on him; he *won't* get away."

As if in slow motion, the speeding Ford made an impossible turn into a blind alley. The police car skidded past the opening of that alley.

"Come on! Turn this heap around! We gonna lose him!"

The young officer desperately wanted to impress his superior officer. He swung the police car hard to the right then hard to the left into another U-turn.

"NO!" The older cop shouted as the police car careened out of control then into several empty trash cans, stalling out the car.

As the dust settled, the rookie officer said sheepishly, "Sorry, sir."

Field Training Officer Ketcham just rolled his eyes, let out a sigh, then hung his head as the man in black made his big escape.

***

Hours later, the rented Ford was safely returned. The man in black was severely shaken. The events of the night had taken a toll upon him. The drugs and pistol that had been taken off the thug were disposed of from the south side of the Manchester Bridge in Richmond, which had limited vehicle traffic this time of night. The bundle was weighted down and thrown into the James River along with his clothing and his beloved sap-gloves, which he had used for many years. The money found on the young thug would be evenly divided between two people that he knew most deserved it. The man in black was now officially retired from further covert missions.

Chapter 35

Marcus took the next three weeks off for a much-needed vacation. He was juggling too many of life's stresses - Neci's desertion, Tamala's convalescence, Rip's elusiveness, financial burdens, and other disturbing matters he tried not to dwell on - to be able to focus safely at work. He dodged phone calls and visits from everyone. Both Sergeant Wessel and Sneak called Marcus. Sergeant Wessel left a message that someone left a large sum of money for the 13-year-old Tyreese and his mother which was greatly needed. Sneak left a similar message that Tamala also had had a generous amount of cash given to her.

Eddie called and left several messages which comforted him that he still did not know about Neci and him. One of Eddie's messages even mentioned finishing the restoration on the Mustang in the spring. In that same message, he also told Marcus about Lamar being found beaten and robbed outside his home, and that Lamar was in 'bad shape.'

With one particular telephone call from the Logan residence, Marcus thought,   *hoped* that it was Neci calling, so he snatched up the phone in a weak moment. Marcus was crestfallen when he heard Eddie's voice on the other end of the line. Eddie invited him over to a Super Bowl party that he was planning for this upcoming Sunday. Marcus only accepted the invitation to get Eddie off the telephone. Seeing Neci again would only make getting over her that much harder.

Chapter 36

Some people may call it police instincts, a "gut" feeling, others may refer to it as an inner voice, an intuition, or maybe a premonition. Whatever the word for it, the feeling that Marcus was experiencing on the early morning of Super Bowl Sunday was one of impending doom. That day something extremely bad was going to happen; it was going to be a horrible date. Marcus felt that strong foreboding deep within his soul when he had awakened on this cold and clear Sunday morning.

By the afternoon the temperature soared into the low 60's, Marcus had completely forgotten about the dread that was evident earlier. Now as he worked in the kitchenette, wearing a Ravens football jersey over a long sleeved black cotton shirt and jeans, he was preparing one of his special dishes - spinach dip.

Eddie never asked Marcus to bring anything to the party but Marcus felt that it would be a polite gesture. He placed the dish in the refrigerator, did some light cleaning, then looked at his watch. *Only 1:05 p.m. Shoot! It's still early!* Marcus thought. Eddie told him to come over anytime, but Marcus thought he would get there after 6:00 p.m., when most of the guests should have already arrived for the kickoff.

Marcus was sure that Eddie invited over most of the squad with the exception of Sergeant Sargent. A large group of screaming, cheering, and drinking cops would probably reduce any uncomfortable tension or feelings between Neci and Marcus. He would keep conversation with Neci to mere pleasantries, 'Hello', 'How've you been?', 'Nice seeing you again', etc. After which time, Marcus would then try to enjoy the game between the Patriots and Giants. That is, *if*

Neci stayed for the party at all; she may have planned for another disappearing act like the first time he came to the Logan home.

Marcus went to his couch and turned on the TV set in an attempt to quell the excitement of seeing her again. After several minutes of flipping through the numerous channels, he decided to take a brief nap before the event. He quickly dozed off into a dreamless nap as a marathon of *The Andy Griffith Show* played in the background.

***

Nearly three hours later Marcus was startled out of his slumber, almost falling off the couch as the ringing telephone brought him back to life.

Marcus sleepily reached for the phone on the side table as he continued to stretch out on the sofa. "Yeah?"

The husky voice replied, "Hi, Marcus."

As always the familiar feminine voice brought him to his full senses. "Hey, Neci. Surprised to hear from you." Marcus's pulse rate increased as he tried to contain his excitement. He used the remote to turn off the TV.

Neci got to the point of her call as she said, "This morning Gerard told me that he'd invited you over for a party this evening. I, I'm calling to ask you *not* to come."

"*What?*" Marcus sat up on the couch disappointed. "Neci, I'm trying to accept you not wanting me in your life. I'm just coming over as a guest, a friend of Eddie's, that's all." Marcus did not even believe his own lie but hoped that she would; seeing Neci again was all he wanted.

"You don't understand-"

"Oh, I *understand*, Neci. I understand you no longer want to see me, ain't a damn thing I can do about that! I'm an invited guest coming over to enjoy the Super Bowl with my partner. It's got nothing to do with you." The hurt of losing Neci could clearly be heard in Marcus's voice. Marcus instantly regretted his lack of temperance.

"Let me finish, Marcus. I'm trying to-"

"What's there to finish?! You made it clear a few weeks ago, Neci! I'm not going to go against *your* wishes! Eddie's a friend, *my* partner, he invited me over! I'll be visiting him. I won't bother you, *trust me*!"

"*Stop* interrupting me, Marcus! I don't *need* this shit right now!"

(SILENCE)

After exhaling sharply, Neci continued in a much softer voice, "I didn't call to argue with you, Marcus. I mailed you a letter yesterday. I've had lots of time to think about…some things. I've made some tough decisions since we've last spoken. I thought that sending you a letter would maybe…clear up a few things."

Marcus was still upset and asked sarcastically, "*What*? You wrote me a *Dear John* letter? It's a little too late for that, Neci! It's clear you want me out of your life!"

"Please, Marcus, don't *yell* at me!" Neci calmed herself then said, "I don't like us being like this! I've called to warn you, about Gerard."

"*Warn* me?" Neci had his full attention now. "I'm confused."

"Gerard's acting…I don't know, *strange*."

Marcus asked with interest, "What do you mean by 'strange'?

"Well…umm…I think Gerard knows, he knows about us, Marcus."

Marcus's stomach dropped in fear. "What? He said something to you?"

"No...it's just his behavior - overly nice, weird smirks, always smiling at me. He told me you were coming over to watch a game, something about a party. I have a funny feeling about it, him inviting you over...I think he wants to confront you - *us*. There isn't going to *be* a party, Marcus."

Marcus's mind flashed back to how he felt this morning - the dread of impending danger. "But he hasn't said anything to you...about suspecting anything?"

"Like I said...not really; it's just a feeling I've got. I don't think it's a good idea for you to come over here, Marcus."

"Neci, don't *worry* about it then. Eddie sounded normal to me over the phone. He even left me a few messages. Trust me, Neci, Eddie doesn't suspect a thing. *Stop* worrying."

Neci had to convince Marcus to stay away from the Logan home. Suddenly, a thought occurred to her. Telling Marcus about the dreadful past in Cantil, California would convince him. Convince him that Eddie was volatile and for that reason could not be trusted. Telling Marcus about the horrible secret would maybe convince him of Eddie's fragile state of mind and persuade him to stay away. She had seen Eddie like this in Cantil, and now over the past few weeks he was exhibiting the same behavior. Eddie was about to explode in the most violent way, just like in California! The secret that Neci had been holding in for so long was about to be revealed.

"Marcus? I need for you to listen to me for a moment. I...this is going to be difficult for me to say, but you must know something about me, about Gerard. Something *not* so good." Neci was sitting in the sunroom wearing an oversized white sweat shirt with UCLA across the front in light blue lettering trimmed in gold, a pair of tight Levi jeans, and black boots. She was trying to gather her thoughts and summon up the courage to tell Marcus what he needed to know.

Marcus heard the apprehension in Neci's voice and became worried. "Neci, what's wrong? Can't be that bad; we've all done stuff...I won't judge you, so just tell me what's on your mind."

After a pause, Neci said, "Gerard and I left California under...not so favorable circumstances."

Neci gave a deep sigh and forged ahead. "Gerard had this...this thing, Marcus. Wait. Let me start from the beginning. Gerard worked in a police department in the Township of Cantil, the Red Rock Canyon Police Department. Very small, close-knit, family oriented community, everybody knew *everybody*. Well, Gerard made lots of friends there...in the police department. We were having problems...in the bedroom, *sexually*. Gerard wanted to add what he referred to as 'spice' to our sex life. He came up with this idea...he wanted to see me...see me have sex...with another man. He thought that inviting another man into bed with us would be a nice little turn-on to spice *things* up...'just for kicks', he said. Gerard *got off* on watching me...with other *men*. Then once Gerard and I were alone...he'd...he'd have sex with me. I hated it all, made me sick to my stomach.

"Over a period of time, he...Gerard had me sleep with several of the officers on the force, Marcus. He just wanted to watch us...he *wasn't* gay, he'd never have contact with the men. He just...*loved* to watch. I, I only did it because...because I wanted to please Gerard, it was stupid, I know." Neci sighed softly then continued, "After a while it became a habit for us to perform this *thing*. Him *watching* as other men touched me made me ill at times, but I loved Gerard so much, Marcus. You probably can't understand this."

Marcus was in complete shock as he listened to Neci's unbelievable story. At that moment, he did not have the voice to speak even if he wanted to.

Neci went on to say, "I would've done anything for him, *back then*. Gerard's voyeurism ended after a while, he started to become jealous. Anyway, Gerard got *so* jealous that he ended it. It was so sick, Marcus. The things Gerard had me do with them...it was just...abnormal." Neci paused.

Marcus slowly sighed. As he found his voice, he expressed, "I...I really don't know what to say, Neci." The pit of Marcus's stomach was burning. He wanted to vomit. He felt his throat closing off; he was barely able to breathe.

Neci said shamefully, "Marcus, that's not the worst of it...it gets a *lot* worse."

Marcus mumbled, "It's okay. I...I'm listening." The young cop was oblivious to the fact that he was squeezing the phone receiver tightly as a slow rage built toward his partner.

"There was this one guy who shared our bed...his name...well that doesn't matter, but I continued seeing him behind Gerard's back." Tears flowed down Neci's face as she went on, "This officer came on to me pretty hard; after things stopped, he wanted to keep seeing me. He said all the right things, Marcus. He fed my ego and Gerard had stopped giving me affection. We, this man and I, got caught one night; Gerard was supposed to be working but came home early, and- "

"Eddie caught you with this guy?" Marcus tried to ask in a calm voice but failed.

"Yes, it…was…just awful." Neci sniffed as she cried silent tears.

Marcus felt as if he was being cheated on all over again…except now it was Neci doing the cheating instead of Tamala.

A heavy sigh and soft crying from Neci could be heard clearly over the phone now. She continued more calmly, "It was a really bad time, Marcus, a bad time in our marriage. Gerard and this officer fought after he walked in on us, and he, my wonderful and *brilliant* husband, *beat* him so badly that he…the man almost died. Gerard's bosses threatened to charge him and of course fire him. In response, Gerard threatened to go to the local press about the…the other officers sleeping, having sex with another cop's wife, *me*…it would've been an awful scandal for everyone involved, especially the police department. I still have nightmares of this coming to light. Could you imagine my parents or my colleagues finding out?

"Anyway, Gerard was going to provide the names of everybody involved; there was even a sergeant and a lieutenant who…participated. The chief of police, upon hearing about Gerard's threat to go to the media, backed off. He even decided not to press charges against my husband for beating the officer. The good old chief wanted to protect the reputation of his police department…along with his son."

Marcus asked, "The *chief's* son?"

"Yes, the chief's son. His son was the officer that I continued the affair with, and the one Gerard put in the hospital. The chief even gave Gerard a glowing recommendation to the Woodland County Police, just to get us out of town. Marcus, I said all of this to get to this point: Before Gerard caught this officer and me, he was acting strange, just like he is now - the constant smirking, suddenly wanting to do things for me, as if he knows he's about to *lower the boom* on me - on us! Gerard somehow knew that I was seeing this man and waited patiently for an opportunity to catch us. I don't want the same to thing to happen to you."

Marcus could hear Neci crying softly. "Did Eddie hurt you, Neci? Back when he...caught you with that guy?"

Neci whispered, *"No.* Just treated me like...like *shit* afterwards."

Marcus shook his head in disgust. He frowned then swallowed hard still not understanding any of this. "Why did you continue seeing him, that cop, if it made you feel so...so bad?"

Neci really could not explain her actions; the 'why' of her continuing to see Officer Todd Bowman was even now a mystery to her. It was just something to do, she thought at one point. "I guess I did it because...maybe because of the stress of it all...it just became a habit...a bad one. Todd, the officer, he pushed and pushed then I finally gave in. Back then any attention was better than none."

Marcus, recalling Neci's words from a previous telephone conversation asked, "You told me that you can only give your heart to one man, you've never slept with more than one guy at a time. And you said that you didn't take lovemaking lightly, you valued it that much! I-I...don't understand, Neci." Marcus felt betrayed and jealous. He struggled to direct his increasing rage toward Eddie, not Neci.

Neci sighed, "No, Marcus. I meant what I said to you, but-"

"I'm listening, Neci!"

Neci was becoming upset with Marcus's berating. She recalled clearly what she had said to Marcus about giving her heart only to one man. In Cantil, her heart belonged to her husband whom she loved deeply. She only had sex with other men to please Eddie, not herself. It was clearly a different situation...and a different time. Neci did not, however, feel like defending herself to Marcus at that moment. Wiping her tears, Neci gave a frustrated sigh then said, "Marcus, like I said, I only continued seeing this other guy because he was persistent. I, I did it because of stress...I wasn't happy...and as I said before, this thing with Todd just developed into a bad habit, so I kept sleeping with him-"

Marcus angrily asked, "Is that what I was, a 'bad habit'?"

The question hurt Neci to her core causing more tears to flow. "That's, that's not fair, Marcus. What...what we shared was *different*. You have no right to *say* that."

"No *right*? How am I supposed to feel, *Neci*? You stopped seeing me, then unload this *crap* on me. You want me to say 'It's alright, baby? I understand?' *Bullshit*! It hurt not seeing you over the past few weeks! Been praying that you'd call! Been moping around here, in my apartment, feeling like my world has ended! You meant the fucking *world* to me! You're my every thought, you're constantly in my dreams! It *hurts*, Neci! I'm tired of being shitted on! Nothing's going right in my life! *NOTHING*!"

Neci cried out, "*I'm sorry, Marcus*! It was *never* my intention to hurt you! I knew you'd end up *hating* me...that was the one thing I couldn't stand - you *hating* me! I wish...I wish that I *was* perfect for your sake! I only told you this to protect you from Gerard! I had no choice!" Neci struggled to gain control of her fear and pain as she then whispered sadly, "Just, just don't…*hate me*, Marcus."

Marcus listened to Neci's heart-wrenching confession and profuse crying. Compassion for her began to set in slowly. He closed his eyes and took several deep breaths to calm himself before speaking. Marcus then looked ahead, staring at nothing as he said, "Look…*look, baby*…I don't hate you, Neci. If anything, I lo-"

"Hold, *hold on*, Marcus!" Neci heard a car drive up.

Marcus heard Neci sniffing as she placed the phone down. After a few seconds she returned and frantically said, "Marcus! Gerard's back from dropping the boys off at the babysitter. Please don't come over here! Let me try and fix this! *I've got to go!*"

Marcus sat shocked holding the dead phone to his ear. Neci had hung up on him. He slowly placed the handset on the stand then got up shakily. The phone conversation seemed to have taken all of the strength out of him. There was only one alternative. He caused this strife for Neci, so it was up to him to take it away. Marcus walked to his bedroom to grab his coat. After putting it on, he made his way to the front door then stopped abruptly.

Marcus ran back into the bedroom to retrieve his police issue Glock .45 pistol, a move that he would later regret for the rest of his life. He placed the weapon in his waistband at the small of his back, covering it with his long football jersey. He did not want Eddie to hurt Neci. If Eddie was going to confront anybody, Marcus was going to be the target. He would take full responsibility for the affair. Marcus then raced out of the front door; he had a date with destiny as rage filled his soul, yet again.

Chapter 37

During Marcus's commute to Woodland County, he prayed that Neci's suspicions of Eddie's knowledge of their affair were misconstrued. Marcus recklessly thought, *his strange behavior of late could be due to any number of things*. Marcus ignored the fact that Eddie, at the very least, believed that his wife had been unfaithful. He further hoped that once at the Logan home, he would see cars belonging to their coworkers parked up and down the street, and Eddie yelling 'sweet.' This would all dispel any worried notions that Eddie was using the party as a ruse to confront the guilty couple.

***

Almost an hour later, Marcus pulled up in front of the Logan home and sat as his car idled. He saw that Eddie's and Neci's vehicles were both parked in the driveway. The green Jetta's passenger side door was standing open. Marcus frowned as he further noticed the front door to the house wide open. He glanced up and down the block; the street was mostly deserted of vehicles other than those of the residents living along Cutler Street. Marcus drove off and headed to the paved alley leading to the rear of the Logan home. He turned off the alley entering the yard. He parked just before the detached garage housing the Mustang. Besides Marcus's Toyota, no other cars were parked in the backyard. *Maybe Neci's right, there isn't a party after all*, Marcus thought nervously.

Continuing to sit in his car, Marcus took off his jacket and found that he had sweated through his football jersey. He then reached behind him and pulled out the pistol from his waistband. He held the weapon down out of sight as he cautiously watched the back of the house. He envisioned

Eddie charging out of the patio doors like a raving madman waving a gun at him, but in reality the home showed no activity at all. It appeared as if no one was home.

Marcus's mind's eye suddenly had a vivid image of Neci lying in a pool of blood and Eddie slumped in a chair with a self-inflicted bullet wound to the head - a murder-suicide. He quickly shook away the morbid vision and then glanced down at his Glock. With shaky hands, he quickly made sure that a round was chambered into the barrel of the sleek pistol. He found the weapon ready for action in the unfortunate event of Eddie becoming violent. He returned the pistol to the small of his back then turned off his car.

Marcus glanced to his front left at the garage and wondered if Eddie was laying wait for him there. *God, I'm paranoid. Eddie doesn't know a thing about Neci and me*, he thought. Marcus peeped at his watch and then said, "It's almost five, still pretty early, people will be arriving any moment." His statement did not bring comfort to him as the thoughts from this morning began to creep back into his mind. It would be dark very soon so his visibility would be limited. Marcus exited the Camry then quietly shut the door as he walked to the garage glancing cautiously through the grimy windows, unable to see fully inside. He saw portions of the restored Mustang sitting in the usual spots. As he continued to scan the interior of the garage, Marcus saw, rather *felt*, movement in the corner of his eye to his right and toward the house.

Several feet away, Eddie was sliding open the patio door. "Hey, *Marcus*, what took you so long?!" Eddie was grinning, just his normal self. He was wearing a Miami Dolphins sweatshirt and blue nylon sweat pants. His blond hair was slicked back in an uncharacteristic fashion and he was unshaven but Eddie's classic dimpled smile was on his handsome face.

Marcus tried to relax then plastered a fake grin on his face as he answered, "*Eddie*, longtime no see!" Marcus began walking to the house.

"Checking out the Mustang? Sweeeeet, huh? She's a beauty, man. *Hey*, you coming back to work anytime soon? Tired of riding with different clowns every night, hell, next *Sargent* will be trying to ride with me!"

Marcus, chuckling over the comment, finally reached the deck to meet Eddie. Eddie embraced him. "Come on in, partner." Eddie led the way into the kitchen. "I gotta run out to the car and grab some more food and drinks but Neci's in the sunroom so go make yourself at home. I'll be back in a few." He patted Marcus on the back then went to the front of the house and out of the door.

Marcus scanned the kitchen. He saw various dessert items, veggie dishes, and meat trays. There were decorated cupcakes shaped like footballs on the table. Marcus breathed a sigh of relief and then mumbled, "I *knew* she was overreacting." He looked through the open doorway to his left and walked into the sunroom where Neci was supposed to be waiting.

***

The spacious sunroom and great room were still bright with sunlight despite the impending dusk outside. The large TV was on and turned to face the sunroom windows. The channel was tuned to the Super Bowl pre-game show. Commentators debated over which team had the better offense and collectively hinted that the Giants would become the new Super Bowl champions.

As Marcus entered the large room, he observed Neci seated with her back to him, typing on the computer. He saw that she wore a white sweatshirt and blue jeans; her beautiful hair flowed down her back. Marcus was relieved to see that she was okay; Eddie had not harmed her. He did not want to scare her so he gently cleared his throat, "Hemmmp-emmm."

Neci, wearing reading glasses, slowly turned in her chair. Neci saw Marcus drive up earlier so was not surprised to see him. She also heard Marcus and Eddie talking in the kitchen. She removed her glasses revealing red eyes. As she set the glasses on the desk, she said without emotion, "You shouldn't have come, Marcus." She sighed then stood up and walked to him. Neci appeared haggard but was as beautiful as ever to Marcus. They embraced warmly. She said softly, "I've *missed* you so much, Marcus."

It felt so good to hold her again. Marcus whispered in her ear, "Couldn't stand the thought of you being here alone. If Eddie really did plan to confront you I wanted to be here. We're in this together, Neci." He then stole a kiss, and she yielded fervently to his boldness as their tongues danced once more; the tension from the telephone conversation was forgotten.

Afterwards, Neci pulled back facing Marcus with a weak smile. She responded, "That's just like you, Marcus, always wanting to be the protector, my *shining knight*. But really, you still shouldn't have come." Upon hearing Eddie come back through the front door, the lovers broke their embrace then stood at a respectable distance. They heard Eddie rummaging in the kitchen.

A short time later, Eddie walked into the room carrying a covered tray with his winning smile, "*Dude*, we're about ready to start this little party." He took the tray to the sitting area of the sunroom and set it down on a small table. Eddie then sat on one side of the tan leather two-piece sectional sofa. "The game'll be on in a bit. Let's socialize a little. Come on, Marcus. Have a seat over here; you too, honey." Eddie patted the sofa insisting that the two sit with him.

Marcus walked over to him and sat down on the matching tan leather loveseat across from his partner. Neci followed then hesitated when she got to them, she looked left at Eddie then right at Marcus. She stood frozen for a second not knowing who to sit next to. Eddie settled it for her as he said gently, "You sit with me, sweetheart." Neci complied joining her husband as she sat closest to the window. Eddie smirked at Marcus as if he had won a victory.

Marcus noticed the smirk and grew uncomfortable. To break the moment, Marcus asked, "So, Eddie…when are the rest of the guys coming?"

Eddie gave a short haunting laugh then said, "Didn't you know? This is a private party, Marcus - just you, my wife, and me, a happy little *threesome*."

Marcus felt a cold shiver go up his spine as he sensed danger. Neci looked dreadfully afraid as she glanced secretly at Marcus then cautiously at Eddie.

Eddie looked down at the covered tray he had carried in then exclaimed happily, "Let's see what we got here!" He lifted the plastic white cover off of the rectangular serving tray revealing sliced fruit - apples, pineapples, mangos, oranges, and kiwi. Looking out of place, a lone apple lay whole among the fruit wedges.

Marcus did not see any of those items because his attention was focused on the large knife that Eddie picked up off the tray.

As the TV played in the background, Eddie grabbed the lone dark red apple as he said, "I *love* apples, Marcus." Using the large knife, much too big to use on fruit, Eddie began slowly peeling the apple. The apple peel curled down Eddie's wrist, resembling a red coiled snake. He then proceeded to cut the meat of the apple, putting a slice in his mouth. "*Mmmm-yum*. Man…this *is* juicy!"

Marcus noticed that Eddie had accidentally cut himself on his right thumb. To Marcus's horror, Eddie began to lick at the cut.

"*Oh*, guess what, buddy? I found out who's fucking my wife." Eddie picked up a folded napkin on the white tray to reveal a tape recorder. Both Neci and Marcus were stunned by the man's statement and by the small Sony digital voice recorder. Eddie dropped the apple, still holding the knife, then picked up the silver recorder. The apple dropped to the carpet with a muffled thump and lay forgotten.

Marcus said, "Eddie, maybe this isn't the best time to- "

"*Wait!* Listen to *this shit*!" Eddie raved then clicked on the recorder filling the sunroom with a crisp digital recording:

Marcus's voice: *Making love to you felt so right, Neci. You know, I can still taste you on my tongue.*

Neci's voice: *Marcus, you're getting me hot, so behave.*

Marcus's voice: *Your pussy tasted so good, Neci. I've never tasted anything so delicious in my life.*

Neci's voice: *It's mean of you to get me this way.*

Marcus's voice: *What way? Say it, we're both adults here. Speak freely.*

Neci's voice: *Wet.*

Eddie turned off the tiny recorder with a loud audible click. The intimate telephone conversation that seemed so long ago exposed betrayal. None of the trio said a word for a moment. A great silence filled the air. The tension was thick. Eddie enjoyed the effect the recording had on the conspirators. Neci began to sob quietly as she stared into the growing darkness outside of the window facing the backyard. Marcus stared cautiously at Eddie who smiled back at him; he was still holding the knife in one hand and the recorder in the other.

"I've got plenty more of these, Marcus, plus lots of other evidence against you and my wife. I did pretty good, huh?" Eddie sat the recorder back on the tray then held the knife menacingly toward Marcus. "What should I do about this?" Suddenly Eddie looked up reflecting on another moment of time. "You know? I caught Neci doing this before, Marcus. When I worked in California, I also found out that she *fucked* my ex-partner there." Eddie turned his gaze back to Marcus. "My wife has a history of throwing her pussy at other men; *sweeeeet* ain't it?"

Marcus answered, "Neci told me all about it, Eddie." The smile disappeared off Eddie's face as he continued. "She specifically told me about your *abnormal* behavior, *your* sickness. You making her sleep with other men so you could *watch*! That was *fucked* up, Eddie. So if you gonna tell the story, *partner,* tell the *whole* story."

Eddie suddenly laughed as he focused back on Marcus. "Ha-ha! Whoa! Let me get this right. Neci told you all about our good times in Cantil, huh?" As if a light switch had been turned off, Eddie spat with anger, "The *thing* is it didn't excuse her from *fucking* my friend, my partner! Just like it don't excuse her from *fucking you*, Marcus!"

Marcus could see the rage setting into Eddie's face. His blue eyes seemed to flash red with fury. Marcus knew he had to act and act quickly. Somehow he must get Neci out of harm's way. Eddie was dangerously close to her with that knife. Marcus made his decision – he had to act right then.

With great speed, Marcus drew his Glock and pointed it at Eddie. "Put down that knife, *Eddie*! Then we can talk about this - man-to-man."

Neci gasped. She looked from one man to the other.

Eddie laughed, "Awww-*man*! You got me, Marcus! Damn, you got me cold, brother! You whipped that thing out pretty *quick*! Sweeeeet!" He smiled wildly then said with coldness, "*What*? You going to shoot me now?"

"Drop the *fucking* knife, Eddie." Marcus did not know whether or not he could actually shoot Eddie unless of course he tried to harm Neci. Fear gripped him.

Eddie dropped the knife which bounced across the carpet and close to Marcus's feet. Marcus was distracted as he watched the knife fall harmlessly. Taking his eyes off of Eddie was a mistake.

Eddie's right fist slammed hard against Marcus's face. Neci screamed. The ex-boxer fell stunned to the floor releasing his firearm as the table upended throwing fruit everywhere. Marcus was dazed and confused as he felt someone suddenly by his side trying to help him set up. He looked up and saw her - Neci.

Neci looked shaken as she asked, "You okay, *Marcus*?"

Marcus could only nod as he tried to reorient himself. The ringing in his ears subsided, and he looked back at Eddie who now stood facing them - with the Glock pistol pointed their way.

Eddie looked back and forth between the two as the lovers realized the predicament they were now in. "You guys look so *sweet* together." His voice suddenly hardened, "Get the fuck away from my wife!"

Neci stood to face her husband then pleaded, "Stop this *now*, Gerard, before someone really gets hurt! *Please*!"

Eddie asked, "So, tell me, Neci. Did Marcus *dick* you better than me?"

Neci just stared at her enraged husband; she began nervously twisting her hair.

Eddie glanced down at Marcus but said to his wife, "You *really* love this backstabbing piece of *shit*, don't you?!"

"Gerard, please...just put that *thing* down!" Neci saw that the gun was pointed at her.

Eddie glared back at Neci. "Answer me! Do you love him?!"

After several tense seconds, Neci reluctantly answered, "Marcus...is a wonderful man." Neci then whispered, "He's...been a good friend to me, *and you*. Now...stop this *craziness*."

"Do you love him? And don't *fucking* lie to me," Eddie said through clenched teeth.

Neci became teary-eyed as she stared directly into Eddie's eyes. She whispered, "*Yes*."

Marcus could not help but to admire Neci at that very moment; she bravely professed her love for him in the midst of her armed husband. Marcus glanced at Eddie. He did not like the sudden expression of shock on his partner's face as Eddie gaped at his wife. Even though Marcus was still slightly dazed, he tried to step in front of Neci.

Eddie did not expect Neci to *really* tell the truth. He could not believe his ears as he frowned, appearing to have misunderstood his wife's response. Rage suddenly overtook him - too many disappointments and failures. His parents were ashamed of him, he had lost a lucrative NFL contract, pain was his constant companion and pills and alcohol drove him. He needed the attention and comfort of many women to keep his confidence up, becoming an actor was not in his future and now he had lost the most precious thing in his life - Neci. Eddie could take a lot of things, but his wife loving another man was not one of them. He squeezed the trigger.

The sound of the .45 semi-automatic pistol was deafening inside the Logan home. Time seemed to have stopped for a split-second. Eddie had a look of surprise and horror on his face as he held the smoking gun. Marcus's eyes were wide with wonderment from the muzzle-flash as he continued to lay dazed on the floor. Neci was in denial as the punch of the powerful weapon propelled her backwards, taking her off her feet. As she hit the carpet near Marcus, the searing pain in her chest slowly set in.

"*Noooooooooo!*" was all Marcus could say as he went to her. He checked for a wound but could not readily find one. Marcus's whole body quaked as he gently swept back Neci's long hair from her face. He searched her face for any signs of life or pain. He was relieved to see that at least she was conscious and breathing. He whispered, "Neci, it's…it's going to be alright."

Neci slowly looked at him and smiled. She nodded then closed her eyes tightly against the pain, groaning.

"*Where*, Neci? Tell me, where does it hurt?" Once again, Marcus looked on and around her body and no longer had to ask. He could see the crimson fluid, the blood beginning to soak the front of her chest, seeping through the white sweatshirt. With great difficulty, he frantically tore off Neci's thick shirt, trying desperately to keep his sanity. Nothing was sexy about the lavender laced bra she wore as he gawked at the entrance wound to her upper right chest. He looked for an exit wound but found none. The bullet was still inside of her.

Marcus used a hand to put pressure on the chest wound. He knew that Neci was in danger of not only bleeding to death, but her lungs could quickly collapse and disable her breathing. He wanted to do anything to stop the life from flowing out of her. "It's going to be fine, Neci. We're going to get you some help."

Neci slowly opened her eyes then clutched Marcus's arm and said weakly, "My, my boys, Marcus. Get my…boys. Need my children…" The pain seemed to spread like fire within her. She closed her eyes then moaned again releasing her grasp of him.

Marcus shakily said, "Let's take care of you first. Then-then we'll get the children."

Neci opened her eyes then whispered, "Don't forget…my…my heart."

Marcus misunderstood her as he said, "You're going to be okay…the bullet missed your heart."

Neci shook her head slowly and said, "No-no…the heart…promise to…" she paused to take a breath then swallowed, "…*always* keep it with you."

Marcus, now understanding her, he quickly held up his other arm allowing her to see the heart pendant dangling from the gold bracelet, "Yeah, baby, *see*?"

Neci nodded and looked lovingly at him. He slowly drew his face closer to her then kissed her gently on the forehead. She smiled ever so weakly saying, "A kiss…for my soul. I…I love it when you…do…" Neci's eyes fluttered shut as she quickly lost consciousness.

Marcus jumped when he heard the .45 roar twice more!

Eddie yelled with tears in his eyes, *"Get away from my fucking wife!"* The pistol was pointed at the ceiling; plaster fell everywhere, a white dust cloud filled the room. The strong odor of gunpowder was in air. Eddie then aimed the Glock at Marcus. "I mean *now*!"

Marcus implored the man as he continued to attend to Neci's bleeding gunshot wound, "*Please*, Eddie! We need to get her some help! Call 9-1-1!"

"The next bullet goes through your *wife-stealing* head. *Move* away from my wife, *I'll* help her!" Angry tears streamed down Eddie's face as he moved closer to the pair; he was now only a couple of feet away from Marcus.

Marcus knew that he must once again make a decision or Neci would surely die.

Marcus reluctantly released the pressure from Neci's wound. He slowly got to his feet, and the gun followed him. As soon as Marcus stood up, he lunged for the weapon and grabbed it. The weapon boomed once more as one of the large windows behind him exploded from the massive blast, missing Marcus's left temple by inches.

The two strong men fought for control of the gun. Eddie pulled the trigger once again. Something else crashed inside the room, destroyed by the .45 slug. Marcus felt his strength waning, as Eddie tried to point the weapon back at him. Marcus was unable to take the Glock from Eddie's powerful grip. Wrenching the weapon from his grasp was simply no good. With one option left, Marcus pushed the gun towards Eddie, hoping to scare him into dropping the weapon. Suddenly, Eddie pushed with all of his weight against Marcus. Marcus felt his body moving backwards toward the gaping hole of the broken window. The pistol was now pointed at Eddie. Both men had fingers on the sensitive trigger.

"Arrrggghhh!" Eddie pushed Marcus with increasing speed and strength closer to the window, passing Neci's lifeless body. Before Eddie would seal Marcus's fate, the deadly .45 pistol roared one last time.

In one moment Marcus saw the hatred in Eddie's plaster-covered face but in the next second, that same face exploded – Eddie's hair, skin, skull fragments, brain matter, and blood covered them both. Marcus saw Eddie's body fall backwards like a rag-doll. He himself felt his own body continue backward from the force out of the shot-out two-story window. As he floated in the air, Marcus heard sirens as he glimpsed the darken sky, and the rear of the house. The last thing Marcus Williams felt that evening was the jarring but painless impact of the grassy knoll below. A peaceful darkness engulfed Marcus as he held tight to the Glock pistol that had just killed his partner.

Chapter 38

Several days later, as a light snow shower fell lazily to the hard cold ground, Marcus was released from the VCU Medical Center on an afternoon in February. A red sports vehicle drove into the parking lot of Chester Estates then stopped in front of the apartment complex. Sneak, behind the steering wheel, asked his lone passenger, "You sure you can make it up on your own, Marc?" He stared at the battle wounds and bandages on his friend.

"Yeah, man. I can make it okay. Thanks for all your help. I'll need a ride tomorrow though. They towed my car from…from Neci's place. You know for evidence and stuff. They're releasing it back to me."

Sneak was lost for words but wanted desperately to cheer up his good friend then said, "Just call me, man, if you need to talk about it. I'm here for you."

"Thanks, Sneak." Marcus was preparing to exit Sneak's brand new Infiniti G35 sports coupe.

Sneak tried to cheer Marcus up. "Marc, you look like that motherfucking actor."

"I know, I know, *Taye Diggs*. I get it all the time."

"*Naw, man.* I was gonna say you look just like that big baldheaded, muscular, cocked-eyed dude in Ice Cube's movie *Friday*. You know, the ugly guy on the bike? You a shorter version of *that* dude. *Shit*, y'all look like family, if you ask me."

"Ain't nobody *asking you*, Sneak." Marcus tried not to laugh as he shot up his middle finger causing another bout of chuckling from his friend.

As Sneak's laughter died down he said, "Man, I'm serious though. You need anything call me. That court thing gonna be some tough shit, just know they ain't gonna convict you. Remember, Marc, you're innocent. I *damn* well know you didn't murder nobody!"

"Thanks, Sneak. I'm sure it'll all work out, and I'll call you if I need anything. But I'm okay."

Seconds later, Sneak said reluctantly, "Umm...Staci told me Tamala was released from the hospital a few weeks back, before, you know...*this* thing happened with you. I bet she's still just as bruised and battered as you are." Marcus just stared straight ahead, with no response. Sneak continued, "Tamala's a good woman despite the shit y'all been through over the past year. Be nice if y'all try to...at least be friends, maybe not right now, but...you know...umm, later perhaps." Sneak added, "It's a damn shame Henrico PD ain't caught up with that asshole who *we know* beat her up. They should've seen right through her weak story in the first place. 'Nuff of my rambling." Marcus did not have the energy or nerve to tell Sneak that justice had been served on Lamar Phelps.

Marcus remained silent, continuing to stare ahead refusing to converse on that sensitive subject. Then after a minute or so he looked over at his friend and said despondently, "Sneak, I'll let you know how things go...with court and all. I'll call you tomorrow."

"Okay, Marc. Take care now."

"Later, Sneak."

Marcus, carrying a white plastic hospital bag containing his belongings, finally got out of the sleek red sports car, shutting the door. He walked away at a snail's pace but suddenly stopped then turned facing the car again. As he stood under the cold gray sky, which matched his mood,

Marcus and Sneak stared briefly at one another. The wet snow plastered Sneak's windows little-by-little. Marcus gave his friend a weak smile. Sneak, seeing no happiness in that smile, nodded then drove off heading back to Richmond via I-95.

Marcus, alone in the parking lot, stood dazed. He was totally oblivious to the moderate vehicular traffic along Route 1 and the patrons inundating the Wawa next door. Finally, as if awakened from a dream, he turned and walked gingerly to the stairs leading up to his home as the frigid temperature cut through his clothing. He could see his breath in the cold February air as he paused to check mailbox #9. Marcus was not surprised that the box contained more past due bills and an assortment of junk mail promising to make life easier if you bought a certain product. He shook his head thinking, *Life just goes on despite the hardships in life. Bill collectors still want their money while others want to keep you in debt, damn!*

After entering his apartment, Marcus placed his belongings and the mail onto his kitchen counter. He saw the red light blinking on his answering machine. A brief check of the caller ID unit showed that most of them came from Tamala's home, her workplace, or hospital room she occupied recently. The rest of the calls appeared to be from various friends or telemarketers - the usual. Marcus looked around the small apartment wondering how he was going to make it with no job, very little money, and no one to share it with. Marcus kind of chuckled at the last thought, *no one to share it with*. He started to shuffle to his bedroom but something caught his eye, stopping him in his tracks. The bright pink envelope stood out prominently laying intermingled among the other mail on the kitchen counter. Marcus thought with a frown, *funny that I didn't notice it before when I grabbed my mail from the box.*

Suddenly, every fiber in his body screamed for him *not* to pick up that envelope. Marcus was confused by his fear of the piece of mail. Ignoring the warning from his inner voice, Marcus's hand slowly reached for the pink envelope out the assortment of parcel. He turned the mail over and read that it was obviously addressed to him. No return address, but his address was written in fine script, appearing to be that of a woman's. Marcus just stared at the pink envelope with melancholy, heartbreak, and fear, knowing exactly who sent it. *But when, how?* He thought.

After what seemed like an eternity, Marcus finally carried the piece of mail over to the couch where he slowly sat down. His hands began to quake as whiffs of Neci's perfume came out from within the envelope; memories of her rushed through his mind. He struggled to hold his emotions in check, trying to will the painful, but happy, recollections away.

As Marcus sat in front of the blank TV within the dimness and quietness of his cold apartment, he suddenly remembered vividly a statement Neci made to him during that telephone call on the afternoon just before the shootings: *I mailed you a letter yesterday. I've had lots of time to think about...some things. I've made some tough decisions since we've last spoken. I thought that sending you a letter would maybe...clear up a few things.*

Marcus slowly tore open the flap to the bright, colorful envelope smelling Neci - her scent, her perfume, much stronger this time; that broke his heart even more. He slowly unfolded the white pages of the scented letter. A letter from his love...from his Neci:

My Dearest Marcus,

The weeks apart from you have been painful. I constantly think about you, about us. Gerard said you've been on vacation. I was so sorry to hear about Tamela (spelled right?).

I don't want you to think that I'm upset with you for not telling me about Gerard's suspicions. That with Juny seeing us, just brought me to the breaking point. My fear got the best of me. You really don't know my husband, and what he's capable of. He has a side to him that can be rather scary to say the least! We can talk about that soon. I've done some things in my past that I'm not proud of. I'm not perfect though you make me feel like I am. (smile)

I've missed you, Marcus. I've missed your handsome face, your warm reassuring smile, and your gentle touch. God, I've more than missed the way you've made me feel. Your kisses and our lovemaking take me away! When I'm in the safety of your arms, nothing can harm me. I have peace and happiness with you. Feelings I've never truly had. As you probably could tell, I've had lots of time to think. I've made one of the toughest decisions ever made in my life.

Marcus, I'm leaving Gerard and moving back home with my Dad and Mom this summer. He doesn't know about it yet. It's the best decision for my children and me. The fresh start will also give us, you and me, a chance to be together. Yes, I said (wrote) us. (smile) I'm in love with you, Marcus Williams! With every beat of my heart, my love flows for you. Sounds sappy, huh? I hope that doesn't scare you away.

Well, I hear movement upstairs. I have so much more to say but have to cut this short. I'm writing this in the sunroom which is my peaceful place in the house as the sunrays bring warmth. It promises to be a good day. It'll be even better now that I've finally conveyed my feelings to you. I belong to you now! Give me time to straighten all of this out. I'll be in touch very soon. Miss you. Once again, I love you!

Yours Always,
Neci "Maria" Johnson (changing my name back too)

Saturday, February 2, 2008
5:35am

Marcus stared at the heart-wrenching letter for several moments as he swallowed back tears. He felt empty inside, devastated all over again. Marcus had nothing else to give physically or emotionally as *her* words permeated his soul. Neci truly had Marcus's heart. After she died, so died his heart.

Marcus calmly refolded the small pages placing them back into the envelope. Despite the time of day, it was time for bed. Walking back to his bedroom, he slowly stripped down to his undershirt and boxers then climbed into bed, still holding the letter. He tried to see her face again as he closed his eyes in concentration. His mind's eye would not cooperate as darkness prevailed instead. He held himself deep underneath the sheets, curled up like a small child as his drought of tears finally ended.

Marcus had not cried since the death of his mother just before he entered the police academy years ago. But today Marcus cried over the break-up with Tamala; teardrops flowed over the death of his best friend and partner, T. C.; tears also fell due to the fact that his partner's killer had gone unpunished; Marcus was even woeful because he crossed the line with Lamar Phelps, Tamala's lover; he bawled harder as he thought about Juny and his little brother Karl, who would now grow up parentless because of him; then intense grief overtook him for ending the life of another police officer, Eddie; even more sorrow engulfed him over the possible loss of his career; but first and foremost Marcus cried tears of pain and sadness over Neci, the woman who died with his heart, his love - his life.

Now, the weeping man struggled to respond to Neci's written words of devotion, "I love…you too…Neci *Maria* Johnson." Marcus Antonio Williams shed tears for all of those things, and more. Eventually, he drifted off into a deep dreamless sleep, clinging desperately to Neci's letter…his last and final connection to her.

EPILOGUE

Present Day

I ponder the proverb: *Time heals all wounds*. That phrase rings false. This cold air-conditioner in my patrol vehicle almost fooled me into believing that I was back in my cold apartment, crying my eyes out, on that bleak snowy day well over six months ago now. Even as I sit here in my patrol unit circling (like a hungry vulture) the Rolling Hills Mega-Mall Complex, on a hot-ass blistering July Sunday evening, I still carry Neci's letter in the pocket of my uniform shirt. Even though her perfume has faded from the letter slightly, the effects (both longing and sadness) that I experience from reading it are as strong as ever. I also wear the gold bracelet with Neci's gold heart attached. I promised her that I'd always have it with me - I intend to keep that promise. I don't think I'll ever love another woman as much as I love her. I miss Neci so very much. Even now my heart aches for her. Neci's memory will stay with me until I die.

I glance at my wristwatch and see that it's almost 6:00 o'clock; the mall's closing now so shoppers are beginning to make their way to their vehicles. The white Toyota SUV with Rolling Hills Security Force plastered on the sides clearly identifies my new employer as I round the corner of Hecht's for the last time today - *thank God*! Yes, now I wear a different uniform, that of a mall security officer.

Losing my police job was hard in the beginning but I'm getting use to not being a cop anymore. The hardest part of being in this security uniform is seeing a Woodland County police cruiser patrolling the mall area. Not that I'm embarrassed or ashamed of being a security guard, it's just...I miss being in that Woodland County patrol car and wearing that navy blue uniform. - the uniform of a cop.

The Woodland County Commonwealth Attorney's Office dropped the manslaughter charge against me. Later I found out that Neci made a statement, during her grave condition, to Detective Diedre Carson who was assingned to the case. She told her that Eddie shot her. But I *am* guilty of one crime - what I did to Lamar Phelps. Phelps's whereabouts are presently unknown.

As I park the mall's SUV in the 'Security Vehicles Only' space, my thoughts go to Tam. She's recovered fully from her injuries. We've talked on the telephone on a number of occasions. Sneak, from Richmond PD, kept pushing me to at least call and check on her. One call led to another, now we talk about twice a week.

Tam and I realized that we both had a lot of unresolved issues that have never been addressed, at least in an adult fashion. She and I should've voiced our true feelings rather than arguing all the time to no avail. Maybe if we'd voiced things, none of this mess would've ever happened. At any rate, the engagement ring currently lays in the bottom of my cluttered nightstand drawer. Who *knows* what the future holds for *it*.

As I turn off the security vehicle and am about to get out, my cell phone vibrates. I view the text message, and my heart nearly stops. I'm speechless. Now my pulse is quickening, my adrenaline is rising and sweat drips down my slick head stinging my eyes as I try to figure out my next move.

This may be my only chance, my last chance. Petersburg, Virginia, room 33 at the Imperial Inn, the second motel on the left after turning right onto Rives from 95, *past* the Texaco is where I must go. Take the Rives Road exit, Exit 47 from 95 South. End of text.

I sit for several minutes in the now-hot security vehicle to calm myself as I watch the other security officers park their patrol units and proceed to the office inside the mall. I get out of the SUV and rush to my car, not even bothering to report in at the office and change clothes.

As I enter my car, I look at my wristwatch: it's 6:15. I look over at the security vehicle that I just left. There is something inside the SUV that I need. I walk back to the unlocked security vehicle and open the rear compartment. I use my key to get inside the gun safe stored there. I glance to see if I'm being watched. People are ignoring me; I proceed with my plan. I pull out the sleek large black gun case which holds the Heckler and Koch MP-5 submachine gun. The H&K MP-5 has three-30 round magazines of 9mm rounds. That weapon, plus my issued Beretta 9mm pistol that I now have on my right hip, should be enough firepower. My stomach's in knots right now. I close the rear hatch to the SUV then calmly walk back to my car. I start it and quickly drive out of Woodland County heading to Petersburg - and the elusive Rip.

"Thanks, Weenie. I owe you big." My informant came through. After all this time, I'm going to come face-to-face with Rip, Rakeem Harper, the man that killed my best friend, my real partner.

As I travel to the Cockade City filled with both apprehension and fear, I'm only sure of two things - one, T. C.'s looking down over me, and two, no matter what happens to me, I know that my Neci loves me and I'll forever love her, despite the fact that she was...*My Partner's Wife*.

The End

It may not be Histeria Lane, but these desperate housewives are fed up with their neglecting husbands. Their sexual needs take precedence over the millions of dollars their husbands bring home every year to keep them happy in their affluent neighborhood. While their husbands claim to be hard at work, these wives are doing a little work of their own with the bedroom bandit. Is the bandit swift enough to evade these angry husbands?

In Stores!!

NEGLECTED SOULS

Motherhood and the trials of loving too hard and not enough frame this story...The realism of these characters will bring tears to your spirit as you discover the hero in the villain you never saw coming...

In Stores!!!

Jimmy and Nina continue to feel a void in their lives because they haven't a clue about their genealogical make-up. Jimmy falls victims to a life threatening illness and only the right organ donor can save his life. Will the donor be the bridge to reconnect Jimmy and Nina to their biological family? Will Nina be the strength for her brother in his time of need? Will they ever find out what really happened to their mother?

In Stores!!!

Betrayal, lust, lies, murder, deception, sex and tainted love frame this story... Julian Stevens lacks the ambition and freak ability that Miko looks for in a man, but she married him despite his flaws to spite an ex-boyfriend. When Miko least expects it, the old boyfriend shows up and ready to sweep her off her feet again. She wants to have her cake and eat it too. While Miko's doing her own thing, Julian is determined to become everything Miko ever wanted in a man and more, but will he go to extreme lengths to prove he's worthy of Miko's love? Julian Stevens soon finds out that he's capable of being more than he could ever imagine as he embarks on a journey that will change his life forever.

In Stores!!!

The police in New York and other major cities around the country are increasingly victimizing black men. The violence has escalated to deadly force, most of the time without justification. In this controversial book, noted author Richard Jeanty, tackles the problem of police brutality and the unfair treatment of Black men at the hands of police in New York City and the rest of the country.

In Stores!!!

Just when Darren thinks his relationship with Tina is flourishing, there is yet another hurdle on the road hindering their bliss. Tina saw a therapist for months to deal with her sexual addiction, but now Darren is wondering if she was ever treated completely. Darren has not been taking care of home and Tina's frustrated and agrees to a break-up with Darren. Will Darren lose Tina for good? Will Tina ever realize that Darren is the best man for her?

In Stores!!

Ronald Murphy was a player all his life until he and his best friend, Myles, met the women of their dreams during a brief vacation in South Beach, Florida. Sexual Jeopardy is story of trust, betrayal, forgiveness, friendship and hope.

In Stores!!!

Tina develops an insatiable sexual appetite very early in life. She
only loves her boyfriend, Darren, but he's too far away in college to satisfy her sexual needs.
Tina decides to get buck wild away in college
Will her sexual trysts jeopardize the lives of the men in her life?

In Stores!!!

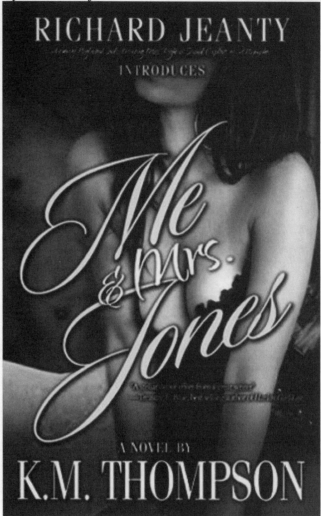

Faith Jones, a woman in her mid-thirties, has given up on ever finding love again until she met her son's best friend, Darius. Faith Jones is walking a thin line of betrayal against her son for the love of Darius. Will Faith allow her emotions to outweigh her common sense?

In Stores!!!

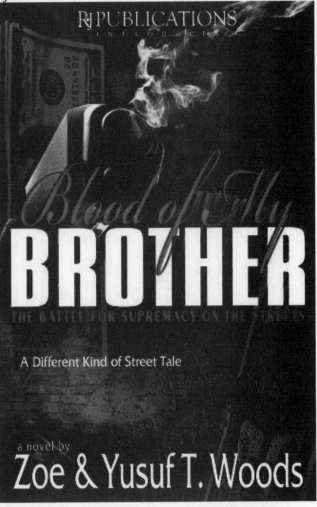

Roc was the man on the streets of Philadelphia, until his younger brother decided it was time to become his own man by wreaking havoc on Roc's crew without any regards for the blood relation they share. Drug, murder, mayhem and the pursuit of happiness can lead to deadly consequences. This story can only be told by a person who has lived it.

In Stores!!!

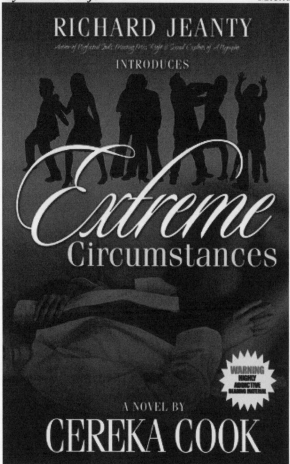

What happens when a devoted woman is betrayed? Come take a ride with Chanel as she takes her boyfriend, Donnell, to circumstances beyond belief after he betrays her trust with his endless infidelities. How long can Chanel's friend, Janai, use her looks to get what she wants from men before it catches up to her? Find out as Janai's gold-digging ways catch up with and she has to face the consequences of her extreme actions.

In Stores!!!

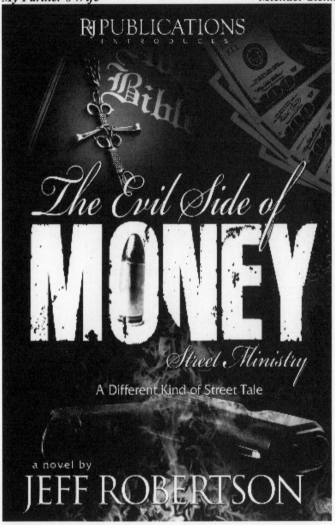

Violence, Intimidation and carnage are the order as Nathan and his brother set out to build the most powerful drug empires in Chicago. However, when God comes knocking, Nathan's conscience starts to surface. Will his haunted criminal past get the best of him?

In Stores!!

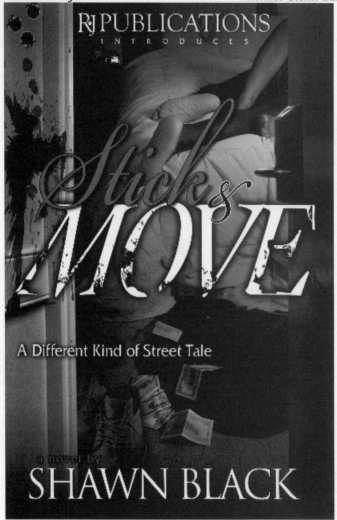

Yasmina witnessed the brutal murder of her parents at a young age at the hand of a drug dealer. This event stained her mind and upbringing as a result. Will Yamina's life come full circle with her past? Find out as Yasmina's crew, The Platinum Chicks, set out to make a name for themselves on the street.

In stores!!

Ashland's mother, Bianca, fights hard to suppress the truth from her daughter because she doesn't want her to marry Jordan, the grandson of an ex-lover she loathes. Ashland soon finds out how cruel and vengeful her mother can be, but what price will Bianca pay for redemption?

In stores!!

Malcolm is a wealthy virgin who decides to conceal his wealth
From the world until he meets the right woman. His wealthy best
friend, Dexter, hides his wealth from no one. Malcolm struggles to
find love in an environment where vanity and materialism are
rampant, while Dexter is getting more than enough of his share of
women. Malcolm needs develop self-esteem and confidence to
meet the right woman and Dexter's confidence is borderline
arrogance.
Will bad boys like Dexter continue to take women for a ride?

Or will nice guys like Malcolm continue to finish last?

In Stores!!!

RICHARD JEANTY

INTRODUCES

WARNING HIGHLY ADDICTIVE READING MATERIAL

Cater to Her

A NOVEL BY
SEAN MITCHELL

What happens when a woman's devotion to her fiancee is tested weeks before she gets married? What if her fiancee is just hiding behind the veil of ministry to deceive her? Find out as Sean Mitchell takes you on a journey you'll never forget into the lives of Angelica, Titus and Aurelius.

In Stores!!

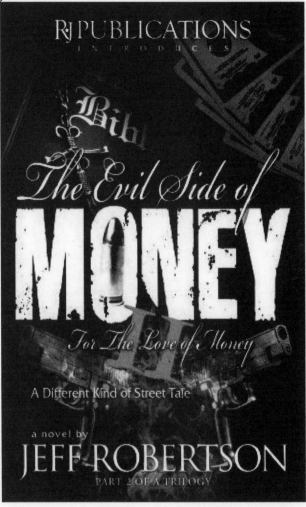

A beautigul woman from Bolivia threatens the existence of the drug empire that Nate and G have built. While Nate is head over heels for her, G can see right through her. As she brings on more conflict between the crew, G sets out to show Nate exactly who she is before she brings about their demise.

In Stores!!!

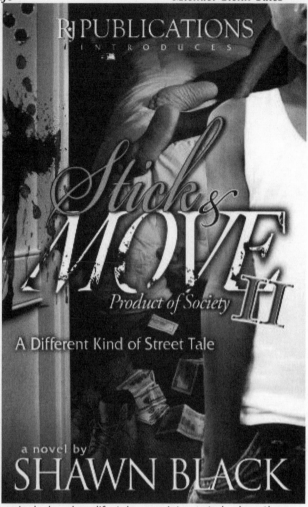

Scorcher and Yasmina's low key lifestyle was interrupted when they were taken down by the Feds, but their daughter, Serosa, was left to be raised by the foster care system. Will Serosa become a product of her environment or will she rise above it all? Her bloodline is undeniable, but will she be able to control it?

In Stores!!

An ex-drug dealer finds himself in a bind after he's caught by the Feds. He has to decide which is more important, his family or his loyalty to the game. As he fights hard to make a decision, those who helped him to the top fear the worse from him. Will he get the chance to tell the govt. whole story, or will someone get to him before he becomes a snitch?

In Stores!!!

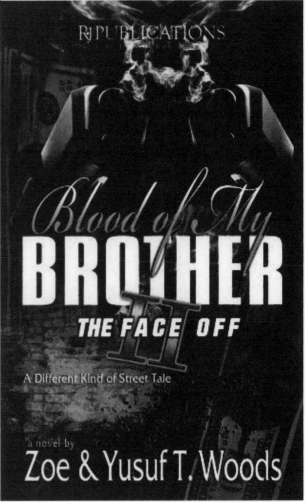

What will Roc do when he finds out the true identity of Solo? Will the blood shed come from his own brother Lil Mac? Will Roc and Solo take their beef to an explosive height on the street? Find out as Zoe and Yusuf bring the second installment to their hot street joint, Blood of My Brother.

In Stores!!!

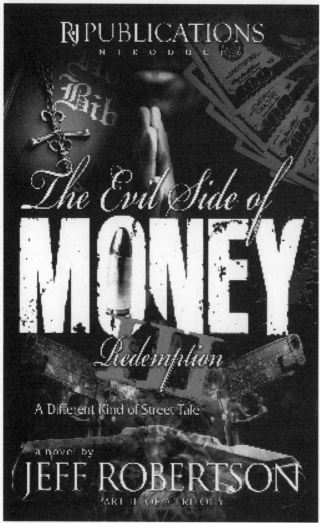

Forced to abandon the drug world for good, Nathan and G attempt to change their lives and move forward, but will their past come back to haunt them? This final installment will leave you speechless.

Coming November 2009

Nafys Muhammad managed to beat the charges in court, but will he beat them on the street? There will be many revelations in this story as betrayal, greed, sex scandal corruption and murder unravels throughout every page. Get ready for a rough ride.

Deon is at the mercy of a ruthless gang that kidnapped him. In a foreign land where he knows nothing about the culture, he has to use his survival instincts and his wit to outsmart his captors. Will the Hoodfellas show up in time to rescue Deon, or will Crazy D take over once again and fight an all out war by himself?

Coming March 2010

While Yasmina sits on death row awaiting her fate, her daughter, Serosa, is fighting the fight of her life on the outside. Her genetic structure that indirectly bins her to her parents could also be her downfall and force her to see that there's no way out!

Coming January 2010

The drama continues as Deshun is hunted by Angela who still feels that ex-girlfriend Kayla is still trying to win his heart, though he brutally raped her. Angela will kill anyone who gets in her way, but is DeShun worth all the aggravation?

Coming September 2009

Buck Johnson was forced to make the best out of worst situation. He has witnessed the most cruel events in his life and it is those events who the man that he has become. Was the Johnson family ignorant souls through no fault of their own?

Coming October 2009

When an Ex-con finds himself destitute and in dire need of the basic necessities after he's released from prison, he turns to what he knows best, crime, but at what cost? Extortion, murder and mayhem drives him back to the top, but will he stay there?

In Stores !!!

What happens when someone falls insanely in love?
Stalking is just the beginning.
In Stores!!!

My Partner's Wife

In this twisted tale of seduction, Marcus Williams finds himself taking refuge in the arms of a woman completely forbidden to him after he discovered his cheating fiancee s sexual trysts. His life spirals out of control after the death of his partner while the killer is still on the loose. Marcus is conflicted about his decision to honor his partner or to completely allow his heart to decide his fate. Always the sucker for love, Marcus starts to fall head over heels for his partner s wife. However, with more deaths on the horizon, Marcus may soon find himself serving time with the same convicts he had been putting behind bars.

In Stores November 2010

Deceived

Rhasan Jones was given a second chance at life when he moved from his slum ridden North Carolina neighborhood to Newport News, VA to live with his grandparents. It didn't take long for him to figure out all the ghettos in America were just the same. After being introduced to a crack epidemic sweeping the nation, he met Cross, a crazed New Yorker who would stop at nothing for his thirst for life's finer things...

In Stores December 2010

Going all Out

When Pharoah megtg Tez, he thought he was helping by putting him on. But he never anticipated that tez would turn to a lunatic. A blood thirty dude, Tez kills at will with no regard for life and no one is off limits. Pharoah now has to watch his back because Tez is out of control...

In Stores January 2011

Hoodfellas III

Deon and his crew are forced to return back to the States. However, lurking in Deon's mind is revenge for the death of his fallen crewmembers. This personal vendetta has to be settled before Deon and the Hoodfellas can have peace of mind, but at what price will revenge come?

In Stores March 2011

PUBLICATIONS
BRINGING EXCITEMENT, FUN AND JOY TO READING

Use this coupon to order by mail

1. Neglected Souls, Richard Jeanty $14.95 Available
2. Neglected No More, Richard Jeanty $14.95 Avail
3. Ignorant Souls, Richard Jeanty $15.00, Available
4. Sexual Exploits of Nympho, Richard Jeanty $14.95 Available
5. Meeting Ms. Right's Whip Appeal, Richard Jeanty $14.95
6. Me and Mrs. Jones, K.M Thompson $14.95Available
7. Chasin' Satisfaction, W.S Burkett $14.95 Available
8. Extreme Circumstances, Cereka Cook $14.95 Available
9. The Most Dangerous Gang In America, R. Jeanty $15.00 Avail.
10. Sexual Exploits of a Nympho II, Richard Jeanty $15.00 Avail.
11. Sexual Jeopardy, Richard Jeanty $14.95 Available
12. Too Many Secrets, Too Many Lies, Sonya Sparks $15.00 Avail
13. Stick And Move, Shawn Black $15.00 Available
14. Evil Side Of Money, Jeff Robertson $15.00 Available
15. Evil Side Of Money II, Jeff Robertson $15.00 Available
16. Evil Side Of Money III, Jeff Robertson $15.00Available
17. Flippin' The Game, Alethea and M. Ramzee, $15.00 Available
18. Flippin' The Game II, Alethea and M. Ramzee, $15.00 Available
19. Cater To Her, W.S Burkett $15.00 Available
20. Blood of My Brother I, Zoe & Yusuf Woods $15.00 Avail.
21. Blood of my Brother II, Zoe & Ysuf Woods $15.00 Avail.
22. Hoodfellas, Richard Jeanty $15.00 available
23. Hoodfellas II, Richard Jeanty, $15.00 Available
24. The Bedroom Bandit, Richard Jeanty $15.00 Available
25. Mr. Erotica, Richard Jeanty, $15.00, Available
26. Stick N Move II, Shawn Black $15.00 Available
27. Stick N Move III, Shawn Black $15.00 Available
28. Miami Noire, W.S. Burkett $15.00 Available
29. Insanely In Love, Cereka Cook $15.00 Available
30. Blood of My Brother III, Zoe & Yusuf Woods Available
31. My partner's wife 11/2010
32. Deceived 12/2010
33. Going All Out 01/2011
34. Hoodfellas III 03/2011

Name_____

Address_____

City_____State_____Zip Code_____

Please send novels circled above; Shipping and Handling: Free
Total Number of Books_____
Total Amount Due_____
       Buy 3 books and get 1 free. Allow 2-3 weeks for delivery
Send institution check or money order (no cash or CODs) to:
RJ Publications
PO Box 300771
Jamaica, NY 11434

PUBLICATIONS
BRINGING EXCITEMENT, FUN AND JOY TO READING

Use this coupon to order by mail

35. Neglected Souls, Richard Jeanty $14.95 Available
36. Neglected No More, Richard Jeanty $14.95 Avail
37. Ignorant Souls, Richard Jeanty $15.00, Available
38. Sexual Exploits of Nympho, Richard Jeanty $14.95 Available
39. Meeting Ms. Right's Whip Appeal, Richard Jeanty $14.95
40. Me and Mrs. Jones, K.M Thompson $14.95Available
41. Chasin' Satisfaction, W.S Burkett $14.95 Available
42. Extreme Circumstances, Cereka Cook $14.95 Available
43. The Most Dangerous Gang In America, R. Jeanty $15.00 Avail.
44. Sexual Exploits of a Nympho II, Richard Jeanty $15.00 Avail.
45. Sexual Jeopardy, Richard Jeanty $14.95 Available
46. Too Many Secrets, Too Many Lies, Sonya Sparks $15.00 Avail
47. Stick And Move, Shawn Black $15.00 Available
48. Evil Side Of Money, Jeff Robertson $15.00 Available
49. Evil Side Of Money II, Jeff Robertson $15.00 Available
50. Evil Side Of Money III, Jeff Robertson $15.00Available
51. Flippin' The Game, Alethea and M. Ramzee, $15.00 Available
52. Flippin' The Game II, Alethea and M. Ramzee, $15.00 Available
53. Cater To Her, W.S Burkett $15.00 Available
54. Blood of My Brother I, Zoe & Yusuf Woods $15.00 Avail.
55. Blood of my Brother II, Zoe & Ysuf Woods $15.00 Avail.
56. Hoodfellas, Richard Jeanty $15.00 available
57. Hoodfellas II, Richard Jeanty, $15.00 Available
58. The Bedroom Bandit, Richard Jeanty $15.00 Available
59. Mr. Erotica, Richard Jeanty, $15.00, Available
60. Stick N Move II, Shawn Black $15.00 Available
61. Stick N Move III, Shawn Black $15.00 Available
62. Miami Noire, W.S. Burkett $15.00 Available
63. Insanely In Love, Cereka Cook $15.00 Available
64. Blood of My Brother III, Zoe & Yusuf Woods Available
65. My partner's wife 11/2010
66. Deceived 12/2010
67. Going All Out 01/2011
68. Hoodfellas III 03/2011

Name_____
Address_____
City_____State_____Zip Code_____

Please send novels circled above; Shipping and Handling: Free
Total Number of Books_____
Total Amount Due_____
     Buy 3 books and get 1 free. Allow 2-3 weeks for delivery
Send institution check or money order (no cash or CODs) to:
RJ Publications
PO Box 300771
Jamaica, NY 11434